THE
ITALIAN'S BARGAIN
FOR HIS BRIDE

CHANTELLE SHAW

THE RULES OF THEIR
RED-HOT REUNION

JOSS WOOD

MILLS & BOON

First Published in Great Britain 2021
by Mills & Boon, an imprint of HarperCollins*Publishers* Ltd,
1 London Bridge Street, London, SE1 9GF

www.harpercollins.co.uk

HarperCollins*Publishers*
1st Floor, Watermarque Building,
Ringsend Road, Dublin 4, Ireland

The Italian's Bargain for His Bride © 2021 Chantelle Shaw

The Rules of Their Red-Hot Reunion © 2021 Joss Wood

ISBN: 978-0-263-28274-0

12/21

MIX
Paper from
responsible sources
FSC™ C007454

This book is produced from independently certified FSC™ paper
to ensure responsible forest management.
For more information visit www.harpercollins.co.uk/green.

Printed and Bound in Spain using 100% Renewable Electricity
at CPI Black Print, Barcelona

THE
ITALIAN'S BARGAIN
FOR HIS BRIDE

CHANTELLE SHAW

MILLS & BOON

MILLS & BOON

PROLOGUE

'PALOMA IS A RISK!'

Franco Zambrotta slammed his hand down on the desk.
'She has spent most of her life in England, disconnected from her Italian heritage. Her ill-advised marriage swiftly followed by a divorce proved that she is headstrong. In my opinion, Marcello's granddaughter is not suitable to take charge of Morante Group. I am sure I do not need to remind you, Daniele, that the company is a global brand with a multibillion-dollar annual revenue. It cannot be entrusted to a girl who has no experience of running a business.'

'With respect, Franco, your opinion on this matter is irrelevant.' Daniele Berardo spoke in his customary, calm manner, hiding his dislike of the other man. It amazed him that Marcello Morante, the founder of Morante Group, who had been renowned for his charisma as much as for his brilliant business acumen, had been related to the distinctly charmless Franco.

In the past twenty-four hours since Marcello had collapsed on the golf course and died on the way to the hospital, Daniele hadn't had a chance to assimilate the loss of the man who had been his mentor and close friend. His priority was to ensure that the media did not learn of Marcello's death before his granddaughter had been informed.

But Paloma Morante, the sole heiress to her grandfather's vast fortune, had disappeared.

The conversation with the man Paloma called Great-Uncle Franco was pointless and a waste of Daniele's time when he urgently needed to find her, but his enigmatic expression revealed none of his frustration as he said imperturbably, 'It was Marcello's wish that Paloma would eventually succeed him. However, he stipulated in his will that if he died before his granddaughter was twenty-five, Morante Group must be managed by the board of trustees until Paloma comes of age to take control of the company. Do I need to remind you, Franco, that your duty as the president of the board is to work in collaboration with the other trustees and run Morante Group until Paloma's twenty-fifth birthday?'

Franco snorted. 'Several of the board members have expressed their concern that Paloma lacks the qualities of leadership. I intend to call for a vote of no confidence in her and propose that I am instated as Marcello's permanent successor.'

The imperceptible tightening of Daniele's jaw was the only indication that he was disturbed by Franco's threat of a power struggle. He had never trusted Marcello's much younger half-brother. Franco was the product of their mother's second marriage after Marcello's father had died relatively young, it was rumoured from a drug overdose. Marcello had been the sole Morante heir and later had given his half-brother a senior role in the company. Admittedly, Paloma's only experience of working at Morante Group had been during a gap year while she had been at university. It was possible that Franco would win a majority vote from the board of trustees to displace her. Daniele recalled the last words Marcello had said to him.

'Will you promise to take care of my granddaughter?

I have come to regard you as the grandson I never had, Daniele. I beg you to think of Paloma as your sister and protect her from the sharks who will want a piece of her when I have gone.'

How was he supposed to think of Paloma as his sister? Daniele wondered grimly. He had tried not to think about her at all for the past three years.

Paloma had been a coltish teenager the first time he had met her, although even then she had shown signs that she would be a great beauty. Daniele had noticed her, but he had been trying to rebuild his life and hadn't paid her much attention.

When Paloma was twenty-one, she had come to Livorno on the west coast of Tuscany to take up an internship with Morante Group. The luxury leather goods business had grown to be a market leader, in part due to Daniele, who had established the company's online presence.

Daniele had been blown away by the beautiful young woman Paloma had become. He pictured her slender figure, chestnut-brown hair and milky pale skin as perfect as the finest porcelain. Paloma possessed an inherent elegance that spoke of her aristocratic heritage spread across three European countries. Her grandfather was a marchese. Marcello's wife, who had died tragically young, had been the daughter of a French duke, and Paloma's English mother was linked, albeit distantly, to the British royal family.

Daniele had found it impossible to resist the chemistry that had flared between him and Paloma. He had tried to keep his distance, conscious that he was twelve years older than her, and his position on the board of Morante Group made him her superior at work.

But on the night of a grand ball held in Marcello's opulent palazzo, Paloma had flirted with him, and when she had instigated a kiss, Daniele's self-control had cracked, and he'd succumbed to her sensual allure. He could still recall how soft her lips had felt beneath his. But he had been brought to his senses by the certainty that her grandfather would not have approved. Marcello had often spoken of his hope that Paloma would make a good marriage within the Italian nobility.

Daniele had not seen Paloma since that night when he had rejected her, but he had often found himself thinking about her. She had lodged like a bur in his skin, and for the past three years, his fascination with her had not faded. However, he was determined to keep his promise to Marcello to act like a brother to Paloma. But first he had to find her and break the terrible news that her grandfather had died.

He knew she lived in London, where she kept a low profile. She had adamantly refused her grandfather's plea to have a bodyguard. But Marcello's death meant that Paloma was a billionairess. Her life was going to be different from now on, and she would have to accept the protection of a security team.

Daniele had been given Paloma's contact details by Marcello's PA, but her mobile phone was switched off. When he'd called her landline number, he had been informed by her flatmate that Paloma was away at a yoga retreat somewhere in Ireland.

'Paloma should be here at Morante Group's headquarters.' Franco's terse voice interrupted Daniele's thoughts. 'You asked me to delay making a formal announcement of Marcello's death to give his granddaughter time to prepare for the inevitable media attention. But I will not wait any longer and risk the news being leaked to the press. Strong leadership is vital at this time.'

'You must understand that Paloma is shocked and distressed.' Daniele was sure she would be devastated, but he was not going to admit to Franco that he did not know her whereabouts, or that Paloma was still unaware of Marcello's death. 'I insist that she must be given more time to come to terms with her loss. Only the board of trustees and a handful of medical staff who treated Marcello know he is dead. I have taken out a legal injunction to prevent anyone talking to the media without my permission.'

'You had no right to go behind my back,' Franco said furiously.

'I had to act quickly to ensure the stability of the company. Marcello appointed me as lifelong vice president of the board in recognition of my loyalty to him and Morante Group.' Daniele knew that Franco had disapproved of Marcello's decision, and now he wondered if Marcello had suspected the other man might try to seize control of the company. 'In the next few days, I will bring Paloma to Livorno so that she can make a statement to the press.'

'I am Paloma's only living relative apart from her mother and I would like to offer her my condolences if you will tell me where she is.' Franco's tone had changed, and he showed no sign of his earlier hostility, but Daniele did not warm to him or trust him.

'I must respect Paloma's desire for privacy.' As he strode out of Franco's office, he was planning to visit every damn yoga retreat in Ireland, in search of the missing heiress.

Daniele's phone rang and he quickly answered it when he saw that Paloma's flatmate, whom he had spoken to earlier, was calling him. 'Laura?'

'Mr Berardo, I lied when I said that Paloma is in Ireland. She works for a charity and is teaching at a school in west Africa. There has been civil unrest and violence

in Mali for many years, and Paloma didn't tell her grandfather what she was doing because he would worry about
her. As a safety precaution, we set up a code word, and if
Paloma ever sent me the code, I was to call you and tell
you that she is in Mali.'

Daniele frowned. 'Why did Paloma ask you to call *me*?'

'She said that her grandfather trusts you implicitly and
she has faith in his judgement.' The urgency in the young
woman's voice sent a ripple of unease through Daniele.
'A few minutes ago, I received a text from Paloma and
it's the code word. I'm worried that she is in some kind
of trouble.'

CHAPTER ONE

PALOMA PEERED THROUGH the tiny window in the hut. All she could see outside was dusty desert, a few scrubby trees and the glint of the gun, slung across the shoulder of one of her captors, who was guarding the compound.

The adrenaline that had pumped through her when two masked gunmen had burst into the school where she had been teaching a class of young Malian girls had helped her to remain calm when she'd been bundled into a truck and driven away. But the hours she'd spent locked in the stifling hut, with barely enough food or water, were taking their toll and she felt scared and helpless.

At least she had managed to send a text to alert her flatmate in London before one of the gunmen had seized her phone. Laura should have contacted Daniele Berardo by now. But realistically, how could a computer geek help her in her present situation? Paloma thought bleakly. Not that there was anything remotely geeky about Daniele, she acknowledged. With his stunning good looks and potent sex appeal, he could be a film star rather than an IT expert and owner of the biggest tech company in Italy.

Her stomach muscles clenched as she visualised Daniele. The press had labelled the self-made multimillionaire Italy's most eligible bachelor, and his handsome face with a faintly sardonic expression appeared regularly in the gossip pages. Invariably he was photographed with a different beautiful woman on his arm. Paloma had spent more time than she was comfortable admitting searching for Daniele on social media sites. The last time she had actually seen him in the flesh had been three years ago.

Despite the intense heat inside her prison, Paloma shuddered as she recalled the most humiliating moments of her life. When Daniele had asked her to dance at a ball hosted by her grandfather, she should have realised that he was simply being polite. She'd had a massive crush on Daniele since she was a teenager, and the champagne she'd drunk during the evening had made her feel daring and encouraged her to press herself up close to his whipcord body when he'd placed his hands on her waist while they danced.

His terse comment that she needed some fresh air as he'd escorted her out of the ballroom had not burst her romantic bubble. They had been alone in the garden and Paloma had curved her arms around his neck and tugged his face towards her so that she could press her lips against his.

Daniele had stiffened, and his hands had gripped her arms as if he'd meant to pull them down. His mouth had been hard and unyielding, like the man himself. But then he'd made a harsh sound in his throat that had sent a coil of heat through Paloma as Daniele had taken control of the kiss. His lips had moved over hers with devastating mastery as he'd explored her mouth and owned it, owned her.

She had held nothing back, and the intensity of her passion had shocked her. But even more shocking had been when Daniele had suddenly wrenched his mouth from hers and set her away from him.

'That should not have happened,' he'd said in a cold voice that had stung her like the lash of a whip. 'Your grandfather would expect a better standard of behaviour from both of us. I suggest we forget that this regrettable incident ever took place.'

Burning up with embarrassment, Paloma had fled back to the house, and she'd left Italy the next day without seeing Daniele again. For the past three years, she had only visited her grandfather when she'd been certain that Daniele would not be in Livorno. Even her decision to marry Calum barely a month after their first date had, in hindsight, been partly to prove that she was over her infatuation with Daniele.

But Marcello had made no secret of the high esteem in which he held Daniele. Paloma hoped he would try to help her because of the affection he felt for her grandfather. Guilt tugged on her fraught emotions as she imagined how worried Nonno would be if he learned that she had been snatched by armed men. One reason for her decision to come to Africa on a volunteer scheme had been the admiration she felt for him. Marcello was a renowned philanthropist and he had established the Morante Foundation, which supported charity projects in Italy and around the world, funded by a percentage of the profits from his business, Morante Group.

Paloma had grown up knowing that she would inherit the company one day. When her father, Marcello's only son, had died in a tragic accident, her destiny had been assured. But her grandfather was likely to remain in charge of Morante Group for many more years, and Paloma had wanted to make her own way in the world, and experience different aspects of life, before she took on the responsibility of heading the company. She had become a fundraising manager for a children's charity, supporting communities in Africa. But spending every day in a comfortable office had felt distant from the problems in Mali, where there was widespread poverty and a lack of education, and she had seized the chance to teach at the school where she could make a real difference to the lives of her pupils.

What was going to happen to her? Paloma wondered fearfully. She'd hardly slept since she had been snatched and she was exhausted. Her head drooped down until her chin rested on her chest. She must have dozed, and woke with a start to the sound of a vehicle racing across the compound, and the terrifying noise of gunfire. Immediately her heart began to thump, and she jumped to her feet just as the door of the hut was flung open.

A figure dressed in khaki-coloured combat clothes and a balaclava covering his face, with two narrow slits cut out over his eyes, stood in the doorway. The man—Paloma guessed from his height and powerful build that he was male—was not one of the kidnappers who had taken her from the school. But his manner was authoritative, and she guessed he could be their leader. He was armed with an assault rifle and she instinctively backed away from him.

'Come with me,' he growled.

She must have imagined that he sounded vaguely familiar. Fearfully, Paloma backed away from him. 'Who are you?' Her voice shook as she heard the *pop-pop* of gunfire outside the hut.

Without another word, the man lurched towards her, scooped her off her feet and slung her over his shoulder. It happened so fast that Paloma did not have time to struggle. He carried her out of the hut, and she heard rough male voices. Once again, she had a sense of familiarity, but her brain had frozen, and she could not understand what was being said.

There was the sound of an engine revving, and then she was thrown into the back of a truck and her head hit the metal floor with a *thunk*. She attempted to sit up, but her captor leapt into the truck, slammed the door shut and flung himself on top of her as the vehicle was driven off at speed.

'Get off me!' Paloma braced her hands on the man's chest and attempted to push him away, but it was like trying to shift a granite boulder. She had trained in martial arts for years, but the reality of trying to defend herself against someone who was so much bigger and stronger than her was impossible. The knowledge that she was at her captor's mercy fired her temper. 'Pick on someone your own size, you *jerk*. Do you get a thrill from overpowering a defenceless woman and children?'

She remembered the terror on the faces of her pupils when the gunmen had burst into the classroom. 'What have you done with the girls from the school? Let them go,' she pleaded. 'Their families can't afford to pay a ransom. I am more valuable to you than a group of schoolgirls. My grandfather is a rich man, and he will pay for my release, but only if you allow the girls to go free.'

She glared into the man's eyes that were the only part of his face not covered by his balaclava. Eyes the golden-brown colour of sherry glittered back at her. Paloma became aware of his hard thighs pressed against her, and beneath her hands, she felt the definition of an impressive six-pack through his shirt.

Unbelievably she felt a flutter of awareness in the pit of her stomach. Not just awareness, but familiarity. Her subconscious mind recognised the impressive musculature of the male body stretched out on top of her, and her senses stirred when she breathed in the evocative scent of his aftershave. Only one man had ever elicited such an intense response in her.

She must be hallucinating, Paloma decided. Her captor couldn't be… She grabbed the edge of the man's bala-clava and tore it off his face. Her eyes widened in shock. *'Daniele!'*

'Ciao, cara,' he drawled in his sexy, accented voice that made her toes curl inside her trainers.

When Daniele had carried her out of the hut, he must have spoken in Italian to the driver of the truck. Paloma spoke Italian fluently, but English was her first language, and she'd been unable to think straight in the tense situation.

She gasped when she heard a metallic thud on the side of the truck.

'Vai più veloce!' Daniele told the driver urgently.

Paloma knew he had told him to go faster. Fear cramped in her stomach when she realised that the thud-ding sound was bullets striking the metal truck. They were being chased by the other gunmen who were shoot-ing at them.

She stared up at Daniele and it occurred to her that he was lying on top of her to protect her with his body if a bullet came through the window. The gleam in his eyes caused her heart to miss a beat.

'I don't understand,' she said shakily. 'You're a com-puter geek.' She had only ever seen him at Morante Group's offices or at her grandfather's opulent palazzo. Daniele had always worn a designer suit and been impec-cably groomed. Now he reminded her of a pirate with his black hair falling across his brow and thick stubble cov-ering his jaw.

'I did not realise that you had such an unflattering opinion of me,' he said drily.

His face was so close to hers that Paloma felt his breath graze her cheek. She could not look away from his sensual mouth as memories flooded her mind of being expertly kissed by him. The weight of his body held her pinned to the floor of the truck, and a purely feminine instinct made her splay her thighs a little so that her pelvis was flush with his.

His jaw clenched, and he flexed his arms and abruptly pushed himself off her. 'Stay where you are,' he ordered before he rolled across to the side of the truck, aimed his rifle out of the window and fired several rounds. *'Evvai!'* There was satisfaction in his voice. 'It's safe for you to sit up,' he told Paloma. 'I shot out a front tyre on the other truck. The men who kidnapped you can't harm you now.'

'Who *are* you?' she muttered.

'I trained as a soldier in the Italian Army and belonged to the Ninth Paratroopers Assault Regiment. The regiment is a special forces unit, like the SAS in the British Army.' There was quiet pride in Daniele's voice. 'An injury I sustained while I was on active service put an end to my military career, but I kept in touch with some of the other paras. When your flatmate told me you were in trouble, I contacted the school in Mali and learned that you had been kidnapped.' His mouth tightened. 'The country is notoriously dangerous, and kidnapping, especially of foreigners, is a serious threat. It was irresponsible of you to come here.'

'I was aware of the risks,' Paloma muttered. 'But there is a shortage of schools and teachers in Mali, and without access to education, children's life chances are reduced. Teaching was a practical way that I could help.' She pushed her hair out of her eyes, certain she must look a bedraggled, sweaty mess. Reaction to her ordeal was setting in, and the censure in Daniele's voice added guilt to the mix of her emotions. 'I didn't expect you would put your life in danger to rescue me. Thank you.' She flushed as she acknowledged how inadequate her words were.

'I promised your grandfather I would protect you,' Daniele said curtly. Instantly Paloma felt that she was a liability. She had sometimes felt stifled by Nonno's over-protectiveness. 'I was assisted by some of my old army friends,' Daniele told her. 'We had a tip-off that led us to where the gunmen were holding you and I planned a rescue mission. In a few minutes we will arrive at an airstrip where a plane is waiting to fly us out of here.'

'Does my grandfather know what happened to me?'

'No.' Daniele turned his head away and stared out of the window. Paloma had the feeling that he was avoiding her gaze.

'Thank you for keeping my kidnap ordeal from Nonno,' she said huskily. 'I had made up a story that I was spending time at a wellness retreat because I didn't want him to worry about me.'

'There is something I must tell you.' Daniele swore when the truck jolted on the uneven ground and Paloma fell against him. She put her hands on the solid wall of his chest to steady herself and was aware that his gaze had dropped to where her sweat-damp T-shirt was clinging to her breasts. To her horror, she felt her nipples harden, and she quickly shifted away from him. 'I'll talk to you when we are on the plane,' Daniele said roughly.

A sense of dread dropped into the pit of Paloma's stomach at his serious tone. They had reached an airfield and the truck pulled up next to a plane. She put her hand on Daniele's arm. 'Talk to me now.'

He exhaled slowly. 'There is no easy way to break the news to you, *cara*. Marcello is dead.'

Her heart stopped. 'It's not true. It can't be.' She searched Daniele's face for reassurance that she had misunderstood him but found none. 'Nonno is not a young man, but he is remarkably fit and healthy for his age.' It *had* to be a mistake. Paloma could not accept what Daniele had told her.

'I'm sorry. I realise what a shock this is for you. Your grandfather had an aortic aneurysm. In layman's terms, it means that the main blood vessel from his heart ruptured. We were playing golf when he collapsed with chest pains. I immediately called the emergency services and the medics fought to save him, but he died before he reached the hospital.'

'Were you with him when…when he died?' Paloma choked. Her throat was clogged with tears as the terrible truth sank in that she would never see her beloved Nonno again.

'I was,' Daniele assured her.

'I'm glad he wasn't alone.' Guilt felt like a knife through her heart. She should have been with her grandfather. He had tried to persuade her to move to Italy and become his assistant at Morante Group to prepare for the role that would one day be hers. She'd assumed that she had plenty of time to spread her wings first. Paloma swallowed a sob. 'When did Nonno collapse?'

'Two days ago. I've managed to keep a news blackout and only a handful of people know about Marcello's death.' Daniele hesitated. 'It is possible that someone on Morante Group's board of trustees arranged for you to disappear.'

Paloma stared at him. 'Why would any of them do that?'

'You are the sole heiress to your grandfather's fortune,' Daniele reminded her. 'The money comes to you straight away, and when you are twenty-five, you will take control of the company, as Marcello decreed in his will. But if something should happen to you, half of your inheritance is to be paid to the Morante Foundation charity and the other half will be divided equally between the eight board members, including your great-uncle Franco, but not myself. Your grandfather gave me a lifelong position on the board, but I am not a beneficiary of his will. In the event of your death, the other trustees stand to become multimillionaires, and the board will decide who to appoint as the new head of Morante Group.'

'I'm young and healthy, and nothing is likely to happen to me.' Paloma bit her lip when Daniele rolled his eyes. 'You said yourself that kidnapping of foreigners is common in Mali.'

'I suppose it *could* be a coincidence that you were seized soon after Marcello died, but in my experience, coincidences are rare,' Daniele said cynically. 'If your flatmate hadn't alerted me, I would not have known where to look for you. But someone knew the Morante heiress was in Mali, and I believe that person hoped to prevent you from claiming your inheritance.'

CHAPTER TWO

DANIELE RAPPED ON the bedroom door but got no response. He tried the handle but was not surprised to find that the door was locked. The previous evening, he had brought Paloma to a hotel owned by his close friend whom he trusted implicitly. In the penthouse suite, Paloma had locked herself in one of the bedrooms and Daniele had heard her crying for hours.

He had paced up and down the corridor outside her room, wondering if he should offer to try to comfort her as he had done after her father had been killed in a speed-boat accident eight years ago. Paloma had been sixteen and still a child in Daniele's eyes. A rapport had grown between them when he'd shared his experience of losing his own father when he had been a teenager.

But Paloma was no longer a schoolgirl, a fact that Daniele had been all too aware of when he'd flung himself on top of her in the back of the truck to protect her from the bullets that the kidnappers had been firing indiscriminately. His jaw clenched as he remembered how his body had reacted to the feel of Paloma's soft curves beneath him. He had been shocked, frankly, by the kick of awareness in the pit of his stomach.

At thirty-six, he was way past the age of behaving like a hormonal adolescent. He dated selectively and enjoyed women's company both in and out of the bedroom, although he had never felt an inclination to marry. It said a lot about him, Daniele acknowledged. He had guarded his emotions since he'd been five years old and watched his mother drive away from the family home. She had promised to visit him often, but she'd never come back. Eventually Daniele had given up staring out of the window in the hope of seeing her car turn the corner of the road. It had been an early lesson that promises were easily made and just as easily broken. A few years later, he had been invited to visit his mother, who had remarried, and he'd met his little half-brother. But since then, Daniele had not had any further contact with that side of his family for twenty-seven years.

He pulled his thoughts from the past and knocked on the door again. 'Paloma, you need to eat. I've arranged for dinner to be served here in the suite.'

'I'm not hungry.' Her voice was muffled. 'I want to be alone.'

Daniele frowned. He had given Paloma's grandfather his word that he would take care of her, which meant he must help her to secure her place as the head of Morante Group.

'You are not the only one who is devastated by Marcello's death,' he said gruffly. 'I share your grief. But you are your grandfather's successor, and he would want you to show strong leadership of the company. I ordered some clothes for you from the hotel's boutique. I'll leave them outside the door.' His words were met with silence. 'There are things we need to discuss, and I do not intend to talk to you through the door. Don't make me break it down.'

'You wouldn't dare.'

'I never make idle threats, *cara*.' Daniele walked back to the sitting room, cursing as his leg throbbed. The old injury was a permanent reminder of the events that had led to him meeting Marcello Morante. Ten years ago, he had paid a heavy price for saving Marcello's life, but Marcello had in turn saved Daniele from the dark place he'd fallen into and given him the chance of a glittering future.

The grief that Daniele had suppressed since his old friend's death felt like a knife blade through his heart. He took a bottle of beer from the fridge and opened it before he stepped out onto the balcony. Now that Paloma was safe, he could finally focus on the man who had meant so much to him.

With his last breaths, Marcello had told Daniele that he'd thought of him as a grandson. It was ironic, Daniele brooded, that his real grandfather, who had disowned him when he was a child, had died only days before Marcello. Daniele had not mourned his mother's father, and in fact, he'd only met the Conte Alfonso Farnesi on one humiliating occasion when he had been made to feel that he was muck on the sole of his grandfather's shoe.

Daniele had been nine when his mother had unexpectedly invited him to the Farnesi estate near Florence. She had not been in contact since she'd left four years earlier and she'd divorced Daniele's father and remarried. There had been photos in the newspapers of her and her new husband, who was from an aristocratic banking family. Some while later, it had been reported that she had given birth to a son by her second husband.

Daniele had been desperate to see his mother and excited to meet his half-brother, Stefano. But the visit had gone badly. He'd felt awkward when he'd walked into his grandfather Alfonso's imposing villa where his mother and her new family lived. On the walls were paintings of grand-looking men and women. The House of Farnesi had been an important family since the time of the Renaissance. But it had been made clear to Daniele that his portrait would never hang alongside his glorious ancestors. His father was a common soldier, and his grandfather was determined that the Farnesi blue-blooded lineage would not be tainted by a low-born grandson.

Under ancient nobility laws, titles were passed down through the male line. But if, as in Conte Farnesi's case, he had a daughter, but no son, the title could skip a generation and be passed to the first male grandchild. By rights, that should have been Daniele. But during that infamous visit, Alfonso had announced that he'd disinherited Daniele and made Stefano his heir.

Daniele forced his mind away from bitter memories of his childhood and took a long swig of beer. The title of Conte was only a courtesy, as official recognition of Italian nobility had ended decades ago. He'd assumed that he had come to terms with being overlooked by his grandfather and rejected by his mother. But before he'd left Italy for Africa, the newspapers had been full of reports of the death of the seventeenth Conte Farnesi. Much gushing prose had been printed about Alfonso's successor, his grandson Stefano, who would take the surname Farnesi.

Daniele had studied the newspaper photo of his mother looking proudly at his half-brother and he'd been surprised at how much it still rankled that he was not good enough for her. He had made a fortune by using his brain and working hard, and his online affiliate marketing company, Premio, was ranked in the top ten most successful businesses in Italy. But despite his achievements, his mother would never be proud of him because his father had not belonged to the nobility.

Daniele heard footsteps behind him. He turned around and inhaled sharply as he watched Paloma walk towards him. During her kidnap ordeal, she had worn the same

T-shirt and shorts for days, but despite looking tired and dishevelled, she had still been beautiful when Daniele had rescued her from her captors.

This evening she was utterly breathtaking. The clothes that had been delivered from the hotel's boutique were typical holiday wear. Paloma was dressed in a long, kaftan-style garment made of fine white cotton, with delicate gold embroidery along the V-shaped neckline. A wide belt of the same material emphasised her tiny waist. As she walked, the side splits on either side of the skirt parted to reveal her slim legs.

Daniele heard the thunder of his pulse in his ears and was conscious that his blood had surged down to his groin. The kick of awareness was even stronger than he'd felt in the truck when he had stretched his body out on top of Paloma to shield her from the gunmen's bullets. He could not tear his gaze from her long, chestnut-brown hair that fell midway to her waist and gleamed like raw silk in the light from the lamps on the balcony. The lemony scent of shampoo, mingled with the subtle, floral fragrance of her perfume, assailed his senses and his pulse quickened.

He was struck by the realisation that the pretty teenager he had first met nearly a decade ago, and even the naive but achingly lovely twenty-one-year-old intern Paloma had been three years ago, had not prepared him for the exquisite and sensuous woman who halted in front of him.

Her dark eyelashes swept upwards and eyes the intense blue of lapis lazuli glared at him. 'You always were as cold as a block of ice, Daniele.'

He was fascinated and relieved to see the pink flush that highlighted Paloma's delicate cheekbones. Her face had been ashen when he'd half carried her into the hotel, but now the evidence of her temper was a good sign. She would need to be strong. Marcello was a hard act to follow, and Daniele did not know if Paloma was up to the task, but it was his duty to give her the chance to find out.

'I have lost my grandfather, who I loved more than anyone in the world.' Her voice shook. 'Would it hurt you to show a little compassion?'

Daniele's eyes dropped to her lips, which trembled slightly before she pressed them together. He sensed she was struggling to control her emotions, and he was furious with himself for imagining covering her lush mouth with his. Paloma was out of bounds, and the quicker his libido accepted that fact, the better. He wondered what she would say if he admitted that, far from being a block of ice, he was on fire. Fortunately, he was a master at concealing his thoughts behind an enigmatic expression.

'I gave you the space that I thought you needed, but time is against us,' he told her. 'You must be at Morante Group's offices tomorrow to make a formal announcement of Marcello's death. We will fly to Italy on a private jet first thing in the morning.'

She frowned. 'You mean we are not in Italy? I'd assumed it was where we were headed when we left Mali, but I was thinking about Nonno, and I didn't take much notice of anything else.' Paloma stepped closer to the balcony rail and looked out. Night had fallen, and the moon was a huge silver ball reflected in the pool below. 'I can see palm trees. Where are we?'

'Tunisia. A friend of mine, Enrique, owns the hotel. Another ex-army friend piloted the plane that was used in the operation to rescue you. I decided against taking you to Italy until I'd had a chance to try and find out who was behind the kidnap plot. For your safety, only Enrique knows that you are staying here.'

'You have useful friends,' Paloma murmured wryly. She slanted Daniele a look when he came to stand beside her. 'I keep hoping that I will wake up and find it was all a dream. Being kidnapped, and then you turning up to rescue me.' She swallowed. 'Nonno dying. It all seems unreal. I can't believe that the two events are linked. The political situation in Mali is unstable and militia groups have a history of attacking civilians.'

'The gunmen who snatched you from the school were not Malian nationals.'

'How do you know?'

'A couple of my guys stayed behind in Mali to carry out surveillance. The gunmen were picked up by the police but refused to say who they were working for.' Daniele exhaled heavily. Paloma needed to understand the seriousness of the situation. 'The kidnappers escaped from custody, or, more likely, someone was paid to allow them to go free. Who was behind the plot to kidnap you? That's what I'd like to know.'

'I don't believe anyone on the board of trustees could be involved. They are...' she bit her lip '...were Nonno's friends and I have known them all my life.'

Daniele shrugged. 'At least two of them have financial problems that would be resolved if you were not around and your grandfather's fortune was split between the board members.'

'It's always about money,' Paloma burst out. 'People believe that wealth brings happiness, but not in my experience. I'm convinced that my family is cursed. Nonno adored his wife, but my grandmother died giving birth to my father. Papa was only forty when he was killed in a speedboat race. Now my grandfather has gone too, and you say that my safety is threatened because I am a rich heiress. Sometimes I wish I could walk away from it all,' she muttered.

Daniele tore his gaze from Paloma's breasts rising and

falling swiftly beneath her dress, and silently cursed his damnable attraction to her that he was determined to resist. 'If I don't get you to Livorno by tomorrow, your wish may come true.'

'What do you mean?'

A knock on the door of the suite gave him the excuse to shelve the conversation for a while. 'That will be dinner,' he said as he ushered Paloma inside and held out a chair for her to be seated at the table. A waiter came in, pushing a trolley laden with dishes. Once the food had been served, the wine poured and the candles on the table lit, the waiter left them alone.

Daniele was relieved when Paloma picked up her fork and started to eat some couscous and roasted vegetables. She looked fragile, and he found himself wanting to comfort her, hold her. His jaw clenched as his body responded to the idea of taking her into his arms so that her small breasts were crushed against his chest. Marcello had asked him to protect Paloma, and Daniele was determined to honour his friend's last request.

'I noticed you were limping just now,' she commented. 'Have you hurt your leg?'

'I was shot…'

Paloma dropped her fork and it clattered against the china plate. 'You mean you were hit by a bullet when the gunmen were firing at us! Why didn't you tell me? It's my fault you are injured.'

'It's an old injury,' Daniele quickly assured her. 'It happened years ago when I was in the army. My kneecap was shattered, and I had several rounds of surgery to rebuild it. Most of the time it's fine, but I landed heavily on my knee when we jumped into the truck to get away from the kidnappers.'

'Was your injury the reason you left the army?'

'Yes, unfortunately.' He looked across the table and saw Paloma's eyes widen at his curt reply. 'The army was my life. I had wanted to join up since I was a kid, to honour my father.'

'I remember you told me that your father died while he was a soldier, serving in Bosnia.'

'He was part of the peace-keeping force and was killed by a sniper.'

'So you became a soldier like your dad. What happened to you?'

'One of my missions in the special forces was to work undercover. I was sent to infiltrate a Mafia gang who were responsible for several high-profile kidnappings and murders. I discovered that Marcello Morante was the gang's next target and managed to alert the authorities in time to foil the plot. Your grandfather was safe, but my cover had been blown, and the Mafia boss ordered my execution.'

Daniele hesitated when Paloma gasped. Nausea churned in his stomach as memories flooded back. Counselling had helped him to process what had happened, but he would never forget the sickening terror he'd felt when the gang had discovered his identity, and he'd been certain he was going to die.

'I was driven to a remote field and shot,' he explained unemotionally. 'The injury was deliberately not immediately fatal so that I would slowly bleed to death.'

'Oh, Daniele.' Paloma's soft voice tugged on something buried deep inside him. An unexpected longing for tenderness that he quickly dismissed. In his heart he would always be a soldier, and perhaps a part of him would always be the boy who had watched his mother leave. 'How did you survive?' Paloma asked.

'I managed to crawl across the field after the assassins had driven away.' For years afterwards, his nightmares had dragged him back to the darkness and the agonising pain of his shattered knee as blood had poured from the bullet wound. 'I came to a farmer's track, and by a million-to-one chance, some tourists were lost and had stopped to look at the map. They patched me up and drove me to the nearest hospital. If they had found me five minutes later, it would have been too late, and I would have bled out.'

'I had no idea that you nearly lost your life to keep my grandfather safe. It explains the bond that existed between you and Nonno.'

Daniele shrugged. 'I was doing my job. I didn't know Marcello then. But he found out that I had prevented him from being kidnapped, and he came to see me. I had just learned that, despite numerous operations, my knee was permanently damaged, and my army career was over. I was twenty-six and felt like my life was over.'

He grimaced. 'Marcello offered to pay me compensation, but I was a surly devil and told him what he could do with his money. I didn't want handouts, and I was determined to make my own fortune. I had always been interested in computers and programming, and while I'd been in hospital for months, I'd developed a smart payment app for mobile phones. Remember, this was ten years ago, and the idea was innovative. Marcello agreed to invest in my start-up company. It was an instant success, and three years later, I became a millionaire when I sold the business. Your grandfather persuaded me to join Morante Group as an IT consultant, and I established an online marketing presence that helped to make the company a global brand.'

'Nonno said you dragged Morante Group into the twenty-first century,' Paloma murmured. 'I know he admired you.'

'I was honoured to have had your grandfather as my friend. He was a great man. But the same cannot be said about Franco Zambrotta.'

Paloma had finished eating, and she took a sip of wine before setting her glass down on the table. 'What have you got against Uncle Franco?'

The red wine had stained her lips. Daniele's gaze lingered on her lush mouth and he wondered if she tasted as intoxicating as she had three years ago. He would never find out, he resolved grimly. Marcello had made him responsible for Paloma, and in the past twenty-four hours, Daniele had formed a crazy plan that would allow him to keep her safe and protect her position at Morante Group. But he could not let his inconvenient desire for her undermine his self-control.

'Your great-uncle intends to call for a vote of no confidence in you,' he said abruptly. 'If he gains the support of the majority of the board of trustees, you will effectively be fired, or at least sidelined, and Franco will put himself up as joint chairman and CEO of Morante Group.'

Paloma's eyes widened. 'He can't do that, can he?'

'I'm afraid he can. If he is voted in as the new head of the company, he intends to reduce the annual donation to the Morante Foundation. You probably know that your grandfather insisted on forty per cent of the business's profits being paid to the charity.'

'A policy that I am determined will continue. I can't believe the other board members would agree to pay less of the profits to the charitable foundation that was so important to Nonno.'

'They might if Franco offers a financial sweetener to the trustees. Legally he could pay them bonus dividends during financial restructuring of the company. But in order for that to happen, the board would first have to replace you with Franco. Under the terms of Marcello's will, Franco will be the acting head of Morante Group until your twenty-fifth birthday. That's in December, isn't it?' When Paloma nodded, Daniele continued, 'Franco will have eight months to win the support of the board.'

'If my grandfather had wanted Uncle Franco to succeed him, instead of me, he would have altered his will. The fact that he didn't must mean that he had faith in my ability to run the company. Surely the board will abide by Marcello's wishes?'

Daniele sighed. 'You are an unknown quantity. Perhaps if you had moved to Italy when you finished university and worked at the company as Marcello had hoped, you would not have been seen as an outsider.'

'I'm not completely clueless. I have a master's degree in business. However, I realise that I lack the necessary experience to run Morante Group. I'd expected Nonno to be around for years to advise me.' Paloma's voice wobbled. 'Now I find myself responsible for the business that my grandfather started before I was born. He was both chairman and CEO, but I'm thinking of splitting the roles and appointing a CEO who will lead the executive management team.'

'I suppose that might allay some of the board's concerns. But there is still the matter of your marriage.'

Paloma flushed. 'My marriage was a mistake. I don't understand why it should matter to anyone else, especially as I am now divorced.'

'I heard it was an expensive mistake because you had not asked your husband to sign a prenuptial agreement before the wedding,' Daniele said drily. He told himself it was a coincidence that the last time he'd got extremely drunk had been the night he'd learned of Paloma's surprise marriage. 'Franco has made the point that if you succeed your grandfather and were to rush into another marriage, your new spouse could be entitled to half of Morante Group's assets in a divorce settlement.'

Paloma's long lashes swept down to hide her expression. 'There is a saying—once bitten, twice shy,' she said curtly. 'I have no intention of marrying again.'

'That's a pity,' Daniele drawled, 'because I strongly advise you to marry me.'

CHAPTER THREE

'VERY FUNNY,' PALOMA MUTTERED. Inside, she was cringing with embarrassment at Daniele's mention of her marriage that had lasted barely long enough for the ink to dry on the register. Worse still, it had been Daniele's rejection that had sent her rushing back to England instead of relocating to Italy as her grandfather had wanted her to do. She'd met Calum soon after her return to London and been flattered by his attention.

Paloma pushed away uncomfortable memories of her ex-husband and forced herself to look at Daniele. 'This is not the time for jokes.'

'It wasn't a joke. I am making a serious proposition.' He held her gaze, and in the glow of the candlelight, his eyes were the golden colour of amber. Lion's eyes, Paloma thought. Daniele reminded her of a predatory big cat. He gave the impression of being relaxed as he leaned back in his chair, but there was something intrinsically powerful about him, and his eyes gleaming beneath his thick black lashes were watchful and alert.

He was unfairly gorgeous, in faded jeans and a cream shirt, unbuttoned at the neck to reveal a sprinkling of black chest hairs. His shirtsleeves were rolled up to the elbows, showing his darkly tanned forearms and the glint of a discreetly expensive-looking gold watch on his wrist.

Paloma was aware of a melting sensation in the pit of her stomach that only Daniele had ever induced. He must be about thirty-six now, but there were no silver strands in his raven's-wing dark hair. She fancied that his face was leaner, harder, the sharp cheekbones more defined. His mouth was perfection and offered the same sensual invitation that had led her to behave uncharacteristically recklessly three years ago.

It was a good thing she had got over her juvenile crush on him, Paloma assured herself. 'Explain yourself, Daniele,' she demanded. 'The last time we met, it was obvious you couldn't bear to touch me. I don't flatter myself that you actually *want* to marry me.'

He looked startled for a moment before his features became unreadable again. 'I have racked my brains to find another way that I can protect you and your interests with Morante Group as I promised your grandfather I would do. A temporary marriage until you are twenty-five is the best solution I can come up with.'

'I don't need your protection,' Paloma said stiffly. She understood that Daniele was acting out of the deep loyalty he felt for her grandfather, but her pride was stung by his obvious reluctance to have any sort of involvement with her. 'Being kidnapped was the most terrifying ordeal I have ever experienced,' she admitted. 'But I don't buy into your conspiracy theory that someone on the board of trustees wants me out of the way.'

'Setting aside the question of who was behind the kidnap plot, Franco Zambrotta is serious about seizing control of the company. I have heard from a private source that he is gaining support from more board members.'

'How would it help me if I married you?' It was out of the question. Nothing would persuade Paloma to agree to

Daniele's astonishing proposition, but she was curious to know the reason behind it.

'Marcello made me vice president of the board, and I am popular with most of the trustees, with the exception of Franco and one or two of his close cronies. I believe the majority of the board will approve of our marriage for two reasons. Firstly, I have the business experience that you lack, and I can prepare you for when you take control of the company. Secondly, if you are my wife, there will be no chance of you marrying without a prenuptial agreement in place to safeguard Morante Group's assets.'

'Are you saying you would be willing to sign a prenup?'

'Certainly. In fact, I'd insist on it. A legal agreement would be drawn up to protect the entirety of your inheritance and the company's assets. I already own a highly successful business and I am wealthy. I don't want your money or your company, *cara*.'

'You must want something from me. Everyone always does,' Paloma said flatly. Ever since she had been old enough to understand that she was an heiress to a vast fortune, she had felt set apart from her peers and wary of people's motives for wanting to be her friend.

Across the table, Daniele gave her a speculative look. 'I don't deny it would be advantageous for me to marry the granddaughter of a marchese. You were born into one of the oldest Italian noble families and your heritage gives you a certain status in society that I, as an entrepreneur who made my fortune through hard work and innovation, can never attain.'

'And that matters to you?'

'It matters to my mother,' Daniele said in a grim voice. 'Her aristocratic family disapproved of her marriage to my father because he had no title and was, in their opinion, a common soldier. My grandfather threatened to cut my mother out of his will unless she divorced my father and cut all ties with me, which she did.'

Paloma stared at Daniele. Her parents had divorced acrimoniously when she was a child, and her mother had been awarded custody, but she'd seen her father fairly regularly. The break-up had been a painful time. How much worse it must have been for Daniele when his mother had cut him out of her life. 'How old were you when she went away?'

'Five. My father brought me up, but he was often sent away on military postings, and I spent a lot of time with my grandmother. When my father was killed, I lived with my grandmother because my mother refused to take me back. She'd remarried and had another son. My half-brother recently became the new Conte Farnesi following my grandfather's death.'

Paloma took a deep breath. 'So you would be willing to marry me to impress your mother with an aristocratic bride?' It was stupid to feel so hurt, she told herself. Daniele was no different from everyone else who valued her for her financial worth or, in his case, her pedigree.

'The marriage would be advantageous to both of us. I would help you to secure your position as head of Morante Group,' he reminded her.

Paloma leapt to her feet. She needed to get away from Daniele before her emotions overwhelmed her. 'If necessary, I'll sign a statement saying that I will not marry anyone without the approval of the board of trustees.' It took all her effort to keep her voice steady, but she was damned if she'd let Daniele see how humiliated she felt. 'I know that my grandfather had the best intentions.' She blinked away tears as she thought of Nonno, the only person who had truly loved her. 'But to him I was always a little girl. I'm not. I am an adult, and I don't need your help or protection.'

She marched across the room and paused in the doorway, turning her head to give Daniele a fulminating glare. 'You will have to find yourself another aristocratic bride. If we were the last two people on the planet, I still wouldn't marry you.'

The pool had been warm when Paloma had started swimming. She'd powered through the water, completing lap after lap while she focused on her breathing to block out her chaotic thoughts. Now, though, she was tired, and the water felt chilly. There had been several other hotel guests swimming or sitting on the poolside when she'd arrived. But when she looked around, she discovered that they had gone, and she was alone.

The pool area was surrounded by trees and shrubs, and the darkness preyed on Paloma's imagination. Was Daniele right, and the men who had seized her in Mali were working for some unknown person who wanted to prevent her from claiming her inheritance? *Be logical*, she told herself sternly. Daniele had said that no one knew she was staying at the hotel in Tunisia. There were not hordes of kidnappers lurking in the shadows.

All the same, she wished she'd told him she was going to the pool. After dinner she had fled to her room, reeling from his shocking marriage proposition. But she'd felt restless and had decided to go for a swim. There had been a swimsuit among the clothes that Daniele had ordered from the hotel's boutique. Paloma had heard him talking on his phone when she'd slipped out of the suite.

Her teeth were chattering when she swam to the edge of the pool. But as she was about to climb up the steps, she heard a rustling noise from the bushes, and she froze.

The memory of the terrifying moment when the gunmen had burst into the classroom in Mali stretched her over-wrought emotions to breaking point. Was someone aiming a gun at her, his finger on the trigger as he waited for her to climb out of the pool? The leaves on the bushes shook, even though there was no breeze. Heart pounding in her chest, Paloma opened her mouth and screamed.

Immediately she heard footsteps running across the terrace and saw Daniele's reassuringly big and powerful figure charging towards the pool. He halted next to the steps and his eyes glittered in the darkness. 'What happened? Are you hurt?'

'There's someone in the bushes over there.' She was shivering so badly with a mixture of cold and fear that she could barely get the words out. The story Daniele had told her of how he had foiled a Mafia plot to kidnap her grandfather had stuck in her mind. Nonno's death meant that she was now incredibly rich and a target for criminals who might try to snatch her and demand a ransom for her release. 'Be careful,' she urged Daniele in a shaky whisper as he strode towards the shadowy area at the edge of the terrace.

'Who is there?' he demanded. Paloma held her breath when there was more movement from the bushes. Daniele let out a low laugh as a cat leapt out and landed on its four paws on the tiles. 'There's your culprit. Stray cats are a problem around the hotel complex.' The cat gave them a disdainful look and stalked away indignantly.

Relief surged through Paloma. Her emotions were on a knife-edge and something inside her cracked. She climbed out of the pool and buried her face in her hands as sobs shook her slender frame. Once again, Daniele had put himself in potential danger to protect her. He hadn't known that it was a cat, not a gunman, concealed in the bushes. Daniele was the only person she could trust, and she did not resist when he placed his arm across her shoulders and drew her against his muscular body.

'*Va bene, cara,*' he murmured. 'You are safe.'

She felt safe with him. Paloma made a choked sound of protest when Daniele moved away from her, but he returned almost instantly to drape a towel around her shoulders and began to rub her dry.

'Are you feeling warmer?' he asked after a couple of minutes of brisk rubbing.

'A bit.' Her skin was tingling from his ministrations with the towel. She ought to object that he was treating her like a child, but when he pulled her into the circle of his arms once more, she sank against him, feeling the warmth of his body through his shirt transfer to her. He smelled divinely of sandalwood cologne, and she heard the strong thud of his heart beneath her ear when she rested her head on his chest.

'You have been through a lot recently. The events in Mali and the sudden loss of your grandfather. You're in a state of shock.' Daniele's deep voice rumbled through Paloma, and she was soothed by the light touch of his hand as he stroked her hair back from her face.

Nonno was the only person who had made her feel cherished. Her mother led a busy life socialising with her jet-set friends, and as a child Paloma had mostly been left in the care of nannies or sent away to boarding school. Visits to her father had been marred by his jealous mistresses who had resented any attention he had shown his daughter. Paloma had learned to be self-sufficient at a young age, but the truth was she had been lonely all her life. A poor little rich girl was how the tabloids had described her when speculation about the size of the divorce settlement she'd given Calum had made the headlines.

She did not want to think about her ex-husband's cruel deception, or the promises he'd made so glibly but had never intended to keep. She could not bear to think of her darling Nonno, the only person who had valued her for who she was, rather than how much she was worth. Standing in the shelter of Daniele's arms, Paloma closed her eyes and allowed her senses to take over from her conscious thoughts.

The call of the cicadas was a noisy chorus in the still night air, and the fragrance of jasmine growing in pots on the terrace was sweetly sultry. Paloma became aware of a subtle change in Daniele's breathing and felt the quickening of his heartbeat. She was conscious of how much taller than her he was, and of the latent strength of his muscular physique.

In contrast, she felt small and weak like a kitten. Of course she wasn't weak. Her great-uncle Franco and the other board members would discover that she was determined to claim her place at the head of the company she had inherited. But that fight would happen tomorrow. Right now it was bliss to be in Daniele's arms while he threaded his fingers through her long hair.

In a flash, Paloma's dreamy state of relaxation disappeared, replaced with an intense awareness of the man who had featured in every one of her adolescent romantic fantasies. The tiny hairs on her skin prickled and the ache low in her pelvis urged her to press herself closer to Daniele. Her breasts felt heavy, and she wondered if he could feel the hard tips of her nipples through the clingy material of her swimsuit. She tilted her head so that she could look at his face and her heart missed a beat when their eyes met and held. A nerve flickered in his cheek and his dark brows met above his glittering amber gaze.

'Paloma...' There was a warning in his gruff voice,

but she could not look away from him or break the connection that throbbed between them. Three years ago, she had made the first move and pressed her lips against his, only for him to spurn her. Now she watched Daniele's dark head descend and her pulse leapt when it seemed that he was about to kiss her. His warm breath whispered over her lips. She could not move, could hardly breathe. Her lashes swept down to hide the longing she was sure he would see in her eyes.

He swore, his voice low and harsh, and abruptly dropped his arms down to his sides so that she swayed on her feet when he stepped back from her. Daniele raked his hand through his hair. 'Go inside. Quickly.' He bit out the command.

Paloma hugged the towel tightly around her. She could not control the tremors that racked her body as reaction to what had happened—or nearly happened—set in. Self-recrimination churned in her stomach. *Idiot!* Why had she stared at Daniele like a lovesick teenager, hoping he would kiss her? He had made it clear that his marriage proposition was so he could fulfil his promise to her grandfather to take care of her. He saw her as his responsibility, nothing more.

He frowned when she did not move. 'For God's sake, go back to the hotel—*now*. And, Paloma,' he said curtly when she turned away from him. 'What just happened. It was nothing. We are both in shock and grieving for Marcello. It's hardly surprising that our emotions are running high.'

Daniele watched Paloma run back to the hotel and was tempted to follow her to make sure she reached the penthouse safely. But he had a more pressing need to discover who had been spying on them. He hadn't imagined the sudden glare of a camera flashbulb from the shadowy area next to the pool. At least it had jolted him to his senses, he thought grimly.

What the hell had he been thinking when he'd pulled Paloma into his arms? But in fairness, when she had broken down and sobbed heartbrokenly, her vulnerability had tugged on something inside him, and his only thought had been to comfort her. He hadn't counted on the fact that Paloma had been a threat to his peace of mind for years. His libido had responded to her softly curvaceous body and her small breasts pressed against his chest. The temptation to kiss her had made him forget the promise he had made her grandfather. Worse, he had momentarily forgotten that Paloma was in danger.

Silently cursing his lack of control, Daniele pulled his phone from his pocket and called the hotel's owner, Enrique, before he made a thorough search among the bushes and trees surrounding the pool terrace. As he'd expected, whoever had been hiding there had gone. Minutes later, he heard a voice behind him.

'Paloma has returned to the penthouse. I have assigned a security guard to patrol the corridor outside the suite,' Enrique told him. 'What's the problem?'

'Someone knows she is here.'

'I don't see how that is possible. You were both checked into the hotel under false names. Do you think one of the other guests recognised Paloma?'

'The only time she left the suite was tonight when she came down to the pool.' Daniele's jaw clenched. He would have tried to stop her if he'd known she planned to swim. Fear had cramped in his stomach when he'd discovered that Paloma was not in her room.

'I've stepped up security around the hotel,' Enrique said. 'Do you still believe that one or more of the trustees of her grandfather's company want Paloma out of the way?'

'It's an undeniable fact that they would all benefit financially. Her great-uncle has made no secret that he wants control of Morante Group, but would he arrange to have Paloma kidnapped?'

'Money and power are strong motivators. What about you, Daniele? What is the motivation for your involvement with Paloma?'

'I promised her grandfather as he was dying that I would take care of her.'

Enrique chuckled. 'Keep telling yourself that, my friend. I have seen the way you look at this woman.'

'You are imagining things,' Daniele drawled. 'Marriage and babies have made you soft.'

'I admit I'm crazy in love with my wife. You should try it.'

Daniele snorted. 'I saw what being in love did to my father. He never got over my mother leaving.'

As Daniele walked back to the hotel, his mind was on his parents' marriage, which had been doomed from the start, according to his grandmother. Nonna Elsa had described his mother as having had airs and graces, and she'd thought herself too good to live in the cramped apartment that had been all Daniele's father could afford.

Claudia Farnesi's brief infatuation with a handsome soldier had resulted in pregnancy and a marriage that had been against her aristocratic family's wishes. She had abandoned her husband and young son and returned to a life of wealth and luxury. But Daniele knew his father had never stopped loving his mother, and he'd watched the once happy man become sad and bitter. Why would anyone risk their heart and happiness on such a fickle emotion as love? Daniele brooded. Love was a weakness and he had never understood its appeal.

They flew to Italy the next morning on a private jet that Daniele had chartered and landed at Pisa airport, where a chauffeured limousine was waiting to take them to Livorno. The seaport was one of the largest in the Mediterranean. Years ago, Marcello had bought a fleet of six cargo ships and established Morante Shipping as a subsidiary company of Morante Group. Livorno was also home to the barracks of the Italian special forces regiment that Daniele had once belonged to. Coming back to the town always evoked memories of his time as a soldier, and he still missed the army that had become his family and given him a sense of belonging.

The car headed towards the historic old town and drew up in front of a grand, neoclassical building that housed Morante Group's headquarters. Paloma had barely said a word since they had left Tunisia, but now Daniele heard her catch her breath.

'The press conference is arranged for midday,' he told her. 'Franco has offered to make the public announcement of Marcello's death if you feel unable to.'

'I'll do it. I am my grandfather's successor and I want to pay tribute to him. It feels strange coming here, knowing that Nonno is not in his office. I don't think it has really sunk in yet that I will never see him again.' Her voice was unsteady.

Daniele shifted closer to her, intending to place his hand over hers, but he thought better of it and leaned back in his seat. Comforting Paloma had not gone to plan when he had found her by the pool, he reminded himself derisively.

Last night she had looked young and impossibly innocent, with her wet hair hanging down her back and her face bare of make-up. Today she was the epitome of elegance, in a black sheath dress that emphasised her slim figure. Vertiginous stiletto heels drew attention to her long legs, and her handbag bore the distinctive MGL logo of the Morante Group leather accessories range. Her hair was swept up in a chignon and her face was discreetly made up. A pair of oversized sunglasses shielded her expression, but Daniele sensed that her grief for her grandfather was raw when they entered the office building from where Marcello had amassed his business empire.

They went straight to the hospitality suite where members of the press had gathered. Paloma was composed when she gave a statement announcing the sudden death of Marcello Morante, the founder of Morante Group and the Morante Foundation, a renowned philanthropist and her beloved grandfather.

'Signorina Morante, can you confirm who is to replace Marcello?' a journalist asked.

'I will become the head of Morante Group when I am twenty-five. Until then, according to the terms of my grandfather's will, all decisions pertaining to the company will be made jointly by myself and the board of trustees.'

'Are you concerned about taking on the enormous responsibility of running the company when you are so young and inexperienced in business?'

'I am my grandfather's heir. It was his wish that I would succeed him, and I will do my best to honour his faith in me.' Paloma stood up and cast her cool gaze over the group of journalists before she swept out of the room. Her regal bearing denoted her aristocratic heritage as the granddaughter of a marchese. But Daniele knew she would need more than her impressive family background to win the support of the board. He opened the door of the boardroom and stood aside to allow Paloma to pre-cede him into the room.

The eight trustees sitting around the table were all male, and all were getting on in years, Daniele surmised. Marcello's loyalty to his old friends, even though a few of them should have long since retired, had been his one weakness. Morante Group would benefit from the new ideas and fresh approach that Paloma might bring, but could she count on the support of the board? Raised voices had been audible from the corridor and it had sounded as though a fierce debate had been taking place. Paloma's arrival prompted an awkward silence.

Franco Zambrotta stood up and crossed the room. 'Paloma, my dear,' he greeted her warmly, but Daniele was not taken in by the other man's smile that did not reach his eyes. 'It was good of you to leave your home in England…' Franco's hesitation was deliberate, to remind the other trustees that Paloma did not live in Italy '…and come here to give a charming public tribute to Marcello. I speak for all the trustees when I say that we understand how devastated you must be at his death. You are not in the right state of mind to make decisions about your future with the company.'

Paloma tensed, and Daniele wanted to tell Franco to give her a break. He hadn't expected the other man would show his hand so early. 'There is nothing wrong with my state of mind, Tio Franco,' Paloma said crisply as she walked up to the chair at the head of the table where her grandfather had used to sit. 'My future with Morante Group is not up for debate. Nonno's will clearly states that he wanted me to succeed him.'

'I am certain that Marcello expected to live for many more years, and he would have trained you to eventually take his place.' Franco's smile had disappeared when he returned to his seat. 'The trustees have been discussing whether I, as the president of the board, should take charge of Morante Group.'

'But that would be going against my grandfather's wishes,' Paloma argued.

One of the other trustees, Gianluca Orsi, spoke. 'We had the greatest respect for Marcello. But his affection for you, his only grandchild, meant that he overlooked your lack of business experience and your impulsiveness. For instance, your decision to marry without ensuring that your assets were protected.'

Before Paloma could respond, Franco said gravely, 'There is another, more serious matter. It has been brought to my attention that you have a personal involvement with the vice president of the board.'

Daniele glanced at Paloma's puzzled expression. His eyes narrowed as he looked at the projector screen on the wall where an image had appeared. Now he had proof that there had been a person hiding in the bushes next to the hotel pool in Tunisia. His gut clenched at the thought that whoever had been there last night could have aimed a gun at Paloma instead of a camera lens. Had someone paid whoever had taken the damning photo of him and Paloma? And could that someone be Franco?

'The photograph was sent to me by an anonymous source.' Franco looked around the table at the other trustees. 'You can imagine the damage that would be caused to the reputation of Morante Group if the press got hold of the picture and published it.'

CHAPTER FOUR

PALOMA FELT AS though she was trapped in an endless nightmare. Her kidnap ordeal, her grandfather's unexpected death and now this. She squeezed her eyes shut and prayed that the image of her and Daniele wasn't real. But when she cautiously lifted her lashes, the picture on the screen was still in front of her. The photo had been blown up to almost life-size and appeared to show them sharing an intimate moment beside the swimming pool in Tunisia.

Daniele's arms were wrapped around her waist, while her body, clad in a skimpy swimsuit, was pressed up against him. But it was the yearning expression on her face that made Paloma wish she could sink into the thick pile carpet on the boardroom floor. The photo had captured her in an unguarded moment when her lips had been parted in an invitation for Daniele to kiss her.

She felt too embarrassed to look at him. She was conscious of the disapproving glances from the group of men around the table and her face grew warm. 'It's not what it looks like,' she stammered.

Franco crashed his hand down on the table, making Paloma flinch. 'What it looks like is a gross breach of policy with regard to the professional conduct of employees and representatives of the company. If the photograph were made public, I have no doubt the shareholders would be horrified by the evidence that you are having a casual affair with Daniele and the disrespect you have both shown for Marcello, days after his death and before he has been laid to rest. To protect the good name of Morante Group, I propose that the board should vote against you succeeding Marcello and appoint me as chairman with immediate effect.'

For a moment Paloma seriously considered if she should walk away from the company as her uncle and the rest of the board clearly hoped she would do. The trustees were elderly men who were set in their ways and likely to oppose any new ideas she tried to introduce. It would be easier to hand power over to Franco.

Maybe she wasn't good enough to take her grandfather's place anyway. Doubt piled upon doubt as her old insecurities surfaced. She'd never been good enough for her mother, who had wanted Paloma to be a party-loving socialite, and she hadn't been good enough for Calum, who had married her when he'd been in love with someone else.

But she had meant everything to Nonno. Paloma had never doubted her grandfather's love for her, and she owed it to him to fight with every means at her disposal for her right to succeed him as the head of the company and the charitable foundation that he had worked tirelessly for. The jumble of thoughts inside her head cleared, and she sucked in a deep breath as she prepared to take the biggest gamble of her life.

'It's not a casual affair. I am going to marry Daniele,' she blurted out. Nine pairs of eyes swung in her direction, but she was only conscious of his glittering amber gaze focused intently on her. 'We have had…feelings for each other for quite a while.' Paloma knew that if her plan backfired she was going to look very foolish in front of the board, whom she needed to impress. 'Naturally, my fiancé was the person I turned to for comfort while I grieved for my grandfather.'

'Is this true?' Franco asked Daniele. 'Marcello never mentioned that you are engaged to his granddaughter.'

Paloma held her breath, remembering her angry response when Daniele had suggested she should marry him. How she regretted her stupid pride. He had been right when he'd warned her that her great-uncle was determined to seize control of the company. Her future at Morante Group was in Daniele's hands.

Her gaze dropped to his strong, tanned hands resting on the table. Hands that had burned through her swimsuit when he'd held her against his whipcord body. But his touch had been unexpectedly gentle when he had run his fingers through her hair. She forced her eyes up to his face and wished she knew what he was thinking behind his enigmatic expression. His silence stretched her nerves to snapping point.

'I trust you are not implying that my fiancée is lying, Franco,' Daniele said curtly. 'Marcello's sudden death was a shock to all of us. Paloma and I decided to postpone announcing our engagement because of the deep respect we both felt for her grandfather.' His voice was icy, and Paloma could have sworn that the temperature in the boardroom had dropped by several degrees.

Daniele fixed his hard stare on each of the trustees in turn. 'Your concerns about Paloma succeeding her grandfather are unfounded. I will support and guide her in preparation for when she takes control of Morante Group on her twenty-fifth birthday. You are all aware that when I established the company's online presence, new markets were opened up in Asia and profits soared. Marcello demonstrated his trust in me by appointing me as a life-long member of the board. Now I am asking you to trust that, with Paloma as my wife, we will work as a team to take the company forwards to an exciting and successful future.'

God, he was good! Paloma was almost convinced of Daniele's sincerity, and it was evident from the approving nods from many of the trustees that he had won them over. Nonno had joked that Daniele could sell wine to a vintner, she remembered ruefully. She must not forget that his marriage proposition was a cold-blooded arrangement that would benefit both of them.

Daniele stood up and walked around the table towards Paloma. She could not tear her gaze from him. His elegant suit was undoubtedly bespoke, and the superb tailoring drew attention to his broad shoulders and long, lean frame. The sensual musk of his cologne evoked an ache low in her pelvis.

Her eyes widened when he drew her to her feet and lifted her hand up to his lips. He brushed his mouth lightly over her knuckles, and a sensation like an electrical current shot through her fingers and up her arm. She felt her nipples pinch and prayed they were not visible beneath her dress.

'I am sorry, *carissima*, that events have forced us to reveal our marriage plans,' Daniele murmured. His eyes gleamed when he met Paloma's startled gaze. 'You are the only woman on the planet who I want to marry.'

She blushed when he gave her a mocking smile, but she needed his help, and so she resisted the temptation to grind her stiletto heel into his foot. 'And you are the only man for me, *caro*,' she simpered. Daniele's lips twitched, but when he turned to address the board of trustees, his expression was serious.

'We had intended to wait until after Marcello's funeral before revealing our relationship. The photograph is an invasion of our privacy, and I will call in private investigators to try and discover who was behind the attempt to discredit us.' Daniele's eyes narrowed on Franco before he continued. 'Paloma chose not to wear an engagement ring until our relationship became public, but now there is no reason for me to wait to put my ring on her finger.'

With mounting disbelief, Paloma watched as Daniele reached into the inside pocket of his jacket and withdrew a small leather pouch. The ring he tipped into his palm was poignantly familiar. An oval-shaped sapphire surrounded by diamonds, it had belonged to her grandmother who had died before Paloma was born. Her grandfather had treasured the ring, and she had no idea how Daniele had come to have it in his possession.

'Paloma, *tesoro mio*,' Daniele murmured. She froze when she realised that he was actually going to propose to her right there in the boardroom. His deep voice was as soft as a velvet cloak against her skin. 'Will you marry me and make me the happiest man in the world?'

She knew that Daniele was putting on an act, and there was no explanation for why her pulse was racing. Paloma's mind flew back to when her ex-husband had proposed. Calum had used every cliché. A romantic dinner at her favourite restaurant, a bouquet of red roses, and he had even dropped down onto one knee when he'd presented her with a ring, but not his heart, she had discovered soon after the wedding. Would she ever receive a marriage proposal from a man who loved her for herself? she wondered with a pang.

She forced herself to smile at Daniele. 'I will.'

For some reason, her hand trembled when he slid the ring onto her finger. Incredibly, it fitted perfectly. Paloma stared at the exquisite piece of jewellery and felt an urge to tear it off. Marcello had given the ring to her grandmother, and theirs had been a true love match. The pretence that she and Daniele were in love felt like a travesty of the deep emotional bond between her grandparents that had been evident in their wedding photographs. Nonno had loved his wife for his entire life, even though her death had parted them far too soon, and he had never remarried.

The gentle ripple of applause from at least some of the trustees jolted Paloma from her thoughts, and her heart missed a beat when she discovered that Daniele had moved closer to her. He placed his hands on her waist and drew her towards him. Her breath became trapped in her throat when she realised his intention. His amber eyes were focused on her mouth as he dipped his head and brushed his lips across hers.

The kiss was over almost as soon as it had begun, but it seared Paloma down to her soul. She fleetingly tasted Daniele's warm breath, and his raw, male scent evoked a sharp tug of desire in the pit of her stomach. When he lifted his head, it was all she could do not to cling to him. The unsatisfactory kiss had left her aching for him to claim her mouth with hungry passion as he had done three years ago.

'Bravo!' Gianluca heaved himself rather stiffly to his feet, and most of the other trustees followed suit and offered their congratulations. Only Franco and the two men on either side of him said nothing.

'I am curious, Daniele, to know how you will prepare Paloma for leadership of Morante Group at the same time as running your e-commerce company,' Franco said tersely. 'You cannot be in two places at once.'

'I have an excellent executive team working for me at Premio.' Daniele shrugged. 'My business interests are varied, but for the past ten years, I have been involved in some way with Morante Group and the Morante Foundation.'

He looked at Paloma. 'The first decision you and the board must make is whether to cancel the charity foundation's gala ball that is meant to take place next weekend, two days after Marcello's funeral. Will it be too soon to host what is essentially a celebration while you are still mourning your grandfather?'

'Nonno would have wanted the ball to go ahead,' Paloma said with conviction. 'All the tickets have been sold, and refunds will have to be given if we cancel. The event raises a huge amount of money for the Morante Foundation and the many charitable causes it supports.'

Daniele nodded and turned to the trustees. 'I suggest a show of hands if you agree with Paloma.'

The vote was carried unanimously, although Franco had been the last to raise his hand, Paloma remembered after the board meeting had finished and she and Daniele were in the car on the way to her grandfather's palazzo, a few miles along the coast in the pretty resort of Tirrenia.

She simply could not believe that her great-uncle or any of the other trustees had been behind her kidnapping in Mali. Everything that had happened in the past few days seemed unreal. It felt like a lifetime ago that she had been teaching at a school in one of the poorest regions of Africa. Now she was the heiress to an enormous fortune and, thanks to Daniele, her position in Morante Group was more secure. But she'd had to agree to a fake engagement to the sexiest and most infuriatingly enigmatic man she had ever met.

She glanced at him, sitting beside her in the back of the limousine. Like her, Daniele had not spoken since they'd left Morante Group's offices, and he seemed to be lost in his thoughts. Paloma studied his chiselled profile, and her heart skipped a beat when he turned his head and caught her staring at him.

'That will be something to tell our grandchildren,' he drawled.

'What will?' She gave him a puzzled look.

'The story of how in the middle of a board meeting you propositioned me to marry you.' He grinned at her affronted expression. 'And how, to save you from embarrassment, I officially proposed.'

'Marriage was your idea. You know I only agreed to it to stop Franco seizing control of the company,' she said sharply. 'I don't *want* to be engaged to you. Obviously, we are not going to have any children and therefore grandchildren.'

'Don't you want to have a family of your own?'

An image flashed into Paloma's mind, of herself cradling a baby with jet-black hair and amber eyes. Daniele's son. She shook her head, feeling hot-faced and flustered, aware that he had been teasing her. 'Perhaps I will have children one day. But it's beside the point. We don't have to get married.'

Daniele raised an eyebrow. 'We don't?'

'All we have to do is keep up the pretence that we're engaged until I am twenty-five, when I can take charge of Morante Group as Nonno's will states. My birthday is in eight months. It's not unusual for couples to take a year or more to plan the perfect wedding, and it won't seem odd if we announce that we will marry next year.'

'By which time, you will have inherited your grandfather's company, and no one on the board of trustees will be able to make a leadership challenge.'

'Exactly.' Paloma gave a sigh of relief that Daniele saw the sense in what she was saying.

'You seem to have forgotten that we made a marriage bargain,' he reminded her. 'I stated my terms for helping you and I expect you to marry me. You will be able to claim your place as the head of Morante Group, and I will have an aristocratic wife with a pedigree that goes back centuries.'

'You make me sound like a thoroughbred broodmare,' she muttered.

Daniele gave her an amused look. 'You are much prettier than a horse, *cara*.'

Those mesmerising amber eyes of his glowed like the embers of a fire. Heat surged through Paloma at the startling idea that he was flirting with her. His throwaway *'cara'* tugged on her heart, even though she told herself he probably used the affectionate term with his—if the gossip columns were to be believed—legions of lovers.

'Why do you want a wife with a title?' she asked him. 'You told me that it mattered to your mother, but why do you care what she thinks after she abandoned you when you were a child?'

Daniele looked uncomfortable and raked his hand through his hair. 'I suppose it was seeing reports in the newspapers that my grandfather had died, and my half-brother has succeeded him as the new Conte.' He shrugged. 'Pride drives me to want to remind my mother that she has another son besides Stefano and to show her that I have made a success of my life without her support. There is another reason why it is vital that we marry.' Daniele's voice hardened. 'The prenuptial agreement stating that I will not receive any of your money or possessions when we divorce must be kept a secret. Publicly we will let it be known that if something should happen to you, I will inherit the fortune left to you by your grandfather and automatically become the head of Morante Group.'

Daniele lifted his hand and captured her chin between his fingers, gently turning her head so that her eyes met his. 'I need you to trust me, Paloma. As your husband, I will be your next of kin, and anyone thinking of threatening your life in order to get hold of your inheritance will have to get rid of me too. But I won't let anything happen to you,' he said quickly when she gasped.

'Do you really believe I am in danger?' Paloma felt sick when Daniele nodded. The idea that someone valued her inheritance and control of the company more than her life was a crushing blow to her already shaky self-esteem. She wished she could hide away on a remote island, but if she turned her back on Morante Group, whoever had arranged for her to be kidnapped would have won. 'Marriage to me could put your life in danger. Why would you be prepared to risk your safety?' she asked Daniele huskily.

'My final words to your grandfather before he died were to promise to protect you. Like you, I have no wish to marry, but I'm afraid there is no other way.'

Daniele could not have made it any clearer that he would prefer to walk barefoot through a pit of vipers than walk up the aisle with her. His incentive was that she was the Morante heiress, and he hoped that by marrying her, he would gain his mother's acceptance. Paloma stared at the ring he had placed on her finger. An engagement ring was meant to be a symbol of love and commitment, but for all its beauty, the sapphire ring was a reminder of the marriage bargain she had made with a man who regarded her as his duty and nothing more.

'Was it by chance that you came to the board meeting prepared, or had you planned to announce our engagement to the trustees?' She held out her left hand and, in the bright sunshine streaming through the car window, the diamonds surrounding the sapphire sparkled with fiery brilliance. 'I am curious as to why you gave me this particular ring.'

'I'm sure you know that Marcello always carried your grandmother's engagement ring with him, as he did on the day we played golf together. He gave me the ring when we were in the ambulance and said he wanted you to have it.' Daniele frowned. 'Your grandfather could not have foreseen the circumstances in which I presented you with the ring, but I believe he would understand that a fake engagement and marriage are the best way I can protect you.'

Daniele knew he had not been completely truthful with Paloma about the ring. He stared unseeingly out of the car window, remembering when Marcello had pressed a small leather pouch into his hand.

'I will soon be with my beloved Isabella,' the dying man had rasped. 'I have kept her ring next to my heart since she was taken from me. You have it now, and one day you will give the ring to the woman who possesses your heart.'

It was never going to happen, Daniele brooded. He would not allow his heart to be possessed by any woman. Although the circumstances had been different, both his father and Marcello had lost the women they'd loved, and they had been heartbroken for the rest of their lives. Daniele did not want to be consumed by a grand passion. He preferred to be in control of his life and his emotions.

It was right that Paloma should have her grandmother's engagement ring. He had kept it in his jacket pocket, intending to give it to her before her grandfather's funeral. But when Franco had seemed poised to take control of Morante Group, Daniele had needed to act fast, to convince the board of trustees that he would marry Paloma and prepare her for when she succeeded Marcello as the head of the company.

The car slowed as it approached the entrance to the grounds of the palazzo. Daniele was puzzled when he saw that the ornate iron gates were open and there was no security guard in the gatehouse. A sweeping driveway lined with slender cypress trees led to the palatial building that had been the home of the noble Morante family since the sixteenth century.

Paloma climbed out of the car and preceded Daniele up the flight of stone steps to the front door. 'It feels as though the place has been abandoned,' she said with a catch in her voice. 'I suppose it's my imagination because I know that Nonno won't stride out of his study to greet me.'

The door was opened by the butler. 'There is only me and my wife, Giulia, here to take care of the house,' Aldo explained when Paloma and Daniele stepped into the opulent entrance hall. 'Yesterday, all the other household staff received letters informing them that they no longer had their jobs. I have just seen a news report on the television that Signor Morante is dead. Please accept my condolences, *signorina*.'

'It must be a mistake,' Paloma said. 'My grandfather would not have wanted his staff who had worked for him for years to be sacked. Who sent the dismissal letters?'

'They had been signed by Signor Morante. Everyone was upset because your grandfather had not given any indication that he was displeased with the staff.'

'But Nonno died a week ago.' Paloma looked at Daniele. 'He couldn't have sacked the staff. So who did?'

'What about the security team?' Daniele asked the butler. 'Were they dismissed too?'

Aldo nodded. 'With the announcement of Signor Morante's death, I am concerned that thieves might try to break into the house while there are no security personnel patrolling the grounds.'

'It's a bit odd, isn't it?' Paloma muttered as she followed Daniele into the salon.

The dismissal of the security staff was more than odd. The hairs on the back of Daniele's neck prickled. 'It's not safe for you to stay at the palazzo. I'm guessing you keep clothes here for when you visit.' She nodded, and he said briskly, 'Go and change your clothes and pack a bag.' He pulled out his phone. 'I need to make alternative arrangements.'

'This is my home now and I won't be scared away from it,' Paloma said in a determined voice. 'Besides, the charity ball will be held here, and I need to help with the preparations. My grandfather always took a personal interest in the fundraising event.' She bit her lip. 'If you really think that someone on the board of trustees wants me…out of the way, we ought to call the police.'

'And tell them what? For all we know, your grandfather might have decided to sack the staff and signed the dismissal letters before he died. They would have taken a few days to arrive in the post.' Daniele could not hide his frustration. 'No actual threat has been made against you while you have been in Italy and the police will not have the authority to investigate your kidnapping in Mali. You are my responsibility.'

Daniele could tell from the way Paloma's eyes had darkened to indigo that an argument was brewing. 'I will rehire the palazzo's staff and the security team in time for the charity ball, but until then, I'm taking you to my farmhouse near Lucca. Be ready to leave in half an hour.'

'Are you always so overbearing?' Paloma gave him a

mutinous look. 'I appreciate your help, but I don't want you to think of me as your responsibility.'

It was vital that he did, Daniele brooded. Otherwise his thoughts might turn to how desperately he wanted to kiss Paloma's lips, which were currently set in a sulky pout. When he'd grazed his mouth over hers at the board meeting, it had taken all his willpower to resist deepening the kiss. But even the brief taste of her sweet breath had had an instant effect on his body, and he'd quickly stepped away from her before she had become aware of his rampant arousal.

Things were likely to get worse once they were married, he acknowledged grimly. In public they would have to put on a convincing act that their marriage was real to keep Morante Group's shareholders happy. Daniele's gaze was drawn to Paloma's pert derrière when she turned and walked away from him. He cursed beneath his breath. *Deal with one problem at a time*, he told himself. Right now he needed to take her to where he could keep her safe while he tried to discover what the hell was going on.

'What is happening?' Paloma asked some forty minutes later when she emerged from the car and stared at the crash helmet Daniele held out to her. He had driven them from the palazzo to a garage in a nearby village.

'We'll swap vehicles and travel to the farmhouse on the bike in case anyone is looking out for the car. Here's a leather jacket for you to wear. It should fit.'

'I suppose another of your ex-army friends left the motorbike and gear here for us,' she said drily. 'It's a good thing I'm wearing my jeans.'

The sight of Paloma's sexy figure in skintight denim was not a good thing for Daniele's blood pressure. Earlier in the day, she had looked sophisticated and untouchable in a designer outfit. Now her long hair was loose and spilled down her back like a curtain of silk. The leather jacket she'd slipped on gave her an edgy, rock-chick look that made Daniele's hands itch to touch every gorgeous inch of her.

'Climb onto the back of the bike and put your arms around my waist,' he growled, before he jammed his helmet onto his head and started the motorbike's powerful engine.

The sun was setting, and the Tuscan scenery was breathtaking, with the undulating hills dappled in gold and the pointed spires of the cypress trees casting long shadows. Daniele felt his tension ease and he relished the sense of freedom he felt on the motorbike as he opened up the throttle. He should spend more time out of the office, he brooded.

For the past decade, he had been driven by his determination to make his fortune, and deep down, he'd hoped that his mother would admire his achievements. He had told Paloma it was pride that made him want to impress his mother, but he acknowledged that he was still haunted by her rejection. If his mother hadn't loved him, would any woman truly love him? He'd told himself he did not want love in his life, but there was an emptiness inside him that money and success could not fill.

His self-made wealth had not gained him Claudia Farnesi's acceptance. But marriage to Paloma would make him a member of one of the most prestigious families in Italy and give him status in the highest echelons of society. Surely, his mother would be impressed by the son she had abandoned when Daniele had been a boy?

CHAPTER FIVE

'WELCOME TO MY HOME,' Daniele said after he'd parked the bike in front of the farmhouse and dismounted.

'This is beautiful.' Paloma removed her crash helmet and swung her leg over the saddle. 'No one would guess the house was here, nestled between the hills. There's not another building for miles.' She turned her stunning blue eyes towards him. 'I had you down as a city type, and I've seen photos of you emerging from nightclubs and casinos in the early hours with your latest mistress wrapped around you,' she said with some asperity.

Daniele grinned. 'There is no need to be jealous, *cara*. When we are married, I will be exclusively yours.'

'I'm not *jealous*.' Two patches of scarlet flared on Paloma's cheeks. 'I couldn't care less what you get up to in your private life.'

'Neither of us will have a private life for the next few months.' His tone became serious. 'Our marriage must appear to be real, which means that I am the only man you can be associated with.'

'*I* don't have hordes of admirers.' She grimaced. 'Not genuine ones, anyway.'

'What do you mean?'

'When men look at me, they see a cash cow.'

'That's not true.' Daniele had heard genuine hurt behind her flippant remark, and a hot tide of anger swept through him. Who had made Paloma feel that she was only valued for the size of her inheritance? Had it been her ex-husband? Daniele did not know the reason why her marriage had broken up, but there had been wild speculation in the British press over the size of the financial settlement Paloma had given her ex.

She had become a millionairess at eighteen when she'd taken control of the trust fund left to her by her father, who had died two years earlier. Now she had inherited her grandfather's vast fortune. Daniele frowned when he remembered that Paloma believed everyone wanted something from her. Was he any better? his conscience demanded. He was not interested in her money, but he wanted the position in society that being married to Paloma would give him.

'Why did you choose to live in the middle of nowhere?'

'Actually, I don't spend as much time here as I would like. My business is based in Rome and I have an apartment in the city. But I was drawn to the remoteness and tranquillity of this place. Like many soldiers who were sent to war zones, I value peace.'

'I didn't realise you had served abroad. Where did you go?'

'Afghanistan.' Memories flashed through Daniele's mind. The heat and dust, the constant threat from IEDs, his own very personal dread of being shot dead by a sniper. Like father, like son. He took a deep breath and pushed away thoughts of his best friend, Gino, who had not returned home from war.

The farmhouse was his sanctuary, and Paloma was the only woman he had ever brought here. But he'd reasoned that it would be easier to keep her hidden in the heart of rural Tuscany than if he took her to Rome or Florence.

He ushered her into the house and wondered what she would make of its rustic charm after the opulence of the Morante palazzo. Why did he care what Paloma thought? Daniele wondered irritably. He did not need to impress her. Their marriage bargain would benefit her as much as it would him.

'I don't employ any full-time staff here,' he explained. 'A woman from the village comes in a couple of times a week to keep the place clean. The freezer is always well stocked, and I've arranged for someone to deliver fresh produce. You are probably used to being waited on by servants, but you'll have to muck in. I can cook, although nothing more adventurous than steak and eggs.'

Paloma followed him into the bright kitchen, where an old-fashioned range stood against one wall. The wooden table in the centre of the room looked as ancient as the house. 'You can leave the catering to me. My grandfather insisted that I spent six months at a Swiss finishing school, and I learned cordon bleu cookery as well as the many other accomplishments expected of an aristocratic bride. That's the reason you are going to marry me, after all,' she said drily.

Daniele met her limpid gaze and laughed despite himself. The attraction that had simmered between them since he'd rescued her in Africa sparked into a blaze. Three years ago, Paloma had been shy, and her obvious crush on him had been distracting. He had been determined to ignore the chemistry between them, telling himself that she was too young and inexperienced. He'd felt sure that her grandfather would not approve if he'd had a relationship with Paloma, and so he had avoided her as much as possible. Until he'd kissed her back at the ball and been forced to admit to himself that he'd avoided her for an entirely different reason—that she tested his self-control to its limits.

Since then, Paloma had developed a strong will and a fieriness that Daniele admired. Added to that, she was the sexiest woman he had ever laid eyes on. An erotic image flashed into his mind of Paloma naked and spread across the kitchen table, her long hair tumbling over her breasts and her lips set in a pout that he would enjoy teasing apart with his tongue.

Dio! He turned away from her and pretended to study the bottles in the wine rack to hide the betraying bulge in the front of his jeans. His role was to protect her, he reminded himself. He had discovered a vulnerability to Paloma that warned him to keep his distance.

'You have a lot of misconceptions about me,' she murmured. 'While I was at university, I lived in student digs, and in Mali, my accommodation was basic. I shared a bedroom with a family of cockroaches.'

Daniele knew he should go to his study and switch on his computer. He had several major deals in the pipeline, and usually he would be impatient to get back to work. Instead he opened a bottle of Chianti, found a couple of glasses and pulled out a chair at the table while he watched Paloma investigate the kitchen cupboards and fridge and assemble a pile of ingredients for dinner.

'Why did you go to Africa? Was it simply a laudable desire to help underprivileged children, or were you running away?'

She flushed. 'Perceptive, aren't you? Volunteering as a teacher in Mali was important to me. But you're right—it gave me a chance to escape from the fallout of my divorce. I felt so stupid that I had been taken in by Calum's lies.' Paloma picked up a knife and chopped some mushrooms with unnecessary force.

'Why did you marry him?'

'I thought I loved him and that he loved me. I was wrong on both counts.' She drank some wine. 'The short version of the story is that Calum was in love with another woman. I discovered later that their relationship had broken up shortly before I met him. He was a barman at a pub near to the London offices of the charity where I worked.'

Paloma paused and took another sip of her drink. 'Calum was handsome and fun to be with. He was unaware that I was an heiress, or so I thought.' She sighed. 'My mother never lets me forget that she is Lady Coulton, and that I am the granddaughter of an English earl and an Italian marchese. She was desperate for me to marry a man with a title. Nonno was putting pressure on me to move to Italy and work with him at Morante Group. When I eloped with Calum, it seemed romantic and exciting, but soon after I'd married him, I realised I had made a mistake when I discovered that he had deliberately fooled me.'

She drained her glass and pushed it across the table for Daniele to refill it. 'Calum *had* known that I was wealthy after an Italian barman at the pub recognised I was the Morante heiress. He was attracted to my money, but a few days before our wedding, his ex-girlfriend told him that she was pregnant with his baby. Obviously, I knew nothing about it then. Calum went ahead and married me, anticipating that he could expect a sizeable divorce settlement.'

Paloma took another long sip of wine. 'I'd stupidly married him without a prenuptial agreement because I believed we would be together for ever. But weeks after the wedding, he resumed his relationship with his girlfriend. Their baby was born a few months later while Calum was still technically my husband.'

Daniele frowned. 'Under those circumstances, it was reasonable for you to file for divorce. Your husband had never been committed to the marriage and I am surprised that a judge awarded him a financial settlement.'

'I didn't fight his claim for money in court.' A pink stain spread over Paloma's face. 'Calum had some raunchy photographs of me on his phone. When we were dating, he'd persuaded me to take pictures of myself in the nude and send them to him. I know, I was an idiot,' she muttered when Daniele swore softly. 'He'd promised he would never show them to anyone. Calum agreed to a quick divorce if I gave him the house in London that I'd bought as our marital home, plus an additional financial settlement. If I refused, he said he would pass the photos to the tabloids.'

Daniele discovered that he had unconsciously clenched his fists as he imagined meeting Paloma's ex-husband. 'You could have had him charged with blackmail, which carries a prison sentence.'

'I couldn't risk the pictures being made public. My grandfather would have been horrified, and I couldn't face further humiliation. I just wanted out of the marriage, so I agreed to Calum's terms.' She gave a bitter laugh. 'Now you know the miserable details of my marriage and why I am in no rush to do it again.'

Once again, Daniele's conscience pricked that he would benefit from marrying Paloma. The situation was not the same as her first marriage, he assured himself. He'd been honest with her and he had not pretended that their marriage would be anything other than a business arrangement. But now more than ever he was determined to ignore his inconvenient attraction to her. He could not risk any kind of involvement with Paloma that she might misconstrue as something more than sexual desire.

He left her to prepare dinner while he went to unstrap their bags from the back of the motorbike and carry them upstairs to the bedrooms. When he returned to the kitchen, Paloma was serving up mushroom risotto. She had tied her long hair in a ponytail, and her cheeks were flushed from the heat of the range, and perhaps from the wine. Her glass was empty. Daniele opened a second bottle of Chianti. They could both do with loosening up after the fraught past few days.

While they ate, he kept the conversation on neutral topics. The dark smudges beneath Paloma's eyes were a sign of the strain she had been under recently. She had grown up used to a life of privilege, but there were no airs and graces to her, and she insisted on helping clear up the kitchen. Afterwards, she opted to watch a film in the sitting room. Daniele went to his study to call Enrique, who operated a security and private investigation business from his hotel in Tunisia.

Enrique had no further news on who had been behind Paloma's kidnapping, but he'd compiled detailed reports on the members of the board of trustees, their families and associates. Daniele skimmed through the information Enrique had emailed to him and frowned when he saw a name he thought he recognised.

'What do we know about Alberto Facchetti?'

'He is the son-in-law of one of the trustees, Gianluca Orsi. Facchetti owns a haulage business transporting freight through Europe. Do you want me to dig deeper?'

'Sì, grazie.'

Returning to the sitting room, Daniele halted in the doorway when he saw Paloma lying on the sofa. Her hair spilled over the cushions and her impossibly long eyelashes made dark fans on her porcelain skin. Her lips were slightly parted, and the steady rise and fall of her breasts beneath her clingy top indicated that she was deeply asleep.

Her intriguing mix of innocence and sensuality sent his pulse haywire. He considered covering her with a blanket and leaving her to spend the night on the sofa. But her neck was at an odd angle and she would be stiff in the morning. Swearing beneath his breath, Daniele lifted her into his arms.

She weighed next to nothing. Her hair felt like silk against his skin, and her perfume—something lightly floral mingled with muskier notes of amber wood and patchouli—evoked a dull throb in his groin. Jaw clenched, he carried her through the house and up the stairs to the second floor. Opposite the master suite was a guest bedroom with en suite bathroom. He shouldered the door and touched the switch on the wall to turn on the bedside lamp before he laid Paloma on the bed.

She had not stirred. Daniele looked at her skintight jeans and frowned. 'Paloma.' He gently shook her shoulder. 'You need to get undressed.'

Her lashes swept upwards, and she regarded him with her startlingly blue eyes. Deep enough for a man to drown in. 'Is that an invitation?'

'Of course it isn't,' he said curtly. He was furious with himself for his inability to control his body's response to Paloma's sleepy, sexy smile.

'Keep your hat on. I was joking.' She sat up and ran her fingers through her mass of chestnut hair. 'I know you are not attracted to me.'

'You know that, do you?' Daniele growled, fighting the temptation to show her how wrong she was.

Paloma rubbed her brow. 'Ow, my head. I think I may have drunk too much wine.' She tilted her head to one side and fixed her mesmerising gaze on him. 'If you did find me attractive, you would have kissed me properly today, instead of acting like I have a highly contagious disease.' She giggled when he scowled. 'You'll have to do better to convince everyone that our marriage is real. Maybe you should practise kissing me.'

She would tempt a saint, let alone a mortal man. He tore his gaze from her lush mouth and stepped away from the bed. 'Tomorrow you will be glad that I would never take advantage of a woman who has had too much to drink,' Daniele drawled. 'I'll bring you some water. If you're going to be sick, make sure you get to the bathroom in time.'

Down in the kitchen, he opened the back door and dragged the cool night air into his lungs. He had made a promise to Marcello that he would protect Paloma, he reminded himself. This was just another mission. His special forces training had taught him to detach his emotions from a situation and focus on the job. He should not feel a violent urge to rearrange Paloma's ex-husband's features with his fist in retribution for how badly the guy had hurt her.

You must want something from me. Everyone always does.

How the hell was he supposed to remain detached after he had seen the wounded expression in Paloma's eyes? How had his life suddenly become so crazily complicated? Daniele wondered as he filled a jug with water.

When he went back upstairs and knocked on the door before entering her room, he caught a flash of white silk negligee and an expanse of slender, tanned thigh as she leapt into bed and pulled the covers up to her chin.

She watched him warily when he placed the jug on the bedside table. 'Thank you.'

'Goodnight.' He switched off the lamp and turned to walk out of the room.

'Daniele, don't go.'

He exhaled heavily. 'You are going to hate yourself in the morning, *cara*.'

'I'm scared the kidnappers will break into the house and seize me like they did in Mali.' Her voice shook, and her vulnerability felt like a knife in his heart.

'No one knows where you are,' he said gruffly.

'You said the same thing in Tunisia.'

The damn photograph. Who had been lurking in the bushes by the pool? A member of the paparazzi who'd got lucky when he'd spotted the Morante heiress? Or was there a more sinister reason why the photographer had been there? With a faint sigh, Daniele lowered himself into the armchair next to Paloma's bed. 'I won't let any harm come to you. Go to sleep, *piccola*.'

Oh, no! Paloma slowly opened her eyes and decided that death would be preferable to her pounding headache and the cringingly embarrassing memories of her behaviour the previous night. It was bad enough that she had bored Daniele with the humiliating details of her marriage. Thankfully, she hadn't told him everything. Her self-confidence had not recovered from Calum's rejection on their wedding night and her secret that she'd never con-fided to even her closest friend.

But she had confessed to Daniele about those awful photographs. Calum had been manipulative when he'd persuaded her to send him photos of herself in the shower. 'Sexting is part of a modern relationship,' he'd told her. 'Seeing pictures of your sexy body makes me feel closer to you.' Stupidly, she had believed his lies.

Paloma shoved the painful memories of her marriage back into the compartment in her mind marked *Do Not Open*. Goodness knew how many glasses of wine she'd drunk last night. The alcohol had made her feel relaxed and it must have gone straight to her head, but it did not excuse her suggestion that Daniele should practise kissing her.

He had looked appalled, and he'd shot out of her room faster than a cheetah that had spotted its lunch. But he had returned to reassure her that he would protect her. She turned her head on the pillow and felt relieved that he was not still sitting next to the bed.

She was ashamed of herself for being so pathetic. Her life had been spinning out of control for the past few days, but she had to get a grip, Paloma told herself sternly. It was not surprising that Daniele had accused her of being immature. How *could* she have asked him to stay with her? But her fear had been genuine. So many disturbing things had happened recently, and the dismissal of the security staff from the palazzo had been the final straw.

She staggered into the bathroom, and after she'd had a shower and swallowed a couple of painkillers, she felt almost human again. It was early in the morning, and the view out of the window of the soft mist over the hills, and the sky streaked with hues of pink and gold as the sun rose, urged her to go outside. She pulled on yoga pants and a matching bra top and braided her wet hair.

Stepping quietly out of her room, she looked across the hallway and saw that Daniele's bedroom door was open. He was sprawled on the bed, the sheet draped across his hips. The regular rise and fall of his chest told her that he was asleep. Her heart missed a beat as she wondered if he slept naked.

Get over him, she ordered herself. She would marry him because it was the only way she could prevent her great-uncle Franco from seizing control of her grandfather's company. But her fake marriage to Daniele would end on the day she turned twenty-five. She grimaced as she imagined the tabloid headlines when she divorced for a second time.

Unlucky in love! Or perhaps, *Money can't buy happiness!*

Both statements were true, she thought bleakly. Although of course there was zero chance of her falling in love with Daniele.

In the kitchen, she made a fruit salad and added a dollop of thick yoghurt. Two cups of black coffee gave her the caffeine hit she craved, before she opened the door and stepped out into the courtyard, blinking in the bright sunshine.

A shadow fell across the cobblestones, and she froze in terror. Her heart felt as if it were about to explode inside her chest. Was the person hiding around the corner of the house planning to snatch her, or worse? Had they been sent by whoever had organised her kidnapping in Mali? Blinding white fury took over from her fear. She was tired of being a victim.

She remembered the advice from her martial arts, self-defence instructor. *Hit first, hit hard and run fast.*

It felt like a lifetime but her thought process had taken seconds. When the figure stepped out of the shadows, Paloma leapt forwards and brought her leg up, ramming her shin—the hardest part of her leg—into his groin. She heard him groan as he doubled over. The sun was in her eyes and she could not see his face. She held her left arm out in front of her in the block defence position and brought her other arm up to strike the assailant's throat with her clenched fist.

He grabbed her wrist, catching her off guard so that she toppled to the ground with him, and her body landed on top of his. She yelped in pain when he forced her arm behind her back and captured her other hand in his as she tried to jab her fingers in his eye.

'You crazy wildcat!' Daniele's eyes blazed with fury. 'Where the hell did you learn Krav Maga techniques?'

'I didn't know it was you.' The adrenaline surging through Paloma fuelled her temper. 'Why were you creeping around? You were in bed asleep. I thought I was going to be attacked, so I attacked first.'

'You're lucky I didn't seriously hurt you. I may never father children,' Daniele muttered, wincing when her pelvic bone pressed against his groin. 'Your kick was right on target.'

She bit her lip. 'I'm sorry.'

'I go for a run most mornings. I didn't want to disturb you, so I left the house by the exterior stairs.'

Paloma glanced over at the set of stone steps on the side of the house and realised that they led directly up to his bedroom. She looked down at Daniele. Her shock was fading, and she was intensely aware of his muscular body beneath her. She noticed that the dark stubble on his jaw was thicker with a night's growth. His amber eyes gleamed with an intensity that made her wonder if he could read the thoughts inside her head. She hoped not, because those thoughts were inappropriate, considering their current position. Her tense muscles were softening, and it would be too easy to melt into him so that every dip and curve on her body fitted snugly to his lean frame.

'You can let me up,' she muttered.

'Not so fast.' He released her wrist that he'd been holding behind her back and moved his hand down to the base of her spine, clamping her against him. 'Tell me how a fragile English rose is proficient in a martial arts combat system developed by the Israeli army and used by military special forces in many countries.'

Her eyes flashed. 'I'm not fragile. I brought you down.'

'Only because I hadn't expected to be confronted by a ninja warrior.'

'*You* introduced me to Krav Maga years ago. I had been visiting my grandfather at the palazzo and he told me about the IT genius he'd employed to develop Morante Group's online marketing. Imagine my surprise when, instead of the computer nerd I was expecting, I saw a fit guy on the lawn, practising martial arts. You made it clear that you had no time for an annoying teenager, but you explained that Krav Maga combines boxing, judo and ju-jitsu.'

'You thought I was fit?'

She blushed. 'You know I did. When I left boarding school and went to university, Nonno was concerned for my safety, and to keep him happy, I signed up for some self-defence classes. The local gym ran a Krav Maga course for women. Today was the first time I'd ever been in a situation where I was able to defend myself and I'm proud that I kept my nerve.'

Paloma felt empowered. She had been terrified when she'd thought an intruder was in the courtyard, but she'd pushed past her fear and used the self-defence techniques she had been taught. 'Obviously, if I'd known it was you, I wouldn't have gone into attack mode,' she told Daniele apologetically.

He moved suddenly and rolled them both over so that she was briefly lying beneath him before he stood up and offered her his hand to pull her to her feet. His eyes narrowed on her face, and she sensed that he was about to say something, but then he gave a slight shake of his head. 'You did well,' he said gruffly. Paloma felt ridiculously pleased by his praise. 'Come into the barn and show me what else you have learned.'

The barn must originally have been used to store farm equipment, but now it was a well-equipped gym. Daniele walked over to an area of the floor covered with thick mats. 'The best way for any woman—or man, for that matter—to keep safe is to avoid confrontation if possible. That's especially true for someone of your petite build. There is no shame in running away.'

'I confronted you when I believed you were a threat, and I won,' she said indignantly.

'I hate to burst your bubble, but I knew it was you and I controlled my reaction. If I hadn't, I might have killed you,' he said grimly. 'As soon as you had delivered the kick, you should have run as fast as you could. However, it is true that the element of surprise can give vital minutes in which to escape from an attacker.' Daniele moved behind Paloma. 'Imagine that I am an assailant and I'm about to drag you into a dark alleyway. What are you going to do to get away from me?'

His arms shot around her in a bear hug, but she instantly dropped into a squat position, making it harder for him to pick her up. Remembering her training, she lunged forwards and at the same time thrust her elbow backwards into his abdomen.

'Good,' he grunted. 'The assailant would be off guard. But if he grabbed you like this—' Daniele seized her by her shoulder and spun her round to face him '—you'd have no choice but to defend yourself. Make a fist,' he instructed. 'Strike mainly with your top two knuckles. Go on, hit me in the stomach.'

Paloma stared at Daniele. She had been fascinated with him since she was a teenager. However, none of her romantic daydreams had featured her punching him. 'I don't want to hurt you.'

He gave her a sardonic look. 'There's no chance of that happening.'

She sensed there had been a double meaning in his words to let her know she couldn't hurt him, either physically or on an emotional level. It infuriated her to admit that he could probably break her heart if she were ever foolish enough to allow him anywhere near that vital organ. She wanted to slap the arrogant expression off his face. Instead she drove her fist into his abdomen. It was like hitting a brick wall and he did not flinch.

'Again,' he said. 'An assailant would not be expecting you to show aggression. Fight like you mean it. Fight for your life, Paloma.'

For the next half an hour, Daniele alternately praised and criticised her as he put her through the hardest training session she'd ever done. She was breathing hard when he finally signalled that they had finished, but she noted that he was not in the least out of breath. He was a superb athlete. She leaned back against the wall and her gaze was drawn to Daniele's powerfully muscular body in grey running shorts and vest top. His skin was darkly tanned, and his legs and forearms were covered with fine black hairs that Paloma guessed also grew thickly over his chest.

He was blatantly masculine and utterly gorgeous. Her insides melted every time she looked at him. Their eyes met and held, and she sensed an undercurrent of awareness between them. There had been something raw and sexy about working out together and getting hot and sweaty. She understood why he had challenged her. He'd wanted her to react and let her anger out. Her marriage and divorce from Calum had robbed her of her self-worth. Being kidnapped, and the continuing threat to her safety, had made her feel disempowered. But Daniele had given her the opportunity to prove to herself that she was strong, mentally and physically.

He moved closer to her and laid his hand flat against the wall next to her head. His amber eyes glowed like the smouldering embers of a fire. 'I agree with the suggestion you made last night,' he murmured. 'Our marriage must appear to be genuine, and in public we will have to act as though we can't keep our hands off each other.'

His deep voice with its sexy accent sent a delicious shiver through Paloma. She licked her dry lips with the tip of her tongue. 'Do you mean you want to practise… kissing me? You didn't give that impression last night.'

'You'd had too much to drink, and I couldn't take advantage of you. But now…' His warm breath tickled her ear as he pulled her towards him and lowered his head. 'Will you object if I kiss you?'

She couldn't speak. Could barely breathe. He dominated all of her senses, and anticipation made her heart pound. His face was so close that she could count his eyelashes, but his mouth hovered tantalisingly out of reach. Realising that he was waiting for her to make a response, she gave a tiny shake of her head, and finally his lips met hers.

The kiss exploded through Paloma. Heat and fire. Her head fell back as she offered her lips to him, and he took everything and demanded more. This was nothing like the cool brush of his mouth over hers after he had announced their engagement at the board meeting. Daniele's arm tightened around her waist and he sank his other hand into her hair, drawing her against him so that she was conscious of his hard thighs and the tantalising ridges of his abdominal muscles.

He deepened the kiss, sliding his tongue over the shape of her lips before he dipped into her mouth in a flagrantly erotic exploration that drew a low moan from her throat. Paloma had *never* been kissed like this. Never felt such an intensity of desire that brought her body to urgent life. Her nipples, jutting beneath her clingy top, were so hard they hurt. Between her legs she ached with a need she barely understood. Her ex-husband had crushed her confidence with his mental cruelty, but now the startling idea occurred to her that perhaps she wasn't frigid, and maybe Calum's inability to make love to her had not been entirely her fault, as he'd claimed.

Paloma was totally absorbed in the sensations that Daniele was creating with his mouth and hands. He feathered his fingertips down her spine and spread his fingers over her bottom. When he hauled her even closer to him, so that her pelvis was flush with his, she caught her breath as she felt the unmistakable ridge of his arousal beneath his shorts.

He lifted his head and his amber eyes burned into her. 'If we act this convincingly in public, we will be in danger of being arrested for indecency,' he drawled.

Of course he was acting, and so was she. The salutary reminder of their marriage bargain doused the fire inside Paloma. She managed a nonchalant shrug when he stepped away from her. 'I guess we will have to suffer a few kisses if it means that we both get what we want.'

His gaze narrowed. 'I apologise if you found kissing me an ordeal.' He walked over to the punchbag suspended from the ceiling and pulled on a pair of boxing gloves. 'I'm going to continue working out.' It was a dismissal. Paloma felt his gaze follow her when she walked towards the door. 'You were an excellent student, by the way.'

She glanced back at him. 'At martial arts or kissing?'

A grin broke across Daniele's stern features and for a moment he looked almost boyish. 'Both, *cara*.'

CHAPTER SIX

THAT KISS WAS branded onto Daniele's psyche and he had thought of little else for the past four days. He'd had a good reason to kiss Paloma, he brooded. Tonight the Morante Foundation's charity ball was to take place at the palazzo, and they would be seen in public for the first time since the news of their engagement had broken in the media, the day after Marcello's funeral.

The funeral had been a small affair. Paloma and Franco were Marcello's only family, and he'd left instructions in his will for a few of his closest friends to attend the ceremony in the private chapel in the grounds of the palazzo. Paloma had been pale but composed, but when Daniele had seen tears slip silently down her cheeks, he'd taken hold of her hand, and she had curled her fingers tightly around his.

The practice kiss at the farmhouse had been necessary. It would be no good if Paloma shrank away from him when they were in front of the curious eyes of the shareholders and the long lenses of the paparazzi photographers, Daniele assured himself. His jaw clenched as his body responded predictably to the memory of Paloma's lithe body pressed up against him. He had felt her nipples as hard as pebbles and heard the soft gasp she'd made when she'd become aware of the burgeoning proof of his arousal. It had taken all his willpower not to tumble her down onto the floor and strip off her sexy gym pants. He had longed to drive his swollen shaft between her thighs and claim his soon-to-be wife. And he'd sensed from Paloma's ardent response to his kiss that she was not as immune to him as she would like him to think.

But if they embarked on a sexual relationship, it would only complicate the situation, Daniele decided. It was crazy how, when he'd made a teasing remark about grandchildren and she had responded that they would not have children, he had pictured a baby with chestnut-brown hair and the bluest eyes—his and Paloma's daughter. He had assumed he would never have a family. At least he had never met a woman who he would want to be the mother of his children and he'd believed he was not cut out for the commitments of marriage and parenthood. He functioned better alone, and there were plenty of attractive women willing to share his bed if he desired company.

Daniele pushed away the idea that a man could achieve his ambitions, make his fortune and have the world at his feet, but still feel lonely. He walked through the grand rooms of the palazzo where the portraits of generations of the noble Morante family adorned the walls and tried to shrug off the feeling he'd had when he was a boy, that he was not good enough for his mother, and now he was not good enough to marry Paloma.

He halted at the bottom of the magnificent, sweeping staircase and every thought was driven from his mind except for one incontrovertible truth. Paloma was beautiful beyond compare. As Daniele watched her walk gracefully down the stairs, his heart missed a beat and his blood rushed south, making him instantly and embarrassingly hard. If their engagement had been real, there was no way he'd be able to keep his hands off her. He clenched his fists by his sides to avoid temptation as he roamed his gaze over Paloma.

Her white satin ball gown with a black floral design was a dramatic showstopper. The strapless bodice had been designed to push her small breasts high and showed off her slim shoulders and the elegant line of her neck. Her hair was piled on top of her head, with a few loose tendrils framing her delicate jaw. Her hairstyle drew attention to her dazzling diamond drop earrings.

When they had stayed at the farmhouse, she had worn little make-up, and in truth, her exquisite features did not need enhancement. But Paloma must be aware that tonight she would be the focus of attention and her appearance was flawless. A smoky shadow on her eyelids emphasised the deep blue of her eyes, and her lips were coated with a scarlet gloss that gave her the look of a glamorous femme fatale.

Oddly, Daniele preferred the more natural version of Paloma. He suspected that few people got to see the intensely private young woman who had shunned the jet-set lifestyle for which her father, a notorious playboy, had been renowned. But in the wake of her grandfather's death, Paloma was one of the richest women in the world and her life would be spent in a goldfish bowl, the subject of constant public scrutiny.

She halted a few steps above the bottom of the staircase and her face was level with Daniele's. Her glistening red lips curved into a smile that did not quite reach her eyes. 'It's nearly showtime,' she murmured. 'The guests will start arriving in half an hour.'

She held up her left hand so that the light from the chandelier above them caused the diamonds surrounding the sapphire ring to catch fire. 'Thanks to the press statement you gave, the news of our engagement is all over the media.'

'We agreed that it would be better to make the announcement before tonight's event,' he reminded her.

'I know,' she said heavily. 'But it makes it seem real. Only our engagement isn't real, and neither will our marriage be genuine. I feel guilty that we are playing a huge confidence trick.'

He shrugged. 'It's either that or allow Franco Zambrotta to seize control of Morante Group.'

Colour winged along Paloma's high cheekbones. 'You will also benefit from our marriage bargain.'

'I don't deny that having you as my wife will open doors and give me access to contacts and networking opportunities to further my business interests.' He would no longer be regarded as one of the nouveau riche when he married the granddaughter of a marchese, Daniele thought cynically.

He had been intrigued when he'd skimmed his eyes down the guest list and seen that a new name had been added. The Conte Farnesi had paid a small fortune for the last ticket to the charity ball. Had the news of his engagement to Paloma been the reason his half-brother had decided to attend tonight? Daniele mused.

'I have arranged for us to have a drink before the party starts,' he told Paloma as he opened the door for her to precede him into the drawing room. The butler popped the cork on a bottle of champagne and filled two flutes before withdrawing from the room. Daniele took a velvet box from the mantelpiece and gave it to Paloma. 'Open it,' he instructed when she gave him a puzzled look.

'Oh, it's exquisite,' she murmured. The choker was made of three circles of white gold with dozens of teardrop diamonds attached to each circle.

'I guessed you would wear the earrings your grandfather gave you on your twenty-first birthday and I had the necklace designed to match them.' Daniele lifted the choker out of the box and stood behind Paloma so that he could fasten it around her neck. The diamonds looked breathtaking against her creamy skin, as he'd known they would.

'Thank you,' she murmured. Her eyes met his in the mirror. 'I get the feeling that the necklace is a statement of possession, and perhaps a demonstration of your wealth to stop any gossip that you are marrying me for money.'

He looked away from her too perceptive gaze and lifted his glass. 'A toast to the memory of Marcello and to the continued success of Morante Group under your leadership.'

Paloma sipped her champagne before she took a piece of paper out of her handbag. 'I devised a questionnaire for both of us to answer.' At his querying look, she explained, 'We will need to know personal details about each other so that we can make our relationship seem convincing. The first question is, how do you like your coffee? I know the answer. You have yours black with one sugar.'

'And you drink your coffee without milk or sugar.'

'I do in the morning, but in the afternoon I prefer a latte, and before bed I like jasmine tea, decaffeinated. We are supposed to be lovers and you should know these things about me,' she insisted when he frowned.

'If we were lovers, I guarantee you would not want to drink tea when I took you to bed,' he growled. A scarlet stain appeared on Paloma's cheeks. He had never known a woman who blushed so readily, Daniele brooded. Paloma's air of innocence was odd, considering that she had been married.

'What is your favourite food?' she asked quickly.

'Sushi.'

'So is mine. That ties in nicely with our cover story. We need to get the details of our supposed romance straight,' she said when his brows rose. 'It will be easier if we say that we met in London. You were there on business and we met by chance in a bar. For our first date you took me to a sushi restaurant.'

'You have clearly given this a lot of thought.'

'Do you have a better suggestion? We can hardly admit to people that we made a soulless marriage bargain so I can take control of my grandfather's company and you might win your mother's affection.'

Her words hit a nerve. 'What are the other questions?' Daniele asked curtly.

'What about your past relationships?' She grimaced. 'You know that I am divorced. Have you been married?'

'No.'

'Ever come close?'

'Not within a million miles.'

Paloma's long, curling eyelashes swept upwards and her vivid blue eyes searched his face. 'Why do you push people away? Do you shun close relationships because you are afraid of being hurt like you were when your mother abandoned you?'

'*Dio!* I don't need your amateur psychoanalysis,' he grated. 'It's none of your business that I have never felt an inclination to marry.'

'I am simply trying to find out if you have left a trail of broken hearts behind you and the chances that I will come face to face with an angry ex-girlfriend.'

He shrugged. 'My past relationships tended to finish by mutual agreement, and I remained on good terms with my ex-lovers. It's my turn to ask you a question. Do you have any secrets that—as the man you are going to marry—I should know about?'

She blushed again and became very busy folding up the questionnaire and putting it back into her bag. 'I don't have secrets. Look at the time! We should go to the ballroom to be ready to greet the guests.'

Daniele wondered why Paloma had lied. Her stiletto heels tip-tapped on the marble floor as she hurried out of the room. He went after her and took his phone out of his pocket when he heard it ping. The message was brief and satisfactory.

All arranged for next week. D

So far, the gala ball had been a great success. At the beginning of the evening, champagne cocktails had been served, before the guests filed into the palazzo's formal dining room for a five-course dinner. The fundraising auction had raised a record amount of money for the many charities supported by the Morante Foundation. Now everyone had gathered in the ballroom, where a jazz band was tuning up. Before the dancing got under way, Paloma was preparing to make a speech.

Her nerves jangled as she walked towards the podium. Her grandfather had been a witty and entertaining public speaker, and in so many ways he was a hard act to follow. She felt a pang of grief as memories of Nonno filled her mind. He had entrusted Morante Group to her, and she was determined to run it to the best of her ability when she took control of the company.

The sight of Daniele standing next to the podium made Paloma's pulse leap. He looked devastating in a tuxedo. Even from a distance, she felt the intensity of his glittering amber gaze. He had been at her side all evening and had acted the role of devoted fiancé so convincingly that the other guests were both charmed and fooled by him.

Paloma had found herself responding to his charismatic smile until she'd belatedly remembered that their engagement was fake. She had made an excuse to visit the cloakroom so that she could bring herself under control. Her reflection in the mirror had shown her flushed cheeks and sparkling eyes. She looked like a woman in love, she'd thought disgustedly as she'd run cold water over her wrists. She had spent a few minutes fiddling with her hair, but she could not avoid Daniele for ever. Reapplying scarlet gloss to her lips had given her the illusion of confidence, even though she did not feel it.

'There you are, *carissima*,' he greeted her. He slipped his arm around her waist. 'I was about to send out a search party for you.' To onlookers he was a smiling, relaxed lover, but when he dipped his dark head closer to Paloma, he said tersely, 'Where have you been? I was starting to worry that you had been kidnapped again.'

'No one could break into the palazzo with all the security measures you have put in place. I'm more protected than the Crown Jewels in the Tower of London.'

'It is my duty to keep you safe.'

For some reason, his words rankled. It was silly to wish that Daniele actually cared about her rather than thinking of her as his responsibility. Paloma pinned a smile on her face and stepped onto the podium to address the guests.

'*Signore e signorini...*' she began.

She kept her speech short, first paying a tribute to her grandfather, followed by a résumé of the company's successful year, and a promise that she and her future husband intended to take Morante Group forwards together. 'Do you have anything you would like to add?' she asked Daniele, who was standing on the podium beside her.

She was startled when he caught hold of her hand and lifted it up to his lips. He turned to speak to the captivated audience. 'Most of you know by now that Paloma and I are engaged to be married. I am delighted to announce that our wedding will take place in one week's time in the spectacularly beautiful location of Isola Cappracio.'

Loud applause rang out around the room. 'You can't be serious,' Paloma hissed to Daniele. His smug smile told her that he was. 'How dare you arrange our wedding without consulting me? I can't marry you in a week.'

'You can and you will,' he said implacably. He dipped his head, so his face was centimetres away from hers, and her heart gave a jolt when she realised that he was going to kiss her. 'Remember what we practised,' he murmured.

'You want me to use a Krav Maga technique and punch you?' she asked in a mock-sweet tone.

His sexy smile stole her breath, and she was as helpless as a rag doll when he pulled her closer and angled his mouth over hers. He kissed her with a mastery that made her tremble. In an instant, she forgot where they were, and that his kiss was as fake as his marriage proposal.

Daniele tilted her backwards over his arm, and Paloma slid her hands around his neck and clung to him while he deepened the kiss. Her senses responded to the spicy scent of his aftershave, the scrape of his rough jaw against her delicate skin and the heat of his hands burning through her dress. Time and place ceased to exist. There was only Daniele and the fire inside her that became an inferno as desire swept through her and centred hot and needy between her thighs.

When he finally broke the kiss, Paloma blinked and was shocked to find that they were standing on the podium in front of hundreds of people. She felt mortified by their very public display. Worse still, she was conscious of the betraying signs of their passion. The hard points of her nipples were visible beneath her satin dress, and there was a smear of scarlet lipstick on Daniele's cheek.

'I've marked you,' she muttered, taking a tissue from her bag and giving it to him. His eyes narrowed so that his expression was hidden behind his thick lashes. He rubbed his face ineffectively. Paloma shook her head. 'Let me do it.' She took the tissue from his fingers and wiped his cheek clean. 'There.' It was strange how the small act seemed as intimate as the kiss itself.

She was thankful when the band started playing and she and Daniele were no longer the focus of attention as the guests moved away from the podium onto the dance floor. 'There must be legal reasons why we can't marry next week.' There was an edge of desperation in her voice. 'I'm sure there must be procedures and paperwork to be sorted out first.' Italian bureaucracy was notoriously long-winded.

'Doubtless you are aware that Isola Cappracio is an independent principality, and different rules regarding marriage apply on the island. I have been a friend of Prince Dragan for many years, since I was his bodyguard when he went on a diplomatic tour to the Middle East. The wedding will take place in the royal castle. The Prince has a highly trained security team, and you will be safe there.'

'You should have asked me first, instead of riding roughshod over what I might want,' she said mutinously. 'It's all happening too fast.' A fake engagement was one thing, but the realisation that in a week from now she would be Daniele's wife sent a surge of panic through Paloma. 'We will divorce when I am twenty-five and I can take control of the company,' she reminded him.

'I have no wish to be married for longer than necessary,' he drawled. 'But be careful what you say in public.

You never know who might overhear our conversation.' Daniele indicated with a slight nod of his head to where Franco Zambrotta was standing nearby. 'Our relationship must appear to be real.'

'I suppose that was the reason you kissed me just now,' she muttered, feeling embarrassed when she remembered how eagerly she had responded to him. She tensed as Daniele slipped his hand beneath her chin and tilted her face up to his.

'If I ever meet your ex-husband, take it from me, he will not enjoy the experience,' he said in a dangerously soft voice. 'I kissed you because you are incredibly beautiful, and the truth is that I find you irresistible.'

He strode away while Paloma was too stunned to think of anything to say. Suddenly she was sickened by the charade they were playing, and she was tempted to follow Daniele and tell him that she could not go through with it. But before she could move, one of the trustees and an old friend of her grandfather, Gianluca Orsi, stopped in front of her.

'Marcello would approve that you are to marry Daniele, and Morante Group's board are relieved by your sensible choice of husband.' Gianluca smiled. 'Daniele will keep you safe and prevent another kidnap attempt.'

Paloma chatted to the elderly man for a few minutes, but after he had walked off, she felt puzzled that he'd known about her kidnap ordeal. She had not told anyone what had happened in Mali, and she supposed that Daniele must have told Gianluca. One thing was certain: she would lose the support of the board of trustees if she did not marry Daniele. They believed that Morante Group would be safe with him to guide her, and over the next few months it would be up to her to prove she was a worthy successor to her grandfather.

As for the wedding happening next week, Paloma's heart lurched. She had forgotten that Isola Cappracio was a popular wedding destination and the process for marrying there was simpler than in other European countries. The island was a sovereign state in the Adriatic Sea, located towards the coast of Croatia. Historically, Isola Cappracio had been fought over by Italy and Croatia, until the fourteenth century, when it became an independent state controlled by the Da Verano family. However, the principality had continued to have strong links with Croatia, and the mother of the current ruler, Prince Dragan, was Croatian.

'My brother is a lucky man.'

The voice came from close by Paloma and pulled her from her thoughts. She looked uncertainly at the man who she'd noticed had been watching her and Daniele during dinner. 'Brother?'

'Daniele Berardo is my half-brother,' the man amended with a faint smile. He was not as tall or as physically imposing as Daniele, and nothing like as good-looking, but Paloma noticed a slight similarity between the two men's facial features. 'I am the Conte Farnesi, but please call me Stefano,' he said. 'And you of course are Paloma Morante.' He looked across to the far side of the ballroom, where Daniele was chatting to some guests. 'I came to the ball hoping to have a chance to congratulate you and Daniele on your forthcoming marriage.'

Paloma frowned. 'Does he know you are here? He didn't mention you or suggest that he could introduce you to me.'

Stefano sighed. 'The truth is that I have only met my half-brother a handful of times at social events. I am eight years younger than Daniele, and I guess we have little in common. He made it plain that he has no time for me. I can't really blame him, seeing as I inherited the title that should by rights be his.'

'It's not your fault that your grandfather made you his heir and overlooked his eldest grandson,' Paloma murmured.

'Obviously, Daniele has told you about our family situation. He blames our mother for leaving him behind when he was a child, but the story is more complicated than he knows.' Stefano offered Paloma another tentative smile. 'It is clear to see that you and Daniele are in love. Perhaps marriage will help to soften his attitude towards his family.'

Paloma wondered what Stefano would say if she revealed that Daniele was marrying her in the hope of impressing his mother, who had ignored him for most of his life.

'Can I get you some more champagne?' Stefano offered.

She gave him a rueful smile. 'I have learned from experience that I'm less likely to embarrass myself if I stick to one alcoholic drink in an evening. I was about to go outside for some fresh air.' She glanced around the ballroom. 'Are you here with a wife or partner?'

'To be honest, I am trying to avoid the twin daughters of Visconte Prizzi. My mother has decided that, now I am twenty-eight, I should think of marrying, and she is of the opinion that either of the twins will be a perfect wife for me.' Stefano grimaced. 'If you don't mind, I will accompany you.'

Daniele resisted the urge to look at his watch again. It had only been a couple of minutes since he'd checked the time. He was edgily aware that half an hour had passed since he'd seen Paloma walk through the doors at the far end of the ballroom that led out to the terrace. With her had been the Conte Farnesi.

Daniele gritted his teeth and forced himself to smile at the woman standing beside him. Vanda Prizzi, or possibly she was Venetia—the twins were identical in appearance and the tediousness of their conversation—had been prattling on for what felt like hours. A few years ago, the young woman would not have given him the time of day. But the Prizzi family had suffered badly in the recent financial crash and, cynically, Daniele supposed that a self-made multimillionaire was suddenly an attractive proposition.

'People were *so* surprised by the announcement of your engagement to Paloma Morante,' Vanda or Venetia trilled. 'I heard that her first marriage was a disaster. It was expected that when she married again she would choose someone with…' She hesitated.

'Blue blood?' Daniele suggested sardonically. As far as he was aware, no one knew that he was related by blood to the aristocratic Farnesi family. His mother never mentioned publicly that she had an older son, and he had kept it secret that she had abandoned him because he was ashamed by her rejection.

The young woman flushed. 'Well, yes, a husband with a title. Papà says that the old Italian families are in danger of disappearing.'

The heir to one particular noble family was likely to disappear very soon, if he had anything to do with it, Daniele brooded as he looked across the ballroom and caught sight of his half-brother dancing with his fiancée. Did Paloma think that Stefano Farnesi was better husband material than a gruff ex-soldier? A marriage between two of the most illustrious aristocratic families would be popular with Morante Group's board of trustees.

Possessiveness was not an emotion Daniele was familiar with, but as he watched Paloma smile at Stefano, cold rage dropped into the pit of his stomach. His half-brother was exactly the type of high-born member of the social elite that Marcello Morante would have been delighted for his granddaughter to marry. Stefano had received the best education at an English public school, and his exquisite manners were the result of his privileged upbringing in Italian high society.

Daniele had joined the army when he was eighteen. While his half-brother had learned how to mix the perfect martini cocktail, he'd trained to use an assault rifle in a combat zone. Since the injury to his leg had put an end to his military career, he had created his own wealth and success using his IT skills, but he was in a different league from Paloma and Stefano, who were old money.

'What is your opinion?' Vanda—Daniele was fairly certain this twin was Vanda—asked him. He realised that he had no idea what she had been talking about.

'I agree, absolutely,' he murmured, guessing from the woman's startled expression that he had given the wrong answer. 'Please, excuse me. I promised the last dance to my fiancée.'

He strode across the ballroom, and his expression must have warned of his foul mood, for Stefano looked distinctly nervous when Daniele clamped his arm around Paloma's waist. 'You seem to be obsessed with taking what is mine,' he said curtly to his half-brother.

'On the contrary, I am delighted by your engagement to Paloma, and I wish you both every happiness.' Stefano gave a stiff nod before he swung round and walked away.

Daniele looked down and his eyes clashed with Paloma's flashing blue gaze. 'Why were you so rude? Your brother is a nice guy.'

Jealousy was a poisoned arrow in Daniele's heart. 'Is that why you slunk out of the ballroom with him earlier? I suppose you appreciate the Conte's air of refinement.'

'I went outside for some air and chatted to Stefano for a few minutes. It was perfectly innocent. You certainly seemed to appreciate Venetia Prizzi's voluptuous charms,' she snapped. 'Your eyes were nearly falling into the front of her dress.'

'Careful, *cara*, or I might think you are jealous,' Daniele drawled. The band struck up the final tune of the evening, a slow, romantic number. He pulled Paloma closer, ignoring the way she held herself rigid. 'Smile, or the guests will think we have had a lovers' tiff.'

She pressed her lips together as if to hold back an angry retort, but her simmering silence spoke volumes. While they danced, Daniele tried not to think of her soft breasts pressed against his chest, and the narrowness of her waist that he could almost span with his hands. He did not want to remember how unbelievably good her mouth had felt beneath his, and how her unguarded response to his kiss had evoked a voracious hunger in the pit of his stomach.

His intense awareness of this woman, and his inexplicable need to be near Paloma and provoke a response from her, was unlike anything he had ever experienced. Daniele sensed she was struggling as much as he was to resist the sexual chemistry that was almost tangible between them. The pulse at the base of Paloma's throat was thudding erratically, and her pupils were deep black pools that mirrored her desire.

The moment the music stopped, she pulled out of his arms and hurried out of the ballroom. In the entrance hall, staff were handing out gift bags to the guests and directing them to their cars lined up outside on the driveway. Daniele eased his way through the crowd and ran up the staircase after Paloma. She glanced over her shoulder and walked faster along the corridor.

'I'm done tonight, Daniele. I don't want to talk to you.'

'A few minutes ago, you were happy to sing the praises of my half-brother.'

She halted in front of her bedroom door. 'Why won't you give Stefano a chance? It's not fair to blame him because your mother chose him over you.'

'Why are you so determined to champion him?' Daniele growled, goaded by the images in his head of Paloma dancing with Stefano. She had looked happy and relaxed. When she'd smiled at his half-brother, Daniele had felt a sinking sensation in his stomach, the same feeling he'd had when he'd watched his mother drive away all those years ago. 'Perhaps you wish you were going to marry Stefano. After all, he would be a better class of husband,' he said sardonically. 'Unfortunately for you, my half-brother has never been required to work a day in his life, and he knows nothing about running a business like Morante Group.'

Since they had left the farmhouse a few days ago and returned to the palazzo, Daniele had occupied a guest suite along the corridor from Paloma's room. When he strode away from her and opened the door to his suite, she was right behind him.

'I don't want to marry anyone,' she flung at him. Her hands were on her hips and her pretty face was flushed with temper. 'It has nothing to do with class. I don't think you are beneath me because I am from an aristocratic family. I can't help it if you have a hang-up about your perceived social status. And it is not Stefano's fault that your mother loves him but not you.'

Daniele lost it then. Paloma's taunt came too close to a painful truth, and his tight control over his emotions cracked. 'Enough,' he bit out savagely. 'You will marry me and honour the bargain we made.'

Paloma was standing just inside the room. Daniele pushed the door shut and backed her up against it, caging her in with his hands on either side of her head. Her eyes were wide with shock and something else. He recognised her excitement, and his blood thundered in his ears and surged down to his sex.

She had driven him to distraction all evening. Every glance they'd shared, the sensual fragrance of her perfume that had teased his senses when he'd sat beside her at dinner, the melodious sound of her voice that made him think of a cool mountain stream.

'The truth is that we both want this,' he told her thickly, lowering his face towards hers.

She did not deny it, and he felt a tremor run through her when he covered her mouth with his and kissed her with a desperation that, if he had been capable of rational thought, would have appalled him.

CHAPTER SEVEN

HEAT AND FIRE. Just like the other times Daniele had kissed her. But this was not a practice kiss, nor was it a kiss designed to convince the guests in the ballroom that their relationship was the greatest romance since *Gone with the Wind*. This kiss was wild and fierce, with an urgency that sent a shudder of need through Paloma. This kiss was real.

She made a low sound in her throat, a hungry plea for Daniele to deepen the kiss. And when he did, when he thrust his tongue between her lips, she opened her mouth to his demands and kissed him back. The groan he gave was raw, almost feral, and brought her skin out in goosebumps. She answered him with a greedy little moan as he plundered her lips and held her jaw with his fingers to angle her mouth so that it fitted perfectly to his.

Daniele lifted her up and supported her with his hands beneath her bottom. Her back was still pressed against the door. 'Hold on,' he told her hoarsely before he lowered his mouth to the base of her neck and sucked the pulse that throbbed there.

Paloma obeyed him mindlessly, sliding her hands up his chest to grip his shoulders while she wrapped her legs around his thighs. His body was as hard as steel, especially *there* where his arousal was a solid ridge straining beneath his trousers. Molten heat pooled between her legs when he shifted position, bringing her pelvis flush with his.

He must have unzipped her dress without her being aware, and when he tugged the bodice down, her breasts spilled over the top of their satin covering. She was braless, and Daniele's amber eyes gleamed when he stared at her small, pale breasts. 'You are driving me out of my mind,' he rasped, before he bent his head and flicked his tongue over one dusky pink nipple.

She gasped as sensation spiralled through her and thrust her fingers into his hair when he moved across to her other breast. When he drew the taut peak into his mouth and sucked, she sobbed something incomprehensible and felt him smile against her breast.

'Your breasts are as perfect as I imagined them,' Daniele muttered, banishing in an instant Paloma's wish that she were more voluptuous. The tantalising press of his hard arousal against her femininity was proof of his desire. He pushed her long skirt up so that it bunched at her waist and slipped his hand between her thighs, discovering the drenching evidence of her arousal when he stroked his fingers over the narrow panel of her knickers.

She wanted, wanted… Dimly, Paloma recognised that her lack of experience meant she did not know exactly what it was she wanted. But a powerful instinct took over, and her body knew. A tremor ran through her when he eased her panties aside and ran his finger lightly over her opening. 'Please…' She was unaware that she had spoken out loud until Daniele laughed softly.

'I have every intention of pleasing you, *carissima*. You are so responsive,' he said thickly as he parted her silken folds and pushed his finger into her. The effect was instant and shattering. She had no control over the hot rush of pleasure that spasmed deep in her feminine core and rippled in delicious aftershocks through her entire body. At the moment she climaxed, Paloma gave a sharp cry and then buried her face in his neck as the reality of what had just happened made her want to die of embarrassment. She had acted like a naive virgin, which was exactly what she was.

'You *are* hungry, *mia bellezza*,' Daniele growled. The satisfaction in his voice elicited a faint unease in Paloma. 'I'm hungry for you too. *Dio*, I need to be inside you right now.' He fumbled with the zip on his trousers and swore softly. 'Even though I am impatient, I'm not going to have sex with you up against the door. We will be more comfortable in bed.'

He carried her across the room and deposited her on the silk bedspread. His amber eyes scorched her like flames as he pushed her flat on her back and shoved the yards of satin ball gown up to meet the bodice of her dress that had slipped down to her waist.

Paloma suddenly felt exposed with her breasts bared to his glittering gaze. He moved his eyes down to her tiny black panties that were soaked with her arousal. 'These need to come off.' He curled his fingers around the waistband, and with his other hand, he opened his zip and started to free himself.

But the spell had been broken. The fire inside Paloma turned to ash. Unwanted memories forced their way into her mind, of her ex-husband rolling away from her to the other side of the bed. 'I don't know why it isn't working,' Calum had told her sulkily. 'I've never had a problem with other women.'

Calum had not actually said that it was her fault he couldn't make love to her, but the implication had been devastating for Paloma. She had been sure it was because of something she'd done wrong, or something she should have done. She'd felt ashamed by her inability to give her husband sexual pleasure.

What if the same thing happened now with Daniele? If he started to have sex with her, but stopped because she did not turn him on, it would be unbearably humiliating. But perhaps worse would be if he did make love to her. How on earth could she explain that she was still a virgin, despite having been married? He would demand to know why, and she would have to admit that she was frigid. Calum had said she was a pretty shell, but her lack of sensuality made her passionless.

'I can't!' The words exploded from her like the ricochet of bullets hitting metal. 'I'm sorry,' she choked. 'I just can't with you.'

Daniele stilled, and his gaze narrowed on her flushed face. He said nothing and the tension in the room stretched her nerves. Finally he let out a ragged breath. 'It is of course your prerogative to say no.' He spoke in a clipped voice, and his movements were jerky as he adjusted his clothes. 'Out of interest, why did you change your mind?'

Conscious of her semi-naked state, Paloma scrambled off the bed and dragged the top of her dress up to cover her breasts. 'We are not in public now, and we don't need to convince anyone that our relationship is real. While we might want to scratch an itch, in the long run it will be better if we keep our marriage strictly as a business arrangement.'

'Scratch an itch?' His eyes had a dangerous glint. 'You know it was more than that. We have been fighting our awareness of each other since Tunisia. A more likely truth is that you decided not to sleep with me because my father's bloodline cannot be traced back over centuries of Italian aristocracy.'

'That had nothing to do with why I asked you to stop.'

Paloma was struggling to reach behind her back to fasten her dress. 'Will you zip me up, please?' She turned around so that Daniele could close the zip, and her eyes collided with his hard stare in the mirror. Her reflection showed that she was flushed and rumpled, her hair had come half down from its chignon, and her mouth was reddened from his kisses. Daniele, on the other hand, bore no signs of their frantic passion, and the only emotion she could discern on his stern features was boredom.

'You should return to your room,' he told her coolly. 'And in future I suggest that you are clear in your mind what you want before you invite yourself into my bedroom.'

'In future I won't set foot inside your bedroom ever again,' she snapped, infuriated by his arrogance. Lifting her chin, she marched across the room and exited the suite. Slamming the door behind her was childish, Paloma acknowledged, but it allowed her to vent some of her anger. And yet, when she was in her own room, preparing for bed, her body ached for fulfilment, and there was a yearning regret in her heart for what might have been if only she had not been forced into a marriage bargain with the devil.

Daniele stared out of the window of the helicopter as it flew over the azure Adriatic Sea towards Isola Cappracio. The tall white tower of the royal residence, Castello delle Aquile, dominated the skyline. A few minutes later, the chopper hovered above the castle's red roofs before descending to the helipad in the grounds.

Inexplicably, he felt his heart lurch at the prospect of seeing Paloma again after they had spent three days apart. On the morning following the ball, he had chartered a jet to take them to Isola Cappracio. But after introducing

Paloma to Prince Dragan, Daniele had flown to Rome. He'd made the excuse that he had neglected his business lately and there were matters that required his personal attention. In fact, his executive team were dynamic and eager to prove themselves. But he'd hoped that distancing himself from Paloma would give him headspace.

Why had he come on to her with a lack of finesse like a clumsy teenager on a first date? *Dio!* Shame and disbelief at the way he had acted after the ball squirmed in Daniele's stomach. The nagging ache in his groin was a constant reminder of the hunger Paloma had aroused in him. He knew she had been with him at first. Her soft cries when he'd given her an orgasm still rang in his ears.

But then she had rejected him. It was the first time a woman had resisted his lovemaking, Daniele acknowledged wryly. The truth was that ever since he had been a young soldier he'd never had a problem attracting the opposite sex. And when he'd become a successful business tycoon, women had flocked to him. Money was an aphrodisiac, he thought cynically. But Paloma was wealthy in her own right. Had she turned him down because he did not have a title? He recalled that her first husband had been a barman, and she had said that she had been madly in love with him. Daniele sensed that Paloma's ex had destroyed her self-confidence.

Not for the first time, Daniele wondered how his well-ordered life had become so complicated. He showed his identity pass to the guards on duty outside the imposing door of the castle and they stood aside to allow him to enter. Footsteps rang out on the stone floor of the cavernous entrance hall and he saw Prince Dragan walking towards him. The two men halted, and Daniele bowed his head respectfully. *'Vostra Eccellenza...'* he murmured.

The Prince responded with a cheerful lack of royal

protocol and slapped Daniele's shoulder. 'It is good to see you, old friend. Your trip was successful?'

Daniele recalled his restless nights when sexual frustration for his unwilling fiancée had kept him awake. So much for forgetting Paloma. 'It was,' he lied smoothly.

'You must have been impatient to return to Paloma. It is not surprising when she is so charming and beautiful. Your future wife has delighted everyone at court.'

Jealousy felt like a knife blade in Daniele's gut. Was the Prince delighted by Paloma, and she by him?

Dragan looked at him closely. 'I value our friendship, Daniele. Do you think I would try to steal the woman you love?'

Fortunately, Daniele was saved from having to answer when the tip-tap of stiletto heels heralded Paloma's arrival. He turned his head to watch her descend the grand staircase and could not control his body's reaction to the sight of her. She looked jaw-droppingly sexy in a short, flouncy skirt that showed off her endless legs. Her chestnut hair fell in loose waves around her shoulders. As she came closer, the evocative fragrance she wore stole around him like a sensual cloak. But it was her smile that had the oddest effect on his heart rate.

Paloma reached up to brush her lips over his cheek. 'I missed you, *caro*,' she murmured.

He knew she was acting the role of loving fiancée in front of their host, but, inexplicably, Daniele found himself wishing that they were not caught up in a game of smoke and mirrors. With an effort, he resisted the temptation to haul her into his arms and kiss her properly.

'Tell me more about your e-commerce business,' Prince Dragan said as the three of them walked through the castle. 'I understand that you are diversifying into new areas.'

Daniele nodded, glad of the distraction from his intense awareness of Paloma. 'Six years ago, I established Premio as the first cashback company in Italy. I quickly realised the potential to expand and offer other internet services such as insurance and online payments. My latest venture, Premio Worldwide Bank, is focused on SME banking.' He paused when he saw Paloma's puzzled expression. 'Premio Bank provides loans to small and medium-sized enterprises,' he explained. 'I am especially keen to encourage start-up businesses and support entrepreneurs, just as your grandfather helped me when I set up my first business.'

'I had no idea that you own a bank,' she murmured.

Prince Dragan laughed. 'I can guess why Daniele does not spend time talking about his work to you. Lovers have better things to do, *è vero*? Still, you only have to wait two more days until your wedding.'

When the Prince left them, to attend an official engagement, Paloma turned to Daniele. She was clearly on edge. Her tongue darted over her lower lip. 'Don't be annoyed,' she began.

'That is not an encouraging opening to a conversation, *cara*.'

'While you were away, I was in contact with Stefano, and we spoke on the phone a couple of times.'

Something dark and ugly stirred inside Daniele. 'What reason do you have for striking up a friendship with my half-brother?'

'He told me that neither he nor your mother have received an invitation to our wedding. Stefano did not expect to be invited, but he said that your mother is upset by what she sees as a deliberate snub by you.'

'What did she expect?' Daniele said curtly. 'She has ignored me for most of my life. Indeed, it is not widely known that we are related.'

'I thought the wedding would be a chance for you to repair your relationship with your mother.' Paloma's wide blue eyes searched his face, and he had the uncomfortable feeling that she saw more than he wanted her to. 'Our wedding has been labelled by the media as the society event of the year. Shall I tell you what I think?' She did not wait for him to reply. 'I think you withheld an invitation to your mother to punish her because you believe she abandoned you when you were a child.'

'She *did* abandon me,' Daniele gritted. 'She made it plain that she was ashamed of her marriage to my father and ashamed of me.'

'Stefano thinks you should—'

'*Dio*, I don't give a damn what my half-brother thinks. He is bound to take my mother's side because she stayed with him. He did not watch her get into a car and drive out of his life when he was five years old. Stefano never had to wonder why his mother didn't love him, or why he wasn't good enough for her.'

Daniele broke off, as stunned by his outburst as Paloma clearly was by his loss of control. He never, ever revealed his emotions, not even to himself most of the time. Cool and calm—that was what he prided himself on being. But right now he felt like a clamshell that had been prised open to expose his innermost feelings. 'Why do you care if my mother attends our wedding?' he muttered.

'I think you were traumatised when your mother left, and you will continue to be affected by your past unless you can find answers and understand why she went away.' Paloma hesitated. 'You should talk to her. At least give her a chance to explain her side of the story. I'm asking you to invite her to our wedding, Daniele.'

He frowned. 'I'll ask you again. Why are you concerned about my relationship, or lack of one, with my mother?'

'The truth is that I appreciate everything you have done to help me. If it were not for you, I might have disappeared in Mali...' her voice was unsteady '...perhaps for ever. Without your intervention, Franco would have persuaded the board of trustees to appoint him as my grandfather's successor. The wedding will be an opportunity for you to meet your mother on your terms. At the very least, it can't do any harm to invite her and your brother.' Paloma grimaced. 'And before you accuse me of having designs on Stefano, he is madly in love with a chalet maid he met at a ski resort in Switzerland and intends to marry her with or without your mother's approval.'

Daniele exhaled heavily. 'Very well. I will ask my PA to send the invitations by courier. But I won't be surprised if my mother declines to come.'

Paloma did not seem to hear him. She was leaning over the stone balustrade and looking down to the entrance hall at the glamorous woman who had swept through the door, followed by several footmen weighed down with luggage. The woman's voice was audible from the second floor, and probably throughout the castle.

'You there—be careful with that hatbox. I will hold you personally responsible if my hat for my daughter's wedding is crushed.'

'Oh, God! My mother has arrived.' Paloma glanced at Daniele. 'Lady Coulton likes to be addressed by her title unless she gives permission for you to use her name, Veronica. The only person my mother has ever loved is herself. She married my father for his money, and she has done well financially from her four subsequent marriages and divorces. But she cares about me in her way, and, despite her many failings as a mother, I love her.' Paloma's wide blue eyes held Daniele's gaze. 'You are not the only one who had a less-than-perfect childhood.'

'Why do you love her when by your own admission she was an uninterested mother while you were growing up?' he asked curiously.

'Mama is all I have. My only other family member is my great-uncle Franco, who you think might have been responsible for my kidnapping so that he could seize control of Morante Group.' Paloma's wry smile did not reach her eyes. 'I don't doubt that now I have inherited a fortune my mother will want to be my best friend.'

Daniele watched her walk down the stairs to meet her mother and felt a tug in his chest when he remembered that Paloma believed everyone wanted something from her. Including him, his conscience pricked. Marrying her would give him entry to the high ranks of Italian society and put him on a level footing with his mother instead of feeling, as he had for most of his life, that he was beneath her. Paloma had been right when she'd guessed that he hadn't invited Claudia Farnesi to the wedding because he'd wanted her to know how it felt to be rejected, Daniele acknowledged uncomfortably.

'Darling!' Lady Coulton's voice soared to the rafters when she spotted her daughter. 'Forget whatever you are planning to wear at your wedding. I've brought you a dress that will complement my mother-of-the-bride outfit perfectly.'

Her second wedding was a very different occasion from her first, Paloma thought ruefully. She had married Calum in Las Vegas in front of a neon sign and two witnesses whom she had never met before.

'I can't wait for you to be my wife,' Calum had told her.

'We don't need a big wedding with hundreds of guests. Let's go abroad, just you and me.'

Paloma had been flattered by his impatience and had convinced herself that she was in love with him, so she'd agreed to an elopement. By then she had told him that she was an heiress and believed his assurance that he loved her for herself, not her money. But only hours after the wedding ceremony, they'd had their first row when Calum had lost hundreds of dollars in the casino, and he'd been furious when she'd refused to give him more money. He had been too drunk to attempt to make love to her on their wedding night, and that had been the beginning of a nightmare few months as Calum's lies had unravelled.

'Apologies for sounding smug, but I knew the dress would look amazing on you,' Laura said in a satisfied voice.

Paloma dragged her mind from the past and smiled at her friend, who had arrived from England early that morning. 'It's one of your best creations yet. I can't believe you made the dress in three days. You must have sat up all night to finish it.'

'That's what friends are for. Luckily, your measurements haven't changed since I made an outfit for you to wear to Ascot last year and the dress only needed a few alterations.' Laura grinned. 'I can't believe you are getting married in a royal palace, and to the sexiest hunk on the planet. You kept your romance with Daniele Berardo a secret.'

Paloma heard a faint note of hurt in Laura's voice. 'I've known Daniele for years,' she explained quickly. 'He was close to my grandfather. After Nonno died we realised that we…um…have feelings for each other.' She hated lying to her best friend, but Daniele had insisted that, while there was still a threat to her safety from an unknown source, no one must know their relationship was fake.

'It's obvious that you are head over heels in love with your fiancé.' Laura turned away to pick up a pearl-and-diamond tiara from the dressing table and did not see Paloma bite her lip.

She must be a better actress than she'd realised if she had convinced her friend that her feelings for Daniele were genuine. Obviously, she would not be idiotic enough to actually fall in love with him, Paloma assured herself.

Laura placed the tiara on Paloma's head and checked that her chignon was secure. 'You look stunning and chic. Very Jackie Kennedy.'

Paloma studied her reflection in the mirror. The dress was an exquisitely simple design, made from pure white silk, with a high neck and cut-away sleeves that left her shoulders bare. The bodice was fitted over her bust and emphasised her narrow waist before the skirt flowed elegantly to the floor. The only adornments on the dress were tiny diamanté and pearls around the neckline that matched the jewels on the tiara.

'I hope your mother won't make a scene when she discovers you are not in the meringue-like dress she is expecting you to wear,' Laura muttered. 'What was she thinking with that peach-coloured sash and enormous bow?'

'The accessories were to match the colour of her outfit. But Mama has set her sights on a Spanish duke who she met yesterday at a dinner hosted by the Prince. I don't suppose she will take much notice of me.'

Laura went to answer a knock on the door and took delivery of a box from the maid. Inside was a bouquet of white roses and lily of the valley, which she handed to

Paloma. 'Elegant and beautiful just like you. Your fiancé has good taste.'

The card attached to the flowers simply had 'Daniele' written in bold handwriting. Paloma stared at his name and imagined him moving the pen over the card with a decisive flourish. Sweet heaven, she was mooning over him like the silly teenager who had once been infatuated with him.

'It's time to go,' Laura told her. 'I'll scoot along to the chapel ahead of you.'

All day there had been the sound of helicopters buzzing above the castle, bringing guests to the wedding. But now dusk was falling, and the air was soft and still when Paloma walked through the castle grounds to the private chapel beside the lake. An ethereal mist hung over the water and added to her sense of unreality that increased even more when she stepped into the porch of the chapel. The inner door was ajar, and she could see the guests seated on chairs on either side of the aisle. On the floor were hundreds of candles lining the path to the altar, their golden flames flickering like fireflies.

The romantic scene made Paloma catch her breath. It was exactly how she would have planned her wedding to a man whom she loved. But this wedding was fake. When she was twenty-five and could take control of Morante Group, she would no longer need to be married to Daniele. A bubble of hysteria rose in her throat when she realised that she would have two divorces under her belt while she was still in her twenties. If she carried on at that rate, she might match her mother's number of failed marriages.

Guilt and confusion froze her feet to the ground. She couldn't go through with this charade of a wedding. It felt wrong to trick people like Laura, who had worked for hours to make her a beautiful dress, or her grandfather's close friend Gianluca Orsi, who'd had tears in his eyes when he'd told her that Marcello had been proud of her. But once again, Paloma could not ignore the likelihood that she would lose control of Nonno's company and his charitable foundation if she did not marry Daniele, who had the support of the board of trustees.

Her mind was spinning, and she half turned to walk out of the chapel when the tall figure of Prince Dragan joined her in the porch. 'I believe it is usual for couples who are about to marry to suffer from last-minute nerves,' he said gently. 'I've never seen Daniele look so tense, not even when he saved me from a terrorist attack in Egypt.' The Prince's hawkish features broke into a smile. 'He asked me to escort you into the chapel because your father and grandfather are sadly not here. I was unaware that Daniele was a romantic at heart, but he gave specific instructions for the wedding ceremony. The candles were his idea.'

Paloma took another peep through the partially open door and spotted Stefano Farnesi near the back of the chapel. Sitting next to him was an elegant woman who must be Daniele's mother. She could not jilt Daniele at the altar, Paloma acknowledged. It was vital to both of them that the wedding went ahead.

Prince Dragan offered her his arm and opened the door so that they could step into the main part of the chapel. Her eyes flew to Daniele standing in front of the altar. He was resplendent in a midnight-blue suit that moulded his broad shoulders. He turned to face her, and even from a distance, Paloma felt the heat of his amber gaze sizzle through her as she walked towards him to seal their marriage bargain.

CHAPTER EIGHT

DANIELE LEANED BACK in his chair and allowed the hum
of conversation and the clink of glasses in the castle's
magnificent dining room to wash over him. The wedding dinner had been superb, much vintage champagne
had been drunk, and toasts had been made to the bride
and groom. Now the reception was coming to an end and
some of the guests had moved away from the tables and
were standing in groups, chatting. The tinkling sound of
laughter drew his attention to Paloma, who was sitting
beside him and talking animatedly to her friend Laura on
the other side of her.

Paloma. *His wife.* It was odd how easily the two words
sat on his tongue, and stranger still that the wedding band
on his finger felt as though it belonged there. Daniele gave
a slight shake of his head, but he could not forget the mixture of awe and lust that had swept through him when
Paloma had walked into the chapel looking so beautiful
that he'd clenched his jaw to stop himself from gaping at
her like a callow youth with a serious crush. He'd managed to get himself under control for the ceremony, but
when the officiant had pronounced them married and invited Daniele to kiss his wife, he'd almost succumbed to
a primitive urge to throw Paloma over his shoulder and
carry her off to bed.

Heaven knew what her reaction would have been, he thought wryly, remembering how she had used Krav Maga martial arts techniques to attack him at the farmhouse. Daniele doubted that his mother would have been impressed if he'd behaved like a caveman. She would have looked down her elegant nose and disassociated herself from her uncultured eldest son.

He had been surprised when he'd seen Claudia with Stefano Farnesi sitting at the back of the chapel. At dinner they had been seated at a table on the far side of the room and there had not been an opportunity or a desire on Daniele's part for a conversation. Paloma had urged him to talk to his mother, but he did not know what to say to the woman who had been absent for most of his life. The truth, he admitted heavily, was that he felt nervous about meeting his mother, and the possibility that she would reject him again. Inside him there was still the little boy who had watched her drive away.

His phone pinged and he read a message before he leaned towards Paloma. 'Will you excuse me while I go and find somewhere private to make an important business call?' She nodded, and he left the dining room and went into a small sitting room across the hall. A fake wedding was not an excuse to interrupt his ruthless work ethic. Ten minutes later, he pocketed his phone, but as he was about to return to the reception, a woman entered the sitting room.

'Hello, Daniele.'

'Madre.' Daniele's gaze narrowed on his mother's face. Make-up did not disguise the signs of age, or the unexpected vulnerability in her eyes. He had recognised her from a newspaper photo taken at her father Conte Farnesi's funeral. But it was twenty-seven years since Daniele had seen his mother in person and he felt a mixture of emotions. There was anger, but also a deep sadness for lost time that could never be regained.

'Thank you for inviting me to your wedding.' She twisted her hands together. 'You have done well.'

He gave her a sardonic look. 'Does my marriage to the granddaughter of a marchese make me acceptable in high society, and therefore to you?'

She flushed. 'I was not referring to your marriage, although your wife is exquisite and very charming. Paloma introduced herself to me a few minutes ago and said that you had asked to speak to me privately.'

Daniele tensed, realising that Paloma had set up the meeting with his mother. He would make it clear to her that being his wife did not give her the right to interfere in his personal life, he thought grimly.

'I am grateful for the chance to talk to you,' his mother said in a tremulous voice. 'I have followed your career as it has gone from strength to strength. Each time I read about another of your successful enterprises, I wished I could tell you how proud I am of you.'

He shrugged, determined not to be affected by his mother's surprising statement. 'But you have not spoken to me for years. You could have contacted me at my company's offices in Rome or Florence.'

'I did not dare try to speak to you while my father was alive.' When Daniele said nothing, his mother continued shakily, 'It is only now the Conte is dead that I am free to do what my heart has longed to do since I had to leave you when you were a young boy.'

'You *had* to leave?' he questioned harshly. 'Is it not the truth that you chose to walk out of your marriage because your husband could not give you the luxurious lifestyle you had been used to, and you were ashamed of me because my father was a common soldier?'

'That's *not* true.' Claudia clasped her hands together so tightly that the knuckles went white. 'I can guess who told you those lies. Your grandmother Elsa never liked me, and she thought your father had made a mistake by marrying me.'

'It would seem that Nonna Elsa had a point,' Daniele said drily.

'Please, Daniele.' Claudia's shoulders slumped. 'I told myself not to hope that you would listen to me.'

Daniele watched his mother turn towards the door. 'Wait.' He exhaled heavily. 'Come and sit down.' He indicated an armchair, and when she was seated, he lowered himself into the chair opposite her. 'I will listen.'

'My father was a terrible man.' Claudia darted a glance around the room and gave a strained laugh. 'Even though I stood at his graveside, I am still afraid.'

'Of what?'

'Of his ghost. He controlled me for so long that it is hard to believe I am finally free.' She saw Daniele's confused expression. 'I grew up in a gilded cage and the Conte was my jailer. I was expected to make a good marriage to forge a link with another noble family, but one summer while my father was away on business, I met a handsome soldier who was home on leave, and I fell in love.' Claudia sighed. 'When I found out that I was pregnant, I was terrified of the Conte's reaction and relieved when Luigi asked me to marry him. You were born a few months later, but my father was furious and banished me from the family home. I did not care if I never saw him again, but he refused to allow me to see my mother, who I adored.'

'It must have been a difficult situation,' Daniele conceded.

'My marriage was unhappy. Your father spent a lot

of time away on military postings, and when he came home, it was soon obvious that we were not suited. I had married to escape the Conte, but when my mother was diagnosed with a terminal illness, I desperately wanted to be with her.'

Claudia wiped her eyes. 'My father gave me an ultimatum. I could return home to nurse my mother if I divorced Luigi and married the man my father had chosen for me. I begged to bring you with me, but he refused. It was a choice that no woman should ever have to make,' she said huskily, 'but I had been conditioned since childhood to be an obedient daughter. My mother needed me. I knew that your father and grandmother loved you, and so I… I left you behind. But it broke my heart to drive away. I hoped the Conte would relent and allow me to see you. When he did eventually permit you to visit, it was another stroke of cruelty. He told me to choose between you and Stefano to be the Farnesi heir.'

'You chose my half-brother,' Daniele said flatly.

'The stipulation was that whichever son I chose would live at the Farnesi estate and the other would be sent away. If I had picked you, my husband and baby son would have been banished from the Conte's house. I could have gone with them, but my mother was still alive, and I couldn't leave her. Motor neurone disease was killing her slowly and horribly. My husband is a kindly man, but weak, which is why the Conte chose him.' Claudia looked beseechingly at Daniele. 'Stefano was just a toddler. I chose the son who needed his mother most. But I wrote to you often, and even though you never replied, I hoped you knew that I loved you.'

Daniele stared at his mother. 'I did not receive one letter from you. It is hard to believe that every letter you say you sent was lost in the post.' His cynical tone made Claudia flinch.

'I wrote to you,' she insisted. 'Until you were eighteen and I learned from a neighbour of your father who I had kept in touch with that you had joined the army and moved away. Your grandmother had died, and I lost any means of contacting you. Years passed, and I read about an upcoming entrepreneur and IT wizard. I wanted to call you, but I was afraid of your response.' A tear slid down her cheek. 'I thought you might hate me, and I couldn't blame you.'

Daniele's mind was reeling. His mother's story sounded genuine, and he was surprised by how badly he wanted to believe her. 'Why didn't I receive your letters? It can only be because you did not send them, and you are lying.'

'I swear I sent them.' Claudia stood up. 'Perhaps Luigi or Elsa did not want you to read them.'

'My father would not have kept them from me,' Daniele said with certainty.

'No, I don't think so. Luigi was not a vindictive man. But I imagine your grandmother's dislike of me increased after I left.'

Daniele remembered that Nonna Elsa had discouraged him from talking about his mother, and she'd had nothing good to say about Claudia Farnesi.

'I'm sorry, *mi figlio*,' his mother whispered. 'If you did not receive my letters, you must have believed that I had abandoned you. But I prayed for you every day, and I will continue to do so for long as I live.'

Claudia walked out of the room and closed the door quietly behind her. Daniele did not go after her. He did not know what to think. Either she was a liar, or his grandmother, whom he had been deeply fond of, had intervened to prevent him from having any contact with his mother.

How long he sat there alone with his thoughts, he could not say. Eventually he stood up and walked back to the dining room. The guests had gone and there was no sign of Paloma. He caught a glimpse of white on the balcony, and when he stepped outside, he found her leaning against the stone balustrade, her elbows resting on the wall and her chin cupped in her hands.

She was so beautiful. Something inside him cracked and he needed to be close to her, to touch her chestnut hair that she'd let down so that it rippled in silky waves around her shoulders. He ignored the voice in his head that said he'd never needed anyone, certainly not a woman. His mother's revelations had left him feeling raw, and everything he thought he knew about himself, he now questioned.

Paloma turned when she heard his footsteps, and those incredible eyes the colour of lapis lazuli searched his face. 'You spoke to your mother?'

'Yes. Your little ruse worked,' he said drily.

She blushed. 'Are you angry with me?'

He sighed. 'No. I appreciate that you were trying to help.'

'Did it help to talk to her?'

Daniele filled Paloma in on what his mother had told him. 'She could be lying about writing to me regularly throughout my childhood.'

'But if she did send the letters, what happened to them?'

'When Nonna Elsa died, she left instructions in her will that some files she kept locked in a bureau should be handed over to her lawyer. I had no reason to wonder what the files contained, but I'll see what I can find out next week.'

Daniele captured one of Paloma's hands in his and placed his other hand on her waist. She did not pull away, he noted, conscious that his heart was beating faster. 'Will you dance with me?'

She looked puzzled. 'Without music?'

Daniele selected a song from his phone's playlist and propped the device on the balustrade. The smooth jazz number soothed his fraught emotions, but when he drew Paloma closer, she tilted her head and stared up at him.

'The reception has finished and there are no guests who we must convince that our marriage is real. You don't have to dance with me.'

'Yes, I do,' he said gruffly. He wanted to hold her. Wanted a good deal more than to simply *hold* her, if he was honest. But having her in his arms while their bodies swayed in time with the music eased some of his tension—and evoked a different kind of physical tension in him, Daniele acknowledged self-derisively.

He did not understand what was happening to him. He had assumed he would think of his marriage to Paloma as simply another business deal and he was unprepared for the possessiveness that swept through him. Just as inexplicably, he found himself imagining Paloma was his wife for real. He was no good for her, he reminded himself. For so long he'd believed that he had not been good enough for his mother and his heart had turned to stone.

One day Paloma would marry a man who could give her the love she clearly craved and deserved, and she and her husband would have beautiful children and she would be a devoted mother. Daniele pictured a happy family. He felt like a child with his nose pressed against a sweet-shop window, staring enviously at something he would never have and, until now, he'd never thought he wanted.

Dancing with Daniele in the moonlight was dangerous. It made Paloma wish that she were in the arms of a man who loved her, a husband who had married her because he wanted to spend the rest of his life with her. She had thought she could distance her emotions from the wedding ceremony. But when she had stood beside Daniele in the chapel to make their vows, her heart had been thumping.

She had reminded herself that his husky voice when he'd promised to love and cherish her and the warmth in his amber eyes as he'd slid a white-gold wedding ring onto her finger, next to her grandmother's sapphire engagement ring, were a demonstration of his impressive acting skills. It had been the same at the reception when Daniele had dipped his head towards her and listened attentively to what she was saying. In a room full of guests, she'd only had eyes for him.

She did not know why he had followed her onto the balcony or why he'd asked her to dance with him, and she gave up trying to fathom the mind of this enigmatic man. The warmth of his body pressed close against hers entered her bloodstream, and the spicy scent of his aftershave was all around her as they moved in total harmony to the seductive beat of the music. Was the erratic thud of his heart that she could feel when she laid her hand on his chest fake?

A discreet cough from the doorway leading to the dining room broke the magic, and she stepped away from Daniele as one of the castle's footmen explained that he would escort them to the white tower.

'Prince Dragan said it is a tradition for the bride and groom to spend their wedding night in the tower,' Daniele told her when the footman had left them at the bottom of a narrow spiral staircase. 'Our belongings were moved by the staff earlier.'

The stairs seemed to climb up for ever, and Paloma was breathless when she eventually arrived at the top and stepped into a huge, circular room. The domed ceiling was made of glass and the inky sky and countless glittering stars looked close enough to touch. A four-poster bed was hung with velvet drapes, but the top was open so that the view of the heavens was uninterrupted.

Daniele discovered a large en suite bathroom complete with a roll-top bath. He walked off to explore the rest of the tower but returned minutes later, frowning. 'This is the only bedroom. *Dio*, I'm sorry. The Prince believes our marriage is real, and naturally, he assumed we would share a bed. Don't worry,' he said when he saw Paloma's startled expression. 'I'll sleep on the sofa in the dressing room.'

He strode into the adjoining room and closed the door, leaving Paloma alone in the bedroom that had been designed for romance. In the mirror, the reflection of a virgin bride mocked her. Before they had been disturbed on the balcony, she was sure Daniele had been about to kiss her. There had been pain in his voice when he'd told her what his mother had said. Why would his grandmother have hidden the letters from his mother? Had she believed Daniele would be upset to hear from Claudia Farnesi, or had his grandmother acted out of spite because she'd disliked his mother?

Paloma wanted to offer her sympathy to Daniele after the shocking revelations that had torn his family apart and destroyed his relationship with his mother. She saw in the mirror her enlarged pupils and flushed cheeks and knew she was kidding herself. What she wanted was for Daniele to make love to her. Their marriage must continue until her twenty-fifth birthday, months away, but the pretence of being a happy couple was already becoming a strain. Every time they were in public, and he smiled at her with heart-stopping tenderness or gently brushed a strand of hair off her cheek, she fell further under his spell. Each time he kissed her, she wanted more than his kisses.

Without pausing to think her decision through, she tapped on the door of the dressing room and waited for an agonising few seconds before she let herself into the room just as Daniele emerged from what must be an additional bathroom. His hair was damp, and droplets of water clung to his chest hairs that continued down over his flat abdomen before disappearing beneath the edge of the towel he'd knotted around his waist. His gaze collided with hers, and the flare of hunger that turned his amber eyes to liquid gold reassured Paloma that she was not about to make a fool of herself.

He lifted a brow. 'Is there a problem, *cara*?'

'I need help to unzip my dress.'

'Turn around,' he bade her in a clipped voice as he walked towards her.

She took a deep breath. 'It's a side zip.' She indicated the cleverly disguised zip that started under her arm and ran down to her hip.

Daniele's big chest rose and fell swiftly when he realised that she could undo the zip herself. 'What do you want, Paloma?'

'You,' she whispered.

He shook his head, and Paloma felt heat spread over her face as mortification loomed, thinking he did not want her. 'If I touch you, I can't guarantee I'll be able to stop,' he said tautly. 'It was hard enough when you changed your mind last time.' The flames in his eyes scorched her. 'You have to be sure, *cara*.'

'I am.'

Still he made no move towards her. 'I want to have sex with you. *Dio*.'

His rough laugh made her skin prickle.

'Want does not come near to describing how badly I ache for you. But the situation is already complicated.'

'If we are lovers, it might make things less complicated. It will be easier to convince people that our relationship is genuine.' Inwardly, Paloma could hardly believe she was negotiating the terms of making love with Daniele. Having sex, she corrected herself. Love did not feature in any bargain she made with him. 'Our marriage has a time limit,' she reminded him.

'And we are wasting time talking.' His slow smile set Paloma's pulse racing. Daniele closed the gap between them in one stride, and whether by accident or design, his hand brushed the side of her breast as he slid her zip down.

'You will have to lift the dress over my head,' Paloma told him. The silk felt sensuous against her skin when Daniele gathered the long skirt in his hands and eased the material up her body as she raised her arms in the air. She was momentarily swathed in metres of white silk and could not see his face, but she heard him growl when he uncovered her sheer bra with a delicate floral pattern over the nipples.

'You blow my mind,' he said rawly. 'You have no idea how long I have wanted to do this.' He lowered his head and pressed his mouth to the side of her neck, trailing kisses up to her jaw, and finally slanted his lips over hers. He kissed her until she was mindless and aware only of his potent masculinity as she ran her hands over his naked chest and felt the faint abrasion of his body hairs beneath her palms.

He unfastened her bra and let it fall away from her breasts. *'Perfetto.'* His voice was thick, and the fierce glitter in his eyes sent a shiver of excitement through Paloma. Calum's foreplay had been rushed and perfunctory, but she'd believed—because he'd told her—that it was her fault she had not become aroused.

How was it that Daniele simply had to look at her and molten heat pooled between her legs? He cupped her pale breasts in his darkly tanned hands and rubbed his thumbs across her nipples so that they tightened and a sensation like an electrical current arced down to her pelvis. Any worries she'd had that her body would be unresponsive to his caresses disappeared. She was burning up, and impatient for her first sexual experience at long last. But she was reluctant to admit to Daniele that this was new for her. Talking would mean he'd stop kissing her and doing the wicked things with his hands and mouth that turned her legs to jelly.

Paloma trailed her fingertips over Daniele's stomach until she came to the edge of his towel.

'I want to be naked with you,' he growled in her ear.

She hesitated for a heartbeat before she tugged the towel loose and it slipped to the floor. It was not the first time she had been this close to a naked man, she reminded herself. Daniele's muscular, olive-sheened body was a work of art, but his size caused Paloma to doubt that she could carry through what she had started.

'You can touch me as well as look,' he murmured.

A memory flashed into her mind of her attempts to pleasure Calum and her sense of shame when nothing had happened. What if she was no good at this? Her eyes dropped to Daniele's manhood that was already jutting proudly without her doing a thing. Fascination took over from her reserve and she reached out and ran her finger lightly along his hard ridge that swelled even more to her touch. He drew an audible breath, and she snatched her hand away.

'Did I hurt you?'

'Of course not.' He pulled her into his arms and kissed the hollow beneath her ear. 'You are a sensual siren, *mia bellezza*, and you turn me on more than any woman has ever done.'

He pulled her lacy knickers down her legs and slipped his hand between her thighs, smiling against her mouth when he discovered her slick heat. 'Why are we standing here when there is an enormous bed waiting for us?'

Paloma's heart thudded when he scooped her up in his arms and carried her into the bedroom. He laid her on the sumptuous gold velvet bedspread and knelt above her, his knees straddling her hips. He leaned forwards, his mouth claiming hers in a slow, erotic kiss. He pushed his tongue between her lips and coaxed her response, taking his time to seduce her with skilful caresses so that she relaxed, but at the same time she was aware of an urgent throb deep in her pelvis that she knew instinctively only his possession could assuage.

Daniele trailed his mouth down her throat and décolletage and paused to flick his tongue across one dusky pink nipple and then the other, sending starbursts of delicious sensation down to the heart of her femininity. Paloma let her mind go blank to everything but the insistent need that was building inside her.

She watched him reach into the bedside drawer and take out a condom and could not stop herself from tensing a little when she realised that it was actually going to happen. She was going to have sex with Daniele. She'd idolised him when she was a teenager, and she'd never completely got over her infatuation with him. He had not made promises that he didn't intend to keep or pretended that their marriage was anything more than a business arrangement. She knew she could trust him, and it felt right to make love with him.

He lifted himself over her and supported his weight on one elbow while he skimmed his other hand down over her stomach. His thigh nudged her legs apart and his fingers gently parted her. When he eased one finger into her and then a second, she caught her breath, knowing that his manhood would stretch her even more.

'You are ready for me, *cara*,' he whispered against her lips before he kissed her deeply. He filled her senses: the heat of his body, the spicy scent of his cologne mixed with something indefinable and uniquely him. She felt the press of his erection against her opening, and he must have been aware of her slight hesitancy. 'Have you had many lovers since your first marriage ended?'

Startled by the question, she shook her head. 'N...no.'

Daniele smiled. 'So it's been a while since you have done this. We'll take things slowly to start with,' he assured her as he slipped his hands beneath her bottom and lifted her towards him. His eyes blazed into hers, and Paloma shivered with a mixture of anticipation and slight apprehension. She had often imagined the physical side of having sex for the first time, but she hadn't expected to feel so emotionally overwhelmed. Her heart was pounding as Daniele moved and entered her slowly. He paused before sliding his shaft deeper inside her.

It didn't hurt. She experienced a brief discomfort followed by a sense of being filled by him when he pressed forwards. Paloma did not know what she had expected, but a feeling of completeness stole around her heart, and perhaps more worryingly, she felt a sense of belonging to Daniele. He had been on the periphery of her life for ever, it seemed, and she had been intrigued by him and wished that he would notice her.

He withdrew a little way and thrust into her again, oh, so carefully. Once, twice, each leisurely stroke heightening the restless ache in Paloma's pelvis. She wrapped her legs around his back and arched her hips to meet his thrusts that grew more powerful, more intense as he quickened his pace. The rasp of his breaths told her that his magnificent control had been replaced with a primitive urgency for release. She matched his pace and they moved together in perfect synchrony, two bodies as one, hearts pounding, breathing fractured.

'Come for me, *mia bellezza*,' Daniele said hoarsely.

'I can't.' Tears of frustration filled her eyes. She should have known that she would be no good at this.

'Relax and it will happen.' He slipped his hand between their joined bodies and unerringly found her hidden pleasure spot. She gasped as he held her at the brink before he gave a clever twist of his hand and pleasure exploded deep in her pelvis. It was indescribable, wave after wave of exquisite sensation that rolled through her and caused her vaginal muscles to squeeze and relax in the most incredible orgasm that was far beyond anything she had experienced when she'd pleasured herself.

Daniele waited until the spasms that shook her body subsided before he began to move again. He stared into her eyes as he drove into her with hard, fast thrusts. His jaw was clenched, and the skin was drawn tight over his sharp cheekbones. The realisation that this powerful man was nearing the point of losing control evoked a rush of tenderness in Paloma. She clasped his face in her hands and pulled his lips down onto hers. He groaned into her mouth as he shattered spectacularly, and shudders racked his body.

For a long time afterwards, he remained slumped on top of her, and she buried her face against his neck and tried to ignore her certainty that nothing would ever be the same again, that making love with Daniele had changed her fundamentally.

Eventually he rolled off her and propped himself up on an elbow. 'That was incredible, *cara*,' he said softly. 'You blew me away.' He trailed his fingers over her stomach and lower to her thighs and froze. '*Dio*, there is blood. I must have hurt you.' His eyes darkened with remorse. 'I tried to be gentle, but you were tighter than I'd expected.'

Paloma could feel her face burning with embarrassment. 'It's nothing,' she muttered. But as she shifted across the bed, she saw Daniele's gaze focus on the small bloodstain on the sheet.

'Bleeding after sex should be taken seriously. I will arrange for you to see a doctor first thing tomorrow.'

'There's no need.' She huffed out a breath. Her conscience pricked that it wasn't fair to allow him to think he had not taken enough care when he'd had sex with her. 'It's quite normal for there to be a little blood after... the first time.'

'The first time?' Daniele stared at her, and the confusion in his eyes changed to a shuttered expression that Paloma could not fathom. '*Madre di Dio!* You can't mean that you were a *virgin*?'

CHAPTER NINE

IT WAS IMPOSSIBLE, Daniele told himself. He would have known that it was Paloma's first time. Surely he would have felt some resistance when he'd entered her. But he had never had sex with a virgin before and he wouldn't know what to expect. The scarlet patch on the sheet was proof of her innocence. An innocence he had unwittingly taken. Guilt cramped in his gut, and he felt angry, *furious*, at her deception.

'But you were married,' he growled, unwilling to accept the truth of that bloodstain.

'My husband was unable to make love to me.' She avoided his gaze. 'Do we have to talk about it? Why does it matter that I hadn't had sex before? It was all right for you, wasn't it?' The uncertainty in her voice and the glimmer of tears in her eyes tugged on Daniele's conscience. Paloma scrambled off the bed. 'I need the bathroom,' she mumbled before she ran across the room, closing the bathroom door behind her with a loud slam.

Daniele raked his fingers through his hair. His experiences when he had been a member of the special forces meant that he was rarely shocked by anything, but he could not get his head around the idea that he was the first man Paloma had given herself to. Why had she decided to bestow the honour on him? For it was an honour, and one that Daniele knew he did not deserve.

He slid out of bed and strode into the dressing room to pull on his trousers. His wife might not want to talk, but he needed answers. He could not risk being naked near her in case his body betrayed his hunger that was more ravenous than ever when he remembered her cries of pleasure as she'd climaxed around him.

When he returned to the bedroom, he found Paloma perched on the edge of the bed. She was swathed in a fluffy white bathrobe that was too big for her slender frame. Her eyes looked suspiciously pink, as if she'd been crying. Daniele fought the urge to pull her into his arms and kiss the crumpled expression from her lips. 'You owe me an explanation,' he said tautly. 'I suggest you start at the beginning.'

She bit her lip. 'To do that, I have to go back three years. Further, in fact, to when I was a teenager and developed a crush on my grandfather's new computer expert. You knew, of course, and I'm grateful that you were kind to me, especially after my father was killed.'

He nodded. 'Your father's death was devastating for Marcello, who lost his only son and heir. But you had lost a parent when you were at a vulnerable age and I knew what that felt like. I will never forget being told that my father was dead. Grief is a lonely place. You were still a child, and I was glad to share my experience if it helped you to come to terms with your loss.'

Paloma sighed. 'I had led a sheltered life in England, mostly at an all-girls boarding school. When I went to university, I'd never had a real boyfriend, and I felt out of my depth when I was asked out on dates. Things never went further than a kiss at the end of the evening.' She gave Daniele a wry look. 'It wasn't just my naivety. Many of the students on the campus knew that I was an heiress, and I was never sure if guys were interested in me or my money. When I became an intern at Morante Group, and met you again, I fantasised that you were attracted to me. But at the ball you insisted it had been a mistake to kiss me. I assumed you had kissed me back out of pity because I didn't have a partner at the party,' she said in a low voice.

Daniele frowned, remembering how he had been unable to resist Paloma's shy advances. He'd kissed her because he had been fiercely aware of her for weeks before the night of the ball. 'I don't see how this has any relevance,' he growled.

'I felt a fool and rushed back to London, determined to forget you. Weeks later, I met Calum, and his flattery was a salve to my dented ego. In hindsight, I should have known that he was too good to be true,' she said bleakly. 'I was eager for romance and Calum was very convincing. He said he had fallen in love with me at first sight. When I told him I was inexperienced, he assured me that he wanted to wait until our wedding night before we had sex so it would be more special. But even though I believed I loved Calum, I hoped you would feel jealous when you heard, as you were bound to do from my grandfather, that I was married.'

'Are you suggesting I was responsible for your marriage that you have admitted was a disaster from the start?' Daniele controlled his temper with an effort. 'You still haven't explained how you were a virgin.'

Paloma blushed. The clues to her innocence had been in front of him, Daniele thought grimly. She hadn't been leading him on after the Morante Foundation charity ball; she had been terrified. Now he understood the reason for her faint hesitancy when he'd taken her to bed tonight. But she had responded to him with a passion that had matched his own and he hadn't guessed that she was a novice.

'Calum was drunk for pretty much the whole of our honeymoon and the marriage was not consummated. When we returned to London and moved into our new house, I hoped things would improve, but the man who had treated me like a princess before the wedding had become distant and withdrawn.' Paloma avoided Daniele's gaze. 'The few times Calum attempted to make love to me were humiliating. I tried everything. Sexy underwear, massage oils.' She blushed. 'I even bought a couple of sex toys. But nothing worked. He said he'd never had a problem before. It was me. I didn't turn him on.'

'Your ex-husband must have been made of stone,' Daniele gritted. 'Just the idea of you using a sex toy is incredibly erotic. Why did you think the problem was your fault?'

'He said it was, and I felt guilty that I couldn't be a proper wife. Things went from bad to worse. Calum often stayed out all night and I suspected that he was having an affair. I suggested we sought marriage counselling or saw a sex therapist. He laughed and said there was nothing wrong with *him*. And then he told me that he was seeing his girlfriend who he'd been in a relationship with before I'd met him, and she was pregnant with his child.' She grimaced. 'I wondered if his conscience had stopped him from having sex with me because he was going to be a father to another woman's baby. But Calum was the only man I'd ever tried to have sex with, and I believed him when he said I was passionless.'

'*Dio*, if you had responded to me any more passionately, we would have gone up in flames.' Daniele needed a drink. He strode across the room and grabbed the bottle of whisky that had been left on a small table. Paloma shook her head when he offered her a drink. He half filled a glass and took a long sip, feeling the fiery hit of alcohol hit his bloodstream. 'Why did you have sex with me? You made the first move,' he reminded her.

She blushed again. 'Are you saying you were reluctant to make love to me?'

He gave a snort of derision. 'I took you to bed because I was out of my mind with desire. You saw for yourself that you only had to look at me to give me an erection. But why did you give yourself to me?'

'I couldn't bear to wake up in the morning after my second wedding night and *still* be a virgin.'

Daniele clenched his jaw to stop himself from swearing. 'So you used me as a *stud*?' Bile tasted bitter in his throat. He was enraged, believing that he had been manipulated by Paloma. It followed the conversation with his mother when he'd discovered that he had been manipulated by his grandmother Elsa, who he suspected had hidden the letters that Claudia Farnesi said she had sent him during his childhood.

'I would not have had sex with you if I'd been aware that you were a virgin,' he told Paloma curtly.

'Were you lying about it being good for you?' she asked in a low voice. 'You said I was incredible, but I know I'm not.'

'I was not referring to your performance,' he bit out, furious with himself for being affected by the vulnerable expression in her eyes. Daniele vowed to himself that if he ever had the chance he would throttle her ex-husband. 'Sex with you was amazing. But that's not the point. You were dishonest and deceived me.'

'I didn't lie.' She looked away from him. 'I admit I was economical with the truth.'

Daniele drained the whisky in his glass. 'Your grandfather gave me the task of taking care of you, but I have broken my code of honour and integrity by taking your innocence. I thought there was trust between us, but clearly, that is not the case.' It hurt, dammit, that Paloma had kept a huge secret from him. 'You should have told me that you were a virgin, *mia bella, disonesta moglie*,' he said savagely, before he strode into the dressing room and slammed the door behind him.

Paloma's jaw ached from smiling. Thankfully, the wedding brunch hosted by Prince Dragan for those guests who had spent the night at the castle was nearly over. But she doubted she would be able to relax when she and Daniele flew back to Italy by private jet. She had not been alone with him since she'd watched him stride out of the bedroom and they had spent the rest of the night apart. When she'd woken in the morning, Daniele had gone from the tower. He had met her at the door to the orangery and escorted her to the brunch party. Both of them had pretended to be happy newly-weds, but Paloma's heart felt like a lead weight in her chest.

When she'd curled up beneath the covers in that huge bed last night, she'd cried herself to sleep. Her omission to mention she was a virgin had been wrong, she acknowledged. As a result, she had lost Daniele's respect. Honesty was important to him, and he was devastated by the possibility that his grandmother had allowed him to believe his mother hadn't cared about him.

She glanced at him, sitting beside her at the table in the light-filled orangery. He looked gorgeous in pale chinos and a black polo shirt. Dark shades hid his expression and he appeared to be utterly relaxed, while she felt confused and miserable and was desperately trying to conceal her emotional turmoil. Paloma guessed he regretted making love to her, although throughout lunch he'd played the role of attentive husband so well that her heart ached for the connection she had felt between them last night when they had danced on the balcony.

She had foolishly allowed herself to imagine that their marriage was more than a cold-blooded bargain, and when Daniele had made love to her with such tender consideration as well as tumultuous passion, the connection had felt even stronger. But she had been mistaken—again, Paloma thought dismally. Daniele had married her to increase his social status, and he was no different from most other people who wanted something from her because she was an heiress with an aristocratic background.

'Has your husband told you where he is taking you on honeymoon?' Prince Dragan asked. He was sitting opposite Paloma at the table and several times she had been aware of his dark-eyed scrutiny. She hoped he did not notice how she tensed with shock before she forced her muscles to relax and gave a strained smile. A honeymoon was news to her.

'Daniele is keeping the location a secret,' she said in a falsely bright voice.

'It is not a good thing to have secrets in a marriage.' The Prince sounded serious.

'I agree.' Daniele joined the conversation. He draped his arm casually around Paloma's shoulders and she wanted so badly to lean into him and kiss his hard jaw. 'I hope I can be forgiven for planning a surprise for my wife that I believe will make her happy,' he murmured.

Paloma longed to rip off his sunglasses and reveal his expression that might give a clue to his thoughts. Was he sending her an underlying message that he was prepared to forgive her for keeping her virginity a secret? He was impossible to read, she thought despairingly.

'You should have discussed a honeymoon with me.

I don't see the need for one,' Paloma told Daniele later when they were driven away from the castle in a car that had the Prince's royal flag flying from the bonnet. Following the wedding, she had intended to return to the palazzo and stay out of the public eye. Her grandfather's death that had made her a hugely wealthy heiress and now her marriage to Italy's foremost entrepreneur had caused a media frenzy. When the car drove through the castle gates, there was a flurry of camera flashbulbs from the waiting paparazzi.

'The board of trustees would think it odd if we did not follow convention and go away for a short honeymoon. Our marriage needs to appear to be real,' Daniele reminded her. His coolness shattered Paloma's fragile hope that he had planned a trip because he genuinely wanted to make her happy, as he had told Prince Dragan. Her expression must have revealed that she felt hurt, for Daniele said curtly, 'We both knew the rules of the game before we started playing.'

As soon as they boarded the plane, he opened his laptop and was evidently engrossed in work for the short flight. Paloma pretended to flick through a magazine, but inside she felt like an emotional pressure cooker. After the plane had landed and they walked towards the domestic flights arrivals hall, she saw through a window a crowd of photographers waiting for them. Her steps slowed and she gave Daniele a despairing look.

'I can't do this. I can't pretend in front of a bunch of journalists that we are madly in love when the truth is that our marriage is a sham.'

'It's all right, *cara*. You won't have to face the cameras.' The unexpected gentleness in his voice tore at Paloma's heart. She did not know what was happening when Daniele led her down a corridor and into a small room.

'Fortunately, you are wearing trousers,' he said, running his eyes over her white culottes that she'd teamed with an ecru-coloured silk top. 'You look very beautiful, by the way. But it could have been a flaw in my plan if you had worn a dress.'

She was even more perplexed when he handed her a motorbike helmet and a leather jacket. 'I assumed we would catch a connecting flight to our honeymoon destination.' It had seemed likely that Daniele had arranged for them to spend their honeymoon at a fashionable resort, perhaps in Monaco or further afield on one of the Caribbean islands where the paparazzi flocked to snap pictures of celebrities. Such places were Paloma's idea of hell.

Daniele had pulled on his crash helmet and there was no chance for her to ask more questions. They exited the airport building through a back door, and the motorbike was parked outside. She guessed that one of Daniele's ex-army friends had been involved in the plan that allowed them to drive away from the airport without attracting the media's attention.

Once they left the city, the lush scenery of Tuscany was spread out as far as the eye could see. Verdant green fields scattered with scarlet poppies, hints of yellow where the sunflowers were beginning to bloom, groves of gnarled olive trees and tall cypress trees lining the roadside like sentinels, all beneath a cobalt-blue sky. Sitting on the back of the bike, Paloma wrapped her arms around Daniele's waist and clung to him tightly while a kaleidoscope of colourful images flashed past. Her heart lifted even more when they drew up in front of his farmhouse. Hidden in a valley between two hills, it had to be one of the most peaceful places on earth.

'I thought you would appreciate disappearing from public view for a while,' he said when he opened the door and stood back to allow her to precede him into the cool hallway. 'If we had gone to a hotel or holiday resort, we would have had the media circus follow us.' He frowned when she did not say anything. 'But if it is too quiet here for your liking, we can go somewhere else.'

Paloma stepped into the kitchen filled with late afternoon sunshine that danced across the terracotta floor tiles. The copper pans on hooks above the range gleamed and the scent of beeswax polish hung in the air. 'I love the farmhouse,' she said softly. 'I can't think of anywhere I'd rather be.' Or anyone she would rather be with. The thought hit her like a thunderbolt and filled her with panic at the realisation that she could so easily fall in love with Daniele.

She quickly moved away from him and filled the coffee machine with water simply so that she had something to occupy her mind and hands, but she was conscious that his speculative gaze lingered on her.

'Good,' he murmured. 'I have always found the serenity of this place cathartic. A lot has happened to you in a short space of time and I'm sure you miss your grandfather. Plus, I can keep you safe here.'

'I am not your responsibility.' She bit her lip. 'Nonno should not have put that on you.'

Daniele shrugged. 'You are my wife and that makes you my responsibility.' He glanced at his watch. 'I have a few things to do. The files you asked to see regarding Morante Group's business structure and reports by the chief operating officer and other department managers are in the sitting room. If you want to take a look through them, I'll try to answer any questions you might have later.'

Her grandfather's company and charitable foundation were the reason she was married to a lump of granite, Paloma reminded herself when she saw the daunting pile of reports on the coffee table. But she was soon engrossed in reading the history of the company, some of which she already knew, of how Marcello Morante had saved the leather goods business and restored the family's fortune from near bankruptcy brought about by his father's wild lifestyle of drinking and gambling. Her great-grandfather and her father, Roberto, must have had similar characters, she thought ruefully. But she took after Nonno, and she was inspired by him. She was prepared to work hard to make sure that Morante Group and the Morante Foundation continued to flourish under her leadership.

Some while later, Paloma's stomach rumbled, and she went to the kitchen to prepare dinner. Through the window, she saw Daniele chopping logs to fuel the range cooker. He had stripped off his shirt, and his tanned torso glistened with sweat as he lifted the axe and swung it down again. His actions were controlled, and with every swing of the axe, his biceps bulged.

Paloma's mouth ran dry as she watched him, remembering how indescribably good it had felt when he'd lowered his muscular body onto her and made love to her with powerful thrusts. Desire flooded hot and urgent between her legs. When Daniele put down the axe and stepped into the kitchen, she was conscious that her pebble-hard nipples were visible beneath her silky top.

She dropped her gaze from his, but not before she'd caught the gleam in his amber eyes. Lion's eyes. For an instant, his face tightened in a predatory expression, before he turned away and picked up a towel to wipe his hands.

'I heard a car earlier,' she mumbled as she concentrated on chopping tomatoes to make a sauce.

'A friend who knows to keep our location secret brought our luggage from the airport. I took your bags upstairs.' He leaned his hip against the table and watched her assemble olives, onions and basil for spaghetti marinara.

'I found some fresh prawns in the fridge that I plan to add to the sauce.'

'You don't have to do all the cooking.'

'I do if I don't want steak and eggs for dinner.' Paloma's heart missed a beat when he suddenly grinned.

'You remembered that my culinary skills are limited.'

She remembered every tiny snippet of information she had gleaned about him. It wasn't much. Daniele was as much of a mystery as he had always been, and the reality that he was almost a stranger hurt more than it should.

'I'll go and shower before dinner.' He sauntered out of the door, and minutes later, Paloma heard the sound of the shower from upstairs. She would *not* picture Daniele naked, or imagine that they were on a real honeymoon, and she would join him in the shower to play out one of her erotic fantasies where she smoothed a bar of soap over every inch of his magnificent body.

'Are you okay?' he asked when he returned to the kitchen. 'You look flushed.'

'It's from the steam when I drained the pasta,' she lied.

He found plates and cutlery and lit a couple of candles that were stuck into the tops of wine bottles. Paloma thought of the grand dining room at the palazzo and the valuable antique silver candelabrum and decided she preferred the rustic farmhouse kitchen, and the soft glow of candlelight that reflected the gleam in Daniele's eyes. Her fierce awareness of him decimated her appetite, and she felt as gauche and tongue-tied as she had been at sixteen, when she'd been torn between hoping he would notice her and praying that he wouldn't. She was thankful when he asked her about the Morante Group's reports, and they discussed business while he ate with evident enjoyment, and she chased a prawn around her plate.

After dinner Daniele went to his study, saying he needed to make a phone call. Paloma headed upstairs, and the discovery that he had put her bags in the guest bedroom deflated her like a popped balloon. Clearly, he did not want her to share the master bedroom with him. When would she accept that he wasn't interested in her? She ran a bath and afterwards got into bed and read for a while, but when she switched off the lamp, she realised that she could not remember anything about the book.

She woke suddenly and opened her eyes to find the room was dark with just a sliver of moonlight poking through a gap in the blind. Her luminous watch revealed that it was two a.m. The house was utterly quiet, but she was sure she had been disturbed by a noise from outside. It had probably been a fox, or maybe a wild boar, Paloma told herself. But then she heard a sound, halfway between a groan and a shout, that made her blood run cold. It had come from across the hallway. Another shout, louder and even more agonised than the first, had her leaping out of bed, convinced that an intruder had broken into the house and was attacking Daniele.

Heart thumping, she crept out of her room. Her eyes had grown accustomed to the darkness, and she saw a pottery vase filled with dried pampas grass on the hall table. She picked up the heavy vase and heard Daniele groan again. What was the intruder, or possibly there were more than one, doing to him? Paloma felt sick with fear as she cautiously opened the bedroom door.

The slats on the blind were open and moonlight slanted across the bed, where Daniele was sprawled. A quick glance showed that there was no one else in the room. She released a shaky breath and walked over to the bed.

Daniele was thrashing his head from side to side on the pillow and muttering something incomprehensible.

Paloma put the vase down on the bedside table and shook his shoulder. 'Wake up. You're having a nightmare.'

His eyes flew open, but, although he stared at her, she sensed that he did not see her. He must be trapped in some terrible place in his mind. She touched his face and he reacted instantly, capturing her hands in his and flipping her over so that she landed flat on her back on the bed. He loomed over her, his features drawn into a savage expression, but then he blinked and finally recognised her.

'Paloma? What's going on?' His voice was a low growl.

'I heard you shouting, and I thought you were being attacked by…someone,' she faltered. It occurred to her that he might think she'd come to his room to offer herself to him as she had on their wedding night.

His heavy brows snapped together. 'If you thought there was an intruder, why did you come to my room?'

'To help you, of course.' She saw his gaze flick to the vase of pampas grass.

'Were you planning to tickle an assailant to death?' he bit out. 'It's no laughing matter,' Daniele said harshly when she started to smile. 'You should have run away and hidden in the woods, and when you were safely away from the house, called the police.'

'But your life might have been in danger.'

'And so you risked your life for me.' He didn't seem grateful. His eyes blazed with anger. '*Idiota!* These people are dangerous.'

'What people?'

He exhaled deeply. 'I am certain the Mafia were involved in your kidnapping in Mali, and they probably planted the photographer at the hotel in Tunisia who took the picture of us that appeared in the tabloids to discredit you.'

Paloma's eyes widened. 'But why?'

'Because someone wants to prevent you from claiming your inheritance—one way or another. I know how organised crime gangs operate. They would think nothing of killing both of us.'

'You had a nightmare.' She wondered if she should mention the noise she'd thought she had heard outside. But she couldn't be sure of what had woken her, and there were probably foxes and other wildlife prowling around the farmhouse at night, Paloma reassured herself.

She became aware that there was only her silk chemise and the thin sheet between their bodies, and almost certainly Daniele slept naked. His hard thighs were pressing her into the mattress, and she felt a dull throb begin deep in her pelvis.

'Can you let me up, please?' she muttered. 'You're squashing me.'

He rolled off her and switched on the bedside lamp. 'I'm sorry if I scared you,' he said gruffly as she sat up.

'What was your nightmare about?'

He raked a hand through his hair. 'I lost a close friend in Afghanistan. Our military base was attacked, and a mortar shell landed in the compound. One minute Gino was standing a few feet away from me, and in the next he'd gone. He died instantly. It could have been me who had been standing in that spot, and for a long time I thought it should have been me. Gino had a wife and two children back home in Italy, but I had no one. If I had stepped into the compound first, his kids would not have had to grow up without their papa.'

'Oh, Daniele,' Paloma whispered. 'You are not responsible for everyone.'

'I was his commanding officer. I should have gone ahead of him.' He shook his head. 'Usually we received intelligence that we were going to come under fire, but that day we heard nothing until the shell exploded.'

'What happened was a terrible tragedy. But I don't believe that no one cared about you. Your grandmother would have been devastated if you'd been killed, especially as your father had died while he was in the army.'

Daniele gave a harsh laugh. 'My grandmother allowed me to believe that my mother had abandoned me. My phone call yesterday evening was to Nonna Elsa's lawyer. She had left instructions that if I ever found out about the letters my mother had sent, they were to be given to me. The lawyer scanned the letters and sent me digital copies.'

'So your mother *did* try to keep in contact with you when you were a child.' Paloma instinctively reached out and put her hand on his arm. She sensed the effort it took him to control his emotions, but she'd heard the rawness in his voice and could only guess how hurt he must feel by his grandmother's betrayal.

He nodded. 'I have you to thank for helping me discover the truth. If you hadn't insisted on inviting my mother to the wedding, I might never have spoken to her.'

Daniele slid a hand beneath her chin and tilted her face up. His amber eyes blazed, but no longer with anger. 'It was dangerous for you to come to my room,' he said thickly.

Paloma was trembling, but not from fear. It was the way Daniele was staring at her as if he wanted to devour her. 'There was no intruder and no danger,' she whispered.

He lowered his head, and she felt his warm breath graze her cheek. 'I am the danger, *cara*,' he warned her before he claimed her mouth in a kiss of savage possession.

CHAPTER TEN

PALOMA WAS SO BEAUTIFUL, and he was coming apart at the seams. He had held it together for years, since he was a kid, but now Daniele found himself wanting things he'd told himself he could not have and did not deserve. He had been haunted by the belief that his life should have been taken instead of Gino's. Two children had grown up fatherless, but nobody would have cared if he had died in Afghanistan.

His grandmother had been dead by then, but instead of leaving his mother's letters for him to read, she had arranged for her deception to continue after her death. He did not understand why Nonna Elsa had prevented his mother from contacting him, and his sense of betrayal felt as if he'd been shot through the heart. Thank God that Paloma had tricked him into meeting Claudia Farnesi.

He broke the kiss and studied his wife. His. Indisputably. She had given herself to him and he felt possessive and something else a lot more complicated that he dared not define. Paloma was light in the darkness. The only person he had confided in about how his mother had abandoned him as a child—or so he'd been led to believe. And now because of Paloma the tight bands that had wrapped around his heart twenty-seven years ago were loosening.

Daniele stared into her eyes, the intense blue of lapis

lazuli. *Dio*, she had feared he was being attacked by an intruder and had rushed to save him, armed with a flowerpot. What astonished him the most was that Paloma believed he was worth saving. For the first time since he was five years old, he wondered if maybe she could be right.

'I want to make love to you,' he told her softly, aware of an odd sensation in his chest when she blushed.

'You were angry when you discovered it was my first time with you,' she said in a low voice. 'I assumed it was the reason we are sleeping in separate rooms.'

He sighed. 'I was angry with myself. I had no idea you were so innocent, and if I'd known, I would have been gentler. I thought you might need time to recover, and I didn't want you to feel under pressure to sleep with me.'

'You didn't hurt me.' Her tongue darted over her lips. 'I liked having sex with you.'

Dio! Did she have any idea how gorgeous she was with a pink flush on her lovely face and her mouth slightly parted in an invitation that made Daniele's heart thunder in his chest? 'This time will be even better,' he promised. And set about proving it.

He pushed away the sheet and heard her indrawn breath when she saw how aroused he was. She'd had that effect on him for years, and suddenly it was important that he was honest with her.

'Three years ago, I kissed you back because I couldn't resist you,' he said gruffly. 'I had been aware of you all that summer when you were an intern, and I found myself making excuses to visit whichever department you were working in at Morante Group's headquarters. At the ball you looked stunning and sophisticated in a sexy dress, and I couldn't take my eyes off you.'

'If that's true, why did you push me away after one kiss?'

'I knew you'd had too much champagne.' He hesitated.

'I also knew that you saw me as Prince Charming, which I certainly am not. You had hopes and expectations that I couldn't fulfil. I still can't.' It was only fair to warn her.

Something flickered on her face, but it was gone in a flash and her eyes met his gaze steadily. 'You haven't a clue what my hopes are. I don't think I even know any more.' She gave a rueful smile. 'My priority is to take my place as head of Morante Group and the charity foundation, as my grandfather wanted me to do. It's why I married you. In my experience, expectations inevitably lead to disappointment,' she said drily.

Daniele should have been relieved by her words, but bizarrely he wished he could be the man who helped her to realise her dreams. But there was one way he could be certain he would not disappoint her. He caught hold of the hem of her nightgown and pulled it up over her head. Her long hair spilled over her breasts. He threaded his fingers through the silken strands and spread her hair across the pillows before he bent his head and drew one dusky pink nipple into his mouth.

She gave a low cry and arched towards him as his fingers played with her other nipple. Paloma had given him a precious gift, and he wanted to show his appreciation and wonder that she had chosen him in the only way he knew how. This was all for her and, even though his body ached for release, his sole focus was on her pleasure. He claimed her mouth in a slow, sensual kiss and then trailed tender kisses over her throat and décolletage, working his way down her body until he reached the vee of tight chestnut curls at the junction of her thighs.

'Daniele?' she whispered uncertainly.

'Trust me, *piccola*.' He spread her legs wider and settled himself between them, and then he put his mouth on the sweetest part of her and used his tongue to give her the most intimate caress of all.

She trembled and curled her fingers into his hair, but she didn't try to pull him away and her husky cries were music to his ears. *She was his.* The words beat inside his head and his heart, and he did not know what to make of them.

'I'm going to...' She gasped and shook as she climaxed against his mouth. When Daniele lifted his head, he knew he would never see a more beautiful sight than Paloma spread in front of him, her creamy skin and those rosy nipples that fascinated him, her eyes, wide and intensely blue, and her face flushed with sexual heat. His. And he made her so again, quickly donning protection before he positioned himself over her and surged into her.

It felt as if his shaft were encased in a tight velvet glove. It was the only place he wanted to be. He slipped his hands beneath her bottom and angled her hips so that he could drive deeper, and each thrust took them higher. But he made himself wait, although it nearly killed him. Only when Paloma sobbed his name, and he felt the ripples of her orgasm clench around him, did his control shatter and he followed her over the edge.

When he surfaced a lifetime later, she was still there, his wife, her gorgeous body wrapped around him and her head resting on his chest. Paloma was there beside him, and for the first time in his life, Daniele felt at peace.

Paloma opened her eyes to find sunshine streaming through the open blind. For a while she lay still and watched dust motes floating in the golden light. She had spent the night in Daniele's bed, and they had made love twice more before falling asleep. Now she was alone, and the doubts that she'd ignored last night crowded her mind.

Sleeping with him had been a bad idea, but it had been inevitable after he'd admitted that he had desired her when she had been a twenty-one-year-old intern. Three years ago, he'd correctly assessed that she could not have handled an affair and he couldn't live up to the romantic ideal she'd had of him. Now they were married, but romance played no part in their marriage bargain.

Daniele had left her to wake up alone. Maybe he was worried that she was still the girl who had worn her heart on her sleeve, even though he had made it clear that all he could offer was great sex. She was determined not to appear needy.

She would always need him. The thought slid into her mind and refused to budge. Daniele had been a reassuring presence in the background of her life since she was a teenager. He was the only person she had cried in front of after her father had been killed because she hadn't wanted to upset her grandfather even more with her grief. Daniele had comforted her, and he had been her ally and protector when she'd needed him.

It was not surprising that she had been in love with him for years. Paloma froze, fighting a dawning truth. Her youthful feelings had not been an infatuation. Age was not a barrier to love. She was in love with Daniele, but he must never guess how she felt when there was no chance he would return her feelings.

It was suddenly important that he did not find her lying in his bed, as if she had nothing better to do than wait for him. She would show him that she was an independent woman, and he did not have to feel responsible for her just because she had lost her virginity to him. And if deep in her heart she was glad it had been Daniele, she wasn't going to admit it to him or herself.

She hurried back to her bedroom, and as she crossed

the landing, she smelled the heavenly aroma of coffee wafting up from the kitchen. A sound made her stop in her tracks. Daniele was whistling cheerfully and, it must be said, rather tunelessly. It was such a normal thing, but from Daniele, the master of self-containment, it was perhaps an indication that he had lowered his guard a fraction.

Heading into her en suite bathroom, she turned on the shower and closed her mind to everything but the feel of the hot spray on her skin. She ran her fingers through her hair to rinse out the shampoo and gave a startled yelp when a pair of big, tanned hands settled on her hips. Daniele nuzzled the base of her throat and moved his lips up to nip her earlobe with his teeth. A quiver ran through her when he cupped her breasts in his palms and pulled her against him so that her back rested on his chest and his arousal nudged the cleft of her bottom. Erotic memories of the previous night filled her mind, and she was shocked by how desperately she wanted him again.

'I prepared breakfast for you,' he murmured. 'But when I carried the tray up to the bedroom, you had gone.'

'Oh, I'd better come now before it gets cold.'

'It's yoghurt and fruit,' he said wryly. 'My capabilities as a cook don't stretch to a—what is it called?—a full English.' He turned her around to face him, and her heart missed a beat when he gave her a sexy grin. His wet hair was slicked back from his face and the dark stubble on his jaw made him look like a pirate.

Paloma caught her breath when he slipped his hand between her thighs and his fingers found her molten heat. His powerful erection jabbed her belly as he lifted her up and held her against the shower wall. Pushing her legs apart, he entered her with a smooth thrust. 'And now you are full of an Italian,' he murmured, his eyes gleaming wickedly.

She giggled, but soon she was gasping as he took her hard and fast. His urgency matched her own and she dug her fingers into his shoulders as the storm inside her built to a crescendo. His ragged breaths told her he was close, and moments later they climaxed simultaneously. The perfection of the moment and the man brought tears to Paloma's eyes, and she prayed that Daniele would think it was the shower spray running down her face.

'I want to make it clear that we will divorce in the future,' she told him much later, after he had taken her back to bed and they had been too occupied to think of breakfast. Finally they had made it down to the kitchen for lunch, and they were famished and feasting on bread and cheese and tangy olives.

'Have you had enough of me already?' Daniele lifted a brow. 'I did not get that impression when you were being very inventive with a bar of soap in the shower, *cara*.'

Paloma felt herself blush, but kept her gaze locked with his. 'Sleeping together wasn't part of the plan. This—' she waved her hand in the air '—attraction between us won't last.' She needed to remind herself that their marriage was temporary.

Something flickered in his eyes before his thick lashes swept down. 'How can you be so sure?'

'I know your track record with women.' Paloma felt a sharp stab of jealousy as she thought of all the women who had come before her and those who would share his bed after her. She wondered if he would bring them to the farmhouse and spoil them with breakfast in bed, even if it was only yoghurt.

Daniele leaned back in his chair. 'Your birthday is more than six months away and we have to remain married until you are twenty-five. I have learned that life is unpredictable,' he said with emphasis. 'I suggest we enjoy whatever "this" is.'

For as long as it lasts. His unspoken words hovered in the air. Paloma sternly quashed her disappointment that he had not suggested their marriage might continue after she was twenty-five. She did not want to be trapped in a loveless marriage for a second time, she reminded herself. But he was right. No one knew what was around the corner. A few weeks ago, she had been teaching in one of the most deprived parts of Africa. The shocking news of her grandfather's death had turned her life upside down.

'I just wanted you to know that I don't have any expectations,' she told him seriously.

Daniele's eyes narrowed on her face, and he seemed to be about to say something but then changed his mind. 'So we agree to take each day as it comes. I have a plan for the rest of today.'

'Are you going to tell me where we are going?' Paloma asked him a little while later as they strolled through some woodland near to the farmhouse.

'You'll see very soon.' He was as good as his word, and when they emerged from the cool shade of the trees into the warm afternoon sunshine, Paloma heard the unmistakable sound of a waterfall. Daniele led the way along a path that opened out to a rocky area where water gushed into a crystal-clear pool. 'I thought we would swim.'

'I'd love to, but I didn't bring a swimsuit.'

'Nor did I.' He pulled his T-shirt over his head and grinned when Paloma's eyes widened as she watched him strip off his jeans and boxers. 'Your turn to get undressed, *cara*.'

She glanced around her. 'But what if someone sees us?'

'The pool is on my land, and no one will come here. Have you never swum naked in a wild pool before?'

'No. It will be another first that I can thank you for.' She slipped off her skirt and top and hesitated for a heartbeat before removing her bra and knickers. Daniele scooped her into his arms and strode into the pool with her. 'Oh, God, the water's freezing,' she gasped as he lowered her down.

'I'm curious to know how you plan to thank me,' he whispered in her ear.

She moved her hand down his body and discovered that the chilly temperature of the water had not affected a certain area of his anatomy. 'Like this,' she murmured, and he groaned when she curled her fingers around his manhood.

For the rest of the day, they swam in the pool or stood beneath the waterfall and dried off by lying on the flat rocks that had been warmed by the sun. 'Like lizards,' Paloma commented.

'You are a million times more desirable than a lizard,' Daniele assured her, and he proceeded to show her how much he desired her. She had never seen him so carefree, almost boyish, and she fell in love with him even more.

The afternoon by the pool set a pattern for the days that followed. They spent almost every hour in each other's company, much of the time in bed, although they experimented on the sofa and on the gym mats after a martial arts session, and most memorable of all was when Daniele bent her over the kitchen table and made passionate love to her while the dinner burned and stuck to the saucepan.

Afterwards, they fed each other olives and black grapes and drank good red wine. And they talked endlessly. About Morante Group—the chief operating officer sent daily reports that Paloma discussed with Daniele, and she was glad of his opinions and advice. He told her about his e-commerce company and his determination to help young entrepreneurs become successful, and they discovered a shared commitment to promote the charitable foundation that was Marcello Morante's great legacy.

Sometimes in the quiet stillness of the night, Daniele spoke about Afghanistan while Paloma listened without commenting, knowing he needed to let the blackness inside him pour out. And when he stopped talking and pulled her beneath him, she held him tightly and told him with her body the secrets she kept locked in her heart.

One golden day slipped into another and another, and Paloma lost track of time. It felt as though their Tuscan idyll would never end. She should have known that nothing was for ever.

Daniele watched Paloma moving around the kitchen with her innate grace that captivated him. She was wearing one of his shirts that was too big for her and stopped midway down her slender, golden tanned thighs. The knowledge that she was naked beneath the shirt made his body clench. Desire was a fire smouldering inside him that regularly blazed into an inferno. He wondered when he would grow tired of her. For surely he must? In his experience, sexual attraction always burned out.

She stirred something in a bowl and paused to study a recipe in Daniele's only cookbook that Enrique's wife had given him. He'd never opened the front cover.

'What are you making?' He strolled across the kitchen, more because of his need to be close to Paloma than any real interest in the concoction in the bowl.

'Chocolate mousse.' She dipped a spoon into the mixture and held it against his lips. 'What do you think?'

That you are driving me insane. He kept the thought to himself and licked the mousse off the spoon. 'Delicious, but I prefer the taste of you on my tongue, *cara*.' He was fascinated by the rosy blush that winged along her high cheekbones. 'Who taught you to cook? Your mother?'

Paloma laughed. 'Heavens, no. I told you I studied cordon bleu cookery at a Swiss finishing school that Nonno persuaded me to attend before I went to university. I doubt my mother has ever set a dainty foot inside a kitchen. After she divorced my father, she took me to live in London, and we had several staff, including a cook and butler. Mama blew her divorce settlement from Papa very quickly and just as quickly found herself another rich husband. I grew up thinking that money, not love, was the reason why people married.'

She poured the mousse into glass dishes and put them in the fridge. 'Mama always forgot the dates of the school holidays, and invariably she was away on a cruise when my boarding school shut for the summer break. I used to stay with my friend Laura. Her family have a farm in Yorkshire, and her mother, especially, was always so welcoming and kind to me.'

Daniele suspected that Laura's family had given Paloma the love and attention that she hadn't received from her own parents. 'Neither of our mothers were good role models.'

'At least you now know from your mother's letters that she didn't completely abandon you when you were a boy.'

'It doesn't change the fact that she left me behind. I accept that the situation was complex, and my grandfather was a cruel man.' His jaw hardened. 'But what mother would leave their child?'

Paloma stared at him. 'I know I couldn't. When I have children, I will tell them every day that I love them,' she said in a fierce voice. Her words hung in the air, and she jerked her gaze from Daniele as the atmosphere in the kitchen crackled with awkwardness.

It was not a surprise that she hoped to have children, he acknowledged. Of course she wanted a husband who loved her, babies, a family of her own. But they were not things that he could give her. He liked his freedom, at least that was what he told himself. Lately, he'd wondered if their marriage might continue after Paloma was twenty-five. But hearing her state that she hoped to have a family reminded him that he was not the man for her. Deep down, he would always believe that his mother had left him because she had not loved him enough to fight to keep him. If he hadn't been good enough for his own mother, how could he be good enough for high-born Paloma Morante? And then there was his guilt that Gino had died and he'd lived, when it should have been the other way round. The truth was that he did not deserve Paloma, and she deserved a better man than him.

Paloma's colour was high, and she avoided Daniele's gaze. It occurred to him that perhaps she wanted more from their marriage bargain than she'd let him believe. And why shouldn't she want more than a sexual fling? Unbelievably good though the sex was, he suspected she still clung to the romantic ideals that had made him wary of getting involved with her three years ago.

'Let's visit Lucca this afternoon,' he suggested abruptly. The city was not far away. He needed to clear his head, but he could not do that at the farmhouse with the constant temptation to make love to Paloma. Up until now, he had avoided taking her to public places because of his concern for her safety. But his enquiries into who had been behind her kidnapping had not revealed a link to an organised gang. Paloma seemed as keen as him to leave the farmhouse and ran upstairs to change into suitable clothes for a trip out on the motorbike.

After the seclusion and quiet of the farmhouse, the crowds of people in Lucca's narrow, cobbled streets took some getting used to, although Paloma knew that the city was less of a tourist attraction than Florence or Pisa. Pretty, historic Lucca was famous for its medieval city walls that were broad enough for pedestrians and cyclists to use. She and Daniele climbed the steps and strolled along the tree-lined promenade to admire the views of the city.

His strange mood at the farmhouse seemed to have lifted, but Paloma sensed that they both made an effort to act as though they were enjoying themselves. The Renaissance architecture of Lucca's many churches was stunning, and another time she would have loved to climb to the top of the Guinigi Tower to visit the roof garden. But she kept picturing Daniele's face when she'd spoken about having children. His barriers had gone up, and she had an awful feeling that he had read her mind and knew she'd daydreamed of having a baby with him.

They ate at a little trattoria that served amazing wood-fired pizza, but Paloma's appetite had deserted her, and she was relieved when Daniele paid the bill and they returned to the bike. Dusk was falling and a soft mist lay over the fields as the motorbike sped along the winding road that led to the farmhouse. Her crash helmet blocked out sounds, and she was unaware that a car was following them until it drew alongside the bike.

Paloma assumed the car meant to overtake, but it suddenly veered so close that it clipped the motorbike's rear wheel. Daniele accelerated, and she clung on to him tightly when the car came alongside again. There was no doubt it was trying to force the bike off the road. The car's blacked-out windows meant that it was impossible to see the driver. The next few miles being chased by the car were terrifying, and Paloma was certain that Daniele would lose control of the bike and they would crash.

They were travelling incredibly fast, but then he suddenly braked hard and turned the bike through an opening in the hedge and into a field. Paloma looked over her shoulder and saw the car was following them. Daniele was heading towards the copse at the edge of the field. The bike tore into the woods and Paloma closed her eyes, sure they would slam into a tree trunk. But at least the car had been unable to follow them into the trees. Daniele drove on a little further before he cut the bike's engine and they both dismounted.

Paloma's hands were trembling as she pulled off her helmet and she burst into tears. 'Whoever was driving that car could have killed us.'

'I think that was the idea,' Daniele said grimly. He drew her into his arms. 'It's all right, *piccola*. I won't let anyone harm you.'

She stared at him. 'Do you think the lunatic driver was the same person who arranged for me to be kidnapped in Mali?' Fear churned in her stomach when she remembered that Daniele had said he believed an organised crime gang wanted to stop her from claiming her inheritance. 'What are you doing?' she asked when he took out his phone.

'Arranging security measures for when we return to the palazzo. We can't go back to the farmhouse, as it seems that whoever is behind the threats to you is aware of our location.'

Paloma remembered that she'd thought she had heard a noise in the farmhouse courtyard on the night of Daniele's nightmare. 'I'm scared,' she whispered.

Daniele slid his hand beneath her chin and tilted her

face up to his. 'Whoever is trying to harm you must know that we are married and believe that, as your husband, I am the sole beneficiary to your fortune. Only you and I know I signed a prenuptial agreement that precludes me from gaining financially from our marriage. Someone wants both of us out of the way.' He held her closer when she shivered. 'I will protect you with my life, if necessary.'

Because you care about me, or because you promised Marcello that you would protect me? Paloma wanted to ask him. But then his dark head swooped down, and he angled his mouth over hers, kissing her fiercely.

Her senses were heightened from the adrenaline that had surged through her when they had been chased on the bike. All that mattered was that they were alive, and she kissed him back unguardedly, unable to hide her emotional response to him.

When he broke off the kiss at last and stared into her eyes, she trembled anew, thinking she'd glimpsed something in his amber depths that gave her hope that he felt something for her. But there was no time to talk. He pulled on his crash helmet, and she did the same. The journey to the palazzo was thankfully uneventful. There were security guards at the gates, and more patrolling the grounds, Daniele explained when the butler ushered them into the house.

'A bodyguard will drive you to Morante Group's offices tomorrow morning,' Daniele told her. 'I have to go away for a couple of days. I'll inform the police about the incident, but their investigation will take time.'

'Does your trip have anything to do with what happened tonight?' she asked shakily.

He nodded. 'I have contacts from when I was in the special forces and infiltrated a Mafia gang. A couple of people I knew back then became informers, but I have to be careful that I don't put their lives in danger.'

'What about your life being in danger?' Terror gripped Paloma when Daniele strode across the entrance hall towards the front door. 'Is there any point in telling you to take care of yourself?'

He smiled briefly, but he had become an enigmatic stranger once more. 'I suggest you focus on your job running your company, *cara*, and let me do mine.'

With a heavy heart, Paloma realised that first and foremost Daniele regarded her as his responsibility, and the honeymoon was over.

CHAPTER ELEVEN

IT FELT SURREAL to be in her grandfather's office at Morante Group's headquarters, sitting at his desk, in his chair. Tears pricked Paloma's eyes when she picked up a framed photograph of herself taken at her graduation ceremony that Nonno had kept on the desk. She missed him terribly and wished with all her heart that she had moved to Italy after university and worked with him. His business experience would have been invaluable to her, but it was too late to learn from his wisdom and advice. Her grandfather was with his beloved Isabella at last, and Paloma was in charge of his billion-dollar company that employed thousands of staff worldwide.

But she had only been able to claim her position at the head of the company by entering into a marriage bargain with Daniele. For the past two days, she had met each of the board members privately and sought to win their backing for her plan to promote the chief operating officer to the role of CEO while she would be in charge of the charitable foundation. Although she had a master's degree in business, she acknowledged that she lacked the experience to oversee the operations and logistics of the company that were the responsibilities of a CEO.

When she was twenty-five, she would become the chairwoman of Morante Group, as her grandfather had wished. But until then, she still faced a threat from her great-uncle Franco, who wanted to oust her and have himself instated as head of the company. Paloma knew she had to stay married to Daniele for the next six months, but what kind of marriage would they have? He desired her for now, but who knew how long the attraction he felt for her would last?

Her phone rang, and her heart leapt, hoping that he was calling her. 'Laura.' Her disappointment that it was not Daniele on the line quickly faded when she heard her friend's cheerful voice. They had kept in contact with occasional text messages since the wedding.

'How was the honeymoon? It was so romantic that Daniele whisked you away to a secret location. Did you go somewhere exotic?'

'He took me to his farmhouse in Tuscany and it is very beautiful and romantic.' Paloma bit her lip as she remembered long, lazy days when she and Daniele had laughed and talked, and he'd made slow, sensual love to her beneath the shade of the maple tree in the courtyard garden. 'It's no good,' she told Laura in a choked voice. 'I can't keep up the pretence and let you think that my marriage is wonderful when it's all a lie.'

'How do you mean?' Laura asked gently. 'What is a lie? You love Daniele, don't you?'

'God, *yes*! I love him. I wouldn't have agreed to marry him if I didn't love him with all my heart.' The truth hit Paloma with the force of a meteor. She cared about Morante Group, of course, and she was determined to be her grandfather's successor, but she would have found another way to claim her place in the company that did not involve a loveless marriage.

'Daniele doesn't love me, but I hoped he would grow to care for me,' she told Laura on a sob. 'He suggested that we should marry to stop my great-uncle Franco from trying to seize control of the company. Daniele has the support of the board, who were happy that he and I would run Morante Group together for a transition period until my twenty-fifth birthday.'

'But why did Daniele suggest marriage? Unless it was because he wanted to marry you,' Laura said slowly. 'I don't see how a marriage bargain would benefit him. He's very wealthy. A self-made millionaire, I've heard. So it can't be that he was after your money like the weasel you married first time round,' she reassured Paloma.

'He wanted the increased social status that marrying the granddaughter of a marchese would give him,' Paloma muttered through her tears.

'Are you sure he doesn't return your feelings?'

'Quite sure. He made it clear that it's just about sex for him.'

'It's only that I saw how he looked at you at the wedding. As if he couldn't believe his luck that you had agreed to be his wife. Why don't you ask him if he has feelings for you?'

Paloma sniffed and wiped her hand over her wet eyes. 'What if he says that he doesn't?'

'Well, at least you'll know where you stand,' Laura said in her matter-of-fact manner that brought a rueful smile to Paloma's lips despite her heartache. Her friend made it sound so simple. But if she pushed Daniele for an answer to where their relationship was going, she might lose everything.

For the rest of the day, she focused on work, as Daniele had suggested, and became so absorbed in a report on the Morante Foundation's various charity projects that it was early evening when she stood up and stretched after sitting for hours. The work of the foundation had been important to her grandfather, and she would fight any opposition from Franco, who wanted to reduce the amount of business profits paid into the charity.

Once again, it came back to Daniele, Paloma thought despondently. She needed him if she were to have the support of the board and shareholders. But she needed him for much more than that. When they had been on their honeymoon, he had made her happy in a thousand different ways.

He really listened when she talked to him, and he'd given her confidence that she could run Morante Group successfully. He made her feel beautiful and desirable, and she had regained a sense of self-worth that Calum had destroyed. She was becoming the woman she had always wanted to be, and when she remembered how relaxed Daniele had been at the farmhouse, she was convinced that she made him happy too.

She was driven back to the palazzo by her bodyguard, Bruno, a burly ex-boxer who had served in the paratrooper regiment with Daniele. 'The boss said that if I allow a single hair on your head to be harmed, he will take me apart limb by limb,' Bruno told her with a grin that did not disguise his obvious respect for Daniele. 'Tell him that Sofia still hasn't had the baby.' At Paloma's questioning look, he explained, 'My wife is a week overdue to give birth to our second child.'

'Daniele is away at the moment.' She felt a stab of concern that she had not heard from him since he'd left the palazzo.

'Your husband arrived home an hour ago,' Bruno said as he opened the door for her to climb out of the car.

Paloma tore into the house and ran upstairs to her room, intending to change her skirt and blouse that she'd worn to the office for something sexier. But when she opened her wardrobe, it was empty.

The maid came into the room. *'Scusa, signorina.'*

'Where are my clothes?'

'Il signore asked me to move your things into his room.'

The master suite had been refurbished eighteen months ago after Marcello had transferred to a bedroom on the ground floor because he'd found climbing the stairs difficult. Paloma barely noticed the sumptuous black-and-gold decor as she heard the shower in the en suite bathroom running. She slipped into the room and caught her breath when she saw Daniele through the misted glass of the shower screen.

He was a work of art. That body of his: lean and powerfully muscular, the broad chest that tapered down to narrow hips and strong thighs. Through the steam, she could make out the whorls of black hairs that grew thickly on his chest and arrowed over his abdomen to the base of his manhood. So absorbed was she in her appreciation of his masculine form that she yelped in shock when he stretched an arm around the screen and caught hold of her shoulder. He tugged and she found herself pulled beneath the spray.

'I'm wearing my clothes,' she protested. Glancing down, she saw that her silk blouse was plastered against her breasts and her nipples had already hardened in anticipation.

'Not for much longer,' Daniele drawled, stripping her with thrilling efficiency. His mouth was on hers, making hungry demands that she returned with demands of her own as their tongues tangled.

'I missed you,' she gasped as he closed his lips around one taut nipple and sucked hard. 'Did you miss me?'

'Can't you tell?' he said thickly, lifting her up so that

her pelvis was flush with his and his erection pressed between her thighs. 'I need to be inside you now, *cara*.'

She wanted to ask if he had only missed her for sex, but his urgency heightened her own, and when he slid an exploratory finger inside her, she was slick and ready for him. He replaced his finger with his rock-hard length, entering her with a powerful thrust that drove the breath from her body. She wrapped her legs around his waist, and he cupped her bottom in his hands as he drove into her faster, faster. The intensity was too much, and she gave a cry as her orgasm surged through her in wave after wave of pleasure. Daniele pressed his mouth against her neck, and his groan was muffled when he came hard, shudders racking his big body.

Afterwards, Paloma blasted her hair with the hairdryer and slipped on Daniele's shirt. The musky scent of his cologne clung to the fabric, and she breathed deep before following him into the bedroom. He was wearing slim-fit trousers and was buttoning a black silk shirt. 'I asked for dinner to be served at eight.'

'I'd better get dressed.' She smiled. 'You had my clothes moved to your room.'

'Of course. The staff would think it odd if we did not sleep together, now we are married. We don't want to risk a careless comment reaching the press and Morante Group's shareholders.'

Disappointment twisted in her stomach. 'Is that the only reason you want me to share a room with you?'

Daniele strolled towards her with that easy grace of his that reminded her of a jungle cat. 'I proved a few minutes ago that I want you in my bed every night.' His lazy smile faded, and his eyes narrowed on her tense face. 'Am I missing something, *cara*?'

She bit her lip. 'It's just that I thought… I hoped that what we have between us is more than sex.'

'What we have?' He sounded genuinely puzzled, and Paloma's hopes sank like a stone dropped into a pool. She snatched a breath.

'I have feelings for you, Daniele. I care about you. Do you feel *anything* for me?'

His shuttered expression told her nothing. 'You know that I care about your welfare. I will protect you—'

'It's not your protection that my heart longs for,' she burst out. 'I want you to love me…as I love you.'

His silence crushed her daydreams and ground them to dust. *'At least you'll know where you stand,'* Laura had said. Now Paloma knew that she stood alone, as she always had, she thought painfully. Only her grandfather had truly loved her. To claim the company that had meant so much to Nonno, she had married Daniele. But she had committed the unforgivable folly of falling in love with him.

'I was honest with you from the start when I told you that I am not the man to fulfil your hopes and dreams,' he said grimly.

'Is that because you don't want to?' she whispered.

'I can't be the man you want me to be.'

'I want the man you are. Not a different version of you that suits me. Even as a teenager, I never saw you as a fairy-tale Prince Charming. I fell in love with you because you are strong and gentle, fierce and kind.'

A nerve jumping in Daniele's cheek was the only indication that his features had not been carved from granite. 'I have never wanted to fall in love because it doesn't last. What is the point in setting yourself up for disappointment and failure?' He stepped closer to her, but when he placed his hand on her shoulder, she jerked away from him.

'Love doesn't always fail.' Paloma bit her lip at his cynical look. Her family's track record for commitment wasn't impressive, and nor was Daniele's.

'What we have is good,' he insisted. 'Friendship, respect for one another and—'

'Great sex,' she supplied heavily.

His eyes flashed. 'Don't knock it, *cara*. The desire we feel for each other is off the scale.' He dragged her into his arms, ignoring how she held herself stiffly, and threaded his fingers through her hair. 'You won't find such passion with anyone else.'

'It's not enough for me.' She would give up her entire fortune to be able to kiss Daniele's stubbled jaw and have him claim her lips in a kiss that came from his heart. But his heart would never belong to her, and so she eased away from him, and he slowly dropped his arms down to his sides.

'I thought I could be content with a sexual relationship,' she said huskily. 'But you taught me that I deserve better than second best. I deserve love, and one day I know I will find it. I can't make love with you any more and pretend that it's meaningless, that the pleasure I feel when you are inside me is just a physical response. I have to be true to myself. I'll sleep in my own room from now on, and I don't give a damn what the staff make of it.'

Daniele heard the snick of the bedroom door as Paloma closed it quietly behind her. If she'd slammed the door, it would have been easier to dismiss her shocking outburst as overemotional—and emotions on any level were guaranteed to send a shudder through him. But it hadn't been histrionics. He'd heard the hurt in her voice, and he felt guilty that he was responsible.

Dio! She loved *him*. Why, he couldn't imagine. He was

not the man for her, and one day she would realise it when she met someone more charming and gracious, someone more suitable for the granddaughter of a marchese than a gruff soldier who saw love for what it was—an illusion.

He ate dinner alone in the grand dining room and asked the housekeeper to take a tray up to his wife, who had a headache and would not be joining him. Was this how things would be from now on? he wondered. Separate meals, separate bedrooms and separate lives.

When Paloma had asked if he had missed her, he'd allowed her to think it had only been sexual frustration that had kept him awake at night. But the truth was that sex was only part of her allure. He liked her smile and her fierce intelligence, her dry sense of humour that caught him off guard, and her boundless compassion and determination to use her fortune to help others. There was a lot of her grandfather in her. Thinking of Marcello reminded Daniele that his old friend had hoped his granddaughter would marry well.

The next morning, Paloma was already sitting at the breakfast table on the terrace when he stepped outside. It was another glorious summer's day, but Daniele did not notice the cobalt-blue sky or hear the cheerful birdsong in the garden. He had the feeling that it would always be winter now. Paloma's coolness made him long for the warmth of her smile.

'Tio Franco has called an extraordinary meeting of the board of trustees and the shareholders to take place this morning. Do you know what it's about?'

'I have no idea.' He watched her pour coffee from the jug and add a sugar cube to the cup before she handed it to him. The simple intimacy of her action evoked an ache in his chest that he assured himself was indigestion. *'Cara...'* he began.

Paloma pushed away her uneaten roll and stood up. 'We should go. The meeting is due to start at nine o'clock.'

She ignored him in the car on the way to the office. Daniele allowed himself to feel righteous indignation. He had never asked for the complication of emotions in what had started out as a marriage bargain, but their relationship had developed into more than a business arrangement, he acknowledged.

Extra chairs had been set out in the boardroom, and there was a tangible sense of curiosity among the shareholders and board members when they took their seats. Daniele collared Franco Zambrotta when he walked into the room. 'What's all this about? The agenda simply states there is an urgent matter to be discussed.'

Franco looked worryingly pleased with himself. 'You'll find out very soon, Berardo. I never understood why Marcello put so much faith in you. His plan to leave the company in the hands of an inexperienced girl could have been disastrous.'

Daniele looked around for Paloma and saw her sitting in the front row. He strode towards the vacant seat a few places along from her. Franco walked to the head of the room and faced the assembly.

'I called this meeting because an extremely serious matter has come to my attention. Namely the conduct of the two people who hold the highest authority in Morante Group that, in my opinion, constitutes moral turpitude.'

'Are you saying you called the meeting to express a personal opinion?' Daniele asked curtly. He glanced across to Paloma and guessed from her frown that she felt as perplexed as him by Franco's statement.

'I believe it is an opinion that most people in the room will share after hearing the recording I am about to play.'

Franco was holding a tablet and Paloma's voice suddenly emerged from the speakers around the room.

'I can't keep up the pretence and let you think that my marriage is wonderful when it's all a lie.'

'Wait a minute.' Paloma jumped to her feet. 'How did you get hold of a conversation that took place on my personal mobile phone? I demand you turn the recording off.'

Franco ignored her plea, and another voice that Daniele recognised belonged to Paloma's friend Laura came through the speakers.

'What is a lie? You love Daniele, don't you?'

'God, yes! I love him. I wouldn't have agreed to marry him if I didn't love him with all my heart.'

'That's enough, Zambrotta. Turn the damn thing off.'

Daniele saw that Paloma had paled, and her stricken expression made him want to sweep her into his arms and carry her out of the meeting. Her voice from the speakers reverberated around the room and inside his head.

'Daniele doesn't love me, but I hoped he would grow to care for me. He suggested that we should marry to stop my great-uncle Franco from trying to seize control of the company.'

Paloma made a muffled sound. 'Please, Tio Franco, turn it off.'

'I think we have all heard enough,' Franco said smoothly. 'It is clear that the marriage between Daniele Berardo and Paloma was a deliberate ploy to mislead the board and shareholders. I believe the trustees have no option but to terminate Berardo's position on the board and replace Paloma with myself at the head of Morante Group with immediate effect.'

'Not so fast.' Daniele leapt to his feet and turned to face the crowded room. 'I will tell you exactly why I married my wife.'

CHAPTER TWELVE

'It's quite simple,' Daniele told his captivated audience.

And it struck him like a thunderbolt that it *was* simple. He loved Paloma. But he had fought his feelings and denied them to himself and to her because he *really* did not want to fall in love. He had numerous examples of how love was transient. His parents' doomed marriage, his mother, who had left him when he was a child, his grandmother, who had lied to him. Only a fool would fall in love. Or a man whose heart was pounding so hard in his chest as his gaze sought the intensely blue eyes of the love of his life. Paloma. His wife.

'I married Paloma for one reason only. I fell in love with her.' He wondered why she looked away from him. Addressing the shareholders again, he continued, 'The phone recording has made me realise that I did not make it clear to her how much she means to me. But I hope she understands that I would give my life for her.'

'Don't!'

Paloma stood up, and Daniele's heart cracked open when he saw tears streaming down her face. 'I know what you're trying to do.' Her lips quivered and black tracks of mascara ran down her face. She was a heartbreakingly beautiful mess. He took a step towards her, but she spun around and ran out of the boardroom.

She had lost everything. The realisation made Paloma feel sick. Her grandfather's company, the charitable foundation, the support of the trustees. But worst and most devastating by far was that she had lost Daniele. You couldn't lose what you had never had, her brain reminded her. *Oh, God!*

She dropped her hands away from her face and forced herself to breathe as the car drew up outside the palazzo and the driver, Bruno, came round and opened her door. In the midst of her agony, she noticed that he looked tense.

'My wife is in labour,' he told her. 'Apparently it's happening very quickly. Sofia's mother is driving her to the hospital.'

'What are you doing here? Go to your wife and baby.'

'Are you sure you won't need me to drive you somewhere?'

'Go!'

Bruno needed no persuading. Paloma ran into the house and up to the master bedroom that she would never share with Daniele. She packed a small suitcase and scrolled through her phone, searching for the next available flight to England. She had sent a frantic text to Laura explaining that her marriage was over.

The car her grandfather had bought her a few years ago was parked in the garage. She was backing it onto the driveway when a taxi swept through the gates. Paloma's heart missed a beat when Daniele got out and strode towards her. She could not face him after her public humiliation at the shareholders' meeting. How Franco had recorded her phone conversation with Laura was a mystery. The memory of hearing her voice through the speakers stating her love for Daniele sent a shudder of embarrassment through Paloma. But even though she had lost everything that mattered to her, there was a sense of relief that she had found the courage to be honest about how she felt. There was no shame in falling in love. Just heartache.

She gripped the steering wheel tightly when Daniele leaned down so that his head was level with the car's open window. 'I'm going to stay with Laura in London,' she said before he asked.

He looked slightly stunned. 'Did you hear what I said in the boardroom?'

'Of course I heard. Everyone there did, but that was the point, wasn't it? I suppose I should thank you.'

His amber eyes flashed. 'Thank me for what? *Dio*,' he growled, his control clearly under strain. 'Will you get out of the car so that we can talk properly?'

'No. I don't want to talk. There's no point. I know you said all that stuff about being in love with me to try to convince the trustees and shareholders that our marriage is genuine. But I can't live a lie any more. We both know you will never love me.' Tears brimmed in her eyes. She could not bear to break down in front of him. 'I have to go.' She bit her lip when he did not move away from the car. His expression was shuttered as always. 'You have to let me go, Daniele.'

'Is that what you want?' His voice sounded odd, as if he had swallowed broken glass.

Paloma stared through the windscreen. 'Yes.'

Daniele stood up straight and dropped his hand down from the car. 'Then go, *mio piccola*.'

Why had he called her his little one, and sounded so wrecked, as if she had ripped his heart out? It must have been her imagination. Daniele did not have a heart. Paloma wiped her eyes and concentrated on the road. The traffic was busy on the way to the airport. She drove for a few miles on the highway and noticed that a black car was close behind. She kept glancing in her rear-view mirror and became convinced that she was being followed.

Fear cramped in her stomach at the memory of when a car had tried to force the motorbike off the road. She had been so desperate to leave the palazzo that she'd forgotten the threat to her safety, especially as she was without a bodyguard. Making a quick decision, she left the highway at the next junction and sped down a lane leading to a village. The black car was some way behind her. She shot down a side road and pulled over, relieved when she saw her pursuer drive past the turning to the road. Her hands shook as she fumbled in her handbag for her phone. There was only one person she wanted to call.

'*Cara?*'

'Daniele, I'm being followed. It could be the same people who tried to run us off the road near the farmhouse.' Paloma's fragile composure cracked. 'Suppose they try to kidnap me?'

'It's all right. You are safe. The threat to you is over,' Daniele said quickly. 'The kidnappers have been arrested. The leader of the criminal gang is a man called Alberto Facchetti, who is the board member Gianluca Orsi's son-in-law. Gianluca knew the contents of your grandfather's will and he let slip to Facchetti that if you died, the fortune you had inherited from Marcello would be split between the trustees. I guess that after Gianluca had received his share of the money, his son-in-law planned to get rid of him too. I remembered Facchetti's name from when I'd foiled the Mafia plot to kidnap Marcello years ago.' He paused. 'I planned to tell you all of this, but when I got back to the palazzo, I was shocked that you were leaving me.'

'So who has been following me?' Paloma asked shakily.

Daniele hesitated. 'Purely for my peace of mind, I asked one of my security guys to make sure you arrived at the airport safely.'

'Because my grandfather asked you to protect me,' she muttered.

'I would gladly spend the rest of my life taking care of you,' Daniele said roughly. 'There is more to tell you. When your great-uncle Franco learned of the threats against you and the suspicion that he was behind your kidnapping in Mali, he was horrified that you could think he would want to harm you. He is deeply sorry that he had bugged your office and has given an assurance that he will destroy the recording of your phone conversation. Franco withdrew his bid to become the head of Morante Group, and the trustees and shareholders have agreed that you will be your grandfather's successor immediately. I will retain my place as a lifelong member of the board and act as your advisor if you want me to. It all means that you do not have to stay married to me. We can divorce and you will be free to fall in love and find the happiness you deserve.'

Paloma gripped her phone tightly. Tears slid silently down her face. Was this goodbye? Would she ever see Daniele again? 'The things you said at the meeting…'

'Every word came from my heart, *cara*.'

After Daniele had cut the call, he'd switched off his phone. Paloma's silence had told him that he'd lost her, and he would not put himself through the additional torture of hoping she would call back. When he had watched her drive away from the palazzo, he'd felt like the five-year-old boy who had wept when his mother had left.

Being at the palazzo had been unbearable without Paloma, and he had jumped onto the motorbike immediately after she had gone. But it was no better at the farmhouse, where memories of her were everywhere. He lost track of time while he was wrapped up in his thoughts of what a fool he had been to realise too late what she meant to him. He stepped out of the kitchen into the courtyard. The sun was fiercely bright. He should have worn sunglasses. His eyes were streaming. He pinched the bridge of his nose and swallowed the lump that had lodged in his throat. He was a grown man, a tough soldier, and he should not be crying, but he could not stop the tears that seeped from beneath his eyelashes.

Dio, he was in hell. He thought he heard a car, but no one ever came here. The farmhouse had been his sanctuary, but he would sell it. Move on. Get over her.

Sure he would.

He roared like a beast in pain. *'Paloma!'*

'Daniele.'

He turned slowly and knew he had lost it completely. Paloma could not be standing in the courtyard, a vision of beauty in a buttercup-yellow dress, with her hair falling in a silky curtain around her shoulders. 'You...you came back.'

'You sounded...' She stared at his wet face. 'Are you hurt?'

'I'm in agony.' He strode towards her, and his heart kicked because she was real, not a vision in his imagination. 'I stood in front of a room full of people and laid my heart on the line. And you left me,' he said rawly.

A tear slipped down her cheek. 'I thought you said...

those things…to convince the trustees. It was part of the game we have been playing.'

He shook his head. 'It was never a game, although I tried telling myself I was doing you a favour by marrying you so that you could claim your place at the company.' Daniele lifted his hand and touched her hair to make sure she was real. 'I was in the ambulance with your grandfather when he died. He gave me your grandmother's engagement ring and told me to keep it with me and give it to the woman who captured my heart. You did that a long time ago, *cara*, but I was too afraid to admit that I loved you. I was afraid that love wouldn't last, and you would leave.' He swallowed. 'And you did.'

'I came back.' Paloma stepped closer to Daniele and stared at his face ravaged by pain. He had said he was in agony, and it was there in the bleakness of his eyes, the trails of moisture on his cheeks. 'You really love me,' she whispered in awe. He had said he was afraid, and she understood that fear. Love was scary. It took courage to risk your heart and soul, but she knew she was brave enough and strong enough to love this strong, brave man.

'I love you, and you love me, so why are we both crying, my darling?'

Light flared in his eyes, hope and adoration that made Paloma tremble.

'*Tesoro.*' Daniele's voice cracked as he wrapped his arms around her and hauled her against his big chest, where his heart was thundering. '*Ti amo, ti adoro, mio cuore.*'

He rested his brow against hers and simply held her, and their two hearts beat as one. And then he kissed her reverently and with so much love that more tears slipped down Paloma's cheeks.

'Tears of joy,' she told him softly. 'My heart belongs to you, and I will never take it away. It is yours for ever, my love.'

'Show me,' Daniele murmured when he carried her into the farmhouse and up to the bedroom. They showed each other with tender kisses that became fiercer and more urgent as passion caught light and became an inferno.

Love that they both knew would last a lifetime.

EPILOGUE

'OUR FIRST WEDDING ANNIVERSARY.' Paloma smiled at her husband, and her heart missed a beat when Daniele's handsome face broke into a broad smile.

He smiled a lot these days. Gone was the enigmatic man who had kept her at a distance. He shared his thoughts and hopes and fears with her as she did with him. But most of all they shared a love that grew stronger every day.

'Next year I'm going to take you away for a private anniversary celebration,' Daniele told her. 'Just the three of us.' He looked down at the baby boy Paloma was cradling in her arms and his smile became so tender that tears pricked her eyes. They both adored little Luigi, who had arrived a month ago with minimal fuss. Paloma was grateful that she had everything she wanted most in the world—love and a family of her own. Luigi's birth had brought their extended family together.

She looked across the airy sitting room to where the baby's two grandmothers were sitting and chatting. Her mother had descended on the palazzo with enough luggage to stay for a year, although she was only visiting for a week, and a new husband, the Spanish duke she had met at Paloma and Daniele's wedding.

Claudia Farnesi was now a regular visitor at the palazzo, as was Daniele's half-brother, Stefano, who had recently married his pretty chalet maid. Daniele's relationship with his mother was a gradual process, but baby Luigi had helped break the ice. Paloma had decided to work part-time so that she could be with her baby son as much as possible, and she had made Franco joint head of Morante Group. He had been deeply upset that she'd believed he could have been behind her kidnap ordeal, and now he was her firm ally and business advisor, which allowed Daniele to concentrate on his own hugely successful business.

Luigi was asleep, and she laid him in his crib. Daniele caught hold of her hand and led her out onto the balcony, where they were alone.

'Happy anniversary, *tesoro mio*,' he said softly as he opened a small velvet box. Inside was an exquisite sapphire-and-diamond eternity ring that perfectly matched her engagement ring. 'I will love you for eternity.'

* * * * *

If you were captivated by
The Italian's Bargain for His Bride,
why not dive into these other Chantelle Shaw stories?

Proof of Their Forbidden Night
Her Wedding Night Negotiation
Housekeeper in the Headlines
The Greek Wedding She Never Had
Nine Months to Tame the Tycoon

Available now!

THE RULES OF THEIR
RED-HOT REUNION

JOSS WOOD

MILLS & BOON

CHAPTER ONE

WALKING DOWN THE stone pathway bisecting the emerald green swathe of grass, Aisha Shetty sent Ro Miya-Matthews's huge stomach a worried look. They'd just left the St Urban manor house, which would, under Aisha's direction, become a six-star boutique.

Enchanted that this amazing two-hundred-year-old building was going to be her base for the foreseeable future—six months, maybe more—Aisha couldn't wait to see what else St Urban had to offer. She just hoped her new boss didn't go into labour before they reached the old wine cellars, the next stop on their tour of St Urban.

The woman was waddling like a duck…a very pregnant, about-to-pop duck.

'How long to go?' Aisha gestured to her stomach, shortening her long stride to accommodate Ro's waddle.

Ro pulled a face. 'Eight weeks. I'm carrying twins, boys, and they are, apparently, huge.'

Aisha's eyebrows flew up. 'Seriously?'

'Seriously,' Ro replied, placing her hands on her hips and arching her back. Her stomach lifted and, underneath her tight T-shirt, Ro saw her stomach ripple. Ro placed her hand on the bump, her blue eyes soft and full of joy. 'I promised Muzi I'd start taking it easy, so I'm thrilled we managed to finalise your contract and that you are here.'

Aisha thought about the contract she'd signed and had to physically stop herself from dancing on the spot. As one of ten consultants working for Lintel & Lily, an international company dedicated to designing, decorating, renovating, and establishing boutique hotels all over the world, she'd been awarded the contract to implement Ro's ambitious vision for St Urban.

The building renovations were all done and the house stood empty. From wallpaper to the waitstaff uniforms, labourers to the layout of the gardens, it was her job to take this now structurally sound, empty building and turn it into a super-luxurious home away from home.

And if she was successful, she would be in the running for a promotion to Chief of Operations when Miles Lintel, her direct boss, became CEO when her famous and wealthy father retired at the end of the year.

The title of Chief of Operations would come with more pressure, a huge jump in salary, and stress, but she'd finally be able to have a home base, buy a home, create her nest.

She'd been working out of hotel rooms and rented accommodation for nearly ten years, and she wanted to sleep in a bed she'd purchased, look at art she'd chosen, cook in a kitchen she'd designed.

She was tired of being a professional vagrant, a wealthy world wanderer. She'd still have to do some travelling, but she'd have her own home, roots, a city she could call hers. Established in South Africa, the now international company of Lintel & Lily had headquarters in both Johannesburg and London, and either city was an option for her home base.

Since her family—parents and four sisters—lived in Cape Town, she was probably going to choose London. She and her family tended to get along a lot better when there were ten thousand miles and a continent between them.

'Do you like the manager's cottage, Aisha?' Ro asked her, sounding a little worried.

Aisha thought of the two-bedroom cottage tucked into the trees at the back of the property with its amazing view of the toothy Simonsberg mountain. It was the beginning of autumn and the weather was still lovely, but winter was wet and cold in the Western Cape. Her cottage had a wood-burning fireplace, a cosy lounge, and a soft queen-size bed. It was beautifully, tastefully decorated and she'd be fine there.

'It's lovely, thank you,' she told Ro.

Ro's phone buzzed and she excused herself, turning away to take the call. Aisha looked around. Similar to the house, the wine cellar was a whitewashed stone building with a modest gable above its entrance, with oak barrels in a temperature-controlled, cavernous room beneath the ground floor. It was situated on the other side of a grove of oak trees, the leaves of the trees turning gold and orange. The grounds of St Urban were extensive, and a small river ran between the vineyards and the buildings. It was romantic and lovely and there were worse places to spend the next few months.

But Aisha still couldn't wait to settle into her own house, a place that was completely hers, surrounded by the things she'd spent the last ten years collecting. She'd take her time to find her perfect home, her first real home.

She couldn't believe eleven years had passed, give or take a week or two, since she'd last lived in the Cape. Over a decade since she met Pasco, ten years since their divorce. Five years since she last spoke to her parents... and she couldn't remember when last she spoke to three of her four sisters.

Like her parents, who were university professors, the Shetty sisters were all academically brilliant and unbelievably perfect. But Aisha was only on speaking terms with Priya, the only family member to stand up for her all those years ago. Priya, always the peacemaker, was overly excited about Aisha being back in the Cape and kept dropping hints about her rejoining the family flock.

'You can't be the black sheep for ever, Aisha.'

Aisha responded by telling her to hold her beer...

Being the only non-brilliant sibling, and the youngest, she'd always stood on the outside of the family circle, the one who never quite fitted in. At school, she'd been referred to as Hema's, Isha's, Priya's or Reyka's sister, and she doubted any of the teachers knew her real name. Academically average, she walked in their shadows, blinded by their light, constantly falling short of her siblings' many successes.

She'd been their sister, her parents' daughter, and then Pasco's wife. It had taken a teenage rebellion, a crap marriage, and a heartbreaking divorce, working demon hours to establish her career—basically, a long, long time—to become Aisha, and she was damned if she'd put herself in any situation that would make her question her self-worth or her place in the world.

So...no. Throwing herself back into those piranha-infested waters wasn't something she was keen to do.

'As I mentioned, we asked various landscape designers to submit their landscaping ideas and I'd like to sit down with you to discuss them,' Ro said after ending her call. She walked down the side of the building and stopped where the building ended. 'We need to get the plants in so they will be established by the time we open.'

The St Urban boutique hotel was due to open in November, a scant five and a half months away. And there was still so much to do: staff to hire and train, rooms to decorate, a marketing plan to activate. And it was her job to make St Urban picture perfect so that things ran like clockwork from the day St Urban opened its two-hundred-year-old doors to paying guests. Ro Miya-Matthews was paying L&L big bucks to make St Urban one of a handful of six-star boutique hotels in Africa.

She'd established a hotel on the edge of the Virunga National Park, in Rwanda and the Bahamas, in Goa and Bhutan. Despite her being the family dunce—her parents and sisters had genius IQs—she'd done very well for herself, thank you very much. In her eyes, not theirs.

Establishing St Urban as a boutique hotel was a challenge, but one she was more than up to. Especially since there was the possibility of a promotion at the end of the project.

'I'm happy to look at your landscapers' plans,' Aisha replied as they resumed walking. 'Are all the building renovations done?'

Ro rocked her hand up and down. 'The tilers are just finishing up the bathroom in Suite Ten and Suite Five is being painted. The builders have told me they'll be out by the end of the week.'

Aisha was glad to hear it as she was expecting her decorating team, and the steady stream of furniture, to arrive over the next few weeks and months.

They walked around to the back of the building and Aisha immediately noticed one third of the brick wall was missing and had been replaced with floor-to-ceiling windows. She didn't recall any alterations to the cellar in the stack of documents she'd been sent.

'Ro?'

Ro turned to look at her, her stomach leading the way. 'Mmm?'

'This is new,' she stated, stepping up to the wood-and-steel structure. She cupped her hands around her face and peered into the small room through the dusty window, seeing craftsmen sanding the gorgeous yellow wood floor.

'What's going on in there?' Aisha asked her, dropping her hands.

Excitement flashed through Ro's deep blue eyes. 'Ah, that's a bit of a last-minute project.'

'What's the project?' Aisha asked, hoping whatever Ro had planned for the space wasn't too off the wall and wouldn't add numerous items to her already mammoth to-do list.

'I want a high-end, fine-dining restaurant in this space and plan on inviting exciting, interesting chefs to run the place for a limited time.'

A restaurant? For fine dining? What the hell was Ro thinking? And did she know how much work that would involve? Aisha hadn't planned to open a restaurant, for God's sake! It wasn't in the budget either.

Not that money was a problem—thanks to inheriting her biological parents' massive estate, Ro could easily add another million, or five, to the budget.

'The restaurant will accommodate up to fifteen people at a time, and I want an innovative, expensive, talk-about-it-for-ever food experience. A place that will be so exclusive, so amazing it will take months, perhaps even years to get a reservation.'

Oh, dear God. This was worse than she'd thought. One of her first solo projects was the establishment of a fine-dining restaurant in Hong Kong and it had been a job from hell. Thanks to that nightmare, she and Miles now had an agreement: she'd work her tail off for Lintel & Lily and Miles kept her away from restaurants and picky, demanding, arrogant chefs.

The Hong-Kong-based chef had reminded her of Pasco: like her ex, he'd been arrogant, pushy, and extraordinarily self-confident.

Aisha placed her hand on her sternum, trying, as she always did, to push away the spike of hurt, the burst of resentment. Her brief marriage—nine months from the time they met to the time they separated, a year until their divorce—wasn't something she liked to think about. But St Urban was situated in Franschhoek, Pasco's home town, so she supposed it was natural thoughts of him kept crossing her mind.

Aisha didn't keep track of him; in fact, she actively avoided articles about him. But she knew he had a restaurant in Franschhoek village and spent most of his time in New York, overseeing his Michelin-starred restaurants in Manhattan.

The young sous chef she'd met in Johannesburg the year after she left school was now a household name, and a multibillionaire thanks to his restaurants, his range of food and kitchen accessories, and his wildly successful travel and cookery show. He was one of the younger, hipper and better-looking celebrity chefs and was regarded to be a rock star in the culinary world.

He'd created the life he wanted, had achieved more than he'd said he would. Aisha couldn't help wishing he'd put a fraction of his considerable energy and drive into their relationship and marriage. If he'd given her a little of the attention he'd given his career, she wouldn't have walked out on him with a sliced and diced heart. She'd thought he could fix the wounds her family inflicted, but he'd just deepened them, then poured acid into her bleeding cuts.

To find herself, to become whole, to heal, leaving him had been oh-so-necessary. Ro patted her arm. 'Miles told me you'd be fine with this, especially since you'll have help to get the restaurant off the ground.'

What type of help?

'I have someone who will give input into planning the space, and on what equipment will be needed. He's an old friend of my husband's and we trust him implicitly.'

Aisha just managed to hide her wince. Who was this guy and how much did he know about luxe dining restaurants? There was absolutely no point in spending a hundred million plus to establish a hotel for it to be let down by a less than spectacular restaurant.

Establishing an on-site restaurant was an excellent idea, in concept. She could see a tasting restaurant here…small, exclusive, lovely. But the design and the concept had to take inspiration from the hotel, as she explained to Ro.

'I understand that, I do. But my guy has a huge amount of experience and knows what he is doing.'

Aisha saw the stubborn tilt to Ro's chin and sighed. She'd come back to the subject of her consultant chef later. 'Do you have any architect plans? Have you consulted with an interior designer? One of Lintel & Lily's or anyone else?'

'No and no.'

Damn.

Aisha far preferred to work from detailed plans and briefs and she wasn't a fan of freestyling. She didn't like imposing her design preferences on a space that wasn't hers—too much could go wrong!—and chefs, in particular, were a nightmare to work with. They didn't take orders, or even suggestions, well.

What to do? How to handle this?

Aisha heard the low rumble of male voices coming from the side of the building. She watched Ro, standing at the corner of the building, turn and heard her release a long quiet sigh. Her eyes softened and her mouth curved, and a look of pure bliss crossed her face.

Aisha recognised that look, knew it well. It was how a woman in love looked at her man; it was the way she'd looked at Pasco a lifetime ago. She'd loved him completely, as much as any woman could love her guy. She'd thought that if she made him the centre of her world, she'd become the centre of his and he'd give the love and attention she'd been missing all her life.

But Pasco's job was his first love—his only love, his mistress, and his reason to wake up every morning. She'd come, maybe, a distant fourth or fifth, or tenth, on his list of priorities.

A tall man wearing expensive chino shorts and a yellow T-shirt, a perfect foil for his dark brown skin, hurried over to Ro and laid a possessive hand on her stomach and covered her mouth with his. He pulled back and tucked a strand of Ro's hair behind her ear, his expression chiding.

'Sweetheart, you've been on your feet all day. You need to rest.'

'Don't fuss, Muzi,' Ro told him. She gestured to Aisha.

'Meet Aisha, our get-it-up-and-running manager,' Ro told her husband, pulling a face at Aisha. 'Sorry, I've forgotten your official title.'

Aisha grinned. 'Officially, I'm a hotel management consultant, but what you said works just as well,' Aisha said, shaking Muzi's massive hand. 'It's nice to meet you, Muzi.'

'And you, Aisha,' Muzi said. He looked over her shoulder and jerked his head. 'Ah, he's done with his call.'

A tall man stepped around the corner of the house, and Aisha felt the blood drop from her head, her brain short-circuit. The world faded in and out, and Aisha heard a roar in her ears, the sound of an incoming train coming in to flatten her. This couldn't be happening to her...

It could *not* be happening.

'Aisha Shetty, meet Pasco Kildare.'

Oh, man, it was absolutely happening.

His first thought was, *There she is*, the second was that she looked amazing and the third, roaring in behind the others, was that he still wanted her.

When his brain restarted, Pasco, who'd had more practice at hiding his shock than Aisha—hers was the most expressive face he'd ever encountered—stared at her, hoping his expression remained impassive.

But, God, his ex-wife looked good. No, that was a ridiculous statement, she looked spectacular. She was tall and still slim, with a pair of legs that made his mouth water. A tangerine and white dress, her small waist highlighted by a thin leather belt, skimmed her slim frame and ended two inches above her pretty knees, the backs of which were ticklish.

Her hair was longer than it was when she was younger, pulled back from her face and hitting the middle of her back in a tumble of sable-black curls. Her triangular face was, achingly, the same. High and defined cheekbones, a full, lush mouth made for kissing and big black eyes framed by mile-long eyelashes.

He'd thought her lovely at nineteen; she was exquisite now. This stunning woman had once been his wife. He'd made promises to her, she to him, promises neither of them had been able to keep. They'd failed, he'd failed, and failure wasn't something he spoke about or advertised.

Pasco ran his hand over his face, thinking back on their impulsive decision to marry, three or so weeks after they first met. He'd needed to return to Johannesburg to start work as a sous chef under one of the country's best chefs and hadn't been able to see how, with his long hours, they'd manage a long-distance relationship. She'd told him her parents would never give permission for her to leave Cape Town, or for them to live together. Not wanting to lose her, he'd suggested they get married.

She'd surprised him by agreeing and a few days later they'd said their 'I do's in a dingy courthouse.

On a sexual and emotional high, with her reeling from a brutal fight with her parents, they'd left for Johannesburg and moved into his small flat. It had taken him less than a week to realise he was no longer responsible for just himself, he was now responsible for her: her safety, security, and well-being were in his hands. By signing that marriage certificate, he was now a husband and was under contract—in his mind at least—to provide her with stability, a home, and a decent lifestyle.

Remembering his up-and-down childhood, the famines and the feasts, he'd had a mini panic attack at the thought.

All he'd known back then was that he couldn't be like his dad, hurt Aisha the way his dad had hurt his mum. He'd known what it was like to live with uncertainty, to be scared of what tomorrow could bring, and he'd vowed, lying on their small bed in their rabbit-hutch apartment, that he'd be the husband his dad never was. He'd work as hard as he could, be successful, be a man she would be proud to call her husband. He'd show his dad, wherever the hell he was, what true success looked like. How to have it all...

In that small bed, her half lying on him, he'd vowed to give her everything. He'd never give her an excuse to leave him, a reason to walk away, leaving tornado-like devastation behind.

But, ironically, that was exactly what Aisha did.

'Hello, Aisha,' he said, rocked off his feet when her eyes slammed into his. 'It's been a while.'

The last time he'd seen her was when he'd left for work on an early autumn morning, thinking he'd see her later, if not after the lunch service, then when he was done for the day. He clearly remembered the night before she left, how excited he'd been to tell her he'd been offered big money to take an executive chef position at a new exclusive restaurant in London. They were on their way...

He'd brought home a bottle of champagne and he'd guzzled it, telling her of his plans, how he'd use this opportunity to look for investors in his own place. She'd have to stay in South Africa for a few weeks, maybe a month or two, while she waited for her visa, but he'd find a home for them, set it up so it was ready for her when she arrived.

She'd congratulated him, they'd made love and he'd finally fallen asleep, excited about their future. This was his big chance, and he couldn't wait. Life was finally looking up.

He'd returned to an empty flat that night. Initially, he'd thought she was out with friends, a little concerned she was out so late. At midnight he'd been worried, by one a.m., he'd been frantic. At two a.m., he'd considered phoning the police. At two-ten, he'd found her note on his pillow...

The words were still printed on his brain.

Congratulations on your job offer but this isn't working and we both know it. I can't do this, us, any more. Set London on fire, Pas. A.

'Hello, Pasco.'

Muzi's sharp eyes bounced between them. 'You two know each other?'

Pasco couldn't help his cynical smile. 'We were married for about ten minutes a long time ago.'

Muzi's eyebrows lifted. 'You were *married*? Seriously? And why the hell didn't I know?'

Pasco looked at Aisha, who was rocking from foot to foot. At Aisha's insistence, he'd waited in the car while Aisha told her family she'd married him and then left the house, lugging a massive suitcase and cradling a heavy box under her free arm, her brown-black eyes wide with anguish. Her parents hadn't taken the news well, she'd told him, and she didn't know if she'd ever be welcomed back into their house.

They'd planned to visit his parents the same day, but Aisha, upset and emotional, hadn't been up to it and they'd left Cape Town without telling anyone else about their court marriage. Not wanting to break the news over the phone, he'd thought he'd tell his folks when they made one of their trips to Johannesburg, but for some reason they never made a trip that winter. Thinking they'd tell his friends and family when they returned to Cape Town at Christmas—maybe even have a church ceremony and a wedding reception—he never imagined that by September they would be separated, and divorced by Christmas.

Before Pasco could answer Muzi, Ro walked over to Aisha and placed her hand on her shoulder. 'I am sorry, I had no idea you and Pasco were married—' Ro tossed him a hot glare '—and this must be a bit of a shock for you. Let's meet again in a day or two and we can talk about the restaurant, his involvement, and you two working together then.'

He was about to speak when Aisha held up her hand. Her skin was paler than her normal shade of light golden brown, her eyes as hard as a chunk of coal. 'I'm sorry, I've lost you. What do you mean?'

Ro wrinkled her nose and gestured to the renovations. 'You're going to be working with Pasco to get the restaurant up to world-class standards,' Ro told her, looking uncomfortable. 'He's my chef consultant.'

Aisha briefly closed her eyes, and Pasco counted to ten, waiting for her to lose her cool. Aisha was fundamentally unable to step back and look at a situation through an unemotional lens.

'Whether or not Pasco and I were married has absolutely no bearing on my ability to do my job. I am one of the best and most experienced consultants in the company and a quick relationship so long ago will not affect me in the least.'

Both Muzi and Ro released a relieved sigh, and Pasco scratched his neck, surprised at her unemotional response. He couldn't help admiring the way she pushed back her shoulders and straightened her spine. She'd grown up, he thought, become more resilient. But a *quick* relationship? God. Her words pissed him off and he felt like a fly she'd brushed off her sleeve.

'I'm a professional and I'll deal,' she told them. 'On the scale of disasters, this doesn't even blip on my radar.'

Good for her, but he couldn't work with someone who made his heart race, his mouth dry, and who'd derailed his life. He wasn't scared of hard work, relished a challenge, but expecting him to work with his ex-wife—the woman who walked out on him—was asking him for more than he could give. She'd disrupted his life once and he'd never give her, or any other girl, the power to do that again.

But she wasn't a girl any more, she was a woman. In every sense of the word.

A very sexy, very remote, incredibly beautiful woman. And he still wanted her with a desperation he could taste. One that scared him senseless. Another good reason for them not to work together.

'I'm so glad to hear that, Aisha. Thank you,' Ro said, smiling.

Muzi wrapped his arm around Ro's thick waist. 'If you don't need Ro for anything else, Aisha, I'm going to take my wife home,' Muzi said. When Ro didn't complain, Pasco knew she was more tired than she let on. Or maybe they were trying to give him and Aisha some time alone. Who the hell knew?

His temper was simmering, and it wouldn't take much to ignite. He wasn't ready to be alone with Aisha or anyone, so he gestured to the path that would take them back to the hotel. 'Let's all head that way,' he suggested, his words a few degrees below freezing.

Ro sent him a tentative smile. 'Actually, I'd appreciate it if you could show Aisha the restaurant space, tell her what we are thinking,' Ro said. 'That would help me, Pas.'

Pasco turned to look in the direction of his car, wondering how long it would take him to reach it. He wanted to slide behind the wheel, crank the ignition, and rocket away. He didn't need the complication of revisiting the past, wasn't keen to dredge up old memories. To re-examine the past.

Ro waddled over to him—there was no other word for it—stood on her tiptoes and placed a kiss on his cheek. 'Thank you, I appreciate it.'

What? He hadn't said he would!

Ro told Aisha she'd touch base with her later and linked her fingers with Muzi. Pasco watched them go and, when they were out of hearing range, turned to look at Aisha again. Best to make things clear, here and now.

'This is my town, my friends, my part of the world. I'm not interested in working with you and I'm sure your company can replace you without too much trouble,' he said, his voice hard.

It took a few seconds for his words to sink in and, when they did, her eyes flashed and her nostrils flared.

'My job, my career, and I'm not going anywhere,' Aisha told him, her words coated with frustration and annoyance. 'You leave and I'll hire another restaurant consultant. I know more than a few and I don't need you.'

Yeah, she'd made that abundantly clear when she left him. Pasco gripped the bridge of his nose with his thumb and index finger, trying to banish the headache that strolled in and settled down. 'Ro is my friend and she asked me to consult on her restaurant, but I can't work with you. If you need me to, I'll talk to your boss. Give me his number.'

Her mouth dropped open and her eyes glittered with fury. 'You arrogant ass! Who do you think you are? I do not need you to talk to my boss because I'm not going anywhere. And my boss is a woman, you patronising jerk!'

'I just meant...' Why was he explaining? Goddammit! 'I need you to leave, Aisha. Just go.'

'You go!' Aisha whipped back, her temper turning her cheeks rosy. 'I'd rather be bitten by a Cape Cobra than work with you. You're the superstar chef, the one with various fingers in various pies. St Urban is my only pie, so leave it alone!

'I signed a contract, and this job is important to me, crucial to my career,' Aisha told him. She drilled a finger into his chest, so close he could see the subtle shades of colour in her black-brown irises, the tiny scar on the top of her lip. She'd changed her scent and now wore something sharp and sexy, head-spinning. Thoughts of restaurants and hotels receded and memories of her lithe and lovely body, naked of course, flashed behind his eyes. It took every shred of willpower he possessed not to lower his head, to cover her mouth with his, to drag her into his arms.

And if he did that, he might find himself on the receiving end of her right hook. She might look like the older version of the girl he married, but she'd grown up, become tougher, harder, more of a warrior.

He didn't know whether to be furious or fascinated.

Oblivious to where his mind wandered, Aisha shoved her hand into her thick hair and seared him with a hot look. 'I am staying here, and I will do my job, and that includes establishing this restaurant. If you decide to be a part of the process, you will treat me with courtesy and respect. Are we clear?'

When he didn't respond other than to raise his eyebrows, she threw her hands in the air and spun away.

She took a couple of steps before stopping to toss a furious look over her shoulder. 'I have work to do, Kildare, and you are wasting my time.'

CHAPTER TWO

LATER THAT MORNING and back in her office at St Urban, Aisha stepped out of her heels and walked across one of the two Persian carpets in her office towards the bank of windows looking out onto the extensive vineyards. In summer they would be lush and green and in winter they'd looked like little old men resting their arms on wire strands. Right now the leaves were turning and falling, creating little pops of autumnal colour across the lands. Aisha knew Muzi's company, Clos du Cadieux, rented the vineyards from Ro and she recalled reading about a rare, old country wine cultivar Muzi discovered on this property. St Urban, the property passed down to Ro by her infamous biological mother, Gia Tempest-Vane, was where Ro and Muzi fell in love.

It was a beautiful building, and the renovations to the centuries-old house were sensitively undertaken. When she brought the original handcrafted furniture back in, after having the pieces restored and French-polished, and replaced the cleaned paintings, the property would start coming to life. She could see it so clearly: luxury furnishings, amazing art, discreet staff on hand to fulfil the biggest or smallest wish, classical music piping through the common areas of the house, and the beautiful views of the vineyards and mountains enticing the guests to kick back and relax. She could make this place one of the favourite bolt-holes of the rich, famous, and stressed.

She just had to ignore Pasco Kildare while she created magic.

Aisha ran her hands up and down her arms, unable to stop thinking about Pasco. Man, he looked wonderful: sexy and strong. Ten years and a little maturity looked good on him. And just like that, she recalled his clever, mobile mouth on hers, the way he kissed. His large, skilled hands on her skin, how he could make her tremble with just one hot look. It had been so long ago, but it seemed like yesterday. She could still smell the scent of their small apartment when he cooked spaghetti bolognese, the rumble of their tired air conditioner, and the sound of taxis hooting at the crack of dawn.

Memories of their brief marriage bombarded her: their small apartment and the double bed they shared, the small desk tucked into the corner of the living room. Mismatched cutlery and crockery, the old, battered two-seater leather couch he'd found at a yard sale. The smell of his skin and the way his arms held her tight when they slept. He always groaned, then sighed when he slid into her always-willing body. He'd greet her, whether they'd been apart ten minutes or ten hours, by placing his hand on her lower back, pulling her into him—her shirt wrapped around his fist—as he plundered her mouth. He always kissed her as if he was never going to see her again and Aisha now wondered if he'd subconsciously known they would never last.

He'd been in love with his career and she'd been in love with the idea of being married, of being Pasco's wife. At nineteen, lonely, insecure, and looking for attention, she'd desperately wanted to be at the centre of the family she and Pasco created, to walk through life with a teammate, someone who had her back, someone who made her the centre of his world.

She'd met him in a pub, immediately entranced by his innate confidence. He was the guy all the men wanted to be and whom all the girls wanted to be with. She hadn't expected him to notice her, never mind spend the rest of the evening talking to her. He was a chef, he'd told her that night, but wanted his own restaurant, then a bunch of them.

She'd smiled at his ambition, liking the fact he knew where he was going and how he was going to get there. It took her a month to realise Pasco's journey required fourteen-to-sixteen-hour days, and another six months to acknowledge he was a workaholic and he had no intention of slowing down, not even for her.

Maybe things wouldn't have been as bad if lack of time was their only problem, but she'd never been an equal partner in their marriage. Pasco didn't play well in that particular sandbox. He refused to relinquish any control over anything. From finances to the future, Pasco had it all planned, and her input was either ignored or dismissed. And when she did push a point, he distracted her with sex or told her he was tired and didn't want to fight, promising to make time for them to talk. He seldom, if ever, did.

It took a while, but she eventually realised they were driving Pasco's car on Pasco's highway and she was just along for the ride.

After a few dismal months of isolation and loneliness, interspersed with stunning sex, she finally realised she'd left one gilded cage to fly into another.

She'd been a needy, neglected, unseen teenager. And then she became a needy, neglected, unseen wife...

A bird flew close to the window and Aisha jumped at the sudden movement. She'd been lost in the past and she couldn't afford to let that happen. She had to live in the world as it was, not how she wished it to be.

And that meant working with Pasco to establish Ro's vision of a space to host fine-dining, pop-up restaurants. Ro was her client and keeping her client happy was how she was going to impress her boss and the board, and it was her path to promotion. Chief of Operations was as far as she could climb up the ladder of the family-owned business, and she'd be second in command. She could live with that.

For now. Aisha recalled Pasco's demand for her to leave St Urban and snorted. His arrogance was breathtaking. But Pasco had never been shy to state what he wanted; his needs and desires were paramount. Ten years ago, his career took precedence over everything else, and she was expected to fall into line with his plans.

That wasn't going to happen. She would not adjust her plans, change her course simply because he wanted her to, because he demanded it. She'd been raised in a passive-aggressive household—outright conflict was something the Shetty family avoided at all costs—but the subtle war of words, snide put-downs and coated-with-sugar insults had been just as brutal. In her years away from her family, and Pasco, she'd learned to be direct, say no, to push back and stand her ground.

She didn't like confrontation, but neither did she avoid it.

Pasco wasn't going to be able to manipulate her, manoeuvre her, distract her. She'd grown up, thank God.

Aisha tapped her lip with her index finger. This St Urban project was going to be trickier than most because the players in the game were all connected. Ro was married to the most influential winemaker in the country, someone who had an international reputation for excellence, and he was a close friend of the Tempest-

Vane brothers. They were the billionaire owners of various companies, including The Vane Hotel, one of the best in the world. They'd used Lintel & Lily's services before and were regarded as especially important clients.

And Muzi's best friend was an internally acclaimed chef. And her ex-husband. Why was life punishing her like this?

Oh, and while she was questioning the universe, why couldn't Pasco have lost his hair, got flabby and pasty? It was so damn unfair he was more attractive than he'd been as a young man.

At twenty-four he'd been rangy, a little thin, but some time in the last decade he'd packed on the muscle. His shoulders were definitely broader, his thighs thicker, his arms bigger and, yeah, sexier. The man worked out, that much was obvious, hard, and often. His light brown hair was sun-streaked, and he'd taken to wearing a couple of days' growth on his lower face. Aisha wasn't a fan of stubble, but Pasco's scruff looked good on him.

His eyes, a deep, dark green and framed by short, dark stubby lashes, were as penetrating as ever. He was a harder, hotter version of his younger self and her body, dumb thing, wanted to get naked and roll around with him.

She was not going to be that stupid, she told herself. She would not jeopardise her career, her promotion, her dream for a man. She would never allow herself to be an afterthought, and she would put herself first. It had taken her years to become a confident and independent woman, and she'd never allow herself to be needy or insecure— unseen!—again.

If they were going to work together, and it was looking as if they were, they were going to have to decide on some rules. The first of which would be that she couldn't fall for him again…

Number two would be for her to be an equal partner in the decision-making process, something she hadn't been in their marriage.

Rules would give them boundaries, a box to work within, structure…

The trick would be to get Pasco, not a fan of being told what to do, to buy into the concept.

La Fontaine was Pasco's second home and he adored Mimi, the woman who'd adopted Muzi when he was a kid, but, hell, he'd rather pull off his toenails with pliers than attend one of Mimi's famous cocktail parties. But he'd promised her he would, and Pasco wasn't one to break his promises.

Eight hours after running into his ex-wife, he parked his McLaren Artura—a gift from himself to himself—between a vintage Beetle and a classic Rolls, and rested his forehead on his steering wheel, fighting the urge to reverse and head back home. Or to go back to St Urban, find Aisha, and kiss her senseless. And then take her to bed.

He had to stop thinking about her; if he didn't, he might go completely off his rocker. He didn't want to be here, and neither was he in the mood to talk to his friends.

He most certainly didn't want to smile and be the charming, successful billionaire restaurateur with a bunch of Michelin stars under his belt, the chef with the reputation for innovative food and the pursuit of perfection.

People looked at his life and thought it was wonderful, and it was, but, damn, they didn't know what he'd sacrificed to be this successful, to attain his wealth…

They didn't know he sometimes wondered—mostly in

the early hours of the morning when he couldn't sleep—whether it was all worth it.

A couple of years ago, Luka, his first mentor, passed away and Pasco flew home to attend his funeral service. He remembered his daughter's eulogy, surprised to hear that Luka had questioned whether his long hours spent at the restaurant were worth it, whether he'd make the same sacrifices again to pursue his ambitions. His words hit home and Pasco started to think something was amiss in his own life. When he returned to Manhattan, the feeling grew stronger. He was no longer happy in the fast-paced city, his creativity was stunted, and he was going through the motions, stuck personally and professionally.

He thought that maybe it was time to pare back, slow down, try something else. Believing he might be burned out—so many years of working his ass off in the industry would do that to one—and sick of New York City, he'd sold his extremely successful and famous restaurant in Manhattan, expecting to feel better.

He hadn't.

After taking a month off, bored as hell—deeply concerned he was living off his capital and wasn't earning money—he started to regret selling Pasco's, Manhattan. When Digby Tempest-Vane suggested he establish a fine-dining restaurant at The Vane, he jumped at the opportunity. Not content, he then launched a kitchen accessory line. Thinking he wanted to travel, he agreed to a six-part series to explore cooking cultures of the world and he'd thought visiting new places like Mongolia, Morocco and Réunion would make him feel whole.

It hadn't. He had everything he wanted, but he still felt as though something was missing; something hovered just out of his reach.

Maybe he was the type of guy who would never be

fulfilled, who constantly needed a new challenge to keep moving forward. Having a goal and working towards it was what he'd been doing since he was a kid, desperate to be the exact opposite of his completely useless father.

They looked exactly alike, and Pasco was often referred to as his dad's mini-me. He was an almost carbon copy of him and Pasco hated it.

His father was why he was so driven, so desperate to prove himself, utterly determined to ensure he never placed the people he loved in a situation even remotely similar to the one Gerald had put them in.

With their doctor mother, and stay-at-home dad, they were seen to be a stable, solidly middle-to-upper-class family, but few people saw past the facade his dad showed to the world.

At some point in his childhood, Gerald decided to re-enter the workforce. But it wasn't in his father to take a job, and to stick and to stay. No, he wanted immediate and quick success, a shedload of money in the bank as fast as he could get it.

And because he was impatient and impulsive, he reached for every shiny object that passed him by, latched on to anyone who could provide him with the opportunity to make a quick buck. If there was a get-rich-quick scheme out there, Gerald tried it, always using his wife's salary to fund it. He also opened up numerous credit cards in her name, maxed them out, and then remortgaged their house. They lurched from crisis to crisis and Pasco remembered living with low-grade anxiety as a kid, constantly worried the sky would fall in.

As Pasco hit puberty, Gerald became increasingly desperate and massively irrational… And then everything fell apart.

Pasco pushed the memories away and rubbed his face,

the back of his neck. His father had been good for one thing, he reminded himself. Every time he looked in the mirror he was reminded of what he didn't want to be.

He'd vowed he'd never be poor, that he'd create a life of complete stability for everyone he loved. That he'd work hard for every cent he earned and he'd stay out of debt. His houses were all paid for, so were his cars, he had no credit-card debt. He had business debt, but it was manageable, under control.

Control was of paramount importance to him, and he did not trust anyone else to make decisions about his life or business.

He'd learned from his own and his father's mistakes, and he'd never, ever repeat them. Failure was not an option.

Marriage? Tried that and failed. He'd fallen in love with Aisha and after her parents freaked out about their marriage—she was too young, it was too soon, she needed to finish her studies first!—he'd vowed to protect her. Everything he did, every decision he made, was to ensure she had a stable life, that she was financially secure, and would have a husband she could be proud of.

But, after hearing about his fantastic promotion, she'd thrown all his hard work into his face and killed their marriage with a three-line note.

He'd thought they'd be together for ever, but his instincts and judgement were flawed. Trust someone again, trust his instincts when it came to love? Not a chance in hell. As for working with Aisha? Well, when hell froze over. Muzi and Ro had pots of money, and, as Aisha had suggested, they could hire a new chef consultant, it didn't need to be him. He and Aisha had had no contact for ten years so it would be easy to avoid each other for the next six months.

Pasco jumped at the thump on his car window and whipped his head around to see Muzi's face staring at him through the glass. Sighing, he hit the button for the electric window and waited for it to descend. 'What?' he demanded, scowling at his oldest friend.

Muzi placed both his hands on the sill of the car and stared down at Pasco. 'How did it go with Aisha? Everything sorted?'

That would be a hard no. 'Not yet,' Pasco replied.

'Hell of a thing, running into your ex-wife...the wife you kept from your closest friends and, I presume, from your family.'

Pasco heard the bitterness in Muzi's voice and winced. He pushed his hand through his hair, knowing he owed Muzi and the rest of his friends an apology. 'Her parents reacted badly to our news, so we decided to keep it to ourselves for a while. We knew we'd catch flak for being impulsive, for marrying so young, be questioned about whether we'd done the right thing. It wasn't something I wanted to disclose over the phone and that year was hectic for all of us, and we never made it back to the Cape. By Christmas we were divorced, I was living in London and I just wanted to put it behind me.'

'And did you?' Muzi asked.

He'd thought he had, but on seeing her again, hot and inconvenient attraction had come rushing back in, bold and bright. Aisha, then and now, affected him in ways no other woman managed to. And he didn't bloody like it.

Muzi stood up and ran his hand over his face, still looking irritated. 'You and I don't keep stuff from each other, Kildare. That being said...

'Look, I get seeing Aisha again is not ideal, but Ro needs both of you to get the restaurant up and running. She's stressed, overworking herself. Her blood pressure is up, and the doctors and I are trying to get her to slow down, to relax. She won't do that if she thinks you and Aisha are at odds, if she has to find a new executive chef or a new consultant to get St Urban up and running,' Muzi added, his words coated with a layer of worry. 'It sounds like Aisha is going to stick and stay. I need you to do the same.'

Uh…crap. 'I know of at least three chefs who would jump at the chance to be involved in a pop-up restaurant at St Urban.' Pasco machine-gunned his words.

Muzi bent down again and narrowed his eyes, his lips curling into a feral snarl. 'Do not even go there, Kildare. You promised my wife your help and involvement and she's counting on you. *I'm* counting on you. I'm already pissed off with you for not telling me you were married. Do not compound it by letting my pregnant-with-twins, stressed-out wife down.'

Ah…dammit. Muzi knew exactly what buttons to push. He started his car and sent Muzi a sour look. 'Tell Mimi I'm sorry, that something came up.'

Muzi grinned and tapped the roof of his car. 'Will do. Tell Aisha it was nice meeting her earlier.'

Yep, Muzi knew what buttons to push. Pasco's father had let him down a hundred times in a hundred different ways and Muzi knew he'd never do that to the people he loved. And that was the only reason he was heading back to St Urban to talk to Aisha, to figure out a way for them to work together.

Returning to St Urban had nothing to do with him wanting to see her again, to let his eyes feast on her, to feel the pounding in his head, and groin. It had nothing to do with wanting to inhale her gorgeous scent, to discover all the ways she'd changed and the ways she hadn't.

Nothing at all.

CHAPTER THREE

FURIOUS WITH PASCO, and emotionally and physically exhausted, Aisha decided to leave St Urban and head into Cape Town, thinking that sharing a pizza with Priya would be more fun than spending the night in her new cottage and brooding.

After changing into jeans and a lightweight jersey, she tossed her jacket onto the passenger seat and pulled on her seat belt before plugging Priya's address into her GPS. Although she and her third oldest sister talked often, she hadn't seen her in real life for over five years. It was hard to meet when one of you bounced around the world and the other had two small children, a husband, and a busy career as one of the city's best paediatricians.

She and Priya had always had a strong bond and Priya was the one who had knocked her other sisters back in line when she thought their teasing went too far. Priya had never given her Christmas gifts designed to *fix* her—self-help books, literary classics, or gym memberships—and had never called her the loser sibling as her other sisters often had. She was the one who Aisha had called when she'd needed a ride home during her rebellious phase, who had loaned her money when her parents had punished her by withholding her allowance, the only person who hadn't made her feel like a complete fool when she'd asked for help understanding compound fractions.

After the huge family fallout five years ago, Priya was all the family she had.

It would be good to catch up, play with the kids, to get to know her husband, Oscar, a bit better. To feel as if she wasn't completely alone in the world...

Aisha started her car, pulled away, and started down the tree-lined driveway. As she approached the bridge crossing over the small river, she saw the lights of another car approaching her and frowned. St Urban was private property—no one else was supposed to be on the grounds, so who was this person, and what did he want?

A little nervous, Aisha stopped and locked the doors to her car. She watched as the car stopped on the other side of the bridge and killed its lights. She watched as the car door opened upwards—fancy!—and sighed when she recognised the long-limbed figure climbing out of the vehicle.

Kildare.

Exactly the person she didn't want to see. Aisha pushed her head into the headrest and sighed again. She knew she couldn't avoid Pasco for ever, but she'd hoped for a little more time to get her head straight, her raging emotions under control. Nobody, before or since, had affected her the way Pasco did. He made her incredibly angry and sad, and horny and hot and frustrated...

Pasco stopped in the middle of the bridge, his hands in the pockets of his trousers, and stared at her, his expression unreadable. He wore black trousers, trendy trainers, and a soft-looking sweater the colour of thick clotted cream. The sleeves of the sweater were pushed up his strong, muscular forearms. He was strong and sexy and looked oh-so-unhappy to see her.

There was a time when his eyes warmed when he laid

eyes on her, when his standard greeting was a no-holds-barred kiss, before gifting her with an I'm-so-damn-happy-to-see-you smile.

That was then, this was now.

He'd come halfway across the bridge and his actions suggested she needed to meet him there.

All she'd wanted to do was to go to her sister's place, eat pizza, drink wine and chill, catch up. She did not want to go another round with Pasco Kildare.

But she couldn't go forward—his car was blocking the road—and she couldn't retreat because she didn't want him to think she was avoiding him. Her only option was to leave the car and talk to the damn man.

She'd far prefer to drop a concrete block on her foot.

Sighing, Aisha picked up her jacket and left the car. The sun was setting, the temperature was dropping so she pulled on her leather jacket and wandered over to where he stood.

'Things are dire when you have to block the road to get a girl to talk to you, Kildare,' she told him.

'Don't flatter yourself. I was coming, you were leaving, and we can talk here as easily as we can at St Urban.'

Typical Pasco, she thought. The time and place suited him, but it didn't suit her. 'I'm actually on my way to meet someone so can we talk some other time?' She turned to walk back to her car. Pasco needed to learn the days of her rolling over at his command were long over.

'Got a date?'

A frisson of excitement ran up her spine at the hint of jealousy in his deep voice, and Aisha fought the urge to spin around. After counting to ten, then to twenty, she slowly turned and looked up into his moss-green, forest-deep eyes.

'Yes,' she lied without hesitation or a smidgeon of guilt.

Pasco's jaw hardened and his lips flattened. 'Tough.' An owl hooted and he turned his head towards the sound, his eyes scanning the trees.

'I've decided to help set up the restaurant and am considering Ro's offer to be the guest chef for three months when it opens. I'll send you an email as soon as possible concerning the kitchen equipment specs, what decor I want, the layout.'

Again, he was making assumptions without her input, just as he used to do when they were married. 'That's not going to work for me,' she told him, lifting her chin.

'Why not?' Pasco demanded.

'I'm not your lackey and I don't take orders from you. Secondly, I don't *want* to work with you,' she told him. 'I'm going to convince Ro to find another chef to consult on the restaurant.'

Pasco's frustration-filled eyes collided with hers. 'You will do no such thing.'

'Newsflash, you're not the boss of me.' Really, who did he think he was trying to boss her around? His sous chef? One of his waitstaff? Arrogant jerk!

'Ro is stressed and being stressed isn't good for her or the twins. When she hears we can't work together she'll worry and then Muzi will rip off my head.'

'I don't really care what happens to your head,' Aisha told Pasco.

'But you do care what happens to Ro,' Pasco quickly responded.

Dammit, he had her there. Though she'd only just met her, she liked Ro and she didn't want any harm coming to her or her babies.

'Look, I want to work with you even less than you want to work with me, but Muzi is my best friend and Ro means a lot to me. I try not to disappoint the people I love.'

His words were an arrow straight through her heart. 'Except that you had no problem hurting me!'

As soon as the words left her mouth, she wished she could pull them back. She sounded every inch the wronged and bitter wife. Dammit, she shouldn't be feeling anything for him, not after such a short relationship so long ago!

'Hey, you were the one who left me!' Pasco told her, his voice rising.

'And it was so easy for you to let me go!' Aisha retorted.

What was it about this man that made her temper bubble, her tongue fly? Her childhood home was a shouting-free zone—her professor parents preached dialogue and discussion—and she never lost her temper at work, but Pasco managed to blow every one of her fuses. How was she going to be able to work with him if all they did was shout and/or snipe at each other?

Aisha folded her arms against the chill of the autumn night and looked up at the swathe of stars above her head. It was a beautiful night, and she was in the company of a beautiful man, but one who despised her.

She couldn't blame him for that—she did walk out on him without warning, leaving him a note explaining nothing. If he'd done that to her, she would still be angry too.

At the time she'd known that if she'd tried to explain her thoughts and feelings, explain that he didn't *see* her, that she needed time with him, he'd either kiss, charm, or persuade her into staying. She'd tried to talk to him, but he always deflected the conversation or distracted her before she managed to convey the depths of her unhappiness. And on the rare occasions she had managed to get her point across, he'd made no effort to give her the time she'd so desperately needed.

Talking and staying was a habit, and she'd broken that cycle with a note and by actually leaving.

The past was the past and nothing could be changed. But she could get a handle on what was happening now. Especially since the stakes were so damn high. If she did a good job at St Urban, she'd get a promotion. If she didn't, she wouldn't, and she'd stay where she was, spending months and months in strange countries. Another shot at promotion wouldn't come any time soon, if it came at all.

Just calm down, Shetty...and think!

Ro is your client, and she wants Pasco to work with you. You can't ask her to choose between the two of you because, if you did, you'd probably lose. Pasco is her husband's best friend and it seems Ro and Pasco genuinely like each other.

If you want to work at St Urban, then you have to work with Mr Annoying. Also known as Mr Annoyingly Sexy.

Shaking off the thought, Aisha decided she had to treat Pasco as she would any other consultant.

But with stricter rules.

'We need to establish some goalposts, guidelines...' God, what was she trying to say? 'We need to work out the rules.'

'Rules?' Pasco asked, his expression derisive.

Aisha dropped her hand to nail him with a hard look. 'Yes, I know, you are a hotshot chef who doesn't think rules apply to him, but with our history and if we are going to be working together, then we need some.'

'There's only one rule...' Pasco told her, hands on his hips. 'Do what I want, when I want it, and we'll get along fine.'

Had he changed at all? If she had to judge by that comment, then he hadn't, not even a smidgen. Aisha clenched her fists, her fingernails digging into her palms.

She hoped he was teasing her, but in case he wasn't she couldn't back down, be seen to be weak. If she did, Pasco would gobble her up and spit her out. Not happening. 'You really should see somebody to talk about your delusions of grandeur, Kildare.'

She saw a gleam in his eyes she didn't like but decided to ignore it. 'That tongue of yours has got sharper, Aisha Kildare—'

'Aisha Shetty. I dropped your name as soon as I could.'

Pasco responded with a mocking smile. He slid his hands into the pockets of his trousers and raised his dark eyebrows. 'Why did you come back here, Aisha?'

'What do you mean?' Aisha asked him, confused by the swift change of subject.

'Did you do some research, find out that I am good friends with the Miya-Matthewses and apply for the job to establish St Urban to edge your way back into my life?'

Aisha snorted, amused. But then she realised he was being heart-attack serious. Seriously? 'Why on earth would I be interested in doing that?' she demanded, her tone terse.

'Ten years ago, you left me because I was a poor sous chef, and couldn't give you the life you wanted, the life I promised you, but I'm not poor any more. And I have contacts within the hospitality industry that would be valuable to you, people like the Tempest-Vanes, and other hoteliers all over the world. Hooking back up with me would be a smart move.'

Did he really believe she left him because they lived in a tiny flat and because money was tight? How could he think that? She would've lived in a tin shack with him, anywhere in the world, if he'd given her a little attention, some of his time. She opened her mouth but yanked the explanation back. The statute of clarifications had run out a long time ago.

'So, I'm back for your cash and your contacts,' Aisha mused. 'Interesting.'

Seriously? Could he be any more arrogant if he tried? She didn't think so.

Aisha felt the long roll of annoyance, the slow, acidic burn of anger. But because she knew disdain was far more effective than screaming, she sent him a below-zero smile full, she hoped, of pity. 'Yes, of course, I'm here because of you. And only you. My being here has absolutely nothing to do with the fact I am Lintel & Lily's best consultant, on track to be the youngest chief of operations ever appointed. Obviously, my studying my butt off to get my MBA and the years I spent in the field gaining experience in establishing hotels all over the world was all because I have this decade-long master plan of returning to the Cape and sliding back into your life!'

She patted his arm, happy to see his eyes widen in surprise. 'You're so clever for working that out, Kildare. How on earth did I manage to live this long without you and your asinine opinions?'

If he responded with a sarcastic comment, she'd kick him in the shins with the pointy end of her sexy shoes. She held her breath, waiting for his reaction. She expected either a blistering retort or maybe, if unicorns existed, a subdued and quiet apology...

What she did not expect was him to take two quick steps to reach her, standing so close Aisha could feel the heat of his body, see the faint scar bisecting his right eyebrow, a tiny birthmark on his right temple. His car lights fell on his face and his stubble held shades of brown and blond and his eyes were a deep, dark mysterious green, the colour of kelp beds off the Atlantic coast. She could see the passion in his eyes and felt her own bubbling inside. A part of her wanted to turn and run, but her feet were glued to the ground, her body demanding to know his again. She needed to taste him again, to run her hands through his hair, across his broad shoulders.

She shouldn't be feeling this transfixed, so fiercely attracted, but she was. Dammit.

He opened his mouth to speak, but instead of forming words, his mouth covered hers in a hot, frustrated, kill-me-now kiss. She tried to remain unaffected, told her body to stay statue-still, but after ten seconds, maybe twenty, she sank against him, her defences crumbling under his skilled mouth.

He tasted like whisky, felt like home. His tongue twisted around hers and she was back in their apartment, nineteen again and in love, desperate for his hands to skim her body, his mouth to explore her skin. Her hands danced across his back, skimmed over the dip of his spine. She sighed at the hard layer of muscle under his clothes, the softness of his hair as it slid through her fingers.

God, the man could kiss, a heady combination of confidence and competence, desire, and a hint of desperation. Nobody, before or after, came close to the way he made her feel…all loose and lazy yet hyped and heady.

She loved what he did and hated the way he made her feel.

Aisha put her hands on his chest and pushed him away, desperate for some distance between them. He was too attractive, too magnetic, and, despite his being an utter ass a few minutes ago, she wanted him.

So, nothing much had changed in more than a decade, then.

Dammit.

She lifted her head, saw triumph and pure male satisfaction blazing in his eyes. 'You still want me,' he stated, sounding more than a little cocky.

The arrogant, presumptuous, conceited ass! She opened her mouth to blast him and saw him lift one, just one, supercilious eyebrow. He was expecting her to lose her temper, was goading her to do exactly that. He wanted her to be a shrew, to throw a slap, to lose her temper…to make a fool of herself.

She was damned if she would give him the satisfaction.

Right, one of them had to be the adult and she'd drawn the short straw. She straightened her spine and pushed back her shoulders.

When their eyes connected, she folded her arms across her chest and tipped her head to the side. 'I've always known you are a determined, driven guy who likes getting your way, but tonight you've been the absolute worst version of yourself. I hope that's an aberration and not who you are now. But understand this, Pasco…

'You were talking nonsense earlier and you know it!' She waited for a beat, making sure she had his full attention. 'Hear me clearly, Kildare. Nothing you can do or say will stop me from working with Ro, from establishing St Urban as one of the best boutique hotels in the world. And if Ro wants a tasting restaurant on the premises, that's what she will get, with or without your cooperation. We had a very unequal relationship in the past, but I'm not the same meek, mild, and easily led girl I was before. Do not be in any doubt about this…if you bite, I will bite back.'

By the end of her soliloquy, she was shaking, and Aisha hoped Pasco was too mad to notice. Gathering her wits, and her pride, she turned around and headed back to her car, slid behind the wheel, and slammed the door shut. Without looking at him, she executed a quick three-point turn and drove back up the road to St Urban.

Nothing to see here, folks. She'd only kissed, argued with, and lectured the only man she'd ever loved, the man she'd once promised to share her life with.

It had been, by anyone's standards, a hell of a day.

Pasco owed Aisha an apology, a huge one.

He'd been way out of line last night and he felt like an utter ass. She'd been right to call him out and her cool lines, delivered so disdainfully, had cut through all his BS.

He had been arrogant in his dealings with her, and the high point of his idiocy had been suggesting she'd returned to the Cape to be with him. Even more annoying was his small wish that it were true.

Pasco, dressed in his oldest pair of jeans, and his most comfortable boots, walked up the road towards St Urban, looking up at the branches of the oak trees forming a leafy canopy over the road. The trees were flaunting their beautiful colours, red and gold, and bronze, and now and again one drifted down to the road, dancing on the light breeze. His property, a smallholding he'd bought on selling his restaurant in New York, had once been part of St Urban and bordered Ro's place to the east. His house wasn't far from her new abode, the manager's cottage situated in the corner of the property. Instead of walking for a good forty-five minutes, he could've hopped a couple of fences, crossed a paddock, navigated his way through a vineyard, and reached her place in ten minutes.

But the long walk had given him time to think and, God, he knew he needed every moment to work out how he could apologise without sounding like a complete moron.

On returning to his place last night, he'd headed straight for his home office and fired up his state-of-the-art laptop. He'd never, not once, done an Internet search on Aisha in all the years they'd been divorced. He didn't believe in looking back, or torturing himself, so he'd kept his curiosity tightly leashed. He'd initially typed 'Aisha Kildare' into the search engine and couldn't understand why he came up with no results or, to be accurate, nothing relating to her. He realised his mistake and with a thumping heart typed in her maiden name and various images and results jumped out at him. There were testimonials about her work as a consultant—all five stars—a write-up stating she was one of the hospitality sector's most exciting and innovative consultants, and he came across a series of articles she'd written for a trade magazine. Then he visited the Lintel & Lily website and, under their 'Meet Our Team' tab, read the write-up on his ex-wife. She had, indeed, received her MBA, graduating near the top of her class. She'd set up hotels in far-flung, sometimes inhospitable places and was respected for her cool head and her practical streak. She was fast, efficient, and smart, and a valued member of the Lintel & Lily family. Her employees and clients adored her.

Basically, if someone wanted to set up a hospitality-based operation, Aisha Shetty was the person you hired to do that. Ro had employed the best of the best.

And he was, as she'd said, an ass.

An ass who needed to apologise.

Pasco pushed his sunglasses up into his hair and rubbed his tired eyes with his thumb and index finger. Sleep, always elusive, had been non-existent last night. He'd sprawled out on his couch in front of his large-screen TV, watching reruns of old international rugby games, but his full attention had been on the hot-as-fire kiss they'd shared. They'd always had chemistry, but their kiss last night had gone beyond that; they'd been radioactive. Her body, slimmer than it had been when she was younger, had fitted against his perfectly, and her scent, edgier now, had invaded his nostrils and settled in his brain. And her mouth, God, her mouth…her taste. It kicked up a yearning in him to know her again, to discover all the ways she'd changed. And the ways she'd not.

Pasco kicked a stone with his boot and watched it skitter into the grass. Taking Aisha back to bed was not a good idea, in fact, it was a comprehensively disastrous one. They'd tried once, they'd failed. He wasn't into reliving the past, revisiting mistakes. So, no, jumping back into bed with his ex was not a good idea. But he still wanted her, goddammit.

Impulsively, Pasco veered left and ambled down the path leading to the cellars. He walked around to the back of the building to look at the renovations for Ro's restaurant. He slipped through the unlocked door and, standing on the newly sanded floor, looked at the unpainted walls and the magnificent view.

This…

A restaurant like this was his unspoken, deepest, never-spoken-of dream. A small kitchen, doing most things himself. Growing as much produce as he could in his own gardens and orchards, picking it in the morning and using the ingredients for lunch and supper, his entire focus on creating excellent food in a non-pressurised environment, forgetting about stars and rewards and reviews.

In a perfect world and alternate reality of himself, he'd ditch his high-pressure restaurants, his travel shows, and the persona of being the country's first international celebrity chef. He'd read, work on a cook book, wander about in a greenhouse he built, raise chickens and goats, make cheese. He wouldn't run from business to business, project to project, dealing with staff and suppliers, making sure the steep and exacting standards he set were consistently exceeded by himself and his staff.

He was tired, dammit.

But whenever he considered closing down his restaurants, leaving his high-powered life, he felt his heart rate speed up, a hand squeezing his lungs. He knew what it was like to lose everything of value, houses and cars and, yeah, money, knew how devastating it was to have his life flipped upside down in the blink of an eye. Living a simple life, free of pressure and ambition, was a lovely idea, but it was a pipe dream, a mirage.

He needed different eggs in a variety of baskets so that if one venture failed, another would keep him afloat. He needed the pressure, the accolades, the five-star reviews, and the attention because it put distance between him and his father, reminded him he was nothing like the man who was so determined to have the easy life while putting in little to no work. Growing up, all he'd heard was how like his father he was, that they looked the same, talked the same.

He might be his father's mini-me, but working hard, moving fast was his way of showing the world that, below the surface, he wasn't his father's son.

He had pots of money but one bad decision, one financial misstep, could wipe a business out. That was why he had backup plans for his backup plans, ten different slush funds, and why he diversified. If something went wrong with Pasco's at The Vane, he could rely on income from Pasco's, Franschhoek and his share in Binta. If they all went belly up, he could expand his travel and cooking show. He would not be like his mother and be blindsided.

No, stepping back, having a small restaurant, pottering really, was a nutty dream. And he was anything but daft. He'd satisfy those cravings for a small restaurant by helping Ro set up hers and, possibly, running it for a month or two. That would have to be enough.

Pasco left the cellar and headed for the path that would take him to the manager's cottage, conscious of the spark of excitement burning in his belly. Since he seldom felt excited about much any more, he reluctantly admitted he was eager to spend more time with his ex-wife. His all-grown-up, now feisty, occasionally fierce, ten times more attractive than she had been, kissed like she was on fire, ex-wife.

Pasco sighed. God, he was up the creek, his paddle was long gone and hungry alligators were snaking on his ass.

Excellent.

CHAPTER FOUR

ON RETURNING FROM her five-kilometre run through the pear orchard, past the stream, and through the vineyard—showing off its lovely autumn colours—Aisha jumped into the shower and afterwards pulled on a pair of black yoga pants, fluffy socks, and a comfortable, slouchy, off-the-shoulder cotton sweater. She intended to work from the cottage today and the four-seater square dining table in her open-plan lounge, dining, and kitchen area suited her perfectly. She had coffee and, because she'd stopped by a deli and bakery in Franschhoek yesterday, she had enough food to tide her over for a couple of days.

She anticipated a day of immense productivity.

But first, she wanted to take five minutes to relax. She picked up her cup of coffee and walked onto the tiny patio leading off from the kitchen and sat down on the white concrete wall enclosing the small area. There was a small wrought-iron table, but she wanted to feel the sun on her face, so she sat on the wall, back against the cottage, and stretched out her legs. The smell of lavender and thyme, planted in raku-fired pots, wafted up to her and she could hear tractor engines rumbling in the distance.

It was a perfect day, clear, cool, and sunny, and Aisha couldn't take her eyes off the Simonsberg mountain basking in the sunlight. It was like a huge dragon's tooth, raggedy edged, filled with cracks and crevasses. She'd read, somewhere, that it could be hiked, and she'd love to do that. Maybe in a month or two when she had a handle on her work here at St Urban, she'd carve out the time.

You left me because I was a poor sous chef and couldn't give you the life you wanted, the life I promised you...

Last night, after her anger had died down, Pasco's words had kept buzzing around her brain. Where and when did he pick up the notion that money, or lack of it, was the reason she'd left him? Of all the reasons she'd bailed, and there were many—lack of time and attention being the biggest reason—money had never been an issue.

She had been all but excommunicated by her parents, so her uncle Dominic had stepped up and paid for online university modules and, when she could, she'd picked up waitressing shifts at the bistro down the road. They hadn't been rich, but they'd been a long way off poor.

'Stunning, isn't it?'

She wasn't surprised to see him, had even expected him to turn up this morning as he wasn't one to leave an argument unfinished. What did surprise her were the battered, faded jeans hugging his hips, and old, mud-splattered boots. The cuffs on his long-sleeved T-shirt—navy blue and hugging his wide, wide chest—also showed some signs of wear and tear.

But the watch on his thick wrist was a limited edition Patek-Philippe, his sleek and sexy aviator sunglasses were high-end, definitely designer. She couldn't name the brand, but knew they'd be ferociously expensive to buy. His hair was expertly cut and his cologne, dancing on the light breeze, was a compelling mixture reminding her of the sun and the sea, and a blend that perfect cost money. Lots of it.

He looked fit, hot, and take-me-to-bed sexy, but Aisha

had no intention of letting him off the hook. He needed to do some big-time grovelling first. 'What do you want, Kildare?'

His eyes deepened and desire flashed, briefly, in his eyes. Yeah, yeah, she got it, he wanted her, their kiss last night clued her in, but if those were the first words out of his mouth she might throw her coffee cup at him.

Pasco jammed his hands into the front pockets of his Levi's, those huge shoulders rolling forward. 'To apologise, actually. I was off base last night. I was pissed off and frustrated and I should never have said what I said.

'You're obviously damn good at your job and I was way out of line,' he added. 'I'm sorry.'

Aisha, shocked at his sincere apology—the Pasco she knew would rather burn Wagyu beef than apologise—needed a minute to think, so she lifted her coffee cup to her lips and sipped, trying to formulate a response. She'd been expecting another fight—Pasco hated losing—but she hadn't expected an apology.

This was new. And she could either accept it and move on or take the opportunity to needle him a little for his assumptions. *Be an adult, Shetty.*

Aisha nodded. 'Thank you.' She saw him looking at her coffee cup and sighed. 'Do you want a cup?'

'I'd love a cup,' he replied, stepping onto the patio. Aisha swung her legs off the wall and walked into her kitchen, Pasco a step behind. She grabbed a mug and put it under the spout of the coffee machine and checked the level of the beans and water.

'I didn't hear a car, so how did you get here?' Aisha asked him.

'I walked over,' Pasco replied, pulling out a chair. He lifted his eyes at the piles of multicoloured folders on the table and cocked his head to read the tabs. 'I own the smallholding right next door, actually. This cottage is about a ten-minute walk, as the crow flies, from my back door. But I took a long way around and walked up St Urban's drive.'

Aisha turned her back to him, not sure how comfortable she was with him living in such close proximity to her.

Pasco pulled out a dining chair and sat down. 'Franschhoek is my home town so I bought a place here.'

'It's a long commute to Pasco's at The Vane every day,' Aisha said, placing his mug in front of him. It was black and strong, the way he used to drink it back in the day.

He picked up the pottery mug, sipped, and closed his eyes. The corners of his mouth kicked up. 'I see you still drink Ethiopian Yirgacheffe.'

She smiled and shrugged. Money had been short during their marriage but some things, Pasco had declared, could not be compromised on. Coffee, excellent South African wine, exceptional olive oil. 'Some famous chef introduced me to it and got me hooked. I had severe withdrawal symptoms because I couldn't afford it on my student budget, but as soon as I started earning decent money, it went back on the list.'

'That chef taught you well.'

He had. She'd learned a lot from Pasco about food and wine and making love. Aisha, feeling her cheeks redden, remembered his comment from last night and decided to take the plunge. 'Talking about money, you said something last night that shocked me.'

Pasco winced. 'Only one thing?'

She smiled briefly. 'I don't want to fight with you this morning, I don't.' She lifted a finger. 'And we really do have to work out the rules of our working together, Pasco.'

He waved her suggestion away. 'Later. What did I say to shock you?'

'You said I left because you didn't earn enough money, because you didn't give me the life I wanted.'

Pasco nodded. 'I didn't.'

Aisha held his hard stare, needing him to believe what she was about to say next. 'I never left because we were financially strapped, Pasco. That was never a problem. Other things were, but not that.'

'What—?'

'No, that's enough for now,' she interrupted him. She nodded to the window and the awesome view of the sun shining on the mountain. 'It's a beautiful day and I'm declaring a truce. Please?' Not giving him a chance to argue, she switched subjects. 'We were talking about your commute to the city.'

Pasco didn't drop his eyes from hers and she knew he was digesting her words, trying to make sense of them. She caught the impatience in his eyes and knew he wanted to dig, needed more of an explanation. She hoped he didn't push; she really wasn't up for another fight.

Pasco dropped his eyes and when his shoulders dropped, Aisha knew she was safe. For now.

'At some point, we'll pick up where we left off...'

Of that she had no doubt. Just not this morning, thank God. 'I don't live here permanently, I just use my Franschhoek house as a bolt-hole,' he continued. 'I have an apartment in Fresnaye, but my chef de cuisine, or executive chef, runs the restaurant on a day-to-day basis.'

'Nice gig if you can get it,' Aisha said, sitting down opposite him.

'Hey, I've worked long hours for a long time to earn that sort of freedom,' Pasco snapped back.

Wow, his work ethic was a hot-button topic for him.

And, yeah, she knew exactly how hard he worked as she'd been the one waiting for him at home.

Aisha cast around for a neutral topic of discussion, but Pasco beat her to it by tapping on a folder. 'Tell me about St Urban.'

That was an unexpected question. 'I'm sure Ro told you all about her plans for the place.'

Pasco tucked his long legs under the table and his knee brushed hers and Aisha felt the familiar tingle, the hit of connection. Pasco folded his forearms on the table and shook his head. 'I haven't had many discussions about St Urban with her. We've all, Muzi, Ro, and I, been so busy with our respective projects—St Urban, Muzi launching a new wine from a rare cultivar he found on the property and my launching a range of cooking accessories and foodstuffs—that when we do get together the last thing we discuss is work.'

Pasco's wicked grin flashed. 'Honestly, all we've discussed lately is Ro's pregnancy.' He pulled a face. 'I know more about pregnancy and birth plans and multiple births than I need to, thank you very much.'

Aisha smiled. 'It's pretty exciting they are having twins.'

'It's pretty scary because they are having twin boys,' Pasco corrected her. 'I knew Muzi as a kid and he was wild!'

Aisha raised one eyebrow. 'And you weren't?' She pretended to think. 'Weren't you the guy who drove his car through the window of an art gallery in town?'

'You remember me telling you that?' Pasco asked.

She remembered everything he told her about his teenage years, boarding school, and his adventures with Muzi and Digby Tempest-Vane. But he never spoke about his childhood before he came to live in this valley in his early teens. Then again, she never spoke about her family either.

'St Urban, Aisha?' Pasco prompted her.

'Right.' Where to start? She glanced at the folders, wondering where to begin. 'Okay, let's start with the manor house. It was important to Ro, from the beginning, to preserve the elegance and grandeur of the house, so distinctive details like the hand-painted dado rails and the broad yellow wood floor beams, and a million others, have been kept and, if needed, restored. After extensive renovations, the manor house can now sleep sixteen, with six en suite bedrooms and a family suite. She's also converted the smaller guest house and the venue can sleep eight. So we have space to host over twenty people in supreme luxury.'

'Uh-huh,' Pasco murmured. Aisha wiggled in her seat. She'd forgotten what it was like to have all that intense energy and attention focused on her. When Pasco listened, he concentrated. And she knew that, in a week, a month, or a year, he would be able to recite their conversation verbatim.

Unfortunately for their marriage, he'd only paid attention when he'd wanted to, when the subject had interested him enough. Her unhappiness hadn't.

Oh, maybe that was unfair. The truth was more nuanced than that. In hindsight, she thought Pasco hated talking about their problems because then he'd have to admit there was a problem, that there was something he—they—couldn't instantly fix. Unlike cooking, you couldn't toss your wife out and start from scratch.

Anyhoo...

'I'd like the guests to feel like they stepped into their second home so, while everything must be exquisite, it must also feel welcoming. Ro and my boss, Miles, who is currently Chief of Operations for Lintel & Lily, felt the same way and that's the direction they went in. The library will be full of books, the lounges will have plump couches, and there will be fresh flowers everywhere. Luckily, the house was filled with antique furniture when Ro inherited so a lot of the desks, tables, dining tables, and bedposts will go back into their original rooms when they have been restored and polished.

'I'm planning luxury picnics by the river, hiking and mountain-biking trails, a small bar stocking the best liquor money can buy. The guests will be able to drink cocktails on the veranda or under the massive oak tree with the wide spreading branches. Damn, I need a mixologist.' Aisha picked up her phone, opened a document, and tapped in a note to look into whether the budget would support a mixologist.

'Talk dirty to me, Aisha,' Pasco murmured.

Her eyes flew up and connected with his. 'What?' she asked, blushing.

He grinned, and Aisha felt as if she were touching the sun. 'Talk food. Chefs, produce suppliers, menus.'

She leaned back and crossed her legs. 'For the manor house kitchen, I'm thinking farm to table, seasonal, local, lovely. That's all I have, right now. The rest depends on who we hire to run the hotel kitchen.'

'Do you have anyone in mind?' Pasco asked her, running his finger up and down the edge of his coffee cup.

'No, not yet. I'll advertise the position in a month or two, and if I don't find someone suitable I'll work through a recruiting agency.'

'I have one or two ideas on supremely talented people who would jump at a chance to run their own kitchen and who'd be up for the challenge. I can get their résumés to you.'

'Thank you, I'd appreciate it. Muzi is restoring the cellars and he wants to install a winemaker here. He's going to focus on producing wine from the rare cultivar he found. Muzi will also be employing the staff needed for wine tastings and cellar tours. The cellar is so old and such an amazing space and I'd like to find a historian who can give me a history lesson of winemaking in the valley and, hopefully, of St Urban itself.'

'My brother Cam is a winemaker and he's the area's local-history nerd. I'm sure he could give you what you need.'

Aisha made another note on her phone. 'You are proving to be surprisingly helpful this morning, Kildare.'

'Glad to be of service,' Pasco replied, amused. 'Right, let's get down to business... Ro's pop-up restaurant. Where are you with that?'

Aisha looked at him and spread her hands. 'Nowhere because that wasn't something I was aware of until I got here yesterday.'

Pasco pushed back his chair, extended his long legs, and crossed his feet at the ankles. He looked relaxed, yet Aisha knew that under that lazy-looking exterior was a mind running at a sprinter's pace and never stopped.

'The tasting-menu restaurant has been low on her list of priorities. It was an idea we chatted about a little after she and Muzi got together, but never really pursued. Then she fell pregnant and it slipped even further down the list. But a couple of months ago, I told her that I was interested in doing it, but only for a few months. She liked the idea of bringing in different world-class chefs on a rotating schedule.'

So that was how the idea of a restaurant was born. Good to know. 'So why are you getting involved in designing the restaurant?'

'Because I'm good at it and have a rep for sky-high standards when it comes to decor, service and, obviously, the food itself. I like to have, at the very least, input into the design of the restaurant and complete control over the food, the menu and whom I work with.'

'All that and without you putting a cent of your own money into the project,' Aisha said, impressed by his cool confidence and a little frustrated by his arrogance.

Pasco's green eyes slammed into hers. 'I am one of the best chefs in the world and people will book into St Urban just to eat my food.'

Aisha cocked her head and sent him a look from under her lashes. 'You really need to work on your self-confidence and self-worth, Pasco.'

He picked up a pen from the table and threw it at her. 'Cheeky brat.'

Aisha looked out of her kitchen window to the sunlight falling on the mountain and nibbled on the inside of her cheek. 'I'm going to be the point person representing Ro on the project, Pas. Are we going to be able to work together?'

Pasco's expression remained steady and imperturbable. 'Why wouldn't we?'

Oh, let me count the ways.

'Because you are demanding and bossy and determined to have your way. And so am I,' Aisha responded. 'I'm not the person I was before, Pasco.'

'I would be disappointed if you were, Aisha. People are supposed to grow, you know.'

He wasn't getting what she was trying to say. 'But I'm not just going to nod my head and say, "yes, Pasco", "no, Pasco", "three bags full, Pasco". I'm going to argue with you, contradict you, flat out tell you no, occasionally.'

He stared at her, the corners of his mouth twitching. 'I'm becoming more terrified by the moment.'

God, he wasn't taking her seriously. She reached across the table and poked her finger into his biceps. 'You aren't listening to me, Kildare! My loyalty is to Ro and her vision for St Urban. If you want or do something contrary to that vision, I'm going to put my foot down.'

'I know that you will try,' Pasco told her, still smiling. 'Relax, Aisha, we'll find our way.'

She knew that he meant that she'd come around to his way of thinking. Insufferable man! She poked him again. 'Don't say I didn't warn you, Pasco.'

He looked down at the finger barely denting his skin. 'Is that supposed to make an impression?'

She yanked her hand away and scowled at him. He grinned, pushed to his feet, and glanced at his watch. 'Where are you going?' she demanded. 'We still have things to discuss!'

He looked from her to the coffee cup in his hand. 'I was just going to make myself another cup of coffee.'

'Oh,' Aisha replied on an internal wince. 'You could've asked me first!'

'Honey, we've been married and divorced, and I got you hooked on this particular drug, so I thought we were beyond that. Do you want a cup?'

'No, yes, okay.' Aisha speared her hands into her hair and sucked in a deep breath. Twenty minutes in and she was already exhausted. She'd forgotten that dealing with Kildare was like trying to wrestle an octopus. And, off subject, the way those Levi's cupped his butt was enough to make angels drool.

He turned, caught her ogling him and lifted an eyebrow. Aisha blushed, annoyed by his grin and the satisfaction in his eyes.

Yeah, he was a good-looking guy and she wasn't immune. She wouldn't touch, that would be stupid, but she could look. A little. A very little.

'Rules of engagement...' she muttered.

Pasco resumed his seat. 'What are you muttering about?'

Aisha waved her index finger between them. 'We need rules. Last night I tried to talk to you about how we were going to work together and we got distracted.'

'That's one way of putting it,' Pasco drawled.

She ignored his comment and pulled a writing pad towards her. Picking up a pen, she clicked the top a few times before jotting down a few bullet points.

He craned his head to look at her writing and released a frustrated huff. 'Your writing is revolting.'

'Yours, I recall, isn't much better,' Aisha retorted. 'I'm making a note of what we need to discuss...things like the budget, decor ideas, equipment, staff. Oh, and we need a name.'

'Pasco's at St Urban,' Pasco whipped back.

'Uh...'

'I have Pasco's at The Vane, Pasco At Home—that's my brand of kitchen items and foodstuffs—Pasco's, Franschhoek. The name is part of my brand, instant name recognition, and that's what this restaurant, if I sign the contract, will be called,' Pasco said, determination in his eyes.

Aisha wrinkled her nose, knowing she'd already lost this battle. Luckily, she saw the reasoning behind his words and was prepared to hand him this victory.

'Okay, then, let's talk about how and when we're going to meet.' She pulled her tablet towards her and opened her calendar. She turned it to face him and gestured to the mostly blank squares. 'As you can see, I'm pretty free, but that will change shortly. So, pick a date. I think we should meet a couple of times a week.'

Pasco shook his head. 'That's not going to work for me. My schedule changes from day to day. I go where I'm needed, do what I need to do as the day unfolds. The best I can do is give you a couple of hours' notice when I'll be free.'

Aisha felt her jaw drop, not sure she was processing his words correctly. Was he seriously suggesting she build her calendar around him? Did he not realise how much she had to do, the mountain of work ahead of her to get St Urban up to standard? She was already operating under time constraints and that was before she heard about the pop-up restaurant.

But now, like then, Pasco's work came first. Aisha felt the wave of resentment and looked away so that he didn't see how much his blithe words affected her. So, nothing had changed, not really.

And how sad was that?

She could say something—she should say something—but honestly, she was tired and didn't have the energy to fight. Aisha scratched her forehead, worried she was slipping into the patterns of the past, allowing Pasco to walk all over her again.

'I see some things haven't changed.'

He frowned, trying to work out what she meant. Dammit! She hated it when passive-aggressive comments slipped out—she was better than that.

She held up her hand. 'No, that won't work for me. You need to give me definite times when we can meet because I am not sitting around waiting for you to call.'

She waited for his response and wondered if she imagined the flare of respect she saw in his eyes. Probably. Pasco took their empty coffee cups to the sink and when he returned to stand in front of her, he slid his hands into the back pockets of his jeans and nodded. 'Fair enough. I'll see what I can do, but I'm slammed.'

'Make time, Pasco, this is important.'

'Noted.' He darted a look at his watch and sighed. 'Talking of, I need to get to The Vane. I have a meeting and then we are spending the afternoon testing new dishes.'

Naturally, Sundays were never a day of rest for the workaholic chef. Aisha looked at her dining table and sighed. Rocks and glass houses, baby.

At the doorway, Pasco turned to face her and lowered his head, as if aiming for another kiss, or to brush his lips across her cheekbone or forehead. He hesitated and she saw awareness flash in his eyes, a reminder to both of them that what they had before, what was acceptable back then, might not be welcome now.

They had to rewrite the rules, find new ones, toss others. Tiptoe through this minefield.

Keep it simple and, for goodness' sake, keep it professional. She sent him her most impersonal smile. Or at least she hoped she did. 'I'll see you around, Kildare.'

'Don't be like me and work all day, Aisha.' Yep, there was that hint of bossiness she remembered so well.

'Like you, I don't have time to relax, Pasco. I have a million things to do and minimal time to get everything done. That's why I need your cooperation.'

'I'll try my best, Aish.' His eyes met hers and his expression turned rueful. 'I know that I can sound autocratic, but I understand what burnout feels like, Aisha, and I'd hate it to happen to you. So do as I say and not as I do and take some time off to relax.' Instead of dropping a kiss on her temple or on her cheek, he squeezed her shoulder. 'I'll let you know when we can meet again.'

Aisha watched, annoyingly tingly and turned on, as he walked out of her back door. Taking, she noticed, the short route back to his house.

CHAPTER FIVE

ON FRIDAY MORNING, Pasco skirted the back of St Urban's manor house and headed for the old carriage house, which Ro had converted into offices for the hotel manager and the admin staff. Walking inside, he heard voices coming from the end office, wandered down the short hallway, and leaned his shoulder into the frame of the door to watch Aisha pacing the floor of her messy office, her hands on her hips and her back rigid.

'Yes, I understand I have to get the order in today to take advantage of the old pricing structure, but I need to get my consultant to sign off on the order and I can't get an answer from the man!'

That man would be him. Pasco winced. His bad.

He'd had about a dozen emails from Aisha over the past fourteen days and nearly as many phone calls, all of which he'd ignored. Not because he didn't want to talk to her, but because he was worried that once he started down that pitted-with-peril path, he wouldn't be able to find his way back. As it was, he spent far too much time thinking about his stunning, sexy ex-wife.

In between lurid thoughts of what she looked like naked—gorgeous, of that he had no doubt—and imagining what he would do to her if he ever got the chance to see her like that again, he rolled her words over and over in his brain, trying to make sense of what she'd said.

'I never left because we were financially strapped, Pasco. That was never a problem. Other things were, but not that.'

If money hadn't been the problem, then what else had caused her to run? He wanted to know, but also didn't. Their time had passed and there was no point in looking back, but he hated the idea of getting something so important wrong.

He did recall stumbling in after a long shift and seeing her sitting on their sofa, her hands under her thighs and her eyes reflecting trepidation and determination. He'd quickly learned her I-need-to-talk expression and that was, after a busy, high-stress night, the last thing he'd wanted to do. Make love to her, sure, he was always up for that, but talking? Not his thing.

Maybe that was one of their problems: he'd been eager to gloss over their problems and pretend everything was fine. It hadn't been fine. A quick marriage, an even quicker divorce, and years of not communicating proved that theory. Talking about his feelings, *anyone's* feelings, made him feel scratchy, as if he were standing in a leaking bucket on a storm-tossed ocean. Unsure and vulnerable…he hated exposing himself emotionally.

Idiot that he was back then, he'd always assumed she was going to whine that they never had any fun, but fun required money and time, and they were barely keeping their heads above water.

Whenever he saw her I-need-to-talk face, he made it a game to see how long it would take him to distract her, to move her off the subject. Luckily for him, she was putty in his hands and one deep kiss and a thumb across her nipple normally distracted her…

God, he'd been a jerk. Young, arrogant, full of himself.

He was now paying the price for his youthful arrogance because he couldn't stop thinking about the real reason for her unhappiness and needed to know what had made her run. He burned with curiosity and his inquisitiveness annoyed him. He and Aisha were done, nothing remained...

Except his need to make love to her, with her, again. That hadn't gone away. If anything, it was bigger and bolder than before.

Crap.

And, yes, this was difficult to admit, but the more time he spent with her, the urge to be with her grew stronger. He didn't have the time to devote to a significant other—

God!

She was his ex-wife, someone he worked with, why was he attaching the words *significant* and *other* to thoughts of her? He was not getting involved with her again.

Bottom line, he couldn't afford to spend great swathes of time with her, wouldn't give her that much importance in his life.

They. Were. Done.

The only reason he was here, in her office, was because he was on his way to Pasco's, Franschhoek and it was a quick detour to St Urban. And also because the tone of her messages and emails had changed from polite and professional to increasingly irate and he suspected he was dancing on her last nerve. He couldn't be around her without wanting to kiss her senseless, but neither did he want to alienate her.

Aisha Shetty still had the ability to flip his world on its head.

Fifteen minutes... He'd give her fifteen minutes and then he was out of here. He could keep his hands off her for that long, surely?

When the call disconnected, Aisha looked up at the ceiling and released a low, intense scream, her arms linked behind her head.

'Problem?' Pasco asked when her arms dropped.

She whirled around, heat in her cheeks and fire in her eyes. He'd never seen her look so beautiful. 'What the hell are you doing here, Kildare?'

Pasco's eyes dropped to her wide mouth, remembering the feel of those sexy lips under his. 'I thought I saw at least two dozen emails from you demanding that I drop in. This is me, dropping in.'

Aisha pursed her lips and Pasco was pretty sure she was counting to ten. Or maybe, judging by the seconds ticking by, to twenty. 'I have been trying to get hold of you for the past two weeks,' Aisha stated, pushing the words out through gritted teeth.

'I've been busy,' Pasco told her, walking into the room. God, a temper looked good on her, her eyes flashing brown-black fire and her skin rosy with frustration. He jammed his hands in his pockets to keep from reaching for her and hauling her into his arms and slowly stripping her so that he could see her standing naked in the sunlight pouring into the room.

'You are an intensely frustrating man, Kildare,' Aisha told him, pushing her hair back with both her hands.

'So I've been told,' Pasco replied, keeping his tone easy and his hands in his pockets.

He sat down on the hunter-green tufted leather camel-back sofa he presumed came from the manor house. He stretched out his legs and crossed his ankles.

'I have fifteen minutes. Talk.'

Aisha looked at him as if he'd grown six misshapen heads. 'You have got to be kidding me! I need hours and hours of your time!'

'Fifteen minutes is what you are getting.' He glanced at his watch and mock-grimaced. 'Thirteen now.'

Aisha's hand curled around the stapler and he hoped she wasn't going to throw it at his head. Her lips moved in what he was sure was a curse and he relaxed a fraction when she released her grip on the heavy-duty stapler. Glaring at him, she reached for her tablet and tapped it, her luscious lips flat with annoyance.

'That was the supplier of the commercial refrigerators. The prices are set to rise and if we want delivery at the old prices, we have to place an order immediately.'

Pasco forced himself to concentrate. He'd recently come across a new supplier with advanced technology, and he wanted to explore that option. 'I'm still investigating other options.'

Aisha rested her butt on the edge of her desk—wide, old, a bit battered—and glowered at him. She wore a navy jumpsuit teamed with a sunshine-yellow jacket, but the happy colour was totally at odds with her scowling face. 'I gave you this information ten days ago, Kildare!'

He grinned at her growly voice. 'And I'm working on it. Next?'

Hand on stapler again. If he got out of here without stitches, he'd call himself fortunate. 'I received a portfolio containing sketches of the interior decor. We need to decide on a look, especially if you want custom-made furniture and a custom-made bar.'

Fair point. He nodded. 'I'll take the portfolio when I leave, and I promise I'll give you feedback by the end of the week.'

Aisha didn't look convinced, and he honestly couldn't blame her. 'You do know that today is Friday, right? That today is the end of the week?'

'Technically, the end of the week is on Sunday.'

His pithy comment resulted in a low, sexy growl. He hadn't set out to annoy Aisha, but he enjoyed her in-his-face exasperation. She'd been a lot more accommodating as his wife and, if he was being honest here, a bit of a pushover. Grown-up Aisha was tough, feisty and he was as mentally attracted to her as he was physically.

That wasn't good news.

Pasco stood up, walked over to her and stopped a foot from her, briefly closing his eyes as her lovely scent hit his nostrils. He wanted to bury his nose in her neck, between her breasts, to get a full hit of her perfume.

Liar—he wanted far more than just to smell her scent.

Pasco plucked her tablet from her grasp and looked down at her neatly typed, bulleted list on the screen. There were still fifteen or so items they still needed to discuss and, dammit, he'd never be able to do justice to her list in a couple of minutes. She was right, she needed hours and hours of his time. He couldn't afford to give it to her, not when he was holding on to his control by the thinnest of strands.

'Email me this document,' he instructed her, wincing at his rough voice.

'I have! Numerous times!' Aisha retorted, eyes flashing. 'Pasco, you are making this a hundred times more difficult than it has to be. I've set up a fine-dining restaurant before—just step back and let me handle it. You don't have the time, don't seem that interested in it—'

'God. You are lovely.'

She blinked, unsure she'd heard him correctly. 'What?'

He wasn't quite sure where the words, so totally unrelated to their conversation, came from, but they couldn't be contained. Because, God, she was. Gorgeous, that was. With her eyes flashing with irritation and her pursed mouth, she was the embodiment of a warrior princess.

'Your skin is flawless and your scent drives me insane,' Pasco muttered.

Surprise flashed in her eyes, along with a hint of pleasure. 'Thank you, but we were talking about…'

Her words faded away, and all he could think about was that he had to have her mouth under his, his hands on her soft, warm, fragrant skin. He saw desire in her eyes, watched her mouth part, and her tongue darted out to touch her bottom lip. It was obvious she'd lost her train of thought and he was glad he wasn't the only one descending into madness. Aisha sighed, took a step closer to him and it was all the encouragement he needed. He dipped his head slowly, giving her enough time to pull back, and then his lips met hers.

He'd thought he wanted hot and fast, sexy and strong, but he surprised himself by gentling his kiss, skimming his lips across hers in a barely there movement. He felt Aisha tense and he waited for her response, fully expecting her to push him away. But instead of her hands slapping his chest, her mouth softened, her sigh hit his lips and she lifted her hand to curl her fingers around the back of her neck. She stood up on her tiptoes to push her mouth against his, sliding her tongue into his mouth.

Yes…*this*.

Their tongues tangled, his hands skimmed over her back, her butt, her ribcage. This kiss was strange, sweet, tender, so powerful in its simplicity. A man and a woman who wanted each other, the soft torment of tongues colliding, hands stroking… What was more basic than that?

Basic and mind-shatteringly powerful.

They were just a man and a woman who wanted each other, Pasco reassured himself. They'd always had explosive chemistry…it didn't mean anything. It couldn't. But, just in case it did, in case he deepened the kiss and took her on that couch—he was so damn tempted—Pasco lifted his mouth off hers and rested his forehead on hers.

'Where's the portfolio, Aisha?'

Aisha dropped her hands from his neck and stepped back, confusion replacing the lust in her eyes. Pity. But necessary.

She pushed her hair off her face and sucked in a deep breath. 'What?'

'The interior decorator's portfolio of sketches that you want me to look at?' It took everything he had to sound professional, businesslike. How the hell his brain was functioning sans blood, he had no damn idea.

'Uh—' Aisha glanced at her desk, still trying to gather her thoughts.

He spied a large leather portfolio on the credenza behind her desk and stepping away from her took a considerable amount of effort. He picked up the portfolio and held it up. 'This it?'

'Yes,' Aisha replied. She folded her arms and rocked on her feet. She glanced at his mouth, shook her head and straightened her shoulders. Her cool expression told him she was taking her cue from him and was happy to pretend that nothing had happened between them, that they hadn't shared a kiss that had rocked his world. 'But I need to explain—'

Hell, no. He needed to get out of here before he lost the battle to take her on that couch in the middle of the day. Not that he had any problem with midday lovemaking— *Crap, Kildare! Pull it together!*

'I've set up a lot more restaurants than you have. I'll figure it out.' He made a show of looking at his watch. 'Time is up, I've got to go.'

'But—'

Pasco didn't dare look at her again—didn't need to, he

could hear the anger in that one word—and swiftly walked to the door. He jerked the door closed behind him and, two seconds later, heard the sound of that heavy stapler crashing against the wooden door.

Yep, not unexpected. And probably deserved.

Aisha stood in the doorway of a closed health shop and eyed the busy entrance of Binta, a famous oceanfront venue a seagull's cry away from one of Camps Bay's most famous beaches. Every Capetonian and most South Africans had heard of the iconic oceanside spot, a cornerstone of the city's social scene. It was laid-back, vibey, expensive, and casual and on any other day she'd be happy to meet Priya for a drink and a meal as they watched the magnificent sunset.

But, unfortunately for her, Priya was hosting a party for her husband's fiftieth birthday in Binta's private dining area and most of the extended Shetty family would be in attendance.

Marvellous.

She'd tried to get out of attending, tried very damn hard. But Priya had shot down her every excuse. It was Saturday evening so she shouldn't be working anyway, and she was staying in Priya's guest suite so she wouldn't have to worry about driving back to Franschhoek—or anywhere since her sister lived in a massive house just down the road and she'd walked to Binta. Priya had also received reassurances from the rest of the family that they'd leave the past in the past.

Hah. They'd try, but Aisha was expecting more than a few snide comments. She assumed there would be a lot of wistful wishing—*We all wish Aisha followed her sisters into the sciences, but it wasn't to be*—and the backhanded compliments that always made her want to run screaming from the room. Five years ago, her parents were finally on the point of forgiving her for her disastrous marriage when events, more accurately her sister Reyka, conspired to hurtle them back into stony silence.

She'd video-called her folks every month or so for the past two years, brief, light conversations, but this party would be the first time she'd see her parents in the flesh for more than a decade and she was as nervous as hell.

Damn Priya for insisting on her being here. Yes, she understood she couldn't avoid them for ever, that she'd have to see and speak to Hema and Isha, and deal with Reyka, but she didn't want to. It would be much easier to go back to St Urban and work. She had so much to do, a hotel to get off the ground, and she didn't need the drama her family always rained down on her head. She always came away from encounters with them questioning herself and the path she'd chosen; feeling less than, and irritable for feeling that way.

Aisha looked across the road to the ocean and wished, for the first time in a long time, she had a masculine hand to slide hers into, a shoulder to place her head against, a strong arm around her waist. Someone to stand in her corner, someone tough and protective, who wouldn't hesitate to step in when he felt she was being bullied or disrespected. Yes, she was a strong woman—she'd learned to be one—but even strong women sometimes needed to lean, craved some support.

She'd love to have Pasco here…

There, she'd admitted it. He knew nothing about her family, except she had a bunch of sisters and that her parents didn't approve of their marriage. She'd never spoken about them, told him how she was bullied and put down, how alone and unseen she felt. Early on in their relationship, she'd realised their time together was limited, and she hadn't wanted to spend the rare moments they had discussing her childhood.

They hadn't talked much, or at all. Aisha pushed her thumbnail between the tiny gap in her two front teeth as she watched the waves roll onto the beach. He hadn't opened up to her either... God, it was tough to admit that they knew each other's bodies inside out, but not each other's minds or hearts. What drove them or hurt them, made them happy, or what made them cry.

All they'd had was an out-of-control attraction. And it was bigger and brighter than before. She'd tried to ignore it to concentrate on business and had sent him another round of emails and left irate messages for him to get in touch—though, to be fair, he had given her feedback on the restaurant's decor and had authorised her to order some kitchen equipment—but there was still so much to do. On Monday, she intended to hunt him down again and, hopefully, they'd get through more than two bullet points this time.

But if he kissed her again—if she kissed him back—all bets, and possibly clothes, were off.

Aisha glared at Binta's pretty facade. *Just get this done, Shetty. An hour, two, and you can leave. And if you don't drink, you can drive back to Franschhoek tonight.* Gathering her courage, Aisha stepped onto the pavement, the skirt of her long-sleeved ankle-length maxi dress swishing around her ankles. She touched the thin black leather belt encircling her waist, thinking she liked the patterned fabric in white and fuchsia and the black edging at the hem and neckline. It was conservative but a little boho, a lot stylish. She'd pulled the sides of hair off her face and allowed the rest to fall down her back and kept her make-up understated. She looked good, but knew her mum and sisters would find something to criticise.

They always did.

Priya and Oscar stood just inside the door of the restaurant, looking exactly what they were: a hugely successful, beautiful couple living their best life. After Aisha received a hug from Oscar, Priya took both her hands and danced on the spot. 'Isn't this place fantastic? I can't believe we managed to book it.'

Aisha looked over her shoulder into the busy bar and lounge area and lifted her eyebrows on seeing an A-list Hollywood celebrity sitting at one of the tables. Binta was vibey and sophisticated and, judging from the laughter and buzz of conversation, looked like a fun place.

Maybe when her family got too much she could hide out down here and order one of Binta's world-famous cocktails. Something citrusy and wonderful and strong with alcohol. She'd need it, of that she had no doubt.

'Everyone is upstairs. We're just waiting on a couple of guests and then we'll join you upstairs.' Priya saw her wince and quickly added, 'Or you can wait downstairs with us.'

'I'll wait.'

Priya squeezed her hand again before turning away to greet a couple she'd never met before. Aisha stepped back, leaned against the wall, and watched as people, mostly dressed in designer clothes, streamed past them to enter the downstairs bar area. She liked the way the doors folded back, leading onto the patio area, separated from the road by huge arches. The room was also filled with luscious plants that provided the tables with some privacy but didn't impede the view of the beach and the setting sun. It looked like what it was reputed to be: a world-class, vibey joint that was the place to see and be seen.

'Oscar and Priya, I presume?'

Pasco? What the hell?

Aisha blinked, then blinked again, but it was definitely Pasco standing in front of her, dressed in a Prussian blue suit over an open-necked white shirt, brown leather belt, and shoes.

Priya placed her hand in his and smiled. 'Pasco, how nice to meet you at last. This is my husband, Oscar.'

Pasco shook Oscar's hand before tuning to Aisha. 'Hey, Aish, you look lovely.'

Aisha started to tell him he looked lovely too, but quickly shut down that thought. 'Why are you here?' she demanded.

Pasco looked around and shrugged. 'I show up here every few weeks just to keep an eye on the place.'

'Why would you do that?' Aisha demanded.

Pasco looked from her to Priya, and her sister rolled her eyes. 'When you told me you were working with Pasco again, I called Pasco up, introduced myself as his ex-sister-in-law, and asked for recommendations on where to hold Oscar's fiftieth. He suggested Binta and designed a special menu for us,' Priya explained.

Her sister had never been shy about putting herself forward. Aisha looked at Pasco and pulled a face. His slow, heat-filled smile caused her stomach to flip inside out. 'Sorry,' she mouthed and saw his tiny shrug.

The pieces started to fall into place. 'You own this too?' she asked him as Priya and Oscar turned to greet more guests.

'With a partner,' Pasco told her. He gave her a long up-and-down look and silently whistled. 'You do look great, Aisha.'

She fought the urge to swish her skirts as a four-year-old would. Seeing the admiration and lust in his eyes made her feel warm and squishy and rather wonderful.

Then she remembered he'd spent the last week ignoring her again. 'You've been avoiding me,' she accused. 'Why?'

Pasco placed a hand on her back and led her to the stairs. 'Honestly?'

'Yes, of course,' Aisha replied, thinking how wonderful his big, warm hand felt on her lower back.

'Because every time I'm within six feet of you, I have to fight the urge to kiss you senseless...everywhere,' he said as they climbed the stairs.

What did he mean...? Oh, right. Well...um...

'I'm not sure what to say to that,' Aisha admitted after a long silence.

At the top of the stairs, Pasco stopped and looked down at her, his smile rueful. 'It'll be a bloody miracle if we manage to get this restaurant up and running, I admit that.' He gestured to the door down the hall. 'That's where you want to go.'

No, she didn't. Aisha stared at the half-open door and grimaced. 'I'll just wait for Priya and Oscar here.'

'But your family is through there. You look a lot like your mum, by the way,' Pasco said.

Aisha pulled her bottom lip between her teeth. 'Do they know you are here?'

He shook his head. 'No, I don't make a point of introducing myself to guests.' He frowned and pushed back his jacket to slide his hands into the pockets of his trousers. 'Are they still pissed about us marrying?'

'When it comes to me, they are always pissed about something,' Aisha admitted. Hearing footsteps behind them, she turned to look down the stairs and saw Priya and Oscar following another couple up the stairs.

She pulled up a smile for Pasco and lifted her index finger to drill it into his chest. 'We need to talk, to work.

Why don't we meet in a very public place next week and we knock this project on its head?'

Pasco nodded, his smile wry. 'Yeah, okay.' He glanced towards the private dining room, his knuckle skimming her cheekbone. 'If you need rescuing, give me a missed call.'

'Thanks, but I'll be fine,' Aisha told him. 'I don't plan on staying more than an hour, two at the most.'

Pasco dropped a kiss on her cheek, and Aisha ignored her sister's coy whistle as he walked away. She glared at Priya, saw a million questions in her eyes, and placed her finger against Priya's ruby-red lips. 'Not one word, Priya, I mean it.'

Priya nodded, but as soon as Aisha dropped her finger, her words flew out. 'One question, just one! Why the hell did you let that gorgeous creature go?'

Reasons, Aisha silently replied. Many, many reasons.

CHAPTER SIX

PASCO STOOD JUST inside the service door leading to the private dining room, his eyes on Aisha. Thank God Binta's managers were brilliant at their jobs, because he'd been less than useless since Aisha arrived.

Nobody, before her or since, had managed to distract him the way she did.

Pasco moved to allow a waiter carrying a tray of sushi to pass him and immediately stepped forward again so that he could see her clearly. She stood in a group comprising her mother, two of her four sisters, and two other women who were either aunts or old family friends. Fifteen minutes had passed since she'd joined the group and Aisha had yet to say a word. Judging by her carved-in-stone face and fixed smile, she'd taken a couple of verbal hits and her body language had changed from uncomfortable to I'm-so-over-this.

Anyone who looked closely enough could see the misery in her eyes, her tension. It was in her hunched shoulders and in the way she held her champagne glass in a death grip.

Unlike everyone else, Aisha wasn't having any fun...

Damn this. He couldn't stand here and watch her suffer for a minute longer. Turning around, he walked down the short passageway and stepped into the very busy kitchen.

He caught the executive chef's eye. 'Do you have everything in hand?' he demanded.

'Absolutely.'

'Good man. Have you seen Jenna?' he asked, referring to the senior of the two on-duty managers. He was told she was in the storeroom and Pasco headed in that direction. She walked out of the room as he approached it, her arms full of bottles of rum.

'We're having a run on mojitos,' she cheerfully told him.

'Excellent,' he replied. He pushed a hand through his hair, feeling uncomfortable. 'Would you and Sbu be able to cope if I took off?'

She nodded. 'Sure.'

'I'll be on my phone if you need me.'

Jenna flashed him a smile. 'Boss, we often run this place on our own. We're good, I promise.'

He was micromanaging and he knew it. He loved control, having it and wielding it, and stepping back was always difficult to do. But right now, Aisha needed him and this business didn't. 'Thanks. Call me—'

'We won't,' Jenna told him as she sauntered away.

Right. Pasco pulled his phone out of his jacket pocket and pulled up Aisha's number. His fingers flew across the screen as he tapped out a message.

You're not having fun so I'm sending a waiter to you. He'll escort you to the staff car park where I'll be waiting. Do not make me come and find you because you know I will.

Aisha stepped into the small car park at the back of Binta to see Pasco lounging against his McLaren Artura, his long legs crossed at the ankles. Her eyes collided with his and she sucked in a deep breath, barely remembering to thank the waiter for showing her the way. He was such a man, Aisha thought, as she walked towards him. Confident, hyper-masculine, alpha to the core. Intelligent, good-looking and ripped, the man had it all. Could she be blamed for her many X-rated fantasies?

Tucking her clutch bag under her arm, she walked across the small car park, her eyes not leaving Pasco's as he walked around the bonnet of his car to open the passenger door for her.

'Are you okay?'

She wanted to lie but couldn't. 'Better now.'

Aisha settled herself into the passenger seat and moments later Pasco sat beside her. Being with him made her feel stronger and invigorated her. He was like her own custom-made energy drink, a one-of-a-kind battery charger. She turned her head to look at him and found him watching her. Their eyes clashed, collided, neither of them able to look away and tiny fireworks exploded on her skin. After what felt like minutes, she managed a small smile.

'Aren't you supposed to be working?' she asked.

'Honestly, that place is so well run, I feel like I'm in the way.'

'It's not like you to be hands-off,' Aisha said. In fact, she knew that Pasco never shirked his duties, ever. If he said he was going to do something, then he always followed through. Their marriage was his only failure. The thought made her sad.

'Binta doesn't need me, you do.'

Aisha's eyes widened at his statement. He was putting her before work? What was happening here? 'I was with my family,' Aisha stated, keeping her tone light. 'It wasn't like I was facing a firing squad.'

'You hated every bloody minute, Aisha. Don't try and tell me that you didn't,' Pasco muttered, jabbing the start button on his car. The engine roared to life, and she felt its power in her feet, up her spine, deep inside her.

'I hated every minute,' Aisha conceded as he pulled out of the car park into the main road. Aisha watched as heads swivelled towards them, and she noticed the pointed fingers and appreciative gazes his fancy car elicited.

'Where are we going?' she asked, half turning to face him.

'Somewhere where we can talk.' He flashed her a smile as they crawled down the busy road. His smile could power the sun and there was nothing better than feeling it against her skin.

'Public or private?' Aisha asked. She shrugged when his head snapped around. 'C'mon, Pas, we both know that if we go somewhere private, we won't do any talking.'

Pasco turned his attention back to the road and Aisha saw the tension in his jaw. 'Public...*dammit.*'

Ten minutes later, he pulled into a parking space about five hundred metres down the road from Binta. After opening her door for her, he took her hand and led her across the busy street to a small, old-fashioned dusty-pink double-storey house. There were tables on the veranda and servers bustled around like flies on steroids. Pasco ignored the steps leading up the veranda, steered her around the side of the house and up a flight of steel stairs. He pushed a doorbell and after a few seconds, the door clicked open.

An attractive woman dressed in a short black cocktail dress smiled at them. 'Hello, Pasco.'

'Busi.' Pasco dropped a kiss on each of her cheeks before introducing Aisha.

'Are you busy tonight?'

Busi rocked her hand up and down. 'Most of the regulars are at a cocktail party at The Vane, so no, not right now. We'll pick up later.'

Aisha looked across the mostly empty banquettes and tables to absorb the view. Needing to take it all in, she walked away from Pasco and Busi to reach the veranda, taking in the expansive vista of ocean and sky. She had an awesome view of the Lion's Head and Twelve Apostles mountains, and a stupendous view of the beach.

'This is amazing,' she told Pasco when he finally joined her, holding a whisky in one hand and a huge margarita in the other. 'What is this place?'

Pasco guided her to a comfortable two-seater couch. 'It's called The View, for obvious reasons. It's a cross between a boutique bar and a private club. You have to be a member to come here.'

'And do you own this too?'

Pasco sent her a slow smile. 'I don't. And that's why I can relax here.' He lifted his drink and clinked it against her glass. 'Cheers.'

'Cheers.' Aisha took a huge sip of her drink and sighed when the perfect ratio of sweet and sour hit her tongue. She whimpered and wrapped both hands around her glass. 'God, you have no idea how much I need this.'

'So what's the deal with your family?'

She'd been expecting his question, had even thought up a couple of glib responses to divert him. But suddenly, she didn't want to lie or fudge, she just wanted to tell him the truth.

'My sisters are all academics, as are my parents. They are very respected scholars and lecture at the university. They are intensely, ridiculously brainy and I am not. They see success in terms of academic achievements, and I let down the side.'

'That doesn't make any sense, Aisha. You're one of the

most organised, logical people I've ever encountered. And you have a master's degree.'

'In business. It's one of the most common post-graduate programmes around and nothing special. My sisters are doctors and scientists who, as my parents frequently remind me, are making a difference in people's lives. I do not.'

He stared at her, his expression intense. 'That's not all of it.'

No, it wasn't. Aisha took another sip of her drink and rested her head against the back of the couch. 'They are so passive-aggressive, Pasco, I can't deal with them. Sometimes, I just wish they'd yell and scream and get it out, but they don't, they prod and poke and whinge and whine.'

'You seem to have a good relationship with Priya.'

'I do. She never gave me copies of *Maths for Dummies* for a birthday present, or a framed photograph of my sisters all holding their PhDs. And she was the only one who took my side when...' She hesitated, not sure if she wanted to tell him about that ugly incident. No, she did want to tell him, she just wasn't sure he wanted to hear it. She and Pasco weren't good talkers. Lovers, yes. Communicators? Not so much.

'Tell me, sweetheart.'

She sipped her margarita and half turned to face him, dragging her eyes off the view. But, honestly, looking at Pasco was as good. 'After I told them that we divorced, it took a long time for them to reach out to me—well, Priya did, but no one else. Anyway, two years later the lines of communication opened up, but it was very obvious that if I was a disappointment before, I'd sunk to new lows.'

'I'm sorry.'

She shrugged and blinked away the moisture in her eyes. 'Five years ago, it was my folks' fortieth wedding anniversary and I saved up to buy them tickets to visit me in London, as well as a tour of six different cities in Europe. Four-star hotels, private tours, it cost me a freakin' fortune.'

'What happened?' Pasco gently asked, placing his big hand on her thigh. It felt right there, just as it felt right to lay her head on his shoulder.

'About a month before they were due to leave, Reyka, the sister just older than me, got engaged. And strangely, the only time she could hold the engagement party was smack in the middle of my parents' trip. I begged her to postpone it. She wanted me to rearrange my parents' trip, but I couldn't. I'd already paid for everything and to change dates was incredibly expensive. I just didn't have the extra money.'

'How long were they going to be away for?'

'A month.'

Pasco pulled back, frowning. 'She couldn't hold off on having the engagement party for a month?'

Aisha shook her head. 'Apparently not. My two eldest sisters supported her, Priya tried to support me but my parents were forced to choose.'

'And they chose an engagement party that could've been postponed,' Pasco stated. *'Wow.'*

Aisha sat up and reached for her drink. 'Tonight was the first we've been together as a family for ten years. Judging by the way they behaved, I was never married, Reyka wasn't a complete bitch and I didn't lose a whack of money.'

Pasco skimmed his hand over her hair. 'I'm so sorry.'

'It is what it is.' Aisha shrugged and tried to smile. She sat back and draped one leg over the other, leaning her shoulder into Pasco's. For the first time that day, she felt marginally relaxed.

This was a little slice of heaven and she intended to enjoy it. The margarita was cold, the fading sun still warm and a stunning view in front of her. And, for once, she wasn't surrounded by spreadsheets and lists, stressing about what to do next.

Aisha slid her feet out of her shoes and wiggled her toes, sighed deeply and tipped her head back and closed her eyes. She hadn't felt this relaxed for...

'Why did you walk out on us?'

Aisha shot up and spun around to look at him.

Pasco took a sip of his whisky and winced on seeing her shoulders shooting towards her ears. Excellent way of killing the mood, Kildare!

'Wow, that's an out-of-the-blue question. Why are you asking me now, ten, nearly eleven years later?'

Because he needed to know, now. Tonight. 'Why, Aisha? You left me with a goddamn note and nothing else.'

Shame flickered in her eyes, only to be extinguished a second later by annoyance. 'Pasco, I tried to talk to you! I told you I was unhappy, that I never saw you, that I was lonely.'

'I was working, Aisha! Trying to create a decent life for us.'

She took a deep breath, and when she spoke, her voice was calm. Well, calmer than his. 'But that's the thing, Pasco, *you* were trying to create a life for me, for us. We should've been doing it together. You made all the decisions, you plotted a future for us that I didn't have a say in, partly because I never saw you and when I did, we rarely talked. We'd make plans, but they always fell through because your work always, always came first. You never made me a priority and I felt like a visitor in your life.'

He stared at her, shocked. 'Why didn't you tell me you

wanted to leave me? Why didn't you give me a chance to fix it?'

'Pas, I tried to…so many times. But you always told me you were too tired to talk, you changed the subject, or you seduced me. The few times I did get you to listen, my unhappiness never sank in because your behaviour never changed. You didn't make the effort to give me what I needed.' Aisha lifted one shoulder in a helpless shrug. 'Then you took the job in London without consulting me. It was a massive decision, we were moving to another country, but you made the call…all on your own. That was what broke me, broke us.'

He started to argue, only to realise he didn't have a decent defence. He'd done exactly that, made the decisions, planned their life, so damn sure he was doing the right thing. His motives, to provide a secure life for them, for the children he'd imagined having with her—for him to be the exact opposite of his feckless, useless father—were good.

But the execution of those plans, he reluctantly admitted, could've been better. He could've brought her into his confidence more, asked for her input on the plans he'd been making. He'd been so damn arrogant, confident and self-involved.

'I made so many mistakes with you, Aisha, and for that I'm sorry.'

Shock flashed across her face, and he didn't blame her, as apologising wasn't something he often did. Or at all. He pulled a face. 'I'm happy to take responsibility for the part I played in the destruction of our marriage.'

She gave him a shaky smile, obviously taken aback by his apology. Admittedly, so was he. But while they were on the subject, there was just one more thing he needed to say. 'But you could've at least told me that you were leaving, that you wanted a divorce. You should've told me all that to my face.'

To his surprise, Aisha nodded her agreement. 'Absolutely. That was wrong of me and I'm sorry.'

Her sincere, easy apology rocked him. God, they'd been so young and made so many mistakes: his fuelled by pride and stubbornness, hers by fear, loneliness, and insecurity. Pasco raked a hand through his hair. He caught her eye and tried to smile. 'So where do we go from here, Aish?'

Aisha placed her hand on his forearm and squeezed. 'We can't go back, Pasco, but I'd like us to be friends.'

It was pretty difficult to be her friend when all he wanted was to back her against the wall, press his body into hers and ravish her mouth. Fill his hands with her lovely breasts, her mouth with his tongue. He wanted her to wrap her long legs around his hips, wanted to hear her breathy moan as he slipped inside her heat, capture the sound of his name on her tongue as she flew apart.

Yeah, friends. Much easier said than done.

They watched the sunset and an hour rolled into two, then three as they caught up on the last ten years, silently agreeing to skirt topics touching on their marriage and divorce. He told her about his businesses, about living in New York and London. She told him about her promotion, and how much she wanted the position, her own house, to feel settled. They talked about music and books, touched on politics, and laughed more than they expected.

They ate, sharing a seafood platter and a bottle of wine, and when a cold wind picked up, they moved inside and sat at the bar, Pasco watching as Aisha ate a generous helping of tiramisu. Around eleven, they left the restaurant and dashed across the road to his car, laughing as the wind blew her dress up to her knees and blew her hair into her eyes.

Aisha leaned her head back on the seat as she watched Pasco walk around the bonnet of the car, stopping to slip a homeless man some cash. Then she saw his hand go to the inside pocket of his jacket and he removed his phone. He caught her eyes through the windscreen and held up his finger, asking her to give him a minute.

After nodding, she leaned her head back and closed her eyes. Despite spending a really lovely evening with Pasco, she had a tension headache behind her eyes. Because Pasco never got sick, she knew he wouldn't have any paracetamol on him and her stash was in her tote bag, which she'd left at Priya's place. A stupid move because she knew, from experience, that any time spent with her family resulted in a migraine-like headache.

What a night! She'd known the party would be tough to navigate, but she'd never anticipated having a what-happened-to-us? conversation with Pasco.

She'd certainly never expected him to apologise, and the memory made her feel warm and a little wonderful.

They'd both been wrong, both made mistakes. As an adult, with time between then and now, she could admit that and maybe move on. Honestly, they'd been too young to marry, too impulsive, drunk on desire, and naive in their belief that love could conquer everything.

She was glad they'd addressed the subject, shooed the elephant out of the room. Oh, they both could've said more, gone a bit deeper, but they'd covered the important bases. And what would change by doing a deep dive into the past? Precisely nothing.

She wasn't the same person she was at nineteen—thank God—and she'd seen changes in Pasco as well. Good changes. And wasn't that the point of life? Growing and changing, acquiring a little more wisdom?

Pasco back then had been balls-to-the-wall, never really slowing down to think, to consider...he'd just set his eyes on a goal and barrelled onward. It seemed to Aisha that Pasco now was more thoughtful, slower to react, to fly off the handle, more considerate. She'd loved him back then, but she *liked* him today, more than she ever had before.

How far he'd come, how far they'd *both* come, was yet to be determined, but what couldn't be denied was their red-hot attraction. They should deny it, ignore it. It would be smarter for them to try and be friends, especially since they needed to cooperate to bring Ro's vision for her St Urban restaurant to fruition. The problem was she didn't see Pasco in a friendly way...no, Pasco made her think of intertwined limbs on cool cotton sheets, masculine hands under her bottom as he slid inside her, filling up those empty, hollow, much neglected feminine places that hadn't seen any action for the longest time. She wanted to feel his lips and teeth on her nipples, his mouth on her stomach. His tongue licking its way down...

Aisha pushed her fingers deeper into her eyes and released a low moan.

Why was her ex the only one who could suck her in like this, who pulled feelings to the surface she didn't want or require? She didn't need the complication of wanting him or wondering whether he wanted her back.

She was out of practice with men, she freely admitted that, but she sensed he did want her. Just a little. Or a lot. And...damn. While she wasn't opposed to the idea of them being friends, it would make life easier, and she liked the notion of them being lovers more. Temporary lovers, she qualified. A couple of nights here and there to scratch the itch, to satisfy her curiosity as to whether her memories lived up to reality.

You're breaking your stay uninvolved rule, Shetty!

This was madness. She had a hotel and a restaurant to establish, a promotion to earn. She didn't have the time or the energy for a love affair.

No, love had left the building a long, long time ago.

But as hard as she tried, she couldn't get the idea of them having a fling out of her head. What would he say if she suggested upgrading their status from friends to friends with temporary benefits? Her stomach fluttered and she knew, just by that small reaction, that this was the worst of ideas. She and Pasco had never been good at simple and she knew that the chance of the situation becoming intensely complicated was high. It was a bad idea, a terrible idea but...

Damn. It was an idea that, like her headache, wouldn't go away.

Pasco ended his call, slid behind the wheel, and closed his door. He turned to look at her and their eyes collided.

She didn't hesitate, just went for what she wanted, and it was blindingly obvious by the heat and lust in his eyes that he wanted her right back. He met her in the moment, his mouth as demanding as hers, and the world faded away, her entire existence narrowed to their lips, his warm hand on her hip, the way his tongue slid into her mouth and wound around hers, sending a buzz of anticipation skittering through her.

She wanted him. So much.

Aisha responded without thinking, spearing her fingers into his hair, running her other hand under his shirt collar to find warm, lovely, masculine skin. She felt his groan, revelled in it, and fumbled for the clasp to free her from her seat belt. It finally popped open and she reached for

Pasco again, pulling his mouth back to hers. She hadn't had enough, not nearly enough.

His mouth was hot, spicy with whisky, and she needed more of his heat, his heady scent, to explore his wide, hard body. How had she gone for so long without him? How had she survived without this pleasure, with not having his hands on her body, making her feel heady, wild, intensely female? Pasco's hand closed over her breast and his thumb swiped her nipple and she pushed off her seat, desperate to get closer. The gear stick pushed into her hip and she cursed the lack of space.

Pasco pulled back suddenly and dropped a curse before running his hand over his face.

'What?' Aisha demanded, half sitting and half kneeling, her breath coming in quick, sharp pants.

Pasco's eyes—hot, wild, and a little feral—met hers. He lifted his hand and created an inch of space between his thumb and index finger. 'I am this far from taking you here and now.'

'I'm that far from letting you,' Aisha admitted. She placed her hand on his hard thigh and released a ragged sigh. 'The way you kiss, I'd forgotten how good you are.'

'Ditto, sweetheart.' Pasco dragged his mouth across hers, but before they could sink into another wild groping session, he placed his hands on her shoulders and pushed her back into her seat.

Aisha looked at the cars passing them, the pedestrians on the boardwalk, feeling dreamy and very buzzy. Her hand remained on Pasco's thigh, and she drew patterns on the fabric of his suit trousers with her thumb. God, she loved touching him.

Pasco gripped her hand and held her fingers still. She slowly turned her head to look at him. 'You don't like that?'

He half grimaced, half smiled. 'I like it far too much and I'm trying my damnedest not to move your hand higher.'

There was no doubt about what he wanted. His face was flushed and his eyes blazed with desire. She dropped her eyes to his lap and if she'd had any doubt, the sight of his erection tenting his trousers would've filled her in.

'You want me,' she murmured, half to herself and half to him.

'Very damn much,' Pasco growled, his fingers squeezing hers. 'I've never been one for making love in cramped cars in public areas, but you make me lose my mind.'

Heat and lust sparked through her at his growly words, coated in frustration. He was such a man and knowing he wanted her thrilled her to her core. She felt powerful and feminine and confident and...

Alive. Her heart was racing and her lungs were heaving. And that was just from a hot-as-lava kiss. If he made love to her, she might just melt into a puddle.

It was a chance she was willing to take. Oh, there were a million reasons why this was a bad idea, and tomorrow she'd probably regret her recklessness but right now? Right now she wanted more, she wanted everything he could give her.

Aisha turned in her seat to look at his handsome profile, and her heart skipped a beat. 'You have a house around here, right?'

His head whipped around to look at her, hope sparking in his eyes. 'My apartment in Fresnaye is about ten minutes from here if I drive fast.'

'Floor it, Pas.'

He gently gripped her jaw with his big hand and her eyes slammed into his. 'If I take you home, you will be naked ten seconds after I get you in my front door, sweetheart.'

She gripped his strong wrist and sent him what she hoped was a seductive smile. 'Well, I hope so. I wasn't asking you to take me home to play Scrabble.'

Pasco dropped a hard, open-mouthed kiss on her lips before pulling back and hitting the button to fire up his powerful engine. Backing out of the parking space, he skilfully and quickly navigated the still busy streets to the luxurious suburb of Fresnaye.

He made it to his place in seven minutes.

CHAPTER SEVEN

PASCO PARKED HIS car in one of the four bays in his garage and led her from the garage to his front door. Aisha quickened her pace to keep up with him, laughing when he fumbled the inputting of the code to open his eight-foot-high front door. He cursed, slowed down, and jabbed at the buttons again and the door clicked open. Pasco pushed her ahead of him, kicked the door shut with his foot, and then the hall lights came on, illuminating his tense face.

Instead of reaching for her, he pushed his hand into his trouser pockets and stared at her, his eyes darting from her mouth to her eyes and back again. A muscle ticced in his jaw and she could see the tension in his wide shoulders, in the way he held his big body.

Why was he just standing there, looking at her? Why wasn't he doing anything? If he didn't kiss her soon, she might lose her nerve…

She rubbed her hand down her hip, suddenly nervous. 'Why are you just standing there?'

'Back then, it was normally me, *always* me, who initiated lovemaking. You, going for what you want, is a hell of a turn-on. I want you so damn much.'

Great, lovely, she was happy to hear it, but could they get on with it? Aisha stepped forward but stopped when he held up his hand. She raised her eyebrows at him, impatient.

Hesitation flickered in his eyes. 'Are you completely sure?' he asked. 'Because, if we start, I'm not backing off.'

Now that was nonsense, she knew that, no matter how far they went, she could call a halt to what they were doing, and he'd stop.

Though the chances of her doing that were honestly less than zero. She wanted him now, tonight. She didn't know if it was a good idea or whether she'd regret this in the morning, but she didn't care. For once she was going to seize the moment, go with the flow, carpe-the-hell-diem.

'Aish—'

Hesitation still lurked in his eyes—did he think they were crossing too big a line here?—but honestly, she was past caring. 'Shut up, Pas.'

Pasco's eyes didn't leave hers as she stepped towards him to slide her hand under his jacket, above his heart. It was thudding hard, another sign of how much he wanted her, wanted this. She ran her hand down his shirt, marvelling at the muscles under his shirt, the heat radiating off him.

He stayed statue still as she pushed his jacket off his shoulders, allowing it to drop to the slate floor beneath her feet. She had a brief thought that she wanted to see his house, explore his home, but that could come later. She had more important things to do with her time right now.

Aisha looked up at him and stood on her tiptoes to skim her mouth across his before dropping back down to pull his shirt from the waistband of his trousers. Torturing them both, she slowly undid the buttons of his shirt and pushed it apart, placing her mouth on his skin, tasting him. Her hands moved up his chest, over his shoulders as she kissed his flat nipple and dragged her nose through his light chest hair. His arms were big, bulging with muscles as she pulled one hand from his pocket, then the other.

He kept them by his sides as her fingers moved to his belt buckle. She glanced up and the intensity in his moss-green eyes sent a bolt of electricity through her, igniting every nerve ending she possessed.

'Touch me, Pas, I need you to,' Aisha said, lifting her hand to touch his jaw.

Her command—or was it a plea?—released him from his self-imposed stance and his arm encircled her waist and yanked her into him. He bent his knees and took her mouth in a hard kiss that was just this side of savage.

Aisha loved it, loved the need she tasted on his tongue. He wanted her as much as she did him and the thought made her head spin.

With her mouth under his, she pushed his shirt off his shoulders, laughing when it hooked on his wrists. Pasco cursed, and ripped his cuffs apart, and buttons pinged across the hall floor. When he was free, he took her mouth again and hiked her long dress up, releasing a groan of appreciation when his hand encircled the top of her thigh.

He pulled away and buried his face in her neck. 'You taste, feel, so good.'

Aisha arched her neck as his mouth moved down her throat and her chest, and she held her breath as he nuzzled her nipple through her dress and bra. Frustrated with the barriers between them, she quickly undid her belt and, grabbing the edges of her dress, pulled it up and over her head and dropped it. She stood in his hallway in her skimpy black panties and lacy transparent bra and watched Pasco's eyes darken. He slowly, far too slowly, pulled the edge of one lacy bra cup aside and stared at her nipple, before bending his knees to take her into his mouth. She whimpered and combed her fingers through his hair, arching her back to encourage him to take more, do more.

Pasco straightened and pressed his thumb into her bottom lip. 'Bedroom, now.'

She couldn't wait that long. 'Here, now.'

'You're sure?' Pasco asked her. 'If we stay here, it's going to be hard. And fast. And it'll be up against the wall.'

She nodded; that was what she wanted this first time again with him. Hot and fast and wild. Out of control. 'Works for me.'

Pasco nodded and reached into his back pocket and withdrew his wallet. He yanked out cards and cash, plastic and notes falling to the floor as he searched for a condom. He pulled one out, dropped the leather wallet, and reached for her, sliding his hands down the back of her panties.

His kiss was all-consuming, limitless, and Aisha pushed her hands between them to undo his belt, then his zip. She pushed her hands inside and there he was, hot and oh-so-hard. So very Pasco.

From there on, time stood still as hands streaked over flesh, mouths followed. They didn't take the time to undress fully, her panties were pushed aside, his trousers fell halfway down his hips, just enough for him to move. Aisha slid the condom over his long length and a second after she was done, Pasco grabbed the backs of her legs, ordered her to wrap her legs around his, and slid into her in one fluid, fantastic, soul-touching stroke.

He groaned and leaned her back against the nearest wall, his forehead on hers, his face a mask of concentration.

He rocked, she responded, igniting a million detonators, setting off a chain reaction of need and want and passion. Chemistry was too tame a word for what he did to her, how he made her feel. Aisha gasped as he rocked deeper into her, she tightened her legs and pushed down and, deep down inside her, stars collided and galaxies exploded.

God, she'd missed him so much. Missed this. Missed him in her body.

And in her life.

Early the next morning Aisha left Pasco sleeping in his king-sized bed and, after pulling on his button-down shirt, padded across his enormous bedroom, skirted the small lounge within his enormous sleeping quarters, and glanced right and...

Stopped.

How could she not?

The sky was awash with shades of pink and purple, accompanied by the music of the sea drumming the rocks below his deck. Entranced by the magical colours, Aisha walked over to frameless folding doors, found the mechanism to slide them open, grateful when the doors opened without a whisper of a sound.

She needed a moment alone, to stand in the magical light and bliss out on the incredible view.

Aisha walked onto the patio running the length of the apartment, skirted the long lap pool, stopping to dip her toe into the water—it was heated, of course—and leaned her elbows on the glass balustrade, also unframed. She recognised the beach to her right as being Moses Beach, a highly desirable location. From Pasco's apartment one could enjoy outstanding views of the sea, white sand, and the incredible tip of Africa sky.

The only thing that would make this view any better would be a cup of coffee.

And, possibly, a lobotomy.

Exquisite sunrise or not, there was no getting around the fact she'd slept with her ex last night, the man she needed to work with for the next month. Slept with? Ha, no! She'd devoured him, all but climbed inside him. They'd started in the hallway, moved onto the open-plan reception lounge—she recalled massive cream couches and outstanding, vibrant, oversized art—and finally made it to his bedroom, where they'd rolled around on his California king. Lord, they'd even shared his shower, exchanging long languid kisses and indulging in some heavy petting.

Aisha gently banged her forehead on the edge of the glass balustrade, wondering if she'd completely lost her mind. What had she been thinking? Had she been thinking at all?

She'd been here before, been enthralled by Pasco, and she hadn't liked playing second fiddle to his career and his priorities. She'd vowed never to give him—any man—that sort of power over her again. She didn't trust love, couldn't rely on it—it was a lesson her family had taught her and Pasco had reinforced—so she had to focus on what she could control, what she could rely on. And that was her work. Becoming involved with Pasco, even at a purely superficial level, would be a distraction from what she needed to do at St Urban.

She didn't have the time for a fling, for a lover, and she couldn't afford to be distracted. She was so close to the goal she'd set for herself when she first joined Lintel & Lily all those years ago.

She would not let her intense and inconvenient attraction to her ex-husband and current work colleague impact her professionalism. She was better than that. She'd obey the rules.

Aisha looked at the oversized men's watch on her wrist,

saw that it was just past six, and thought about calling for an Uber to run her back to Priya's place so she could collect her car and then she'd head back to Franschhoek. She wanted to avoid any early-morning awkwardness with Pasco and she thought putting a little time and distance between them would be a very good thing.

Running again, Shetty?

She pulled a face at the still gorgeous sky—lighter now—and sighed. She was an adult and should be able to have a reasonable, intelligent conversation with the man who'd rocked her world last night. She was sure, well, mostly sure, she wouldn't do anything stupid, like make love to him on one of those two-seater lounges as the sun rose. One night and she was already looking for another Pasco-induced high. Another and she might become addicted. Aisha sighed.

No, she wouldn't run, but when she mustered the courage to walk back into his bedroom and wake him up—but only after a cup of coffee or three—she'd tell him that their sleeping together was a lapse in judgement, a step out of time, that it couldn't happen again.

They had to work together and to do that they needed to be professional and uninvolved.

She would not let her attraction to her husband—*ex*-husband dammit!—impact her work. She had a promotion to secure, a life to lock in, a house to buy.

She'd learned one lesson from Pasco—along with never making quick decisions and that love was a farce—and that was to put her career first.

He was, after all, brilliant at doing just that.

'Pretty sunrise.'

His voice behind her made her skin prickle, and Aisha turned around to look at him, standing in the doorway to the open-plan lounge, two coffee cups in his hands, steam rising from the surface. He wore a pair of light-weight cotton trousers and his pale grey T-shirt clung to his broad chest. His golden-brown hair looked messy, his three-day-old beard was thicker this morning and he had a pillow crease across his right cheek.

He looked amazing.

Pasco skirted the outdoor furniture, walked over to her, and pushed a cup into her hands. He lifted his to the sky in a silent toast.

'It was lovelier earlier, streaks of deep pinks and purples and golds,' Aisha told him, wrapping her hands around the mug.

Pasco sipped before responding. 'I think this is the best place to watch the sunrise, better even than Table Mountain. I remember visiting a school friend's house in this area when I was about ten or eleven and seeing a sunrise like this. I vowed that I would some day own a house right on the beach.'

Aisha looked over the balustrade on the rocks below. Yep, once Pasco set his sights on a goal, he never relented. Yes, she'd walked out on him, but she couldn't help thinking that he'd let her go so easily that he hadn't fought for their relationship—hadn't tried to talk to her about coming back, hadn't followed her home. Their relationship wasn't something he'd put a lot of effort into. The thought still made her heart hurt.

That was why they would never be anything more than lovers. She'd never hand her heart over to him again.

'I saw the sunset earlier, I woke up as you left the bed,' Paso told her. 'I've been watching you for the past fifteen minutes.'

She didn't know what to say to that, how to respond.

'So, when are you going to talk to me about rules, tell me that this isn't a good idea, that we are work colleagues who shouldn't complicate their lives by getting physically involved, that this was a one-night thing?'

God! She hated it when he read her mind. She fought the urge to either smack or kiss that know-it-all look off his face. But since he'd opened that door, she'd walk on in. 'I don't have to because you said it for me,' she pointed out, pleased at her super-reasonable tone.

'We're adults, Aisha, we can separate sex from work,' Pasco told her, his tone abrupt. 'One doesn't have anything to do with the other.'

'Didn't you say that you were avoiding me because of our attraction? Because you kept thinking about taking me to bed?'

'Fair point,' he conceded.

Aisha looked at him across the rim of her coffee cup. 'We have a history, Pasco, one that doesn't get wiped away with one hot-as-fire encounter. We're divorced, and one night of conversation doesn't put our past to bed. I also need to work with you, and adding sex makes it complicated.'

Pasco sighed and rested his mug on the balustrade. He frowned and rubbed his hand over his face. 'Do you want to have another conversation about the past?'

'I can see that you don't,' Aisha retorted.

'What more is there to say? I was bossy and domineering, didn't spend enough time with you, and didn't make an effort to give you what you needed. You didn't explain what you needed and then you bailed, leaving just a note.'

She wanted to tell him that, if he loved her, he should've *known* she was unhappy. That he didn't look hard enough, that he didn't *see* her.

Before she could lash out, and she wanted to, he spoke again. 'Aish, guys are not good at subtext, we don't read between the lines. I'm a straightforward guy. I might've understood how miserable you were if you sat me down, looked me in the eyes, and used small words. Words like "I'm leaving unless you get your crap together", "I'm miserable", "help me figure this out".' He shrugged. 'But maybe, because I was too young or too conceited or too lazy, it was easier to tell myself that whatever you were feeling would blow over.'

A part of her wanted to blame everything on him; her ego wanted Pasco to be at fault. But that wasn't fair.

Aisha watched as a wave covered the rocks with white foam and gathered her courage to explain. It would be hard, but that wasn't an excuse to duck the issue.

'Everyone in my family is profoundly intelligent and so very erudite, Pasco. They are also intensely rational and, being scientists, none of them is driven by emotion. I am the cuckoo in the nest. I found it difficult to express myself verbally. And I felt everything… I was a walking, talking miasma of emotion.'

She forced herself to continue. 'I'd tried to talk to them but, because we came at issues from entirely different directions—rational thinking versus emotional—we rarely agreed. I invariably walked away from every conversation feeling less than, unseen and, sometimes, stupid.

'I wasn't good at expressing myself so I stopped,' she added. 'I learned to shut down, to keep my thoughts and feelings to myself. Not only with them, but with everyone. I guess I carried that over into our marriage, stupidly thinking that, because you loved me, you'd know how I felt and what I was thinking.'

His hand drifted down her arm. 'You don't seem to have a problem communicating in a business setting,' Pasco commented.

'In the early days with Lintel & Lily, I was passed over for promotion, despite being damn good at my job, not once, but twice. Miles, my boss, pulled me aside and told me that if I wanted to move up, I'd have to learn to state what I wanted, to start communicating better.' She shrugged, remembering how hard, and how frightening, it had been to break those habits from her childhood. She'd come a long way.

Aisha knew his eyes were on her face, could feel his heat, smell his divine scent. She felt exposed and a little raw. She needed to put some distance between them, to wrap her head around everything that had happened: them sleeping together, the part she'd played in their divorce, how they were going to work together with the desire bubbling between them.

She needed space now, and started to walk away, but Pasco snagging her shirt impeded her progress. She whipped around and scowled at him. 'What?'

'Where are you going?'

'Inside to get dressed and then to call an Uber. I want to go back to St Urban. I have work to do.'

'You're pissed off with me,' Pasco growled, frustration in his eyes.

She wanted to agree, but her innate honesty had her shaking her head. 'Actually, I'm more annoyed with myself than with you.' She shrugged. 'I want you to be solely responsible for our marriage imploding and knowing I played a bigger part than I thought is hard to accept.'

Pasco's smile was tender as he pushed his fingers in her hair above her ear, raking back her hair. 'We can dissect the past, take it apart bit by bit, but it won't make a damn bit of difference. What if we decide to forgive each other, forgive our younger, dumber selves and move on?'

She held his strong wrist. 'Pasco...'

He dropped his head to nuzzle her temple. 'I don't want to fight with you, Aisha. We were kids, we made mistakes, both of us. But here we are, older and, hopefully, a little wiser. Let's move on, sweetheart.'

He rested his forehead on hers. 'I'm sorry I hurt you, Aisha.'

What else could she say but... 'I'm sorry I hurt you too.' And she was. Aisha sighed and the cracks in her heart started to knit themselves back together. There'd be scars, but those chasms would heal.

His too, she hoped.

'Spend the day with me,' Pasco suggested, his lips brushing hers. 'I want to drink my coffee and watch the sunrise with you in my arms. Then I want to make you breakfast and take you back to bed. Give me today, sweetheart, one day where we have no past, no future, no worries, no agendas.'

God, she was tempted. So tempted. She wanted that more than she wanted to breathe or for her heart to keep beating. But playing hooky, from life and reality, was a risk and one that might come back to bite her. It might make her want more, far more than she could ever have.

But it had been so long, years and years, since she'd allowed herself the pleasure of a step out of time, to take a day for herself, to spoil herself. And spending the day with a man who made her heart race, her skin prickle, and her mouth water was the ultimate in spoiling herself.

She didn't shop, she didn't take spa days, she didn't take vacations. She worked. She could do this, she was allowed to do this, and, being a big girl, she'd accept the consequences.

'One day, Aisha. Come play with me.'

When he looked at her like that, those deep green eyes

temptation personified, she couldn't resist. And why on earth would any woman want to?

After breakfast—fluffy blueberry pancakes with honeycomb and bacon butter—and another round of soul-stealing, languid, lovely lovemaking, Pasco bundled her into his shower and told her he'd be back in half an hour. She showered, pulled on the long-sleeved T-shirt he'd left her and climbed back into his bed, buried her nose in his pillow, and drifted off to sleep. She woke up an hour later and saw a pile of clothing at the bottom of the bed.

Yawning, she pawed through the pile, finding designer jeans and a white, men's style button-down shirt, a soft leather jacket, belt, shoes, socks, and even underwear. And the sizes were spot on. She dressed and, carrying the low-heeled boots and socks, walked down the hallway, back into the entrance hall—that wall would always have a soft spot in her heart—and into the lounge area. The sun was shining, and Pasco had opened all the doors leading onto the entertainment area and she could hear the waves crashing onto the rocks below. This was a brilliant example of bringing the outside in. Wide awake and not in a sex-induced haze, she could take in the details of his exquisitely decorated apartment, the squishy cream couches with colourful cushions, the enormous flat-screen TV, the wall of books. Sculptures and paintings, some old, some new, added character.

Dropping her boots to the Persian carpet, she padded past a ten-seater indoor dining table—there was another one outside—and found a gourmet kitchen with its cheffy ovens, upmarket appliances, and a huge fridge.

Pasco stood at the island, expertly chopping vegetables. He smiled at her, and Aisha felt her heart roll over.

'Don't you have minions to chop vegetables for you these days?' she asked.

'I do, but I like to keep my hand in,' Pasco told her, his knife flying even as he kept his eyes on her.

Sliding onto a bar stool, she sniffed the garlic-and-herb-scented air. 'What are you making? It smells delicious.'

'I thought I'd test out an idea I had for a recipe while you slept,' he replied, leaning across the island to drop a quick kiss on her lips. He dropped his eyes to her chest and waved the knife at her shirt. 'I'm glad the clothes fit.'

'Thanks for getting them for me,' Aisha said. 'I'll pay you back.'

He ignored her suggestion and Aisha looked around the apartment. 'This is one hell of a place, Kildare. How many bedrooms?'

'Three plus a study, wine cellar, gym, and sauna upstairs.'

Wow. 'When did you buy it?'

He dumped the diced onions into the pot sitting on a sleek stovetop embedded in the island. 'Ah, when I sold my New York place. I came home, looked for a place on the beach, saw this, and put in an offer on the same day.'

'Thereby obtaining yet another of your goals,' Aisha stated. She saw the bottle of orange juice and poured some into the glass he'd been using. She took a long sip and realised that it was freshly juiced. Marvellous.

Pasco nodded, his thoughts far away. 'I guess the house I saw so long ago made such an impression on me because my friend's family had so much and we had so little.' The corners of his mouth lifted in a self-deprecating smile. 'I was always competitive and I didn't like coming second-best.'

Aisha lowered her glass, trying to make sense of his

words. 'I don't understand. You come from money, your dad is one of the wealthiest men in the valley, your mum is a doctor.'

Pasco stirred the onions before gripping the edges of the counter, straightening his arms. 'The man I call my dad, the man I consider to be my dad, is my stepdad. I took John's surname the year I turned thirteen, the year I went to high school. And yeah, he's wealthy, but before we met him we were, at times, dirt poor.'

'I don't understand,' Aisha said, her thoughts swirling. 'Your mum is a doctor.'

'It's an ugly story, Aisha,' he said as he cleaned his board of onion skins.

But it was a story, one he hadn't told before, one she didn't know. Despite their wedding vows, she didn't know much, or anything, about his early childhood, and the fact he was telling her this now both intrigued and scared her. What did it mean? Was this his way of deepening their friendship?

She didn't understand…

Pasco stood up, switched off the stove, and wiped his hands on a snowy white kitchen cloth. 'My father, also known as the sperm donor, studied business management at university, but dropped out in his second year. Shortly after Mum graduated they married, and a year after that I was born. My mum was the breadwinner in our family, so she worked and my dad stayed at home and took care of us and our finances.'

Anger and devastation sparked in his eyes, and Aisha resisted the urge to walk around the island to comfort him, but knew that if she did anything but sit still and listen, he'd clam up.

After a long silence, Pasco spoke again. 'My mum earned good money and my dad spent it on cracked business schemes. God, he tried everything, from making shoelaces to selling mobile phones. He had a food truck and then a butchery. He sold coins off the internet and antique furniture.'

'I'm sensing he wasn't good with money,' Aisha quietly stated, keeping any censure out of her voice.

'He had the attention span of a fly and couldn't stick to anything for more than a minute. He'd borrow money, using my mum's credit, start up a business, and when he was bored, packed it in. Two months later, he'd borrow more money and the cycle would repeat itself.'

Aisha cocked her head to the side. 'Why didn't your mum put a stop to it?'

Pasco rubbed the back of his neck. 'My lovely, stunningly intelligent mother was a fool when it came to my father. She loved him, wildly and intensely. He brainwashed or nagged or conned her into believing that love had to equal complete trust. In what she now admits was the stupidest mistake of her life, she gave him power of attorney over her financial affairs. For someone like my dad, that was like giving a teenager a limitless credit card and dropping her off at the mall. He managed to keep our money troubles from her for the longest time, but I heard his conversations, I knew something was wrong. But he told me not to bother our mum with it, that she was stressed, tired and he was taking care of everything.'

'But he didn't.'

Pasco's mouth thinned. 'No, he didn't.'

His eyes turned distant and dull. Something major happened, an event that kicked them sideways and upended his world. 'What did he do, Pas?'

Pasco raked his fingers through his hair and when he looked at her, she saw the regret in his eyes. It was obvious to Aisha he was wishing he hadn't opened this can of worms, that he could back away and return to normality. Whatever that was.

But this was the first time ever—and how sad was that?—that she'd burrowed beneath his everything-is-peachy surface and she wanted to know how that chapter of his life ended.

Aisha stared at him, willing him to open up, to confide in her. She didn't say anything, knowing he either would or wouldn't confide in her, nothing she did or said would make him do something he didn't want to do.

'His creditors finally caught up with him,' Pasco stated, sounding a little robotic. 'My birthday is a week before Christmas, and they threw me a birthday party. I invited everybody I knew, girls, guys, old friends, new friends. We lived in a nice house…not fancy, but it had this big pool…so we decided to have a pool party. They hired a DJ, and it was the best party ever…up until the debt collectors stormed in and started loading up our furniture and putting tow hitches on the cars.'

Aisha put her hand to her mouth. Dear God.

'They took everything that wasn't nailed down, anything that had even the smallest value. My boombox and our PlayStation, paintings, the jewellery my mum inherited from her mum and grandmother.'

'Why did they take her property?' Aisha demanded.

'My parents were married in community of property so everything was fair game,' Pasco explained. 'We were left with our pets, two cats and three dogs, and a suitcase of clothes each.'

'And this all happened at the party?' Aisha asked, horrified.

'Yeah, I remember an argument between the DJ and the collection agents because they tried to take his mixing equipment. Some of the girls were crying, the boys were laughing. One of our dogs bit one of the removers.'

He tried to smile, but there was no amusement behind the action. 'Eventually, everyone cleared out and we were left in this house with, I kid you not, nothing. Not even a kettle. There was food and they put it onto the kitchen floor. But we couldn't do anything with it because there wasn't a stove, or pots or pans.'

Aisha held her hands to her cheeks, horrified. 'How did your mum respond?'

Anger, hot and bright, flashed in his eyes. 'I'll never forget my mum sitting on the floor of her empty lounge and staring up at my dad. She asked him how much money was in the bank and he said that they were overdrawn. She listed every account, and he answered the same way every time, that there was nothing. The credit cards were maxed out. He had a little cash in his wallet, she had none.'

Pasco folded his arms across his chest and stared past her to the amazing view outside. 'Can we stop talking about this now?'

'Tell me the rest, Pas. Please.'

He looked at her, desperation and humiliation in his eyes. 'I can't, I'm done,' he replied, his voice hoarse. 'I haven't thought about it for years, talked about it since it happened.' He rolled his shoulders back and reached for the pot on the stove, tossing the contents into the waste disposal. 'I'm feeling claustrophobic, let's get out of here.'

She looked at the wide expanse of the deck, the sunlight streaming into his apartment, and felt as if she were standing on the edge of the world, light and free. His house was linked to the land, the sea, and the sky and there was nothing claustrophobic about it.

Pasco wasn't running away from his place but his past, the memories. And she could understand that. He was so

successful now, so financially secure that being reminded
of that awful time in his life—how out of control he felt,
so helpless—had made him feel jumpy.

A part of her wanted to push, to dig deeper, but he'd
given her what he could, and that was far more than he
ever had before.

She nodded and when he held out his hand, she placed
hers in his. 'Where are we going?'

'Out.' He gestured to the bright sunshine and the intense, deep, glorious blue sky. 'It's a stunning day, we are
together, playing hooky, so does it matter?'

When he put it like that, she didn't think it did.

CHAPTER EIGHT

AISHA BROKE OFF a piece of fish and looked at him from her side of the picnic table overlooking the wide, stunning beach. Their helmets rested on the wooden bench next to them and icy bottles of beer dripped condensation onto the wooden table.

She'd pulled her hair back into a loose knot at the back of her neck and the sunglasses he'd lent her kept slipping down her nose. She had a grease smudge on the side of her mouth, and she kept making take-me-now noises as she worked her way through the greasy but fantastic fish and chips.

After spilling his soul earlier—those brown-black eyes were like a truth drug—Pasco vowed to keep the rest of their day fun and light-hearted. Instead of taking one of his three cars, he'd handed her a helmet and put her behind him on his powerful Ducati, thinking it was a truly excellent day to drive the magnificent Chapman's Peak road. Aisha just smiled, plastered her chest against his back, wrapped her slim arms around him, and, following his lead, leaned into the corners, confident in his ability to keep her safe on the dangerous road.

When they stopped, at a viewpoint or for coffee, and she removed her helmet and his sunglasses, he saw excitement sparkling in her eyes and he wondered how he'd lived his life for so long—in both New York and, before that, in London—without days like these. Easy days, loving days, days he never wanted to end. Hearing her laughter coming over his intercom system and enjoying her relaxed body behind him, he'd carried on driving up the coast, eventually stopping for lunch in Pringle Bay, a charming coastal village situated on the famous Whale Route. Instead of a fancy restaurant, he'd headed for a small fish and chips shop and ordered them a takeaway lunch. He wasn't disappointed with the meal; the hake was perfectly cooked, he thought, licking salt off his fingers, tipping his face up to enjoy the autumn sun.

'God, this is good,' she muttered, picking up another chip and waving it around. 'Tell me about Pringle Bay. I've never been here before.'

Pasco gestured to a mountain to his right. 'The town is surrounded by mountains on three sides and the ocean and the bay, as you can see, is awesome.'

Aisha wiped her hands on a paper serviette and took a sip of her beer. 'Who was Mr Pringle?'

Pasco smiled at her. 'That would be Rear Admiral Thomas Pringle to you, sweetheart. The town was established in the late 1700s. There's also a cave around here, which was used by prisoners and runaway slaves as a hideaway in the eighteenth century.'

Aisha's eyes widened. 'Seriously? Can we see it?'

He shook his head. 'It's on private ground and is hard to find. It's in an inlet washed by the sea and you get to it by a rope between rock walls. I think I remember something about someone in the 1890s finding skeletons in the cave.'

Aisha turned sideways on the bench, lifted her feet, and wrapped her arms around her legs. He was happy to sit in the sun, drink his beer and watch her.

Pasco tipped his bottle to his mouth, mentally running

through the last twenty-four hours. Sex with Aisha had been wonderful a decade ago, but last night it had been nothing short of spectacular. She was less inhibited—thank God—than she'd been at nineteen, he more patient, and the combination was explosive. He could still taste her on his lips, could smell her scent, feel her soft skin under her hands…feel himself stirring once again.

He wanted her again. He didn't think there'd be a time when he'd ever not want Aisha. He was drawn to her in a primal, moth-to-a-flame way—wanting her was in his DNA.

He could understand the physical connection—she was a stunning woman who made men's heads turn, their attraction was understandable—but he didn't understand why he'd told her about his dad, about his life before his family moved to Franschhoek. He never spoke to anyone about what his dad put them through, preferred to forget it, to not think about it at all. As far as he was concerned, his life started when they moved to Franschhoek, and John started dating his mum.

But he'd told Aisha about his life before this life, and he wondered why he'd done that. He'd had many lovers since their divorce, but he always kept things simple, not delving into their lives and keeping them from digging into his. When they pushed for more, for a deeper connection, he always, always ended things, stating that he didn't have the time, that his life was too chaotic for a love affair. A few called him on his emotional unavailability, but he didn't allow their tears or anger to affect him.

He didn't talk. Okay, sure, he'd got through two conversations about their marriage with Aisha—yay him!—but those were super-necessary, had to be done so that they could move on. But what was the point of harping on the past? It couldn't be changed by some back-and-forth exchange of words.

Then, strangely, he'd opened up about his dad. But he still hadn't been able to tell Aisha the worst of it. Only his mum, his brother, and his stepdad John knew the next chapter of that godawful saga.

'It's very pretty here. As lovely as St Urban.'

'Mmm. I looked at buying property here when I returned from the States,' Pasco told her.

'To do what?' Aisha asked, turning her head to look at him.

He shrugged. 'I had this idea of buying a plot of land, establishing greenhouses, and running a small farm-to-table place, little work, no pressure. Living the simple life, you know.'

Her eyebrows rose, as if she couldn't conceive the notion.

'I know, right? I don't blame you for your disbelief. I would've gone off my head in six months.'

'Actually, I'm surprised by the wistfulness I heard in your voice. It sounds like that's something you'd like to do.'

There she went again, seeing through his layers. 'It's not me, Aisha. I do better in high-pressure environments.'

'But do you like it?'

He frowned at her. 'Sorry?'

'Do you like running your swish restaurant at The Vane, Binta, the restaurant in Franschhoek? Does it make you happy?'

The returns, the money in the bank did. The security it gave him made him very happy indeed. Being successful, not following in his father's reckless, unsuccessful footsteps, was all that mattered.

'Yeah.'

'Wow, don't go overboard with your response, Kildare.'

Pasco wiped his hands, bundled up their packets, and tossed them into a nearby rubbish bin. Instead of retaking his seat, he walked around the table and sat behind Aisha, his legs on either side of the bench and her hips. He wound his arm across her torso and pulled her back so her back rested on his chest.

She gripped his arm in her hand and sighed. 'It's such a perfect day. I could sit here for the rest of the day, drinking beers and watching the waves, hoping to see a whale.'

'Better chance of that in June,' he told her, burying his nose in her sweet-smelling hair. He looked over her shoulder at his watch and saw that it was past three. He had a conference call scheduled at five with the same investor who helped him set up Pasco's, Manhattan seven years ago. Hank wasn't the type for out-of-the-blue chats and Pasco suspected he'd found an interesting space or stumbled on a new concept for a restaurant.

The restaurant would be in New York because Hank was Brooklyn born and bred and Manhattan was his playground. Hank still hadn't forgiven Pasco for bailing on the Big Apple—in his eyes, it was the only place to be—and he'd made it his life mission to pull Pasco back to the city. Maybe it was time to consider doing that; his local restaurants were now exceptionally well run and he didn't need to be here any more.

He'd see what Hank had to say...

The only thing that made him hesitate was this woman in his arms.

He tensed up, immediately dismissing that thought. *Do not overthink this, and don't get sucked into the romance of this, Kildare, it was one night, one great day. A step out of time.* He wasn't young and idealistic any more and knew that one night in her arms didn't mean anything.

It was great sex—they'd always been compatible physically—and some laughs. It was a way to get each other out of their system. They'd had their chance and there was no going back.

She'd get St Urban and the pop-up restaurant up and running and then she'd go back to...where?

'When you are done with St Urban and get your promotion, where do you intend living?'

He felt her small shrug. 'After my not-so-fun reunion with my family last night, I think it's best if I stay as far away from them as possible, so probably London.'

If he went to New York, it was only a six-hour flight between the cities. It took half a day to fly from London to Cape Town. God, was he really thinking that far ahead? He hadn't even spoken to Hank yet...

But if he wanted to keep on seeing her after her time ended at St Urban, provided they hadn't crashed and burned by then, London and New York were more doable. At least the cities were in the same hemisphere.

One date, one night together and he was already making plans, just as he had ten years ago. He'd seen her in that pub, decided she was going to be his, and set out to make it happen. With other women, he made a move, mostly got what he wanted—a hook-up or a fling—and moved on, not letting her affect his life in any material way.

He was like his dad that way and the thought pissed him off. Going for what he wanted without considering how his actions affected others. The thought made him feel a little sick.

He wouldn't be like that with Aisha; he refused to repeat his past mistakes. He'd be better than his dad, better than he'd been before. She made him feel more, want to be more...

Yeah, she heated his blood, but she also calmed his mind and inspired him to be a better man. But God, walking around with a heart high on emotion *terrified* him.

So he'd tread slowly, slow the hell down, take a breath, try to be goddamn sensible around her.

Talking about sensible...

'We should think about getting back, Aish.'

She sighed, kissed his wrist, and dropped her knees. 'I know. I still need to get my car from Priya and get back to St Urban.'

'And I have a conference call and I need to inspect management accounts.'

Aisha stood up, Pasco followed her to her feet, and they walked towards his matt black Ducati. He handed her her helmet and pulled his sunglasses off the top of her head. 'We need to talk about the restaurant.'

Aisha cocked her head to look at him.

'I realised that if I give you some solid time, we could just get it done. I'll rearrange my schedule so I can give it a few full days next week.'

Aisha nodded. 'That would be great. If we could work over the weekends, then I could work on St Urban during the week.'

He shook his head. 'Weekends are normally busy for me, and we're catering the Tempest-Vane ball in a few weekends. Are you going?' Aisha shook her head. 'Uh... no. What ball?'

'It's their annual ball to raise funds for their foundation.'

'You're confusing me with your A-list friends, and I'm far too busy to socialise.'

Pasco sent her a lazy smile. 'Honey, nobody is ever too busy for a Tempest-Vane ball. I'll arrange an invitation for you—you should come.'

He saw the hesitation on her face. 'You should meet the Tempest-Vanes. They would be great contacts for you.'

'Is this a business invitation or are you asking me to be your date, Kildare?' Aisha asked before slinging one leg over his bike and scooting back.

Yeah, he didn't blame her for sounding a little pissed off. 'I'd love you to be my date, but I have to run the kitchen, so I'll only be able to join you around ten-thirty, eleven. I'll arrange for you to sit with Muzi and Ro, and the Tempest-Vanes.'

He saw her indecision and sighed. 'Hey, I'm cooking and the menu is stunning. You know you can't resist my food.'

She didn't smile. 'Do you want me there?'

God help him, he did. 'Yes.'

'Okay, then, it's a date.' She lifted her finger and sent him a cheeky smile. 'But I'm only coming for the food.'

He grinned. No, she wasn't. 'Noted. And when can we get together to discuss Ro's pop-up restaurant?'

'I have a quietish day tomorrow, but I suppose that won't suit you?'

His heart leapt at the idea of seeing her again so soon. And because Mondays were normally a slow day, he nodded. He had some meetings, but they could be rearranged. 'That'll work. I'll be with you by nine.' He dropped a kiss on her lips before helping to secure her helmet.

He settled himself on his bike, felt her arms around his waist, and sighed. He didn't want this day to end; he liked being with her, having her in touching distance, hearing her voice, smelling her scent. He loved the sex, but the simplicity of her company was as wonderful.

She was still lovely, a little sweet, a lot sassier. Stronger too. There was definitely a balance between them that hadn't been there before. He could, if he needed to, lean on her, knew she wouldn't, this time around, break. Or run. He was less arrogant, he hoped, she a bit more assertive, and he liked them better now, as individuals and as a couple.

This could, if they chose to let it, grow into something…special. Intense. Meaningful and important.

And that terrified him.

Pasco, unfortunately, only made it to St Urban on Tuesday morning. Yeah, he was a day late, but on Sunday evening, after his call with Hank—and yes, he did want Pasco to fly over to inspect a building for a new restaurant—he checked in with his chef de cuisine at The Vane Hotel and, two minutes into his video call, realised Davit was either sick or getting sick. His sickly pallor, tired, dull eyes and his croaky voice made Pasco think his right-hand man was on the point of collapse.

Pasco, worried that Davit would infect the rest of his staff with whatever bug he was carrying, told him to go home. But Davit refused, telling him that two of his station chefs were off work, thanks to the same bug. Pasco didn't hesitate and headed straight for the restaurant. He told Davit to beat it, pulled on his chef's jacket, and got to work. Davit wasn't ready to come back to work on Monday, but luckily, professed himself well enough to resume work on Tuesday.

'Hi,' he said when Aisha waved him into her office. He caught a glance at her face and internally winced. Tight lips, narrowed eyes, clenched jaw…he didn't need to be a rocket scientist to realise she was ticked.

Pasco sat down in the chair opposite her and placed his ankle on his other knee as he inspected the loose braid running along the side of her head. With tendrils falling out, it was a soft and feminine look and was in direct contrast to her flat eyes and irritated expression.

'Are you okay?'

Aisha didn't look at him and neither did she reply. Unease rippled up his spine. He thought he'd try again.

'Ready to head down to the cellar?' he asked, glancing at his watch. It was nearly nine and if they got a solid three hours of work in, he could make the short trip into town and do a spot check at Pasco's, Franschhoek and see what was happening there. He'd noticed an upturn in expenses and a downturn in income and he needed to get to the bottom of that problem.

God, it never stopped.

Aisha linked her fingers together and rested her hands on her desk. 'No.'

Okay. 'When will you be ready? In ten minutes? Fifteen?'

Aisha turned her computer screen towards him, and he pulled his eyes off her lovely face to look at what he presumed to be an online appointment schedule. Aisha jabbed a finger at a red block from yesterday. 'I blocked off that time for you, yesterday. I have a slew of appointments this morning.'

Oh, crap. She was mad at *him*.

'I'm sorry I couldn't be here yesterday, but something came up. Can you not postpone this morning's appointments?'

Aisha scowled at him. 'I could, but I don't intend to.'

Young Aisha would've jumped to do as he asked; Aisha today wasn't budging. Dammit.

'Had you let me know earlier, I would've rearranged my schedule. But you didn't because your time is so much more important than mine.'

'Ro's restaurant is still in a planning phase. My restaurants are not. And if there's a problem, I need to put them first.' He wasn't being unreasonable, was he?

Aisha scanned her screen. 'We can get together to-morrow at four or Thursday at eleven,' she said in a very even, flat voice. He wasn't stupid enough to believe she wasn't still furious with him.

Pasco stood up and walked around to stand behind her. He looked at the appointments on her screen for the next few hours. He silently cursed when he saw she was scheduled to walk the grounds with St Urban's grounds manager. Her second appointment was with a local supplier of cleaning materials and housekeeping consumables and, because they'd want St Urban business, they'd be happy to reschedule.

'I'm sorry, it was rude of me not to give you more notice about my change of plans,' he said, half sitting on the edge of her desk. He nodded to the screen. He was running out of time, and he did need to get to Pasco's, Franschhoek today. 'Why don't you call those people, reschedule and let's get some real work done?'

Aisha stared at him for a minute, maybe longer, and it slowly dawned on Pasco he'd somehow made a bad situation a hundred times worse. How, he wasn't quite sure, but he had.

It was in her eyes, flashing *Abort! Danger ahead!* and in her flattened lips and tense jaw. She pushed her chair back and stood up, pushing back her light jacket to rest her hands on her curvy hips. He'd stroked those curves, kissed the smooth skin above her hip bone, slid his hands around to her truly spectacular butt.

'You arrogant, opinionated ass!'

He wasn't sure what surprised him more, her insult or her raised voice. He couldn't remember Aisha ever yelling before, didn't think she had it in her. During their marriage, she'd always been so even keeled, happy to acquiesce. Occasionally, he'd wished she'd stand up for herself more, but because he didn't have time for arguments, he'd appreciated her willingness to go with the flow. Kitchens were full of drama. He hadn't needed it at home too.

'How dare you stride in here and demand that I rearrange my working day to accommodate you? You might not respect my career—'

Whoa, hold on! 'Of course I respect your career!' he interrupted, standing to face her.

'If you did, you wouldn't have blown me off or sent me a message an hour after we were supposed to meet!'

She waved her hands in a shooing motion, trying to dismiss him. 'It doesn't matter.'

'Actually, it *does* matter. Don't shut down, *talk* to me.'

Her eyes widened at his statement, and she finally nodded. Frowning, she speared her hands into her hair.

'The bottom line is that you don't respect me, my time, or what I'm trying to do here! If you did, you wouldn't walk into my office looking for me to fall into line with your schedule, your wishes.'

Pasco winced. Okay, maybe he'd been a little heavy-handed in insisting she blow off her other appointments to be with him. Because that was what he wanted, her with him. He'd missed her, missed her smile and her voice, missed her in his bed. Missed her scent in his nose, and her body in his arms. His apartment felt empty without her.

'I was needed at The Vane,' Pasco carefully replied. 'My chef—'

'Of *course* you have to put the restaurant first. Your time is so much more valuable than *mine*. Guess that hasn't changed.'

He heard the bitterness in her voice and, worse, the

derision. It pierced him with all the accuracy of a scalpel blade.

'Next time give me ample warning you can't make a meeting. I'm not someone who will wait around for you, Kildare. Respect me and respect my time.'

She brushed past him to cross the room to yank open the door to her office. 'When would you like to meet? Tomorrow at four or Thursday at eleven?' she demanded, gesturing for him to leave.

He saw the militant look in her eyes and internally winced. Knowing there was little point in arguing, and no chance of her changing her mind, he jammed his hands into the pockets of his chinos and walked towards her.

As for another meeting with her, that depended on what he found at Pasco's, Franschhoek today and tonight. 'I'll let you know,' he told her.

She lifted her chin. 'Fine,' she said through gritted teeth.

Pasco sighed, stopped and turned to face her. She was right, he'd been disrespectful today and she was right to call him out. If he wanted to have Aisha in his life, he'd have to do better, think more, stop believing he was the reason the world turned.

He'd been on his own for a long time and was the lord of his little fiefdom. Thanks to his power and success, people kowtowed to him, and he'd become spoiled.

Hell, even if Aisha weren't a factor, this facet of his life, of himself, could certainly do with a great deal of work.

'I really am sorry, sweetheart.'

He saw the surprise in her eyes at his genuine apology, but instead of inviting him back into her office, she slammed the door in his face.

And his respect for her inched upwards.

CHAPTER NINE

THROUGHOUT THE REST of her day, Aisha questioned her reaction to Pasco's lack of consideration, wondering if she'd allowed their past to colour her response to his actions. After all, rescheduling appointments was something she often did, and there had been many times when she couldn't make an appointment because something else arose. It was never a big deal.

But she always had the decency to let the other party know, to explain her actions. No, she decided, Kildare had messed up and she'd been right to let him know he was out of line. And, yes, maybe she had been a little ruder to him than necessary because she felt as if she'd been snapped back into the past and she was nineteen again, pacing their flat because he'd promised to come home early so that they could catch a late dinner. Or she was waiting in the hallway, her packed suitcase at her feet, waiting for him to take her on a weekend away only to find out, hours later, that he had to work. Alone in her bed, crying herself to sleep, because she was so damn lonely and felt neglected and unloved.

But she wasn't nineteen any more and she was a professional woman who stood up for herself.

You are so much stronger than the girl you were, Aisha, and you're not a pushover.

She grinned into the darkness. She'd come a long way.

Aisha scowled at the dark trees as she walked back to her cottage, navigating the path by the torch on her phone.

Tired and headachy, she pulled the pins out of her hair and allowed it to tumble down her back. She shoved the pins into the pocket of her jacket, hunching her shoulders against the cold wind cutting through her clothes. While she'd been nursing her anger at Pasco, a cold front had come in, bringing cloudy skies threatening rain, and a biting wind. She increased her pace, thinking about what she could eat when she got home. She tried to recall what was in her fridge and pulled a face. Apart from a few bottles of wine in her small wine rack—she'd be having a glass or three tonight—there wasn't much in her house in the way of food. She kept meaning to go into the village to stock up, but it kept getting shoved down to the bottom of her to-do list.

Maybe if she headed into town around lunchtime tomorrow, she could catch Pasco at his Franschhoek restaurant, nail down a time for them to meet and pick up some food, either before or after. And when they met again, they needed to have a tension-free, productive conversation about the restaurant. She had to get their working relationship back on track and, to do that, she'd have to keep her distance from him, to put space between them.

When he'd walked into her office earlier, her heart had fizzed and fumbled, stuttered, and stumbled. No man, before and after him, had ever made her feel off balance, shaky, as if she were attached to the charging pads of a defibrillator. Despite being incandescently angry with him, she'd had to grip the edge of her desk to stop herself from leaping into his arms.

His arms were where she most wanted to be. Dammit. She couldn't regret sleeping with him—their lovemaking had been off-the-charts wonderful and she'd enjoyed every minute out of bed too—but she knew it couldn't happen again. Every non-professional encounter she had with him made her want more, encouraged her to throw caution to the wind, allowed him to slip a little deeper under her skin, a little further into her soul.

There was no future for them. There couldn't be. He couldn't see her as an equal partner, would never make her a priority, and she could never settle for anything less.

Friends and fellow professionals, colleagues. That was all they could be.

Aisha walked up to her veranda and yelped when she saw a shadow-like figure in the corner. Then, when her mouth caught up to her brain, she let out a small screech and started to kick off her heels so she could bolt away.

'It's me, sweetheart,' Pasco said, not moving from his seat on the swing in the corner.

Aisha, off balance because she was only wearing one heel, slapped her hand to her chest and released a low growl. 'You scared me, Kildare! What the hell are you doing lurking on my veranda?'

'Waiting for you,' Pasco stated.

Looking down, Aisha located her heel and bent down to pick it up. Standing on one foot, she put her heel back on before stepping onto her veranda. Her eyes flicked over Pasco, noticing he'd pulled on a leather bomber jacket over his shirt and that his hair looked more messy than normal. In fact, he looked exhausted and, she squinted at him in the low light, sad.

'Everything okay, Pasco?' she asked him as she inserted her key into the lock before pushing open the door to her cottage.

'It's after eleven. Do you always work so late?' Pasco

asked from a couple of steps behind her. 'Please tell me that my idiocy today isn't the reason you are home late.'

He looked genuinely contrite, so Aisha shook her head. 'No, this is my life.' Aisha dropped her laptop bag onto the dining table and watched him as he strode into her place, holding a large cooler box with ease.

'Got any wine?' he asked. He lifted the box with one hand. 'I'll trade a massive glass for lemon chicken, roasted potatoes with rosemary, roasted vegetables, and a pecan nut pie.'

Exhausted, she thought about asking him to leave, but her stomach was grumbling and she needed food. Then she looked at Pasco, really looked, and saw his tight lips, his turbulent expression, and the devastation in his eyes.

He looked both gutted and furious, upset and disheartened. Something had happened between him leaving her office and now, something that rocked his world.

'Sit down, Pasco,' she told him, kicking off her heels. Reaching for a bottle of red from her wine rack, she put it on the table and rooted around in a drawer to find the corkscrew. 'Open that and pour us some. The glasses are in the cupboard above the fridge. I'm just going to change into something warmer and more comfortable.'

Without replying, Pasco reached for the wine and Aisha scampered into her bedroom to change into a pair of track pants and an oversized hoodie. She pulled thick socks onto her feet and roughly pulled her hair back into a messy tail.

Aisha sighed as she caught a glimpse of herself in the freestanding mirror in the corner of her room. She looked about sixteen, and sloppy. But this wasn't a date. This was a meal—thank God!—some wine, and then she would send Pasco on his way.

What was he doing here anyway? Had he come to apologise?

Aisha walked back into the open-plan living area and saw that Pasco had not only poured wine, but was also in the process of unwrapping a plate of food. He tested the temperature with the back of his hand, grimaced, and stomped over to the microwave. Aisha had no problem heating food, but Pasco, picky chef that he was, despised the practice.

'Where's yours?' she asked, pulling out a chair and sitting down.

'I ate at the restaurant earlier,' Pasco replied, hitting buttons on the microwave.

He turned and his eyes slammed into hers and electricity—or annoyance, who could tell?—arced between them. He started to speak, but stopped when the microwave dinged. He turned, pulled the plate out, and placed it on the navy placemat in front of her. She breathed in the delicious smells of lemon, lemongrass and garlic, rosemary, and roasted chicken. Heaven, she thought, picking up her cutlery and digging in.

After five minutes of eating, she looked up to see Pasco still standing in front of the counter, his untouched wine glass next to him. He looked broody, tired, and as if he was about to snap.

'While I appreciate the food, I'm still not sure why you are here, Pasco,' Aisha stated.

'But thank you for bringing me food, it's delicious,' she added.

'It was one of the trainee chefs' chance to cook the staff meal at the restaurant. I think he did a decent job.'

More than decent, Aisha thought as she took another bite of chicken. Chewing, she watched as Pasco turned to stare out her kitchen window, wondering what he was looking at as it was pitch-black outside. His shoulders were tight with tension, and he kept massaging his neck, as if he was trying to rub away a knot in his muscles.

'Pas, come sit down,' Aisha told him. He turned to look at her over his shoulder, as if debating whether that was what he wanted to do, before nodding. He yanked out a chair and extended his long legs, crossing his feet at the ankles.

'Again, I am sorry about earlier. I was a jerk.'

'Accepted. So what happened today?'

Pasco leaned back, picked up his glass of wine, and downed it in one swallow. After refilling his glass, he looked at her, his gaze broody. 'My gut has been telling me that there's something wrong at my restaurant in Franschhoek for a while, but I ignored my instincts. Expenses are up, revenue is down, and I've been meaning to get there to find out what's going on, but I've been busy.'

'Couldn't your accountant or business manager investigate for you?' Aisha asked, taking her last bite and placing her cutlery together. 'That was fantastic, thank you. I was so hungry.'

'I could tell,' Pasco said, humour flashing in his eyes. 'That was a man-sized portion. Where do you put it all?'

'Fast metabolism,' Aisha told him. 'The restaurant?'

'My business manager and accountant both told me not to worry about it, that the margins were in the appropriate range and that it was probably just a temporary dip. Nothing to worry about because the manager is also one of my most trusted employees. Jason has been with me from the beginning. We worked together at my first restaurant in London.'

Aisha picked up her wine glass and took a sip, leaning back in her chair.

'When you kicked me out of your office—' Aisha started to protest, realised it was a fair statement, and nodded, refusing to feel guilty. He'd deserved it. But because she didn't believe in holding grudges, she gestured for him to continue.

'I headed over there. I was early, the only one there so I let myself in. I went straight to the office, thinking that I'd do a couple of spot checks. I was about to start when I heard a knock on the back door, the door where the staff enters.'

'Who was at the door, Pas?' Aisha asked when he hesitated.

Pasco rubbed his forehead with his fingers. 'Jason's wife. She had one baby in a pram, another on her hip and I could tell she'd been crying for what looked like days. She asked me if Jason was in, I told her no and her knees buckled, just for an instant. The baby started to wail, the toddler started screaming and it was pandemonium.'

'What did you do?'

'I invited her inside, gave her some coffee. After what seemed like hours, I got the story from her,' Pasco said, his expression bleak.

'And it wasn't pretty,' Aisha stated.

'Jason left her a couple of months ago and hasn't paid her any child support. She's all but destitute. She's being evicted and she came to see him. She needed money to go to her mother in Kimberley.'

'And Jason?' Aisha asked.

Pasco's gaze hardened. 'Well, apparently Jason has a new woman, a new house, and is spending every cent he earns, and that's a lot, on his new girlfriend. He's bought a new car, new clothes for her, furniture, jewellery. All this while his wife can't get any money from him to pay for nappies, formula, and the rent.'

Aisha winced, immediately angry. 'What a dirtbag.'

'Yeah,' Pasco replied. 'But he's a dirtbag I considered

to be my friend. I don't recognise this, recognise him. That's not the guy I know.'

'That's the guy he's being right now,' Aisha told him. 'I presume you gave the wife a wad of cash?'

Pasco nodded. 'I arranged a driver to take her to Kimberley, paid her rent, and gave her money to buy what she needed,' Pasco said, in his furious, growly voice. 'Today was his day off and, in between helping out in the kitchen, I did some spot checks and he's been stealing from me.

'When he comes in tomorrow, I'm going to fire his ass,' Pasco told her.

'Do you have proof?'

'There are some dubious invoices that don't look genuine. I think he's also been double-dipping.'

'Double-dipping?'

'He's claimed cash from petty cash on invoices that were paid on the company credit card. I'll bring in a team of forensic accountants to go through every scrap of paper.'

Aisha rubbed her thumb across his knuckles. 'I'm sorry he hurt you, Pas,' she quietly stated.

Pasco stared at her with haunted eyes. 'He was my first employee, Aish, he's been with me for years. Why do the people closest to you always let you down?'

He wasn't talking about Jason any more, and Aisha knew that the ghosts from the past had their cold fingers around his throat. 'You're thinking about your dad.'

He shrugged. 'How can I not? It's pretty much the same thing he did.'

No, Jason had opened up Pasco's wounds, he hadn't caused them. 'Tell me about your dad, Pas.'

Pasco jammed his thumb and index finger into his eye sockets and rubbed them, as if trying to dispel the memories. But when he looked up, Aisha saw that they were still swirling in his eyes.

'My mum tried hard to make her marriage work, but having her house repossessed was the last straw. We moved to Franschhoek, and my father stayed in the city. It was a tough, tough time. I remember listening to her crying herself to sleep. It didn't help that he wouldn't stop calling her or trying to see us, rocking up at midnight or four in the morning, causing scene after scene and threatening to take us away.

'Mum got a restraining order and instigated divorce proceedings. Then she went to work and put her head down to clear the debts he ran up in her name. She met John, my stepdad, but she refused to accept any financial help from anyone, including her wealthy family. She said she'd been the idiot, so she'd pay the price. We had some visits with him—they were awful because he wasn't that interested in us, he just ranted about my mum most of the time, constantly telling us how he was going to take us away,' Pasco explained. 'Then he dropped off the radar and I was hurt. Confused. And worried. And I felt guilty because John was around and he was great, stable, and interested in us, you know?'

Aisha nodded.

'I white-knuckled it through my last year of primary school, knowing that I was going to Duncan House. My grandfather and uncles all went to the school and my grandfather left money for the fees. That was what got me through that year, the knowledge that I was going to this fantastic school.'

Aisha sucked in a breath, suspecting what he was about to say next. 'A couple of weeks before I was due to start, my mum got a call from the school, asking for a meeting. She went in and when she came out, she was crying…'

Pasco's Adam's apple bobbed.

'Your dad stole that money too?' Aisha gently asked.

He stared out of the window, misery in his eyes. 'My mum, naively, believed he wouldn't stoop so low to take our education fund. But he had that damn power of attorney, and he did. My mum just shrank in on herself, fell apart. She handled losing her house, her savings, but losing the ability to fund her boys' education? That nearly killed her.'

'But you did go to Duncan House,' she pointed out. 'How did that happen?'

He smiled softly. 'After a week of watching my mum cry, John said to hell with it and he went to Duncan House and cut a cheque for both my and Cam's education, for the full five years each. My mum told him to cancel the cheque, that it wasn't his problem, and he told her he didn't have any kids, that he was going to marry her and he had pots of money. He told her he understood her desire to pay off his debts, but we were going to Duncan House and that was the end of it.'

'You must've been so relieved,' Aisha stated.

'Yeah, I was, but I was so pissed off with my father too,' Pasco replied, rubbing the back of his neck. 'I needed to talk to him, to confront him, you know?'

'Did you?'

Pasco nodded. 'I found out where he was living, I don't remember how, and I hitched a lift to the city and went to see him.'

'Go on, Pas,' Aisha said when he hesitated.

'I went to his apartment—God, that's too good a word for the hovel he was living in. I expected a house, something great to show for all the money he stole, but it was a hovel. There was a mattress on the floor, a sleeping bag, and a two-ring stove. No fridge. He said he lost the money in some pyramid scheme, and he was destitute. He asked *me* for money, his twelve-year-old son.

'I just stood there, wondering who the hell he was and how he could make such stupid decisions. I vowed I would never be like him, that I would be the exact opposite.'

A bankload of pennies dropped. That was why he was so driven, so committed to his career. Pasco's need to be successful was his way to heal the psychological wounds his father had inflicted. Aisha stared at him, feeling shocked and sad. 'What did you do?'

'Bolted out of there and called John. He collected me in the city and brought me home.'

Aisha stroked the back of his hand with the tips of her fingers. 'I'm sorry you had to go through that and I'm sorry Jason let you down and yanked all those old memories up again.'

'I don't understand how Jason can walk away from his family without looking back, how he can pretend they don't exist. I've done everything I can to make sure my family is financially secure. They'd never have to work a day in their lives again if they chose not to.'

Aisha tipped her head to the side. 'What do you mean?'

'There's a trust…if my parents or my brother, you, get into financial trouble, there's a massive trust with millions in it as a backup plan.'

'Me?' Aisha squeaked. 'Why am I there?'

He shrugged. 'I started the trust when we first married. Every cent I earned working overtime went into it.' He frowned at her. 'Why do you think I worked all those extra hours? I needed to make sure that you would be okay.'

Aisha buried her head in her hands and shook her head. 'God, Pasco!'

She hadn't needed a saviour or a financial backup plan, she'd needed her husband. She'd needed his time and attention and that was why she'd walked. Yet, because he'd been so disappointed by his father, he went to the other extreme to be the exact opposite. And their marriage fell apart because they were useless at communicating.

His previous actions suddenly made so much more sense to her than they ever did before. He'd become a workaholic, someone who couldn't sit still for more than a second. He needed to work because if he took a minute to relax, he thought he was becoming like his dad, and he couldn't bear the thought.

Pasco was hard-wired to give his businesses everything he had. She now understood his need to succeed, his determination and his drive. It wasn't because he was ruthlessly ambitious, but because he needed to protect the ones he loved, to plot and plan so that he would never let anyone down the way his dad did him.

She understood his impulse to make sure everyone's ducks were in a row, but that wasn't his job. She most certainly didn't need the money in his trust, for him to be her backup plan. How to say this, frame this, without getting his back up?

'Pas, you are not responsible for the actions of others, and it's not your job to clean up your dad's mess.'

'He stole my mum's money...' Pasco hotly replied.

'Yeah, he did.' Aisha took a deep breath, knowing what she was about to say would be hard for him to hear. 'But your mum played a part in letting that happen. And, judging by what you said about her repaying her own debts, she's owned her actions and has accepted her part in the fiasco.

'Your stepfather is rich, your brother is financially stable, I'm fine...none of us *needs* you to be our backup plan, Pasco. You are not responsible for our financial well-being. We have to be able to stand and fall by our own decisions. *Our* choices, *our* consequences.'

He stared at her, turmoil in his eyes. She pointed a finger at him. 'Stop trying to control the world, Pas. Let the people you love, who love you, be your partners and not your responsibility.'

Something flashed in his eyes, an emotion she couldn't identify. She could see he wanted to argue but it was late and she was tired, and she'd given him enough to think of for now.

He'd either see it her way, or he wouldn't…she couldn't impose her beliefs on him.

Aisha stood up, walked around the table, and slung her thigh over Pasco's. He pulled his knees up, his hands instinctively going to her hips. Aisha brushed his hair back from his face and slowly lowered her head, allowing her breasts to sink into his hard chest. Her mouth touched his and she gently nibbled his lower lip. She was mentally exhausted and he, she assumed, was too. It was time to put this day behind them, to relax and recharge. And she knew a very good way to do that.

'Think about what I said. But only much, much later.'

CHAPTER TEN

SERVICE FOR THE Tempest-Vane ball had been a bitch and Pasco was running an hour later than he expected. After a quick shower, he pulled on his black suit, white shirt, and black tie—nothing showy—and headed to the ballroom on the third floor, directly above his busy restaurant. He hesitated, thinking he should check in with his restaurant staff, but knew that if he did he'd be sucked into whatever was happening in the kitchen.

Nobody had called him with an issue, so he'd just let sleeping restaurant dogs lie.

And…he really couldn't wait to get to the ball to see Aisha.

Something had changed since their conversation about his dad at her cottage, and their connection had, despite their busy schedules, deepened. He'd spent a lot of time thinking about what she'd said about his need to be responsible for everyone and everything and thought she had a point. But how to change the habits of a lifetime was still giving him trouble. Being protective was wired into his DNA and he didn't know if he'd ever stop worrying about the people he loved.

Pasco stepped into the lift, his blood fizzing with anticipation at seeing his lover. The past few weeks had been incredibly busy, but they'd managed, somehow, to have a few arrive-late-and-leave-early sleepovers. When they couldn't be together, their early-morning and late-night phone calls got him through the hours until they could be together again.

Their busy lives weren't ideal, but they were making it work, trying to accommodate each other as much and whenever they could. They were certainly communicating better and their lovemaking was…yeah, bloody fantastic. Better than it had ever been.

But he still felt dissatisfied and wanted more. More time, more making love, more conversations about everything and nothing.

More.

It was strange to feel like this and Pasco wasn't sure how to cope with his restlessness. Ten years ago, five, working like a demon got his blood pumping, made him feel ten feet tall. Now all he felt was frustrated. And tired.

The last month had been a perfect storm, with Hank bombarding him with videos of a warehouse space he was convinced would make an awesome restaurant and entreaties to come back to the States. His producers wanted a definite answer on whether he was going to do another season of his popular travel show and he was dashing between The Vane, dropping in on St Urban before heading to Pasco's, Franschhoek, where he'd installed a temporary chef and manager.

He hadn't visited Binta for a few weeks and he was also neglecting his kitchenware line. Frankly, all he wanted to do was ignore all of it and spend some time with Aisha, have a leisurely meal, catch a movie, watch the sun go down behind the Simonsberg mountain with a glass of red in his hand and her at his side.

Maybe a dog lying at his feet.

Pasco rubbed his face, surprised by his longing for domesticity. But there was only one woman he could see as his wife and that was his ex-wife.

Did he really want to do that? Go there? Or was he just overworked and tired? Stressed? But a little voice inside him insisted that his first choice was the only woman with whom he could imagine spending the rest of his life.

Absurd notion—preposterous, really—but it didn't make it any less true. Aisha was it for him.

But they'd tried once, and they'd failed. How could they—even if she was interested in trying again—be together? Aisha was up for a promotion and if she got it, and she would because she was bloody brilliant at her job, she had the option to live in London or Johannesburg. If she moved to London and he didn't move back to New York, they'd only, with their schedules, occasionally see each other.

But seeing each other when they could was better than nothing. But he knew, after a few months of incessant travelling, the novelty would quickly fade, and travelling would become a drag. And, in time, they'd drift apart.

Crap, he simply couldn't find a solution.

Living apart was not what he wanted anyway. He wanted to see Aisha every day, in every light, and in every way. He wanted her in his bed, on his deck when he woke up, to meet her for lunch or an afternoon quickie. He wanted a life with her, he wanted a *wife*.

But to get what he wanted, one of them would have to make a massive sacrifice. He would either have to slow down, or Aisha would have to give up her job. Neither option was possible.

He couldn't slow down; he'd tried that before and he'd been miserable. Aisha had worked damn hard for her promotion, and he couldn't ask her to give that up—that wouldn't be fair.

Devil, meet Deep Blue Sea.

Why did relationships have to be so damn complicated? This was why he'd avoided them for so long: he didn't like thinking this hard. Oh, and he probably also avoided relationships with other women because he was still in love with his wife.

He'd never stopped being in love with her.

Pasco stepped into the lavishly decorated ballroom—white and gold—searching for Aisha in the sea of black-and-white tuxedos and ball gowns. Navy blue seemed to be the favoured colour this year, along with a dark, turbulent grey.

Pasco caught a flash of dazzling, deep pink and sucked in a breath. Stepping to the side, he saw Aisha standing next to the dance floor, talking to Muzi. She wore a ruffled sari, the fuchsia colour eye-popping. A heavily jewel-embellished, teeny-tiny blouse and matching belt gave her traditional outfit a trendy vibe.

And yeah, he loved the deep vee in her blouse hinting at her stunning breasts and, because she had a drool-worthy body, the way the dress highlighted her tiny waist and stunning skin.

Pasco forced his feet to move and when he reached her, he took in the matching colour of her lipstick, her subtle make-up, and the tiny silver bindi placed between her eyebrows. She'd straightened her hair and it fell in a thick black fall of shine down her back.

She looked sensational...strip-her-down-and-take-her-to-bed stunning.

Aisha's blush, Muzi's deep laugh, and Aisha's elbow in his ribs told him he'd said that last sentence out aloud. Oh, well, it was the truth.

Pasco shook Muzi's hand and pulled his friend in for a quick, manly hug. 'How's Ro?' Pasco asked.

'Hanging in there.' Muzi grimaced.

'She's done well to keep those babies in as long as she has,' Aisha told Muzi.

'Yeah.' Muzi pulled back his jacket sleeve to look at his watch. 'It's getting late. I'm off.'

Pasco clasped his shoulder. 'Let us know if anything happens baby-wise.'

'Will do,' Muzi said before striding away.

Aisha sent him a quick smile. 'He's a basket case.'

'He adores Ro and is worried about her,' Pasco replied, watching his friend's progress across the room.

Aisha took a champagne glass from a waiter holding a tray and Pasco ordered a bourbon. She sipped and let her eyes drift across the room. 'Do you want kids?' she asked.

He wasn't completely surprised by her question. He'd seen the longing in her eyes when she eyed Ro's ginormous stomach. 'I haven't given it much thought. But if I did, I'd only want to have them with you.'

Aisha stared at him, shocked. 'What?'

'You heard me,' Pasco replied, jamming his hands into the pockets of his suit trousers.

'But you and I, we're just—' Aisha stumbled over her words and her glass wobbled. He plucked it from her fingers and placed it on a high table and linked her fingers in his.

He dropped his head and placed a kiss on her temple, breathing in her feminine, lovely, too-sexy scent. 'Lovers? Exes? Friends? We're all of that, but we're also so much more.'

'How much more, Pas?' Aisha asked him, her eyes wide with surprise.

Pasco took her hand, pulled her to the dance floor and into his arms. He rested his cheek against the side of her head as they glided around the floor. Their bodies, as always, were completely in sync, and they moved easily together.

'I think we should discuss that, discuss us,' Pasco told her, wincing at the tremble he heard in his voice. Damn, but he was nervous. 'Would rewriting the rules be something you'd be interested in doing?'

He held his breath, scared she'd say no. His heart slowed down, and he forgot to breathe.

'Yes.'

There it was, thank *God*. He released the tension in his shoulders, in his spine, and closed his eyes in relief. 'Can I take you to dinner next Saturday night, somewhere wildly romantic? Maybe we can figure something out, to see if we can get from here to…babies.'

She didn't reply, and Pas could feel tension running through her. He pulled back to look at her, saw her eyes fill with emotion. He couldn't decide whether fear or excitement had the upper hand, but he intended to find out. 'Is that something you want, sweetheart?'

'I don't know what I want, Pas. And feeling like this again scares me,' Aisha softly replied, resting her head against his chest.

'I know, I'm scared too. But maybe we can figure it out together,' Pasco murmured, before pulling her closer and holding her tighter.

Late on Wednesday afternoon, Aisha sat in her office, sifting through résumés of people applying for the top positions at St Urban—permanent hotel manager, chef, food, and beverage manager—but after reading the same résumé twice, she pushed the folders aside, and her chair back, and captured her hands between her knees, frustrated by her inability to concentrate.

Pasco wanted to talk about their relationship. God,

she was in a relationship with her ex-husband... How did that happen?

That had been rule number one, do not fall for your ex, and she'd broken it a hundred times over. What was she thinking? Had she been thinking at all? No, as it had years before, her brain shut down whenever she came within six feet of the man!

Aisha bit her bottom lip and stared at her shoes. She appreciated him wanting to find a way for them to be together, but this time around, she was trying to be sensible, to think things through. She was going to be in the country for another four, maybe five months, and if she got the promotion, she'd have to decide on moving to Johannesburg or London. If she wasn't promoted, she'd be moving on to the next project, which could be in Canada or Cartagena.

Either way, she'd be hours and hours away from Pasco. And yes, she understood that some people managed to make long-distance relationships work, but she didn't see how they could. They couldn't even make it work when they'd lived together in the same apartment.

Yes, they were older and more mature, but realistically, they were already struggling to carve out time to spend together. How would they manage that when they were in different cities, different time zones?

She wanted to be with him, see more of him, but...how?

Her computer indicated she had a video call and, happy to be distracted from her thoughts, which were going around and around, Aisha pounced on it, wincing when she saw it was her mum calling. Unable to cut the call, she rubbed her fingers across her forehead and sighed. 'Hi, Mum.'

'I'm phoning to see if you are coming to dinner, not this Saturday but the next. Everybody will be there.'

Would it hurt her mum, just once, to open a conversation with a *'Hello, darling, how are you?'*?

'I don't think so, Mum.'

'Why not?'

Oh, let me count the reasons.

'Because you all but ignored me at Oscar's party and when I did speak, my opinion was instantly dismissed? Because the family spoke over and interrupted me?'

'We don't do that!'

Oh, enough now! She'd always been careful to dance around her mum's feelings, but she didn't have the time or the energy to massage her mum's delicate ego. Or anyone else's! She was done with bottling up her emotions to make people feel comfortable. 'Mum, what's the point? Really?'

'You're our daughter—'

'Well, it doesn't feel like it! Growing up I felt like the ugly stepchild, never part of the family, and nothing has changed.'

'We don't—'

She sounded a little mortified, but Aisha was past caring. This moment had been a long time in coming. 'Mum, I get it, you're all intellectuals and I don't fit in. I don't get advanced maths or know how to map the neural pathways of the brain. But I'm not an idiot!'

'Well, none of us think you are.'

Aisha scoffed at her tepid response. Really? That was news to her. 'I don't fit into the family, Mum. I never have.'

It felt good to verbalise her long-held hurts, to tell her mother how she felt. It felt a little like poison leaving her system, as if her blood were thinner, her heart able to beat a fraction better.

'That's not true!'

Aisha sighed. 'It's true for me, Mum.'

'If that's how you feel,' her mum stated, her voice stiff with outrage, 'I'm not going to beg you to change your mind.'

'Mum, don't be like that, okay? Everything is fixable, but only if we communicate and compromise. Talk to Dad and give me a call in a day or two if you think we can find another way of dealing with each other. Maybe, instead of a family dinner, it could just be the three of us. What do you think?'

'I'll talk to your father,' her mum muttered.

Honestly, that was more progress than she'd expected.

Aisha lowered her phone, saw the call had been dropped and rested her forehead on her desk. Look at her, taking names and kicking butt! Aisha hauled in a deep breath, feeling lighter and brighter. She was learning about boundaries and what she would and wouldn't accept. She was making others, and herself, take responsibility for their actions and behaviours. She was finally learning to take care of herself.

And damn, it felt good.

Aisha heard the beep of an incoming video call coming in on her computer, pushed her hand through her hair and faced her screen, her hand clicking her wireless mouse.

Her boss's lovely face appeared on her screen and her white teeth flashed as she smiled. Aisha sighed, relieved.

'Hello, Miles,' Aisha said, leaning forward. Thank God for work, the one thing in her life that wasn't complicated.

Miles's smile faded and she leaned forward, her expression concerned. 'Damn, girl, you look like hell! How hard are you working? Are you sleeping?'

Miles, under her sleek and sophisticated facade, was a bit of a mother duck. 'Lots to do, Miles.'

'How's the restaurant coming on?' Miles asked.

Slowly, because she and Pasco often got distracted. But they'd get it done. She wouldn't let down Ro. 'It's coming.'

'I know that I dumped that on you, Aisha,' Miles told her, wincing. 'But I don't want you killing yourself. If you can't manage, I'll send someone—maybe Kendall—to take over the establishment of the restaurant.'

Kendall was young, sexy, and an incorrigible flirt. She'd take one look at Pasco and decide to add him as a notch on her bedpost. Aisha had no problem with Kendall's relaxed attitude to men and sex—her body, her rules—but not when it involved her husband…dammit, her ex-husband.

Uh, no. She'd rather work her fingers to the bone, thank you very much.

'I'll let you know if I get overwhelmed, Miles,' she said through gritted teeth. No, she wouldn't.

'Your call,' Miles replied. 'So, I know it's late notice, but Dad and I are flying into Johannesburg tomorrow evening, and we want to have a strategy meeting all day Friday and Saturday morning. On Saturday night, Dad is hosting dinner at his house for senior management, and he wants you to join us.'

Getting an invite to the chairman of the board's house was a big deal, something that hadn't happened to her before. It wasn't a leap to believe she had a better than average chance of being promoted.

Aisha felt the buzz of excitement and told herself not to gush. 'That would be…' Oh, *crap*. Pasco. They'd made plans for Saturday night, and he'd pulled strings to get into a spectacular restaurant in Cape Town, a place where you had to wait months to get a reservation, and he wanted to talk.

'You have plans…' Miles stated. 'Hot date?'

Aisha scratched her forehead, not wanting to lie. 'Yes, but I'll cancel…'

'Judging by your torn expression, it sounds like meeting him is important to you.'

It was, but was it as important as her job? She wished she could say that it wasn't, but she couldn't. Equally important, maybe.

And that was the difference between her and Pasco: he didn't hesitate to put his work first. No, that wasn't fair, not any more. Pasco was definitely getting better at making her a priority. And how ironic was it she was the one who now had to choose between her man and her work? But she couldn't pass this invite up. Pasco would understand. 'Please thank your dad for the invite, and yes, I'll be there.'

To her consternation, Miles shook her head, her expression pensive. 'We'll be done with business by lunchtime Saturday. Book a flight back for mid-afternoon and you can still make your date.'

Aisha frowned. 'Really, it's fine, I'll cancel.'

'It's a casual dinner, Aisha, not a referendum on your work. And you know that I'm all about a work-play balance. You work too much and play too little so you're going on that date.'

'Your dad won't see it that way,' Aisha protested. Miles's father expected his employees to say, 'How high?' when he said, 'Jump'. She often thanked God that Miles and not her father was her boss—she would've resigned years ago. Aisha was also grateful that Mr Lintel would be retired when—if—she got the promotion.

'Aisha, I'm grateful for your work ethic, I really am. But I worry about your workaholic tendencies.'

She was a workaholic? She snorted. She was an amateur compared to Pasco.

'I worry about you because you don't worry about yourself enough. I'm the one who has to insist that you take a vacation, who practically has to force a pay rise on you. I'm thrilled that you are dating and even more thrilled this man is important to you.'

He was, unfortunately. Always had been, probably always would be.

'Is he based in Cape Town?'

'Yes,' Aisha muttered, wondering why Miles was asking.

'Is it serious?'

Miles wasn't going to let this go. Her boss was a bull terrier when she sank her teeth into something, so Aisha might as well admit the truth and save them some time. 'We were married when I was very young. We've recently reconnected and it's…complicated.'

Miles opened her mouth to speak, closed it again, her lips moving in a silent 'wow'. 'I did not know that.'

Few people did.

'He's a very busy guy, but he's taking me to Michel's on Saturday night to see if we can find a way forward.'

Miles whistled. 'Michel's? You lucky thing, I waited for ever to eat there. Right, that settles it, you're flying back Saturday afternoon.'

'Mr Lintel won't be happy—' Aisha protested.

'I'll handle my dad,' Miles informed her. 'Look, Dad isn't convinced that you are ready to be promoted but I am, Aisha. When I move up into the CEO position, I want you as my operations officer.'

She knew that Mr Lintel had his reservations, but hearing her suspicions confirmed made Aisha wince. Maybe she should cancel on Pasco and go to that dinner.

'Don't even think about it,' Miles warned her. She lifted her finger to point it at her screen. 'You need a life and when you get the promotion, I will be pushing you to find more balance in your life. And if some mad-about-you man wants you to stay in Cape Town, we can make that happen. After Covid-19, we've all realised what can be achieved by working remotely.'

Aisha released a long sigh, a mixture of confusion, relief, and sadness. 'I appreciate that, Miles, I do. I just don't know if things will work out with Pasco. Our relationship has been anything but smooth sailing.'

'Relationships aren't supposed to go smoothly, Aisha. Where's the fun in that? They are supposed to have dips and highs, valleys and summits. How you navigate the obstacles is what matters, how you love each other through the hard times.'

Aisha lifted her eyebrows. 'Did you learn that from the Danish prince you're dating?'

'No, I learned that from watching my folks stay married for close to thirty-five years,' Miles replied.

'Right, that's sorted. I'll see you on Friday in Joburg, okay?'

'Okay.' Aisha glanced down at the pile of résumés on her desk. 'Can I ask you a quick question about St Urban and my search for a general manager...?'

'Sure, hit me.'

God, she loved her job. At least she knew what she was doing there.

Due to Jason's suspected malfeasance, Pasco was working at his restaurant in Franschhoek on Wednesday night and, thanks to the unexpected arrival of a tour bus of English tourists, he saw his plans for sneaking out early to spend the night with Aisha fading away. The tourists were in a mood to party, his kitchen was slammed, and the bartenders and waitresses were run off their feet.

Pasco found himself pulled a hundred directions and when he stepped into the restaurant from the kitchen, he saw Aisha sitting at the bar and pushed away a surge of irritation.

He wasn't irritated by her presence, but by the fact he hadn't seen her since the ball and, thanks to their busy schedules, knew that they wouldn't be able to spend some quality time together before Saturday night.

The freaking sky could fall in but nothing—repeat, *nothing*!—was going to interfere with his plans for Saturday night. And Sunday.

Pasco lifted a hand in her direction, spoke to a waitress, and sighed when one of his regulars stood up to speak to him. It took ten minutes for him to reach Aisha, which was about nine and half minutes too long.

Bending his head, he kissed her temple and wrapped his hand around her wrist. 'Come with me,' he told her.

Aisha followed him through the doors marked 'staff only' and down a short hallway that led to his office. Standing back, he urged her inside, followed her in, and slammed the door shut, twisting the lock. Not giving her time to speak, he lowered his lips to hers, taking her mouth in a need-you-now kiss.

Aisha, so responsive, opened her mouth to his insistent tongue, and he couldn't resist sliding his hand up and under her thin jersey to thumb her already responsive nipple. Why did they put work first when being together, loving each other, felt like this? What was wrong with them?

Pasco felt lust flash through him as she angled her head to allow him deeper access to her mouth, her tongue tangling with his. She moaned, a sexy sound deep in her throat, and dropped her hands from his shoulders to run her fingers across his stomach, letting them drift over his aching erection before settling them low on his narrow hips.

Three hard raps on the door had him lifting his head. 'Give me a goddamn minute!' he shouted.

He heard footsteps fading away and immediately returned to kissing Aisha. Seeing her was an unexpected pleasure and the rest of the world could give him five minutes. Or thirty. Or a couple of hours. What the hell could be so damn important?

Pasco nuzzled her neck and lifted her sweater to her collarbone, tonguing her breast through the lace fabric covering her nipple. He yanked her bra cup aside and took her nipple into his mouth, smiling when he felt her hand in his hair, holding him in place.

She loved what he did to her...and he loved doing it. Win-win. Caught up in the passion between them, he drank her in. Not able to resist, he slipped a hand between her legs to cup her.

'Pas!'

Pasco heard the need in her voice and fumbled with the zip to her jeans so that he could feel her hot flesh on his fingers.

Someone banged on the office door again. 'Boss?'

Pasco lifted his head from her mouth to glare at the door. 'What?' he shouted, annoyed.

'Uh...another bus of tourists has arrived. We need another pair of hands at the bar.'

Pasco groaned and rested his forehead against Aisha's. He closed his eyes and pulled his hands up to rest them on her hips, quietly muttering a string of curse words.

'I just wanted a half hour with you,' he murmured, wrapping his arms around her. 'Thirty minutes, that was all.'

Aisha's hands rubbed his back. 'Bad timing.'

He pulled back to run a hand over her hair. 'Do we have any other type of timing?' he asked, sounding rueful. And a little pissed off.

'Seems not,' Aisha replied, pushing her hands into the back pockets of her jeans. 'And on that point, about Saturday night...'

Pasco saw the apology in her eyes and grimaced. 'You're cancelling our plans?'

He felt the wave of disappointment, a small stab somewhere in the region of his heart. Was this the way she felt every time he cancelled their plans before? Frankly, it sucked.

'Not cancelling, just amending,' Aisha replied.

Pasco released his pent-up breath, relieved. Aisha went on to explain she was leaving for Johannesburg for work and would be returning on the four o'clock flight Saturday afternoon. 'I should probably stay for the chairman's dinner—I was specifically invited—but I'm skipping out.'

For Aisha that was a big deal and he appreciated it. 'No problem. Shall I push the reservation back from seven to eight?' he asked.

'Yes, please.'

She rubbed the back of her neck and he noticed she looked tired. 'Would it help if I collected you from the airport?'

Aisha shook her head. 'No, don't worry. I'm leaving my car there, so I'll just meet you at your Fresnaye apartment. If I land at six, I can be there by half-seven, I imagine.'

She'd still want to shower, do her hair. 'I'll make the reservation for eight-thirty.'

'Thanks.' She glanced at the locked door and nodded. 'You should go, you're needed.'

He was, but he wanted to know why her eyes held a

hint of worry, why the muscles in her neck were hard with tension. 'Everything okay?'

'Sure.' She looked away and Pasco knew she was lying, that she was worried about something. Him? Them? Their relationship? He didn't blame her; he also spent hours wondering whether they were doing the right thing by hurtling into something deeper, something that could drown them. He wasn't any closer to figuring out how they could be together without one of them reinventing their lives, something he wasn't able to do.

No, that wasn't true…he, mostly, didn't *want* to change his life. It was busy and demanding and exciting. He just wished it left a little more time for him to spend with Aisha. And, yeah, he wished that her schedule weren't quite so busy…

Hypocritical, Kildare? Sure.

Pasco heard a roar coming from the bar and knew he had to get back to work. Stepping around Aisha, he unlocked the door. 'I have to get back.'

Aisha nodded. 'Duty calls.'

He slid his mouth across hers and pulled back before he lost control again and told the rest of the world to go to hell. 'See you Saturday.' He ran his thumb across her bottom lip, not convinced she was fine.

Honestly, the weekend couldn't come soon enough.

CHAPTER ELEVEN

AISHA FIDDLED WITH the stem of her wine glass and fought the urge to look at her watch again. It was half-nine and she'd been sitting at this table in Michel's for the past forty-five minutes waiting for Pasco. She felt the inquisitive eyes of her waitress on her and knew that if she met her gaze, she'd see sympathy and curiosity on her face.

Sympathy because, yeah, she'd been stood up, curiosity because few people had the balls to miss a meal at Michel's.

Pasco was one of the few people who would.

Aisha ran her fingertips over her forehead, her elbow on the table. What a stupid, crazy, super-stressful day. The strategy session ran later than expected and she saw Mr Lintel's frown when she excused herself, not happy she was leaving early. When she ran into the domestic departure terminal, her name was being called on the public announcement system. She cleared check-in at speed and ran to her gate, apologising to the unimpressed attendants.

She found her seat on the plane, ignored the dirty looks she received at holding up the flight—*It was five minutes, people!*—and fastened her seat belt. She, and everyone else, expected to hear the engines start but nothing happened. Fifteen minutes later, she was told that the flight was delayed because another aircraft needed to land unexpectedly.

It wasn't an emergency, the air hostess told them over loud groans, but they were expecting a half-hour delay, which turned into forty-five minutes.

On hearing she would be landing in Cape Town later than expected, she called Pasco to give him an update, but he didn't answer his phone. She sent him an email, a text message, and a WhatsApp message, all of which he didn't respond to.

When she landed in Cape Town, she still hadn't heard from him and placed another call; this time his message went straight to voicemail. Unsure what to do—had he lost his phone? Was it dead?—she called Michel's and asked them whether he'd cancelled their reservation. He hadn't so she decided to head straight for the restaurant. Choosing to believe, fool that she was, that he'd be there.

She arrived at eight forty-five and he'd yet to contact her.

Was he hurt? Dead? What the hell was wrong with his phone that he couldn't call?

Aisha looked down at her white shirt, which looked a little limp and not so white any more. She'd bought a red cocktail dress for this occasion, gorgeous shoes, and had planned on curling her hair. She'd rushed from the airport to this fancy restaurant and, feeling limp and looking ragged—and sitting here alone—she stuck out like a sore thumb.

Dammit, Kildare, where the hell are you?

He'll be here, a little voice deep inside her responded, just give him more time.

She'd wait another ten minutes, not a minute more. Aisha took a sip of wine and looked out of the window to watch the waves breaking over the rocks below. The spotlight on the restaurant's roof illuminated the rocky seascape below and Aisha idly watched a crab scuttle across a rock, dodging an incoming wave.

That was how she felt about life with Pasco, as if she were constantly dodging rogue waves.

Aisha sighed. Why had she ignored her rule not to fall in love with him, to keep her emotional distance? When they first reunited, she knew she had to be careful, that he could upend her world again. But instead of setting out clear boundaries, obeying the rules, she'd fallen under his spell again.

Could she have been more of a fool?

Aisha watched as an older woman across the room pulled out a credit card to pay for her and her husband's meal. That was what she wanted, she thought, an equal partnership, give and take, to be able to make decisions with him. She wanted Pasco to respect her career and to support her in it.

And she wanted to spend time with him, eating the whole fruit basket instead of just taking bites of the apple now and again.

But the reality was that if they decided to take another chance on their relationship, and to make it work, one of them would have to slow down. Would Pasco expect her to cut back on her workload without changing his hours? Would she be the one to make the sacrifices, working twice as hard as he did to give their relationship a shot?

Look, she got it, she wasn't stupid. He was a hotshot chef with a billion-dollar empire to look after and that ate up his time. But to have a relationship, one of them would have to concede, to give more than the other, and Aisha knew it would be her.

And if she did that, how long would it take before she started to feel resentful, for her to start nagging him to spend more time with her? How long would it be before she left him again?

What would Pasco give up? If anything?

Aisha dumped some more red wine into her glass and scowled at the empty seat opposite her. Another five minutes had passed, and she'd heard crickets. There was no excuse for his behaviour.

He wasn't dead or hurt, he was probably just ignoring her calls because he'd got sucked into work—at The Vane, in Franschhoek, or at Binta—and he didn't want to deal with her annoyance and anger.

In the morning he'd rock up at her door and apologise, saying he got delayed or his phone died or some other stupid excuse, and he'd try to charm her into forgiving him. If words didn't work he'd kiss her, knowing she was putty in his hands. He'd take her to bed, hoping that some good sex would improve her mood.

To be fair, it normally did.

Aisha felt fury burn away the moisture in her eyes. She'd had a hell of a day, and she'd all but killed herself to make her flight, had driven like a madman to get to this restaurant. She'd left a work event, incurring the chairman of the board's displeasure at her leaving the strategy meeting early—something she wasn't too worried about because she had Miles's support—to make this date with Pasco…

And he'd bloody stood her up.

If she needed a clear message on how life with Pasco would be going forward, this was it, big and bold and written in sparkly, six-foot-high letters.

You are always going to be last on his list of priorities…

She'd been kidding herself to think that anything had changed, that Pasco had changed, that he was ready to make space for her in his life. He was as committed to his career as he always was, he'd shown that over and over again. She'd struggled to get him to pay attention to the pop-up restaurant and when she did make arrangements with him to meet, he stood her up. He'd told her, time and time again, that he decided on his priorities and that his work, and his business interests, came first.

She stood on the outside of his life, only welcome in when it suited him. And didn't that feel familiar? Wasn't that the way she felt with her family? And, God, why did she keep choosing to love people who made her feel unseen, neglected, and less than?

She had to stop that, had to break that cycle. She was worthy of a man who put her first, who moved heaven and earth to be with her. She deserved to be a priority, to be considered, to be seen… She deserved a man who would support her, who would respect her enough to send her a damn message when he couldn't make a date.

Enough!

Enough of waiting for him, hoping for him to change, hoping for more than Pasco was able to give. This stopped now, tonight. She was done with hoping and wishing…

It was time to face the truth. She loved Pasco, she did, but she didn't like feeling 'less than', unsupported, dismissed. She needed to be a priority in his life, to be an equal partner, to step into the inner circle of his life.

It wasn't going to happen, and it was time she accepted that. Yes, she loved him, probably always would, but love couldn't exist in a vacuum and sometimes it simply wasn't enough.

Aisha reached into her bag to pull out her purse and placed enough money under the side plate to cover the mostly full bottle of wine. She pushed her purse back into her bag and her heart went into freefall when she saw her screen light up, showing an unfamiliar number.

She jabbed her finger on the green button and held the device up to her ear.

'Aish? Sorry—'

Aisha heard a man shouting, was Pasco in a *pub*? His voice faded in and out—the signal was terrible—but she heard a 'sorry' and 'in the morning'.

Aisha didn't say anything, she just cut the call, stood up on shaky legs, and pulled her bag over her shoulder.

She'd made him a priority but, to him, she was still an option.

That stopped right now.

The fire at Pasco's, Franschhoek broke out in the late afternoon, shortly after he left Franschhoek to head back to the city for his date with Aisha. By the time Pasco arrived back in the village, the old cottage, with its wooden floors, door frames, and wooden furniture, was fully engulfed. The fire engine took its time getting there, and the firefighters found him, his brother, Cam, his staff and many Franschhoek residents trying to douse the flames with hosepipes and buckets of water.

Frankly, their efforts hadn't made any difference.

Pasco glanced at the mountain, bathed in the early-morning light as he walked the long route to Aisha's cottage after a night of no sleep.

He needed the time to think, to work out what he was going to say to her, how to apologise. After telling Aisha how important this date was, how much he was looking forward to finding a way forward, it had been hours before he thought to call her. On seeing the fire, he'd immediately gone into his solve-this-and-sort-it-out zone, not allowing himself to be distracted. He'd hauled hosepipes and buckets of water, manned the hose of the ancient fire engine, beat at the burning bushes with blankets. He'd comforted his shocked employees and driven those who used public transport home.

He'd had a building and a business to save, and nothing else, at that moment, was important. He'd inherited his ability to focus on one thing, to the exclusion of everything else, from his father, and it made him an incredible chef, perfectionistic and driven. It also made him a lousy human being.

It wasn't that he hadn't thought about her—he had, he'd just pushed the need to contact her away. Caught up with the fire and what he had to do, he'd decided she could wait. But it really wouldn't have taken much to run to his car and send her a message, a quick call…five minutes? Ten? But no, because he was a control freak, he couldn't step away for even that long. Something might happen, he might miss something, he might be needed… As a result, it was after nine before he called her and, although the signal had been terrible, he'd immediately sensed her anger and disappointment.

He'd let her down *again*.

Was he ever going to stop doing that? Was it even *possible*?

Feeling sick and sad, he let his thoughts drift from Aisha to his restaurant and the cause of the fire. He'd heard mutterings about old wiring starting the blaze, or a pan of oil being left on the stove. BS, all of it. He'd had the house completely rewired a couple of years ago and his staff followed protocols at the end of a shift, including the washing and packing away of all used pots and pans. The fryer was emptied of oil and power cut to all the equipment in the kitchen. He knew without a shadow of a doubt that all those protocols had been followed because he'd run the kitchen during the lunch service and he'd checked.

Pasco knocked on the door to Aisha's cottage and waited for her to answer the door. There was only one logical explanation for a fire that burned so hot and so fast and that was that it had had some help from an accelerant.

And there was only one person who was pissed off enough to do that to him. Jesus, Jason.

Aisha answered the door, dressed in a pair of men's style flannel pyjamas, her hair early-morning messy. She frowned at him.

'It's just past seven, Kildare. What are you doing here so early?' she asked, her tone cool and her expression closed off. 'Actually, you know what? I don't care. Just go away.'

Her reaction wasn't unexpected, but because she didn't slam the door in his face, he followed her into the kitchen area, where she immediately headed for the coffee machine. Using the side of her fist, she hit the button to turn it on and checked the level of the water and the beans. She looked as if she'd had less sleep than he had, and he'd had, well, none.

'I'm really sorry about last night, Aisha.' God, did she hear the sincerity in his voice? He hoped so.

'Apologising means nothing if you don't change your actions, Pasco.'

He winced at her freezer-cold tone and instantly knew he'd need a miracle because he'd screwed up. Big time.

Five minutes…why hadn't he taken five damn minutes to call her? What the hell was wrong with him?

Aisha walked past his legs to open the fridge, but his arm shot out and he pulled her to stand between his legs, resting his forehead on her flat stomach. God, she smelled good, her scent cutting through the smell of smoke in his nose.

'Pasco's burned down last night,' he bluntly told her. 'The fire started just after five, we got it under control around eight, eight-thirty.'

When she stepped back, he noticed her eyes were wide with shock. 'Pasco's burnt down?'

He rubbed a hand over his eyes. 'You really didn't know? I thought you would've heard by now—news travels fast in this valley.'

'I've only been here for two months. I'm not plugged into the gossip line,' Aisha explained, her eyes reflecting sympathy and shock. 'I'm so sorry. When? How?'

Pasco filled her in on the details and by the time he was finished, his coffee was cold. Needing the caffeine hit, he put his cup under the spout of the coffee machine and blasted it with steam. 'Between you and me, I think it was Jason.'

Aisha's eyebrows flew up. 'Jason? The guy you recently let go?'

'Yeah.'

'You think he set fire to your place because you fired him?'

'And because I laid criminal charges against him for theft,' Pasco told her, his voice hard. 'He's a hothead, I can easily see him getting drunk and doing something stupid like this. And the fire, so they think, started in the office area. It burned hottest there.

'Didn't you hear me tell you about the fire when I called you last night?' Pasco asked, gripping the bridge of his nose.

She shook her head. 'No, I heard the noise in the background but not much else. You called from someone else's phone.'

'I used my brother's,' he replied, wincing when he remembered the many text messages and missed call alerts that came through when his phone was recharged. 'I tried to call you later, but your phone was off.'

'I switched it off when I left the restaurant,' Aisha said, her tone flat.

Of course she had, and he didn't blame her. He looked at her and shook his head. Despite her hurt, despite him treating her like an afterthought, sympathy brimmed in her eyes. He was starting to think—*know and believe*—he wasn't good enough for her, that he could never make her happy.

The thing was, he was like his dad...selfish, hyper-focused, ruthlessly determined. Okay, he made good monetary decisions instead of bad, combined the determination he inherited from his father with extreme hard work, but at their essence, they were the same. Selfish, relentless, rigid. And both he and his dad had the ability to fall in love with a woman far too good for them. Pasco felt his stomach turn into a lead ball, nausea climbing up his throat. He couldn't help noticing his muscles seemed to be losing strength, that his hands were trembling.

Aisha needed to be his priority, for him to put her first, but as last night proved, when the chips were down, he was too much like his father and unable to put her first. He couldn't keep hurting her—it was unacceptable. He rubbed the back of his head, not sure what to say, to do. He couldn't walk away, but neither could he stay. He wanted to bury himself inside her, lose himself in the taste of her mouth and the softness and fragrance of her skin, but he'd lost the right to touch her.

He stood in no man's land, unable to step forward, and he couldn't go back. He dropped his head, conscious of the burning sensation in his throat, his wetter than normal eyes.

Aisha placed her cup on the dining table and gripped the back of a chair with white-knuckled fingers. He had to look at her, noticing her brown eyes looked darker than usual. Her face was a couple of shades paler, and her mouth was flat with unhappiness.

She lifted her eyes to meet his and slowly shook her head. He braced himself.

'When we first met, I told myself, told you, that we needed some rules, some guidelines to deal with each other. I told myself not to get involved with you, not to let the past colour the future. I didn't listen.'

To be fair, he'd had the same thoughts, but neither did he listen to his inner voice.

'I can't do this, Pasco.'

Her words were what he'd been expecting since first realising that he'd stood her up last night. She wasn't his young wife any more. She was a vibrant, smart woman who knew her own mind and he knew he'd pushed her too far, tested her limits, run out of chances. And he refused to hide behind the fire, use it as an excuse…he'd messed up. Badly. And he'd probably, because he was his father's son, do it again.

Unacceptable.

He was done with hurting her. And if that meant walking away, then that was what he would do.

Pasco stared at her with haunted eyes, his face pale and drawn. That he was physically exhausted was obvious, but Aisha knew he was dancing on the edge of mental exhaustion too. And so, honestly, was she.

They kept knocking the stuffing out of each other, hurting each other, coming close to making it work, but never quite getting it right. It was time to give up, to stop trying. She couldn't take much more Pasco-induced pain.

Or any, really.

Pasco didn't respond to her I-can't-do-this statement, but pain flashed in his eyes and he flinched. Thinking she needed to give him an explanation, she ploughed on, her voice high and tight.

'This dinner seemed to be important to you and it was damn important to me, despite its awful timing. I blew off a meal with the chairman of my company's board to rush back to Cape Town, Pasco! My dinner invitation was a big deal because Mr Lintel never socialises with the common folk. I told Miles, his daughter, that I couldn't go, that I had a date. She understood, she's good like that… she's big into having a balanced life,' Aisha explained.

Pasco flinched and she knew her verbal jab landed on target.

'The strategy session ran over, and I had to excuse myself, something I don't like to do, especially when I'm up for promotion. Anyway, I barely made my flight. Then it was delayed. I tried to call you, but it just rang. I couldn't get hold of you so I rushed from the airport to the restaurant, but you weren't there… Look, I'm sorry about your restaurant, but I'm so damn angry with you, I'm not going to lie.'

Her anger didn't matter, she could nurse it, and her soul-deep hurt, later. She needed to get this out, get it over with and move on.

It's self-care, Aisha, another set of boundaries. You're protecting yourself and you're allowed to do that.

She lifted her hands. 'I'm done, Pasco. Done with wishing that things will change. I know they won't.'

She closed her eyes and shook her head. 'I am not and never will be a priority in your life. Being busy, gathering businesses and bank accounts and trust, making sure that you are nothing like your father is all that's important to you!'

Something in his eyes, a flash of disagreement, but he didn't speak, just kept looking at her with those intense green eyes. For the second time in her life, she was going to walk away from the only man she'd ever loved and, although she knew it was the right thing for her to do, she didn't know if she could bear it. Spots danced in front of her vision and Aisha knew there was a good chance she'd break down completely and beg him to stay.

No... Boundaries. Self-care. Protection.

'Do you know what I realised last night?' she quietly asked. She echoed his body language and folded her arms against her chest, surreptitiously pinching the inside of her arm, directing her mental attention and her pain onto that spot on the tender skin.

'What?' he croaked.

'In trying to be exactly the opposite of your dad, you've turned out to be more like him than you thought.' Distaste flashed across his face, and she was sorry to be the one who hurt him, but he needed to hear the truth. Or the truth the way she saw it.

'You told me that your dad made a habit of reaching for every shiny object that passed by, that he wanted what he wanted, when he wanted it, not caring who it hurt.'

Tumultuous emotions roiled through his eyes and Aisha expected him to respond, to deny her accusation, but, to her surprise, he didn't. He just held her eyes and gestured for her to continue.

'You reach for shiny objects too, Pasco, but yours are work and success and accolades, things to remind you that you are nothing like him. But they are still shiny and you reaching for them still hurts the people who love you, people like me. You'd rather work, intent on gathering money and things, because in doing that you can tell yourself that you're not like him, that you are a success. But in doing that, you're hurting the woman who loves you, the woman who's always loved you, just like your dad hurt your mum. He lost all the money and business, you win it all, but your wives are the ones to suffer.'

Pasco was statute still, his body rigid with tension. All the colour leached from his skin and his eyes were emerald green in his haggard face.

'Jesus! Would you say something, please?' she half shouted, half begged.

Beg me to be yours, tell me you love me...say something to persuade me that you are worth taking a chance on!

He opened his mouth, but slammed it closed again and shook his head. He forced his shoulders up and let them fall, heavy as sin. 'You're right.'

Aisha glared at him. 'That's all you have to say?'

He shrugged again and for the first time, Aisha wanted to hurt him, to shock him into speaking, mentally screaming at him to say or do something to fight for her, to fight for them.

She waited a good twenty seconds, then another twenty, refusing to drop her eyes, to break his stare. Pasco didn't speak.

Right, enough now.

Aisha's voice turned hard. 'I was weak before, Pasco, but I'm not weak any more. I don't need you to provide a life for me, I'm not impressed by your success or your money. I have my career, my own money. I love you, I do, but I can't be with you because I need more than you can give. I need your time. I need you to be present. I need you to *see* me.'

'I *do* see you.'

His words, rough and low, came too late, and were far from convincing. 'You don't, Pasco, not really. You don't see me as an equal partner, someone you're willing to put first, someone you want to put above your need to prove to yourself that you are a better man than your father. Everybody but you knows that, by the way,' she told him.

'I spent my entire childhood not being seen or respected, being dismissed. I won't tolerate that from you, or any man. I refuse to stand on the outside of your life, only to be pulled in when it suits you.'

Aisha forced herself to walk over to him, to touch his cheek with the tips of her fingers. 'Miles has offered to send someone to help me with setting up the restaurant. I think I'm going to accept her offer and let Kendall work with you. You'll enjoy her, she's fun.'

He shook his head, and for a moment, just a moment, she thought he was holding his arms tight across his chest to keep from reaching for her.

'I'm sorry, Aish. I really am,' he managed to croak.

Aisha released a small sob, shook her head and forced herself to walk away.

A long, miserable week later, Pasco stood in the empty warehouse in New York City, trying to ignore his throbbing, aching heart. Hank was rambling on about capacity and seating, telling him how eager the city was for a new restaurant, how the eating scene had changed since Covid-19. He wasn't paying attention, and only heard every fifth word he said.

All he could think about was Aisha's words. *'You reach for shiny objects too, Pasco, but yours are work and success and accolades, things to remind you that you are nothing like him...that you are a success.'*

A successful businessman, maybe, but not a good

human being. He was, in many ways, his father's son and that was a problem and his biggest challenge. He didn't want to be that driven, hyper-focused jerk he'd been.

So why was he here? In New York? He didn't want to live in this city, work a thousand hours a week, be the lauded New York City success story again.

Be honest, Kildare, you're only in Manhattan because it hurt too much to stay in Cape Town. To even be in the same area as Aisha. Because you hoped that flying to New York and listening to Hank's pitch would be a distraction from the suffocating pain and relief from the heavy stone squashing your heart.

God, he missed Aisha. He felt as if he were missing an arm, a leg, his damned spine. The last time they split, he dived into work, focusing his energy on building his empire. This time around, work failed to hold his interest.

After booking into the Waldorf, he'd left again immediately and started walking the city that had been his home for five years. He'd walked for hours and hours, eventually stopping outside the premises of his old restaurant, now an upmarket deli.

He'd earned the first of his Michelin stars there, been lauded for bringing innovative dishes to the jaded food scene. He'd been featured in food magazines and on travel programmes, in fact, his appearance on a travel programme had led to him having his own.

He'd had royalty and rogues eat his food, celebrities of all sizes, shapes, and sorts. His reviews were generally good, and he'd earned many tens of millions feeding the great and good, and not so good, of this magnificent city.

He definitely didn't need to do it again. Pasco looked at Hank, who hadn't taken a breath since jumping into the cab that had brought them here. He wore a thick gold chain around his neck, another on his wrist, and a fat Rolex.

Hank had a magnificent apartment overlooking Central Park, ate out every night, and had a different girlfriend every month. He was a billionaire investor, another collector of shiny objects like businesses and bitcoin.

'I'm telling ya, Pasco, we can make ourselves a fortune.'

He already had a fortune, and that was before he counted the money he'd placed in trusts for his family. He still owned an apartment in New York, another in London, a villa in Greece, and his two homes in South Africa. Apart from his restaurants, he owned a couple of industrial properties and a block of apartments, all of which generated rental income. He received money from his range of kitchen accessories, interest from his fat bank accounts.

'You and I can do great things together. More great things,' Hank amended, smiling. Pasco jammed his hands in the pockets of his suit trousers and looked at the older man.

'Why did you never marry, Hank?' he demanded.

Hank frowned at his out-of-the-blue question. 'Too much hassle, not enough time,' he eventually answered. 'Truth be told, I love my work more than I could ever love a woman. We're the same, you and I.'

Pasco flinched at the observation. Were they? He loved to work, loved his job but…

But he loved Aisha more. None of it meant anything without her. She was what was missing from the life, the empty hole he couldn't fill because it was Aisha-shaped, and the only one able to complete him. So, yeah, if he had to choose between work and her, it would be her. Funny how it took making a complete idiot of himself and flying halfway across the world to look at an opportunity he had no interest in to come to that realisation.

'It's not for me, Hank,' Pasco said, looking around. For someone else, sure, but not him. New York wasn't his place any more; he didn't want to move back here, commit to working fourteen-hour days for the next ten or so years.

Hank didn't miss a beat. 'Okay, what will suit you?'

He had no idea; maybe it was a small restaurant, with simple dishes prepared well, great wine, greenhouses, and herb gardens, maybe not, but it wasn't here, across the pond away from Aisha. What would really suit him was his ring on her finger, his son running into his arms, Aisha's stomach round with their second child.

Maybe it was even doing what he did now, but slowing down, delegating, occasionally taking his hands off the wheel, but always, always going home to Aisha.

What would suit him best was a life that worked for Aisha, with him at her side.

He needed to spend his life being there for her, spending time with her, supporting her, *seeing* her. Making her his sole priority because she was the most important person in his life, ensuring she never felt on the outside looking in again.

Whatever she wanted from him, he'd give to her. She could work, not work, jump in and out of his life—he didn't care!—as long as she was happy, fulfilled, living her best life.

God, he needed to talk to her, to find a way to make this work. He'd been hyper-focused all his life, but winning Aisha back would be the biggest, hardest, most important battle of his life. 'Well, what do you want, Pasco?'

Pasco pulled up a smile for Hank. 'I want to go home, Hank. I want to drink wine with my woman, look at the mountains, smell the fynbos. New York isn't for me any more.'

Pasco felt his phone vibrate and pulled it out of the

inside pocket of his jacket, his eyebrows lifting when he saw Muzi video calling him.

'What's up, dude?'

Muzi, as he always did when he was excited, babbled away in Xhosa. 'Ro's in labour! I'm going to be a dad!'

Pasco's heart jumped and he silently cursed. What the hell was he doing here when all the people he cared about were on another continent, eighteen hours away? 'Oh, man, Muzi, that's so exciting!' he responded in rusty Xhosa. God, his accent was dreadful.

Muzi obviously thought so too because he switched to English. 'She keeps saying that it might be a false alarm, that it's a practice round, Braxton somethings, but I know this is it, Pas. I'm going to be a dad!'

'You are,' Pasco told him, grinning. This was the first good news he'd had all week, the first thing to make him smile. 'I'm heading straight to the airport and I'll leave as soon as I can. Send me a picture as soon as they are born, and I'll come straight to the hospital, okay?'

'Okay.' Muzi placed a hand on his heart. 'I'm not ready for this, Pas.'

Pasco walked to the exit and stepped into the sunshine. But it wasn't tip of Africa sunshine, so it felt wrong. 'You are ready, brother, and even if you weren't, they are on their way. Hang in there, Muzi, and keep me updated, okay?'

'Digby is on his way, so is Keane. And Radd. But I need—'

He needed him, his best friend. Yeah, Pasco didn't need him to spell it out. He needed to get home, to meet the twins, and to share a cigar with his oldest friend.

But even more important than that, he needed to find Aisha and love her for the rest of her life.

CHAPTER TWELVE

THE NEXT DAY, in her cottage, Aisha yanked a bottle of wine out of her fridge and held the cool bottle to her forehead. Lowering it, she squinted at the bottle, saw it was nearly empty, and cursed. She lived in one of the premier wine areas of the world and all she had to drink, after a fairly crappy day, was a few gulps of wine.

Oh, well, it was better than nothing. Dashing the minuscule amount into a glass, she considered what she could eat for supper, realised she still hadn't bought any food, and decided she wasn't hungry.

Well, she was hungry for junk food…she could murder a packet of fries, slam down a huge bar of chocolate. Emotional eating, Aisha?

Sure, she was allowed since she was feeling so damn emotional!

Taking her wine back to the living area of her cottage, she curled up into the corner of the couch and started scrolling through her social media accounts. Her oldest nephew was a chess champion; Hema had been invited to speak at a conference in Germany; Reyka posted a photo of her and her husband.

They looked pretty and perfect and she didn't care. For the first time in a long time, she could shake off the feelings of insecurity and stop judging her life by her sisters' accomplishments and milestones. She had an amazing career, she did good work and her boss valued her. There was a good chance she'd still get the promotion she so wanted. But unlike her siblings, she was nearly thirty and not married, a big black mark.

No, stop! Not being married wasn't a problem, nor a sin. It was perfectly okay for her to be single…

And apparently, so was confronting her mother. That awful telephonic conversation a week or so ago had actually resulted in her and her parents sitting down for a one-on-one meal two nights ago. It had been awkward and uncomfortable, but they'd tried and for that Aisha couldn't be more grateful. She was sure their next get-together would be easier and, in time, maybe she could even reboot her relationships with her sisters. She would never match their intellectual brilliance, but she no longer felt the need to; she was Aisha and she had value.

Her relationship with Reyka was beyond repair and she was okay with letting it go or, in the interest of family unity, being polite but having as little to do with her as possible.

Aisha scrolled through more social media posts, stopping when she saw a photo posted by Ro an hour before.

She sat in a hospital bed, looking tired and pale, her hair a mess, but her eyes glowing with happiness. She held a baby wrapped in a blue blanket in each arm, and her smile could power a nuclear plant. Aisha lifted her hand to her mouth, tears stinging her eyes. She tapped her screen and saw more photos, Muzi kissing her forehead, his eyes closed, a tear on his cheek. Muzi holding his boys, his eyes dancing with excitement. Another picture of Muzi showing his boys to the Tempest-Vanes and other people she didn't know. Aisha stared at the photograph, looking for Pasco. He wasn't in the photograph…

Why not? Pasco was Muzi's best and oldest friend, and he'd never miss the birth of the twins. Was he okay? Why wasn't he there?

He'd probably just stepped out of the room and missed the photo op. Aisha enlarged the photograph of the twins and smiled at their chubby cheeks, curly hair, and rosebud mouths. Both had Muzi's deep, brown-black eyes.

Aisha placed her hand on her heart, her throat tight with emotion. She was so happy for Ro. And Muzi. Happy for their friends, the clan she saw on the screen. Because that was what they looked to be, a group who were each other's safety net and support structure. They were wealthy, sure, stupidly so, but they had something money couldn't buy: they were a tribe, a family, knitted together by love.

She wanted a clan like that, a place where she fitted in. A place where she didn't need a PhD, to present academic papers or to save lives. Somewhere she could just be herself…

She needed friends, a community and, when her heart stopped aching and breaking, in a couple of years or decades, she might even look for a man. She didn't expect to experience a wild and intense love affair again—Pasco was a once-in-a-lifetime force of nature—but maybe she could find a companion, friendship with a man she didn't mind seeing naked.

But the thought of living her life, of being with anyone but Pasco made her feel a little, no, a lot, queasy.

It's just a thought, Shetty, not a stone-carved commandment! Jeez…

In the meantime, she'd work, get St Urban up and running and tomorrow she'd brief Kendall, who'd flown into Cape Town this afternoon, on Ro's restaurant project. Miles had all but told her the promotion was hers, so she'd start looking for a little house, probably in Johannesburg so she could be closer to Priya, a place to call her own. She'd keep herself busy and, in time, her battered and shattered heart would piece itself together.

Everything passed, eventually. She just had to hang on until the pain eased, until her tears stopped, until the sun started shining again.

Aisha felt her stomach rumble and told herself she should eat. She didn't want to, but she needed fuel, almost as much as she needed sleep. Both had been in short supply lately. Forcing herself to rise, she wrinkled her nose, wondering what she could push down her tight throat.

In the kitchen, she pulled open her fridge door and scowled at the empty shelves. Cheese, yoghurt...wilted salad. *Ugh.*

A gentle rap on her door had her turning and, grateful for the distraction, she walked back into the lounge, expecting to see Kendall on her doorstep, as her colleague had said she might stop by this evening to say hello.

She pulled the door open and stared into a long-sleeved, navy-blue T-shirt. She dropped her eyes to see the edges of a leather jacket, long legs covered in jeans, and trendy trainers. She tipped her head back, her eyes slamming into his, deep and forest green.

'You're not at the hospital. You're here,' Aisha said, trying to wrap her head around the fact that Pasco stood outside her front door. Why wasn't he with his best friends and their babies?

She tipped her head to the side. 'Uh, why aren't you at the hospital?'

'After I landed, I popped in, met the twins, and then came straight here.'

'Uh...okay. Why? Everyone you love is there.'

'Except the person I love the most,' he said, lifting one big shoulder. 'It's freezing out here—shall we go inside?'

Aisha nodded, her brain still trying to catch up to reality. When her feet remained glued to the spot, her eyes stuck on his, Pasco put his hands under her forearms and easily lifted her. Walking her backwards, he deposited her inside the cottage and kicked the door shut with his foot.

Looking down at her, he shed his leather bomber-style jacket and tossed his car keys onto the surface of the small table to the side of the door.

'Hi,' he said, his thumb skating across her cheekbone.

'Hi back,' Aisha whispered.

Aisha turned and, feeling a little shaky, sat down on the edge of the grey couch. She pulled a yellow cushion onto her lap and hugged it. She gestured to the chair opposite her and watched as Pasco sat. He immediately leaned forward and rested his forearms on his thighs.

'You said you landed. Where were you?' she asked.

'New York,' Pasco told her, his eyes not leaving hers.

She lifted her eyebrows. 'Why were you in New York?' *And why are you here?*

Lifting his head, he nailed her with an intense look. 'I was there because I was looking at setting up another restaurant. My investor, Hank, found a property and it has potential for an amazing restaurant.'

Aisha's heart dropped to her toes and her blood turned to ice water. She wrapped her arms around her torso and started to shiver. He was going back to the States and, in doing that, hammered the last nail into their already sealed-tight coffin. Why was she surprised and why, oh, why had she expected anything different? She hauled in a deep breath and forced herself to smile. 'Sounds interesting.'

'It's a great space but not for me. Neither is the city.'

She frowned, trying to keep up. 'I don't understand.'

'Another restaurant, anywhere but here, is…how did you put it? A shiny object that I have to have,' Pasco explained, his smile forced. She saw his worried expression and it was his lack of confidence, his hesitation, that kick-started her brain. She'd never seen him looking unsure, uncertain. She didn't like it.

'You were right, I have spent my life doing everything I can to prove to myself that I'm not my father's son. But in trying to be the opposite of him, I became more like him than I imagined. I look like him, talk like him, but I *am* not him. I refuse to be,' Pasco stated, his eyes flashing with intense emotion.

No, he wasn't, not really. Oh, parts of him were, but he was a better guy than his father had ever been. He was the guy who worked hard, who gave his everything, supported his friends, made her feel more alive than she ever had before.

'I just want to be with you, Aish. I'll be a good partner, I promise. I'll give you copies of all my bank accounts and never ask you about yours. I'll change nappies and cook and we will make every major decision together. We'll argue, probably, but I swear I'll listen and I'll always, *always* respect your point of view. I'll respect you.'

It was his turn to ramble, and she found it sweet.

She was about to speak, but Pasco beat her to it. 'I'll move. I'll hand over complete control of Pasco's at The Vane to my chef de cuisine and I won't rebuild Pasco's, Franschhoek. If you get the promotion, I'll move to London or Johannesburg. If you don't get the promotion, I'll follow you wherever you go next.'

Aisha's fingers dug into the fabric of the cushion, and she was sure her eyebrows had reached her hairline. 'Are you offering to give up your career? For me?'

Pasco nodded. 'I'm not saying it will be easy and I'll probably be, on occasion, an ass about it, but if that's what it takes, then I'll do it.'

'But why?'

His eyes drilled into her, almost begging her to understand. 'Because your job is important to you. You've worked hard to establish your career and you love your work. But you are my priority, your happiness is my *only* priority. You're the most important person in my life, hell, you *are* my life.'

And there it was. God, it was sweeter and sexier and more wonderful than she could ever have imagined. But despite her need to throw her arms around him and taste his lovely mouth and lay her hands on all his skin-covered muscles, they still needed to talk.

Be an adult, Shetty. You can get to the fun stuff later.

Pasco released a low, frustrated growl. 'I wish you'd say something, Aisha.'

She mulled over a few sentences, discarded them, considered others. 'I don't want or need you to give up your career or your business for me, Pasco, that was *never* the point. I just wanted to feel I was as important to you, that I had an equal call on your time.' Aisha smiled at the hint of relief she saw in his eyes.

Yeah, Pasco not working would drive them both mad. His thumb skimmed her cheekbone. 'I promise you will never doubt that, or me, again.'

He started to move off his chair, but Aisha held up her hand, silently telling him to stay there. He slumped back and stared at her, his expression a little frustrated. 'Can we have make-up sex now?' he asked.

Aisha smiled, knowing he was trying to lift the tension a notch or two. 'Not yet. I still have things to say.'

Pasco hauled in a breath and straightened his shoulders as if bracing himself to take another verbal beating.

'When you walked inside, you said you loved me. Is that true?' she asked, discarding her pillow and wrapping her hands around her knee.

Pasco nodded. 'I do.'

Two words, so simple, so powerful.

Aisha blinked away the moisture in her eyes. 'I love you too.'

He lunged in her direction, but she laughed and edged down the couch. 'Not yet! Just hold on, okay?'

Pasco glanced at his watch. 'You've got two minutes, talk fast.'

'I'm still up for promotion—if I get it, I'll move to Cape Town. I don't want to stop working and I won't let you stop either, so we will need to adjust our schedules.'

'Done.' He easily agreed. 'A part of me wants to slow down, take it easy, just be. Be with you.' Those were the sweetest words she'd ever heard.

'But we need to make some rules…' he added.

Aisha mock-frowned at him, her lips twitching with amusement. 'You're not good at rules, Pas.'

'I am when I make them,' he told her, cupping her cheek. 'One rule, two parts…we always prioritise each other, and our kids, above work. That's non-negotiable.'

'Agreed.'

'And we make every important decision together. Deal?'

Aisha nodded enthusiastically. 'Deal.'

He smiled at her before looking at his watch. 'We still have a minute and ten seconds left.' His mouth tipped up in that sexy smile she so adored. 'Anything else we need to cover or can I strip you naked now?'

There was just one more thing…

She had a man who loved her, who'd promised to put

her first, offered to give up his business for her, someone who *saw* her clearly. He was a good man, not perfect—perfection was overrated, and she was far from perfect herself—but he was perfect for her.

She pulled in some much-needed air. 'Will you marry me again, Pas? Love me every day and in every way, give me babies and back rubs? Will you talk to me and fight with me and consult with me? Will you build me up when I'm feeling small and pull me back into line when I'm being awful?'

'You're never awful,' Pasco told her, and Aisha swallowed at the look of adoration on his face.

'That wasn't a yes,' Aisha told him on a wobbly laugh. God, maybe she was going too fast again. They'd only been back in each other's lives for a couple of months—maybe she was jumping the gun again, maybe it was too soon. What was she thinking? Talk about history repeating itself...

'I'm sorry, I'm rushing things, rushing you,' Aisha said, waving her hands around.

Pasco moved over to the couch and sat down on the coffee table in front of her and placed his hands on her knees. 'Look at me, sweetheart.'

Aisha raised her head and sucked in her breath when she saw his face. His eyes were tender, his mouth curling in a pleased smile, his fingers warm on her thighs. 'Sure,' he stated, sounding completely confident.

Great, but... 'What are you agreeing to, Pas?'

He curled his big hand around her neck and lowered his forehead to hers. 'Everything,' he whispered. 'And a whole lot more,' he added.

She brushed her lips against his before pulling back. 'One more thing?'

'Make it quick,' he muttered, placing kisses on her jaw.

'Let's not keep our relationship or our marriage a secret this time around, okay? Love needs to stand in the light, not the dark.'

Pasco pulled his phone from the back pocket of his jeans and swiped his thumb across the screen.

'What are you doing, Kildare?' Aisha demanded, caught between laughter and frustration.

He held up a finger and punched the keyboard. He lifted the phone, took a photo of her, and looked down at his screen again. Then he handed her his phone and she looked down at the screen, seeing her messy hair, broad smile, and happy eyes.

She read the series of one-line messages he sent to the group Family and Friends.

My fiancée.

We're getting married.

Again.

You're invited to the wedding.

Aww…

Pasco whipped the phone out of her hand and typed another message before flinging it onto the couch and standing up. As he bent down to pick her up, she read his words and grinned.

Love her madly. Will answer all questions later.

Much, much later.

* * * * *

*Couldn't put
The Rules of Their Red-Hot Reunion down?
Don't miss these other Joss Wood stories!*

How to Undo the Proud Billionaire
How to Win the Wild Billionaire
How to Tempt the Off-Limits Billionaire

Available now!

COMING SOON!

We really hope you enjoyed reading this book.
If you're looking for more romance, be sure to
head to the shops when new books are
available on

Thursday 6th January

To see which titles are coming soon, please visit
millsandboon.co.uk/nextmonth

MILLS & BOON

THE HEART OF ROMANCE

A ROMANCE FOR EVERY READER

MODERN

Prepare to be swept off your feet by sophisticated, sexy and seductive heroes, in some of the world's most glamourous and romantic locations, where power and passion collide.

HISTORICAL

Escape with historical heroes from time gone by. Whether your passion is for wicked Regency Rakes, muscled Vikings or rugged Highlanders, await the romance of the past.

MEDICAL

Set your pulse racing with dedicated, delectable doctors in the high-pressure world of medicine, where emotions run high and passion, comfort and love are the best medicine.

True Love

Celebrate true love with tender stories of heartfelt romance, from the rush of falling in love to the joy a new baby can bring, and a focus on the emotional heart of a relationship.

Desire

Indulge in secrets and scandal, intense drama and plenty of sizzling hot action with powerful and passionate heroes who have it all: wealth, status, good looks…everything but the right woman.

HEROES

Experience all the excitement of a gripping thriller, with an intense romance at its heart. Resourceful, true-to-life women and strong, fearless face danger and desire - a killer combination!

To see which titles are coming soon, please visit

millsandboon.co.uk/nextmonth

MILLS & BOON

Coming next month

DESERT PRINCE'S DEFIANT BRIDE
Julieanne Howells

Lily watched as Khaled came closer, all smouldering masculine intent. Seconds ago she'd been in a snit. Now she couldn't remember why. By the time he reached her she was boneless and unresisting, letting him gather her hand and lift it to his lips.

'*Habiba*, you are beautiful,' he purred.

Beautiful? Her breath fluttered out. Dear Lord, she'd sighed. She'd actually just *sighed*.

He dipped his head. He was going to kiss her. She shivered as warm lips brushed the tender skin of her ear. A delicious, scintillating caress.

But not a kiss.

He was whispering to her.

'Something has come up. Follow my lead.' Louder, for the benefit of the others, he said, 'Mother, ladies, our apologies. An urgent matter needs our attention and we must go.'

Okay. It was part of the act.

'Can I leave you to gather everything Miss Marchant will need for her stay? You have her sizes?' The assistants nodded vigorously. 'And please send a selection of everything you think appropriate.' He turned to gaze adoringly at her. 'Don't stint.'

As if they would. They were staring at him as if he were a god come down to earth, imagining all their commission.

His long fingers curled through hers, warm, strong and wonderfully comforting—drat the man. And then he set off for the private lift they'd arrived in.

Focus, Lily.

He'd said something had come up. Perhaps there was news on Nate?

The lift doors closed. 'What's so…?' Where had that husky note come from? She tried again. 'What's so urgent that we needed to leave?'

'This.' He gathered her close and pressed his mouth to hers.

She should have pushed him away—there was no audience here—but his mouth slanted over hers in a kiss so tantalisingly gentle she leant in. He began a delicate exploration of her jaw, her throat, and found a tender spot beneath her ear, teasing it with a slow swirl of his tongue.

Her fingers sank into his biceps.

When he nudged a thigh between her legs she instinctively rubbed against it, seeking contact where she needed it most.

'Come,' he said.

Yes, oh, yes…

Wait…no. What?

He was walking. He meant her to go with him. He was leaving the lift.

She teetered in her new heels and he drew her protectively against his side. Together, eyes locked, they crossed the foyer and stepped outside into the now familiar intense heat and something else—something new.

With the dazzle of sunshine came camera flashes. A cacophony of voices. Crowding figures.

'Your Highness? Sir? When's the wedding?'

'Lily? Has he bought you a ring yet? When did you know it was love?'

She blinked as the lights exploded, over and over. With a jolt she realised he'd walked them into a press pack—and he knew enough about those for it not to be an accident.

Continue reading
DESERT PRINCE'S DEFIANT BRIDE
Julieanne Howells

Available next month
www.millsandboon.co.uk

LET'S TALK

Romance

For exclusive extracts, competitions
and special offers, find us online:

f facebook.com/millsandboon

🐦 @MillsandBoon

📷 @MillsandBoonUK

Get in touch on 01413 063232

For all the latest titles coming soon, visit
millsandboon.co.uk/nextmonth

MILLS & BOON
Desire

Indulge in secrets and scandal, intense drama
and plenty of sizzling hot action with powerful
and passionate heroes who have it all: wealth,
status, good looks…everything but the right
woman.